NINE..

DAYS

WITHOUT

YOU

a novel

JENNIFER WOODWARD

This novel contains material which some may find upsetting. Please go to the author's website for full details.

Cover art by Elizabeth Ward
Author photo by Brandon Bishop
Cover and interior designed by David Provolo

ISBN 978-1-8383987-0-5 (paperback)
ISBN 978-1-8383987-1-2 (ebook)
ISBN 978-1-8383987-2-9 (hardback)

www.jenniferwoodward.co.uk

For J.D.

I

I'll love you. But just this twice.
—Atticus

1

I step off Shaftesbury Avenue onto a side street and am jarred by the sudden appearance of nipple tassels, whips, dildos and a shop that must sell the ultimate in deviant merchandise as its windows are fully blacked out. The whole twisted little street is packed with sex shops. I had no idea London was so sordid.

I laugh. My first laugh in a long time.

The next turn reinstates a buzzy but respectable London, like I popped out of a seedy white rabbit hole. I locate the upscale Japanese restaurant where I'm due to meet my best friend Lena. Oh, and her work colleagues, even though it's our last night, even though Lena and I haven't had an evening to ourselves all week. I push through the door and scan the room for her. It's buzzing with Friday-night-on-the-town revelers, but she's not here. There's one last seat at the bar. I can't help but feel a little rejected as I squeeze onto the trendy barstool. But what was I expecting? On the plus side, Lena's tardiness gives me a little time to write. I take out my notebook. I uncap my pen. I chew the pen cap. I hail the bartender. "A glass of Sauvignon Blanc, please."

I know my writer's block is connected to the breakup. I don't understand what that connection is, but frankly I don't care. I just want it all to shift, for this depressing segment of my life to end. The bartender places my wine in front of me, and I nod my thanks. Okay. Write anything. Just make a start. I write:

Anything.

"anyone lived in a pretty how town..."

One of my favorite poems but not gonna get me anywhere.

Who am I kidding? Why would I be able to come up with an idea in the few seconds before Lena walks in? The wine's delicious. I'm away from home. I'm in a trendy London hot spot that's brimming with well-heeled folk. All is well. I pull out my phone so that I can log onto the restaurant's wi-fi. I hate waiting for my phone to connect. Then six new texts spill in. Make that seven. Eight. My heart wants it to be Jonathan, but there's only one person who rapid-fire texts me.

Louise

Earth to Louise

How's The Big Smoke?

I had a big smoke last night

I feel like a cow shat on my head and then I ate a cow shit sandwich. And Mom keeps picking on me to get my shit together when really, will her shit ever be together?

Oh, and Dad has a new lady friend. No surprise there.

At least she's not young enough to be our long lost big sis

When are you coming back again???

Can you tell I'm bored?

the whole idea behind you living with Mom was to be bored. But if that's not working out, go get a job

Thanks Louise. I'll put that to the committee

Do you think we really have a long lost big sis somewhere?

Nope. Just us in this nuthouse

Not that you're here

And I'm not at Mom's to be bored. I'm here to realign my life but how the hell can I do that when she harasses me all the time?

What are you doing now anyway?

Working

Stop! You're on vacation!

A playwright's job is never done

You got anything?

> *Yeah. I'm in the middle of being a genius.*
> *Flying back tomorrow. Talk then?*

Maybe I'll come down to the city to hang out
Let's go to that sushi place near you
Or we can order in Chinese and watch a movie?
bc you'll prob b jetlagged

> *K. I'll call you*

I shut off my phone. My little brother Mattie is on the verge of mania again. I know this is what's happening because my stomach starts to ache.

Now I really want Jonathan. He may have partied too much, but he always knew how to make me stop worrying about Mattie. Oh Jonathan. I gave him back the engagement ring. I gave the sweater that smelled like him to the Salvation Army (after sleeping with it for two weeks). And I have not spoken with him once this entire six months. Well, I may have texted him. I did. I couldn't help it. It turned out to be an exercise in humiliation. He didn't reply. So I texted him again. I couldn't help myself. It was awful. I could see that he didn't even bother to read my text until two full days after I'd sent it, and even then he didn't reply. So no, I haven't spoken to him.

I close my eyes and he fills my mind so vividly that I would swear he was here, the warm cocoon of him surrounding me. His smell... can I seriously smell him?

I open my eyes. To my right, a woman sips what looks like a dirty martini. The fresh scent of olive juice. Jonathan loves dirty martinis.

I love Jonathan. He's my martini.

I want to text him so badly it hurts and I am so sick of this hurt. I want it to stop. Someone make it stop. I want to scream cry yell at the top of my lungs. I write in my notebook, "FUCK THIS SHIT."

I hear a chuckle. It's the man on the stool next to me. Reading over my shoulder. I feel his gaze and my face starts to heat. I turn to face him, make direct eye contact. "Can I help you?"

He shakes his head. "I'm so sorry, really cramped quarters, I couldn't help but read…" He indicates my notebook. "Having a good day, then?" He's very nice-looking. Blue eyes, that lovely British accent. "Can I buy you a drink?"

The man clearly wants to flirt and I don't. "I already have one. Thanks."

"Ah. Sorry to bother you." He turns away from me.

I pause and reconsider. Wasn't the point of coming to London to stop moping and have some fun? And here's a great-looking man with his enchanting speech pattern. I put away my notebook. I say, "You're not bothering me. This obviously isn't the place for inspiration."

He turns back to me, smiling. "I'm Charlie."

"Kat."

"Katherine?"

He makes my name sound so elegant, but: "I prefer Kat."

"And you're a poet?"

"Playwright."

"Ah! I thought you'd written out a poem. That's what I get for snooping. Misinformation." His eyes twinkle at me. I smile. "Give me your favorite quote from a play."

"That's tough." I want to impress him. "I guess I'd go with, 'I don't want realism. I want magic.'"

"Who's that?"

"Blanche Dubois. Streetcar?"

"Oh yeah, very good. I've never seen it. Though of course I've heard of it."

"She goes on to say something about how she lies… well, *misrepresents* the truth, in order to give people magic."

Charlie swirls the ice in his drink. "We could all do with a little magic."

"That's what I think." I sip my wine, turn my body to face him squarely. "So what's your quote?"

"Well, I don't have a quote from a play. But I could give you a poem?"

"Sure."

He finds a spot at the ceiling to stare at. "I have eaten the plums that were in the icebox/ and which you were probably saving for breakfast/ Forgive me they were delicious so sweet and so cold."

He keeps his gaze fixed on the ceiling. The poem hangs between us.

When he finally looks at me, his face is candid, as if we've been lovers for decades. I feel like I could kiss him. I manage to say, "We should all have that one memorized."

"Kat!" Lena waddles up to the bar, her very pregnant body only slightly at odds with the sleekness of the place because even seven months pregnant, Lena exudes grace. She's one of those women who looks amazing 24/7/365. And she's the whole package: cool job, French husband, a girl at home, a boy in the oven, and Russian bone structure to die for. If she weren't one of my best friends, I'd hate her. She hugs me. "I see you've already met Charlie."

I ask Charlie, "You're one of Lena's work colleagues?"

Lena assesses the situation in a flash. "Charlie, were you hitting on my friend?"

He smiles down at his now empty glass. "We were discussing poetry."

"I'll take that as a yes." Lena explains to me, "Charlie's a management consultant from a big firm here called JCK. Thankfully his firm does pro bono work so he restructured our London office. I've been following him around all week because I'm going to have to replicate his changes back in Paris." Lena manages the Paris-based team of a human rights organization. She turns to Charlie, "Kat's a playwright in New York. I've known her almost all my life. She's like a sister to me so step wisely."

"I shall consider myself fairly warned." Charlie bows. We both kind of chuckle. His eyes are twinkling away at me. Then he moves on to speak with another colleague.

Lena's inspecting me so I sip my wine and ask, "How's the bump doing?" I know she wants to say something about this Charlie fellow.

I'd bet anything she thinks he's the perfect way to get over Jonathan, but she politely follows my lead and details the kicks of her day.

———

A round table in a private alcove. Ten of us. I'm disappointed that I'm seated across from Charlie instead of next to him. Since I met him about five seconds ago, this strikes me as insane in a desperate-woman-way, so I do my best to pay zero attention to him. Still, I can't help but notice that a lot of compliments head his way. I comment to Lena, "Charlie seems to be the man of the evening."

"He helped our London office make some tough decisions, and as a result of his work it's running much smoother." She pauses. "I've spent a fair amount of time with him this week, and he seems like a great guy. Plus, I found out today that he's single. So you should totally go for it."

"I knew you were plotting something. Not going to happen."

"You should!"

"You know I don't do one-night stands, so… what? I'm going to start dating someone who lives in London?"

"A one-night stand could be just what the doctor ordered."

"Please."

"Isn't the reason you came to stop mooning over Jonathan?"

"I came to see you," I tell her. She looks at me. She knows as well as I do that we've had zero time together. I'm angry, but I also feel bad. Lena works hard. So rather than see who blinks first, I turn my attention to the man sitting on my other side and make small talk. Another one of Lena's human rights colleagues from the London office.

As we chitchat, I think I can feel Charlie's eyes on me. I glance over. His eyes *are* on me. I smile at him. He smiles back.

2

Outside the restaurant, our group chats about who's going where and who will share which cars. After someone asks Lena where we're staying, Charlie offers to drop us at our hotel, saying, "It's right on my way." I pop into the back of his car, relieved when Lena asks him something about work. It's dark and I feel safe back here with no one talking to me. We zoom past row after row of white, charming houses lining tiny, twisting streets. Charlie explains, "The best way to get anywhere in London is with a zigzag."

"You live near our hotel?" Lena asks.

"Well, no," Charlie confesses. "I thought it might be fun to hang out with the Americans on their last night."

He catches my eye in the rearview mirror.

3

"We probably should have gone out for a drink, or even gone to sit in the cheap lounge downstairs, but I really needed—" Lena puts a pillow under her feet then carefully leans back against the golden headboard of our hotel room's queen-size bed. Lena works for a non-profit, so the accommodation they provide is clean but cramped. She closes her eyes. "Ahh."

Charlie shakes his head at Lena then heads towards the small loveseat, the only place to sit besides the bed. I stand there then ask, "Would you like something to drink?"

"A cuppa tea would be lovely," replies Charlie. "Milk, no sugar, please."

"Me too but something herbal," says Lena.

No one speaks. Lena becomes engrossed in her phone. I've got a hot British guy staring at me. Jonathan be damned! I have to be extra careful not to knock over any of the hot drink paraphernalia the hotel has stacked economically onto a very small shelf. I throw Charlie what I hope is a winning smile as I bring the kettle into the bathroom to fill it. Why the hell is Lena on her phone?

As if I've willed her to break the silence, Lena says to Charlie, "So I've been meaning to ask all week, was it really different working for a human rights organization? I'm assuming you're usually at big corporations?"

I'm putting the kettle back into its stand to boil as Charlie replies, "My Company works with a range of clients, and I requested to do some of the pro bono work this year—"

"Well, that worked in our favor!" Lena cuts in.

"That's kind of you to say. And to answer your original question, no. At the end of the day it was not too different. Turns out people are people, no matter the size of their organization."

Rather than squish onto the love seat next to Charlie, I perch on the end of the bed near Lena's feet. I ask him, "What does a management consultant do exactly?" I'm relieved my voice sounds casual.

He gives a small laugh. "That's a good question. I often wonder that myself." We smile at each other. "Basically, I go in and observe the structure and internal workings of companies. I can't evaluate what they need until I see how they've set themselves up and how they're functioning, or, more likely, not functioning. And then I work out how to help them do everything better."

"Doesn't sound like you'd ever get bored doing that."

"I don't, but I spent the past decade in Seoul. I'm thrilled to be working back in London again."

"What was Seoul like?"

"Ahh, it was interesting. I don't drink, and they do a lot of drinking there. Not dissimilar to here but somehow more challenging than here."

Lena pipes in, "Kat loves drinkers so that's too bad."

I'm mortified. "Lena!"

Charlie seems to sit up a little straighter. "What's this?"

"Should I not have said that?" Lena tucks an extra pillow under her head as another text comes in. "Sorry, just getting shit from Jean-Marc about being away from Leo again."

Charlie's attention stays on me. "You love drinkers?"

"Lena's full of it."

She texts and talks. "I'm cutting to the chase. We can't pussyfoot around things now that we're in our thirties. Though I suppose," she sits up, "that given your history with drinkers, you'd prefer a non-drinker. So this is great news."

Charlie looks confused. "Didn't you have a glass of wine at the bar?"

"Yeah. Why?"

"Oh sorry, you're not in recovery."

"Recovery?"

"AA?"

"Oh. No, no. I'm not opposed to drinking. I mean, not that people in AA are opposed to it. I mean obviously, I drink. Not that much though." I sound like a ding-a-ling but continue, "Lena's referring to the fact that I recently broke up with my boyfriend because he was kind of a boozehound."

"Fiancé," Lena adds. "And he did drugs."

"Yeah. Thanks for your input, Lena."

"And I wouldn't say you ended it *recently*, Kat."

Charlie still has his eyes on me, as if ending it with a drinker is riveting information.

Lena goes on, "Nor was he your first barfly."

"Lena!"

"Well, you do seem to have a thing for them."

I can't believe her. We have, of course, discussed ad nauseum how I gravitate towards the personality that goes along with guys who drink a lot. Lena was instrumental in helping me see the light around Jonathan's partying. And how I downplay it by calling it "partying," which is way too innocuous a word for what Jonathan was doing. I admitted she was right. But that was a private conversation!

The water's boiling so I get up to make tea for everyone as I say, "Sometimes you remind me of my mother in all the bad ways."

"Maybe that's why Anne didn't come." Lena eyes me suspiciously.

Anne is our third best friend. She lives and works in LA as an acting agent, a fast-paced job that suits her energetic personality. We all grew up a five-minute walk to each other's houses and now live long-haul distances away from each other. It sucks. I tell Lena, "I don't follow. Anne didn't come because you remind me of my mother?"

"No, because I can't drink right now and you've cut back so dramatically since you and Jonathan broke up that Anne wouldn't have anyone to get wasted with. Is that it?"

"Didn't she have so much happening at work that a weekend in London when she lives in LA was impossible?"

"That's what she said, but I think she's lying."

"Why would she lie?"

Lena's about to answer, but another text comes in.

Lena's right. Anne was lying. But I know better than to get in the middle of that. Charlie doesn't seem rattled by the exchange. On the contrary, he reaches out to take his tea from me and asks, "How long were you and Jonathan together?"

I hand Lena her tea, then sit back down on the end of the bed, facing Charlie. I tell him, "Five years."

"And how long have you been apart?"

"Six months."

He makes a face, as if to say that's not too bad.

"How long have you been not drinking?"

"Seventeen years."

I'm stunned.

Lena looks up and stares at Charlie. "Wow."

I ask, "So you're like… a drinker… who doesn't drink?"

"You could put it that way." Charlie blows at and then slurps his tea, like he's skimming off the cooler top layer.

Huh. This Charlie guy will have drinker qualities—the free spirit, the big thoughts, the fun—but not actually drink? I see Lena look at him with fresh eyes.

Charlie says, "One of the many paradoxes surrounding AA is that the founder, a man named Bill…"

"Yeah?"

"People think he's the most amazing guy, and he was. Before AA, alcoholics ended up either dead or in jail or insane asylums."

"Yeah?"

"Yes, so by founding AA, he made it so that regular people like me, millions of us, can have functional lives. Amazing, right?"

"Sure."

Charlie sips his tea. "But even though Bill created this extraordinary fellowship, he was an ordinary man. Incredibly human. He constantly cheated on his wife."

"Is infidelity *incredibly human* these days?" Lena semi-challenges.

15

She's sunk down into the bed now, her hands cradling her belly. "Excuse me." With great effort, Lena pushes herself up and shuffles to the bathroom.

Charlie turns to me. "I think it's incredibly human. Don't you?"

"Well, a lot of people don't cheat. Maybe it would have been just as incredibly human for him to be faithful."

Charlie rests his teacup on a tiny side table. He tilts his head back ever so slightly, and I see a small scar where his chin meets his throat. Maybe he cut himself shaving or something, but it's a little long for that. He asks me, "Are you saying he's not human because he cheated?"

"I think the human species has all types. And I wouldn't speak ill of the man. I don't even know him."

"He's long gone now."

"Oh."

The toilet flushes. It makes a ludicrously long, shrill squeak. Charlie and I laugh. The sound of teeth being brushed wafts over the dying toilet flush. I stand. "Lena's getting ready to crash."

Charlie stands too, facing me.

And then, fuck. There's a charge between us. It hits me hard. At this moment, right now, I'd like nothing more than to screw the bejesus out of him. But where would we even do it? Next to Lena? Would I leave the safety of our hotel room to roam around London with basically a complete stranger? Besides, I could be projecting this sizzle and I will not make the first move. I will not because I can't bear being hurt again.

With great restraint, pretending I'm a lady, I walk him to the door.

He moves in to hug me. What a hug! He squeezes me so tightly that his chest surrounds mine and doubt vanishes. He likes me. "Can we exchange details?" he asks so pointedly that I feel a rush of giddiness.

But I'm cool as I pull out my phone. While Charlie taps in his information, he keeps glancing at me and he's so close that I can smell him and boy he smells good. He's going to ask me to come somewhere with him right now and really how can I refuse?

Lena emerges from the bathroom. "Oh, you going?" She makes a beeline for the bed. "I may end up calling you with some questions." As she climbs in, she releases a tiny fart. "Oops. Don't mind the heavily pregnant lady!"

The spell breaks. Charlie says, "Bye then."

I smile a little too widely. "It was nice to meet you!" At least I don't follow him out the door. I mean, thank God the door closes and I am on one side and he's on the other. But then… maybe I'm missing out. Maybe I'm being a prude. My hand's on the doorknob about to open it again, but Lena will think I'm insane. No. Lena told me to go for it. I open the door. I glance down the hallway. Charlie's gone. I sigh. "If that guy lived in New York, I'd definitely date him."

Lena doesn't respond. She's down under the covers, lying on her side. I can't see her face. I peek around the side of the bed. Her eyes are wide open. "You okay?" I ask. Lena glances up but says nothing. "What is it?"

She shows me a text from her husband, Jean-Marc. "Honestly, Lena, you don't comprehend the impact your work life has on this family. The situation you've created is unsustainable and I cannot cope with it for much longer."

I'm not sure what to say. Lena married Jean-Marc when they found out she was pregnant with Leo. Anne and I were flabbergasted. It was the most traditional move our friend had ever made. She had been focused on her career career career, had never breathed one word of desire for a husband or children. That was always me. When we asked her why she was getting married, she'd simply say, "I love him."

I quickly change into my pjs, do a cursory brush of my teeth and wash my face. Then I climb into bed behind Lena. "Jean-Marc is just being Jean-Marc and making a point. He's not going to leave."

Lena says, "He's never threatened this before. I mean, he complains that the amount of work I do bothers him…"

"Maternity leave's just around the corner. You'll all have time together, and he'll forget he was ever mad." I stroke Lena's hair the way I used to when we were in high school and she'd get stressed out about exams or the SATs or her early admission to Harvard. Once I hear her breath deepen and know she's asleep, I allow my mind to wander back to Charlie and that hug. Damn. That hug had sex in it. It screamed, "I could do you in a way you've never known possible."

Maybe I should text him when I'm home tomorrow. Maybe he'll text me.

4

Lena's glued to her phone as we taxi to the airport. Every once in a while she glances up as if she's about to say something, and then another text from Jean-Marc comes in and her fingers fly around, getting her very important point across to him in record time. When she eventually leans back and rests her phone face down on her leg, I ask, "You guys okay?"

She exhales, "For now." Then she looks at me. "Are you thinking about Charlie or Jonathan?"

I laugh. "Who's to say I'm thinking about a guy?"

She laughs with me. I take her arm in mine and rest my head on her shoulder. "Well?" she prods.

"Charlie."

"I think that ship sailed."

"He gave me his details."

"The Atlantic Ocean may be a pretty big cock block, but what do I know? Maybe he's working in New York next month and you can have your one-night stand after all."

"I don't want a one-night stand."

"Oh dear."

"What?"

"I can hear in your voice that you've gone all boy crazy again."

"Don't be ridiculous." We pull into my terminal.

"This is just like Billy O'Brian."

"That was 2nd Grade!"

"You wrote him secret love letters that everyone knew were from you and humiliated yourself."

"Please."

"In middle school you carved KC + EK in a big heart on a table and got suspended for vandalism. The list of men in college is

19

insane—Jake, John, the other John, Phil, Jacob, Pete, that exchange student, Marcus, the French guy named Guy—and that was all freshman year and every one of them was *the one*."

"I was with Jonathan for years!"

"Yeah, and you arrived here still obsessed with him even though he pursued his recreational activities with too much passion from the moment you met him—"

"Stop."

"He was in jail for buying drugs, in the hospital with acute pancreatitis, and in your bedroom closet pissing because he thought it was the toilet."

"Please stop! I'm not thinking about him now."

"Because you've replaced obsessing about him with obsessing about a stranger."

"He's not a stranger. He's your work colleague and you suggested I sleep with him!"

"Because that's what you do with your best friend's work colleague, not plan a wedding!"

The taxi driver's watching us in his rearview mirror so I grab my bag, open my door and tell her, "I don't think it's fair of you to pick on me because your marriage is in the shithole." Then I go.

5

I usually walk through my door relieved to be home, but I stewed the whole flight. Fuck her. I perch on my couch, my unopened suitcase next to me. I don't have to text Charlie. But I can if I want. Lena does not get to dump her shit on me. But I won't text him. I will email him. This is far less personal than a text and, therefore, a superior option. I open my email, send another mental *fuck you* to Lena, and type away.

> *Dear Charlie,*
> *Who would have thought that on my last night in London*
> *I'd meet someone as compelling as you?*
> *How are you doing? Work any fun?*
> *- Kat*

Short. Sweet. Complimentary. Flirty yet casual. I'm pretty sure I've hit all the right notes.

After it's gone, I can't see if he's read it, as it's an email. I curse my choice. I unpack and get ready for work tomorrow.

———

Ah, the sheer splendor of the Human Resources Department at Meribal Goldstein. I answer the phones, take care of basic HR issues (travel, maternity leave, etc.), and then direct more nuanced issues to the appropriate muckety-mucks. It's dull but my colleagues are great. They always come to my shows, and if I'm squeezing in rewrites during a quiet spell, no one cares. Also, and most importantly, it's a good-paying job with health insurance, yet when I leave work, my time is my own. Which means I have every night free this week to try and fail to get a new idea going. I sketch scenes, but can't imagine them as part of anything bigger. Everything I write lacks spark. Even if I wasn't producing award-winning drama when I was with Jonathan, at least I was producing.

Fucking Jonathan. Why can't I write without him in my life? I'll text him and see how he's doing. But an email arrives.

Katherine,

Lovely meeting you too. Sorry I'm terrible at staying in touch. I've been working like a madman. It's no excuse—though perhaps incredibly human. What do you think?

Charlie x

What's with the "Katherine"? Of course I recall the sexy effect his accent had on my full name, but I asked him to call me Kat. And more importantly, what the hell is going on with that "x"??? Isn't it a little premature for x's??? I write back.

A lot of humans work very hard and a lot of lazy dolts watch tv all day long. If you're "incredibly human" for working so hard does that make them incredibly inhuman? Or perhaps the human spectrum can contain both industrious men and slackers.

Seriously, how are you?

- kat (not katherine) x

I delete the x, then put it back in, then delete it, then put it back in, hit send. I then check my emails every few seconds for the next hour. No response. Maybe he went into a meeting? Two hours pass. A very long meeting? It's the end of the day. It's not like he suddenly went out of town. Maybe he went out of town? Maybe I misplayed the x.

I push Charlie from my mind. I try to write. I catch myself thinking about Jonathan. I push Jonathan from my mind. I try to write. I google "Billy O'Brian," my second grade crush. I already know he's married with two young children, a dog and a very beautiful wife. He owns a carpet business. Looking at a picture of him grinning in front of O'Brian's Wholesale Carpeting, I wonder if I missed out. I start googling all my exes and ex-crushes. I've done this before but I can't stop myself from doing it again. I finally look at a post of Jonathan and me, engaged, less than a year ago. I don't understand time. I don't understand how I was so close to being done with being on my own. I don't understand why he wouldn't let me take it all back. Who cares that he liked to party? I zoom in and try to see if we were happy. I think we were. Yeah. We were definitely happy.

6

Opening night scares me so I'm hiding in the lighting booth. It's
dark and safe in here. The light board operator is a quiet guy who
keeps to himself. He's happy for me to be here so long as we don't
have to speak. Perfection. Plus the booth is up behind the audience,
so I can watch them all stream in. This is what I'm doing now. They're
eager to check out the lead, a beautiful soap star who wants to be
viewed as a "serious" actor. My agent shows up! I'm surprised. He's
been wonderful at keeping this particular show alive, so I'm not sure
why he rubs me the wrong way. But I don't have time to ponder this
as I see Mattie strut down the aisle.

Oh Jesus. My little brother is 6'4" and broad-shouldered, which
means his size alone impresses. He's spent his life explaining that he
doesn't play basketball. Tonight, he dons a purple cowboy hat and a
yellow plaid flannel shirt. I can't decide if they match or clash. He
looks like a Wild West Easter egg. People turn to stare at him. He
leans in to a couple, way too far in. He's talking and talking then
starts laughing, as if he's laughing at his own punch line. They look
very uncomfortable, staring at him, not interested in whatever he's
saying.

He never did come down from Mom's house in Pleasantville
when I got home from London. In fact, we'd decided that we'd see
each other (and our divorced parents in their respective homes)
tomorrow for Thanksgiving.

A text comes in.

Set looks cool

What're you doing here?

Came to see your big success!

I crash at yours then we take train back home tmrw?

Where you?

24

Behind you. Lighting booth

Mattie turns and looks for me. I wave until he sees me. Then he sticks his tongue out, a little rockstar-esque and I quickly grimace in response, hoping he'll close his mouth. He does, and I pop back down to hide. He texts:

Nervous?

Been here, done that

Not with Marcia Simmons playing Annabel

Still

Set looks cool

Yeah. You said. Enjoy show!

He stops texting me, but I peek up to see that he's still texting someone. Vigorously. The lady sitting behind him leans forward, taps him on the shoulder and says something. This prompts Mattie to remove the purple cowboy hat. Thank God. He places it under his seat, then turns back around to the lady, smiling brightly, and launches into what looks like a speech. I can only see the back of the lady's nodding head, but I can imagine her face, wondering when this guy's going to stop jibber-jabbering at her.

Thankfully, the lights dim. Mattie faces forward. I lie down on the floor of the booth. This is my opening night position. I find it relaxing to listen with my eyes closed, breathing in and out the way they taught me in the acting class I had to take to get my Theater degree. It was the only thing I loved about acting class: lying on the floor and breathing.

I hear my words start to come alive. It never ceases to amaze me that this can happen. That real people recite the words I wrote.

Mattie guffaws.

I pray it's a one-off.

He guffaws again.

He's seen *Annabel* before. In fact, he's seen it every time he could, becoming my first enthusiastic fan back when it originally opened, and this is its 7th revival. Mattie's been at every opening night, even when it was done in a 100 square foot room for an audience of a dozen in Queens. I love him for this. And to be fair, there are some funny lines in the show. But really I'm a dramatist not a comedian. The funny lines are chuckle-funny, not guffaw-funny. And yet Mattie guffaws every chance he gets. Or lets out an equally grating, "Oh ho *ho*!" His vocalizations rise above the usual audience din and scream, "I'm here too! Don't just pay attention to the stage, pay attention to me!"

I feel the familiar mix of anger, guilt and sadness that overwhelms me whenever I'm near Mattie and he's manic. I'm also scared he's driving the other audience members bonkers. I should've brought him back here to the lighting booth with me. Should have kept him safer.

———

Act I ends with a round of appreciative applause. People are into the show despite Mattie's OTT exclamations. It strikes me that I may be the only person bothered by his reactions. Maybe I'm over-sensitive. Maybe Slightly-Flamboyant-and-Loud Matt seems normal to everyone else.

I'm still lying on the ground. A text comes in:

Going so well! Feel really proud of you!

Thx

You coming out here for a drink?

God no

You're ridiculous

c u after

I stay on the ground doing the breathing thing, and it works its trick because suddenly it's time for Act II to begin and amazingly I feel relaxed. I pop up and peek out at the audience members returning to their seats. The worst thing is when people leave the show during intermission. But it looks like all but one person have returned. Mattie.

The light board operator turns to me. "Someone's not coming out of the Men's room, but we're going to start the show anyway."

I nod calmly as alarm bells clang in my head.

I dash down to the restrooms.

As I approach the Men's room door, I hear Mattie scream from inside. I press the door open to find an usher knocking on a closed stall while getting out his cell phone. "Sir? Sir? Can you please try to open the door?" The usher turns to me. "I'm calling 911."

Of course it's Mattie in there. His distinctive cowboy boots under the stall door confirm it. I crawl under and squeeze into the tiny space.

He's sitting on the toilet, jeans down, collapsed into himself, holding his groin for dear life, cowboy hat on the back of the toilet. "Mattie?"

"It's killing me, Kat. Something's really wrong."

I press against the wall so that I can open the door. I hear the usher tell the emergency dispatcher our location. I gently ask, "Can you stand up?"

"Nooooooo." A long, pathetic wail, his eyes squeezed shut. Why is he holding his groin? Could he have testicular cancer? "Oh, Kat. I think I'm dying." He rears his body up and tilts his head back. White powder streaks under his nose.

"Oh Mattie. This is not testicular cancer." As tiny as the space is, I manage to reclose the door, grab a wad of toilet paper and wipe his face. I notice that the top of the toilet paper holder's speckled with white dust, so I clean that too. I whisper, "Pull up your jeans." He does. "Give me what you're holding."

"I don't have anything."

"There's an ambulance coming. Give me what you're holding." He hands me a small dime bag of white powder that's mostly empty, and then another small bag of white pills. I have no idea what they are. I ask him, "Cocaine?"

He rolls his eyes at me.

"Mattie, what is this?"

He whispers, "Meth." Then protests when I flush it all down the toilet, "That shit's expensive!"

"Don't be ridiculous."

He groans like a dying grizzly bear.

I rub his back and tell him, "Help is on its way. It'll be fine." But I'm lying because this is so not fine.

Somehow, Jonathan would have been able to make this better. I don't mean he'd have done anything differently for Matt. He would have made *me* feel better.

7

"Advanced gonorrhea and a severe outbreak of herpes, alongside the beginnings of what looks to me to be a manic episode." The doctor delivers this information about my little brother's sexual and mental health with no nonsense. I cringe. She continues, "He says he's bipolar. Has he been clinically diagnosed?"

I nod. We're out in the hallway, but I'm nervous Matt can hear.

"The gonorrhea treatment is outpatient, but I'm going to recommend inpatient care until he stabilizes mentally."

I say quietly, "Inpatient care sounds right to me."

"We'll have to transfer him to an appropriate facility. Why don't you go and see him now." The doctor gestures into the room we're standing outside.

In his green gown on the white sheets, Mattie looks so vulnerable that my mind flashes back to when he was a child. He used to draw me pictures that were folded inside pictures that were folded inside pictures. In the very center of it all, he always drew a heart.

"Fuck, Louise, this is bad." Matt stares up at the ceiling.

"Yeah," I agree, taking the seat next to his bed. "Doc says you need inpatient care."

"Fuck that." He doesn't look at me.

"Yeah well, let me put it this way, *I* think you need inpatient care."

"Well, that's great, but I don't want it."

"What's going on with the drugs, Mattie?"

He looks at me like I'm stupid. "What do you mean *what's going on*? I'm taking care of myself." I laugh. "It's how I get to normal." He adds softly, "Don't laugh. It really is. Don't tell Mom and Dad."

"Well, how about this. You agree to inpatient care for your bipolar, and I won't tell Mom and Dad about the drugs."

"I don't think you understand. I need them to balance myself out."

"If that's the case then when we get you stable through inpatient care, you won't need them anymore, right?"

He thinks about this. "Yeah. Totally."

"Then I'll talk to Dad. We'll get you in somewhere good."

"You won't mention the drugs."

"I won't."

"Promise?"

"Yeah, yeah, I promise."

I step into the hallway to call Dad. He answers with a jubilant, "Katherine!" He always sounds happy to hear from me. "How's Mattie? Wasn't it great that he came to see the show? I got him that ticket. Did he surprise you?" As I explain the situation, it feels like I'm slowly deflating a three-year-old's balloon. "Shit. Ahh, shit," Dad says.

"Yeah."

"You're with him now?"

"Yeah."

"Well, I don't think he needs inpatient care."

I take a deep breath in. "He does, Dad. He really does."

"Why do you think that?"

"He's dressing flamboyantly, talking to strangers, laughing too loud. He's not in a full blown manic episode, but he's definitely riding beneath one."

"Definitely? Please, Kat, you're not a psychiatrist. Don't diagnose him."

"Dad, we've been through this before. I recognize the signs. He's not taking care of himself! He's clearly been in pain for a while now but let it get so bad he needed an ambulance. Why is he popping into the city when he should be at a doctor?"

"Don't yell at me, Katherine, honey. He wanted to be at his big sis's opening night. What's wrong with that? This is not as dramatic as you make it out to be."

"I'm the one who's here, Dad. And it is this dramatic." There's a silence. I steel myself. "Listen, Dad, he's doing drugs. I promised I wouldn't tell you, but he says himself that he's using them to even himself out. So if we just help him get evened out in a clinic, then he won't need the drugs."

"What kind of drugs?"

"Methamphetamine."

"Shit."

"Trust me, Dad, he needs help."

Dad sighs. "Okay then. Okay."

"What should I tell Mom?"

"Nothing!"

"Dad, come on." I suspect Dad never wants to share information with Mom because he's been angry with her for as long as I can remember, not just post-divorce anger, going back to when we were little. In fact, getting divorced did nothing to abate his anger. How he has managed to sustain this for so long is beyond me. But one of its side effects is that when something crops up around Mattie's care, his initial instinct is to hide vital information from Mom. To placate him, I say, "We'll tell Mom everything except the part about the drugs. That'd just upset her anyway. We'll tell her the doctor recommended inpatient care until he's stable again. He'll be out in no time and it won't be a big deal."

"Exactly, Katherine. No lies."

"No lies."

8

After spending a grim Thanksgiving with Matt in his new psychiatric hospital during which he complained about the food, the staff, that Dad didn't want to stay, that Mom *did* want to stay, that the playing cards were too worn and that the backgammon set was missing a piece, I get back into the city with the very bad idea jammed into my brain that I really ought to see Jonathan for old time's sake. To get up the guts to act on this very bad idea, I don't call Lena. Irrespective of the fact that we haven't spoken since the airport, calls like this don't go to her. Calls like this go straight to Anne. I talked about Jonathan's drinking with both Anne and Lena a lot. I mean, it went on for years. And to put it mildly, Anne was skeptical that this was a strong enough reason to end the relationship. Even when I came clean to her about the amount of drinking and drugs he did, Anne said, "A lot of people party like that, Kat." I told her, "Sure, when they're drug addicts and alcoholics." Anne replied, "Why are you labeling him? He works hard and he plays hard. It's not like he's hurting anyone. It's not like he comes home drunk and beats you up or sleeps around or even breaks things."

So now, when I want to see him, I call Anne. She picks up and asks, "How was London?"

"It would've been better if you'd come. I haven't seen you in ages."

"I'll be back in New York for Bobby's wedding and see you then. Besides, if Lena really wanted to see us she could have made more of an effort than inviting us on a work trip. I mean, for fuck's sake, did she even have any free time at all?"

"You being a touch sensitive?"

"I'll take that to mean she worked non-stop and you barely saw her. Why do you always defend her?"

"Listen, not to change the subject but should I call Jonathan?"

"God, yes."

"What should I say?"

"Just text him 'hi.' Do it right now. It's ludicrous you haven't seen him since last spring."

"It's not like I had a choice. He left."

"Yeah, because you criticized his lifestyle. But it's months later and you're still thinking about him so freaking text him already."

"Last time I texted him, he didn't reply."

"Oh my God, will you stop and just do it already."

I do. He responds immediately.

I wait in the bar of a fancy Tribeca restaurant. I'm wearing a deep purple dress (that Jonathan always said made my eyes look like the ocean) and sexy stiletto boots that I bought this afternoon. I know I look as great as I can, but I'm beyond nervous.

He blasts through the door. His eyes search until they find mine. And when they do, a part of me relaxes that I didn't realize was tense.

Jonathan may not be every woman's cup of tea. His chin's non-existent and he'd be too hairy for some. But he's also in great shape and funny and has those tender brown eyes, and within seconds of seeing me he's holding me and I'm trying not to cry. The bartender, witness to our fervent reunion, hands us each a glass of champagne.

Dinner is a gush of what he's been doing, what I've been doing. I tell him about the *Annabel* revival and how I've been suffering from writer's block. He tells me that he's gotten the money for his latest startup. I don't ask about his drinking or any of that, but he downs the glass of champagne, immediately orders his signature dirty vodka martini, downs it, orders another and downs it as well. All before we even order. Then over dinner, he keeps topping up my still full glass of wine while he singlehandedly drinks the rest of the bottle.

He asks, "Can I come sit next to you, Kat?"

I give him a slight nod.

He slides into the booth beside me. He takes my face in his hands. His fingers (that I know so well they feel like old friends) warm my skin. I lean into their heat and close my eyes. I'm not surprised when his lips touch mine. He stops. I open my eyes and look at him. He explains, "I'm sorry. I probably shouldn't have done that. You're just so gorgeous." I well up. "Baby, baby, don't cry. Don't cry." He puts his hands on my shoulders, gently pushing me back against the booth. He kisses me again, says, "Us breaking up was a good thing. You're right about me. I drink too much. I'm 32, still doing cocaine and not gonna change. I would have wasted your time. Oh Kat, I don't want you to cry so I'm going back to the other side of the table." Carefully, he moves back to his side.

I look up at the ceiling, think about the mascara I'm wearing, and breathe. Tiered art deco chandeliers emit a warm orange glow. Fuck. He even chose a restaurant that's designed from my favorite era. Still looking up, I ask, "But how can it be wrong when I feel so much for you?"

"Baby, I don't know. I don't know. Let's order dessert." He motions for the waiter. But we don't order dessert. Jonathan gets the check and we quickly walk the few blocks to his new place.

———

His new apartment. His apartment without me. Shit. He'd been slumming it with me up in Washington Heights. I mean, it was fine, but we'd always planned to move into a two-bedroom apartment together and now he's gone and done it without me. And it's a Tribeca loft. I mean, I don't want him to be living in a dump, but how can he have moved here without me? How has he even lived *one day* without me? I've spent months and months pining for him, while he just... bought a fancy new apartment! Decorated it! Got on with—

"What's this?" I ask. On his refrigerator door there's travel information. Someone named Jules is flying in this weekend.

"Yeah," he says sheepishly. "My mother's setting me up with this girl. I'm supposed to pick her up at JFK and bring her to a party her family's having where my family will be. It's so embarrassing."

I exhale a quick hot breath.

"Don't worry, Kat. I've seen a picture of her and she's kind of a dog."

"You're a jerk."

"Can I be your jerk?"

And we're straight into his bed, tearing and kissing and grabbing, and all the while I'm smelling the alcohol on him. I move away from his breath, down his body, kiss the chest I know so well. But when I really get down to business, his balls are sweaty with a sort of vodka sweat, and though I'm trying to be sexy, to take him in my mouth, I gag at their smell.

"You all right?"

"Mmm." I work to keep the mood hot because I don't want to stop, I want to be with him, so my solution is to not smell the vodka oozing out of each and every one of his pores. Smelling it turns my stomach and reminds me that I'm probably making a mistake, so I breathe through my mouth. I want to be back in that feeling of home I had when he first embraced me.

Mid-thrust he whispers, "If we get you pregnant, then we'll have to figure out a way of getting along." This makes perfect sense. So I'm suddenly having unprotected sex with him for the first time.

Then as he comes, we both have the same reaction and push him out of me. So he sort of… half comes inside me. Sort of like a half commitment. Symbolic. Pathetic. Depressing. And yet we don't stop there. We do it again, have unprotected sex again. I'm still breathing through my mouth, striving to recapture something. A bond? An energy? A relationship? Whatever I'm trying to reconstruct, it ain't happening. But I give it my all, and then he comes half in and half out of me again. It is the first time in my life a man has tried to get me pregnant. And he only half tried. Twice though. Maybe that's something. Maybe two half-tries make a full try.

I haven't orgasmed. But I don't care. I always cry when I do and

I don't feel like crying now.

We assume our usual positions and I fall into one of those sleeps where I feel like I'm never actually asleep, while he's snoring away. Then suddenly it's morning. I creep home feeling a weird mixture of shame and triumph. It's around the time of month that I really could get pregnant. He's right. We'd find a way. This is what people do.

———

I plop myself down on my couch, and text Lena:

> *Sorry I haven't been in touch and that I was*
> *a little irritated when we said goodbye*

I can see she's read it so I continue.

> *Okay. I was rude. I'm sorry*

I was harsh too and I'm sorry too

> *Can we move on? Bc I either did*
> *something genius or idiotic*

I feel like I'm confessing, especially when I reveal what time of month it is for me, but I dutifully tell her everything that happened last night.

Ms. Too-Busy-To-Speak calls before I'm done tapping it all out. I answer reluctantly because I suspect what's coming. "Hey."

Lena jumps straight in with, "When are you planning to see him again?"

"Well, we didn't really say."

"So, you're not going to see him, say, this weekend?"

I'm immediately cornered, forced to admit, "Well, he has plans this weekend."

"What plans?"

How does she do this? It's as if she knows I know he has plans and is pressing me to fess up. "Well, actually, he has another girl coming down to stay with him. Well, not *stay* with him. He didn't specify where she's staying—"

"Hold on," Lena interrupts. I hear her get up and say, "Mommy's talking on the phone for a minute, Leo." I hear her switch on the television then step into a quieter room. She inhales deeply then says, "Kat. Do you really consciously want to get mixed up in the crazy life of a drunk who doesn't want to stop drinking? Who left you as soon as you suggested that he *cut back*? Whose recreational drug habit is regular? Who will always choose those habits over you? Who has another girl coming to visit him *this weekend*? What are you thinking, Kat? Snap out of it. Thank the Heavens above that you questioned his drinking and he ran away! You deserve a man who's capable of being there for you. Showing up. Everyone does."

"Right."

"I am right! Listen, my maternity leave started, so I'm here at home. But I have to finish up some work as well as go pee for the third time this hour, so I'm gonna make this very succinct: do not go back to him. It was right for you guys to break up and I promise you that some day you'll see that. Okay?"

I say nothing.

"Didn't your show open?"

"Yes."

"Is it going well?"

"Yes."

"How's Mattie?"

"Not great, but getting help."

"So everything is as good as it could be. Focus on yourself, your writing. Get back into your Kat Groove."

"I'm trying but—"

"Put all your energy into yourself and your art and something will shift. Fuck this bull shit you have going on with Jonathan."

"But what if I get pregnant?"

"Go get yourself the morning after pill, Kat. Trust me, it's hard enough to have a child with someone who doesn't have a problem with booze and blow. Call the doc right now and get it. Don't take that chance. It's not fair to the potential child."

We hang up. I know Lena's right, but fuck I really wish she wasn't because I want Jonathan to be the one. I want him him him. I want to be pregnant and us to have to find a way to make it work. Without moving my position on the couch, I call him.

He picks up on the first ring. "Hi baby!"

"Hi. So listen. It's the time of month when I really could get pregnant."

"I can't talk, baby. I've gotta go pick up Jules from the airport." He says goodbye and hangs up.

I cry. I call my doctor and get the morning after pill. I cry anew. Calling Jonathan was a very bad idea.

9

Christmas Eve in Pleasantville, New York. I'm staying, as per usual, in my old bedroom at Dad's house. Mom only has one extra bedroom in her post-divorce house and Mattie's been released from the hospital so he's back at Mom's. He always stays at Mom's, even though they fight all the time and he says he hates living with her. I always stay at Dad's. And even though we never fight, I hate being around his never-ending stream of women. My father's thrilled to introduce me to his most recent lady friend, Red. As Mattie told me, Red is indeed refreshingly older than Dad's usual type, but they act like teenagers. I mean, there's so much PDA. It's disgusting. I don't want to hang out with them on Christmas Eve. Yet Mom has requested time to speak with Mattie, and thought that I'd be with Dad so Christmas Eve was the best time to do this. Of course, if I asked to go over to Mom's it would be fine, but I don't feel like it. On top of all this, Lena and Anne aren't even home for Christmas this year. Jonathan should be with me. He really freaking should. He made the wrong decision. Not just about his drinking. Going to pick up that Jules from the airport. He never even called me back. I feel used. I feel like an idiot. I go to bed early.

Late Christmas morning, my father's side of the family and Mattie arrive for an early Christmas lunch of turkey, cranberry sauce, stuffing, squash, corn, creamed spinach, hot rolls, etc. Thank God Dad's girlfriend left.

Mattie's far too low energy.

Dad discreetly remarks to me, "I think Mattie's doing very well, don't you?"

I raise my eyebrows. "I think he seems completely depressed."

"No, no, he's fine. He's doing great."

"I think he'd do better if he was staying with you."

Dad grimaces. "Not gonna happen."

"He may be on the quiet side now, but he and Mom always end up fighting and then he gets all manic again. Maybe if he stayed with you he could break the cycle."

Dad asks my aunt to pass the buns.

As the meal wears on, Mattie's silence starts to feel more sullen than depressed. Maybe Dad's right and he's fine. Maybe he's just being quiet because he's pissed off about something.

When we leave Dad's to do the half-mile trek to Mom's, Mattie finds his tongue. He fixates on Dad's new girlfriend. "Next time you see her, ask her why the fuck she's called Red."

"I'm not planning on seeing her."

"Yeah, but you probably will so just ask her."

"I prefer to engage with Dad's girlfriends as little as possible." It snowed a few days ago, only a little, but now it's all melted muck that we trudge through.

"I asked," Mattie says.

I laugh. "What the hell did she say?"

"Nothing. That's the thing. She smiled enigmatically."

"Why does he always have to date such weirdos?"

Matt continues, "She could've said, 'It's a nickname I picked up in high school when I dyed my hair,' or, 'It's short for Reddington, a family name,' or even, 'Yup, my parents named me Red. Can you believe it?' But no, she said nothing. Just fucking smiled."

"What a fucking loser."

Mattie snaps, "That's a little harsh, don't you think? I mean, Dad deserves to be happy."

I stop walking. "Excuse me? Why the change in allegiance? Mattie, she's a dingbat! She's dating a guy who doesn't give a shit about her. Let's hope that when Dad seriously falls for someone she'll have a modicum of self-esteem."

"I don't know why you think Dad'll ever fall for someone."

"Of course he will."

"I think he's pretty happy the way things are. Why do you think he doesn't want me back in my old room? I'd cramp his style."

"Don't be ridiculous."

"I'm not being ridiculous!" He's shouting. "I fucking hate it when you say shit like that! I'm the one who's here and I'm telling you, Dad getting play is way more important to him than me staying in my room!" His eyes stream with tears.

"Okay, okay. Sorry. You're right I'm sure. I don't want to believe it, but I'm sure you're right."

"I am fucking right, Louise. You don't know everything, you know. You're not here. You haven't been here for over a decade so—"

"Oh, don't start this again."

"It's true. You left for college and left me here!"

"Did you expect me to skip college?"

"I thought that you'd care a little bit more about leaving me with our parents while their marriage imploded."

"I love you very much, but it's true that I was more than happy to get the fuck out of here and go to college."

He continues, "And now I'm in this fucking outpatient crap and I have to commute. It takes like an hour to get there! I don't have time to do any of the things I like anymore!"

"Like what?"

"Like gardening! I just want to be out in the dirt, digging and planting!"

"It's winter?"

"Jesus fucking Christ, Kat. You think there's not shit for gardeners to do in the winter? You think it's a fucking summer job?"

"I just meant that it's winter, so there can't be much that you're missing."

"Don't fucking talk to me. You don't understand a fucking thing."

We plod along in an unpleasant silence to Mom's. There, we eat a Christmas meal identical to the one we had at Dad's: turkey, cranberry sauce, stuffing, squash, corn, creamed spinach, hot rolls, etc.

Mom flits from the kitchen to the dining room. Once, as she's passing me, she leans in and quietly remarks, "I don't think Mattie's doing very well."

This is the way it always is. Mom thinks he needs help, while Dad thinks he's fine. I guess I always think Mattie's somewhere in the middle because I tell her, "He's fine, Mom," and tuck into the déjà vu meal.

10

Home. Gratefully back home, I glance at my small Charlie Brown Christmas tree. I got it to cheer myself up, but it's making such a mess all over the carpet with its needles that I actually wish I'd skipped the tree this year. I slump down on the couch and soak in the silence that is my apartment, my space away from Mattie and his moods, my parents and their opposition, my space where everything is where it should be. I'm one with the small, sad, falling apart tree.

I'll call Lena. A few weeks ago, Lena gave birth to Coco, a healthy and huge baby girl who's doing very well, but Lena's been struggling with the breastfeeding and the no sleep. As I'm about to hit her number, an email from the now forgotten Charlie arrives.

> *Dear Katherine,*
> *Happy Christmas. I can't sleep so I thought I'd drop you a note to say hello and wish you a very happy holiday period.*
> *It must be strange being American. Everyone out here is obsessed about you and your politics. I hope I'm not misspeaking to say certain American politicians make the entire world a more dangerous place. And it's history now, but Bill Clinton let a stupid lie about sex ruin it all. I always think that if he hadn't lied then so many things could have been different and maybe our world would be a very different place...*
> *Enough of politics. Hope you're well and happy.*
> *Best,*
> *Charlie x*

I don't understand why he's emailing me now, or the still fascinating little "x."

Charlie,
I'm no expert on politics in general and have zero desire to rehash long gone political events on the day after xmas. Sorry.

So I wrote you an email, you wrote back, I wrote back, and then I hear from you <u>six weeks later</u>? And you just ignore the questions from my previous email? That's incredibly annoying. Why did you do that?

I had a very painful (though par for the course) Christmas with my family and don't have time for bullshit. If that's what this is, stop emailing me.

Good night.

ps- I go by Kat, not Katherine. I've told you that twice now.

I hit send. Then I call Lena. I know it's unlikely she'll pick up, but I want an actual chat. I leave a message. I unpack my bag. Maybe a fab idea for a play will pop into my head. It doesn't. Then an hour or so later, I get:

Dearest KAT,

It makes me laugh that you find me annoying, I probably am. I suppose I don't know what we're doing, so I suppose I don't know if it falls into the "bullshit" category or not. I know I met you here in London, liked you, wish I'd kissed you before you left. Flirtation, needing someone, loneliness, seduction, intrigue is all a bit messed up in me. So I suppose I didn't write back in order not to intrigue too much. That being said, why I laughed was that I had already decided that it was annoying you wrote back so quickly!!!

I'm sorry you had a painful Christmas. Family can be the challenge of our lifetime. I've certainly been wounded by mine. But even the most painful wounds can transform, like alchemy. The agony can turn to gold as what you thought were your weaknesses become your greatest human qualities. If you examine those pains, you can learn compassion, kindness and forgiveness. You can understand humanity and the fragility and strength of human life. The challenges of my life have only made it more precious and dear.

I found this poem for you:

I dreamt last night
oh marvelous error
that there were honeybees in my heart,
making honey out of my old failures
(antonio machado)

One of the fears of being sober a long time is turning into a caricature of obi-wan kenobi from Star Wars. My apologies if that just happened. All I'm trying to communicate is that you will be all right. Whatever the pain of Christmas was, you will be all right.

sleep well

Charlie x

ps- Brush up on your politics! Don't take for granted the right to political freedom your forefathers died for!

I read his email over and over and over and over and over.

II

At the touch of love,
everyone becomes a poet.
—Plato

1

Fuck emailing. I text him. He immediately texts back and away we go. I assign his texts their own unique ascending twinkle and every time I hear it, I grin like an idiot. Then one afternoon I read:

> May I ring you?
> Charlie x

And suddenly we're no longer texting. We're speaking every day and I'm in heaven. I rush home from work, cut short time with friends, and stay up far too late because I love talking to Charlie. Funnily enough, we never video call. I ask him once, "Should we turn the video on?"

"No."

"Should we send each other some photos?"

"No, no, no."

"I don't mean X-rated photos. Just so we can see each other."

"No, it's much better on my end that we keep it simple and only talk on the phone."

"Okay."

"Besides, hearing you but not seeing you… there's something rather sweet about it. I worry that a video call would make it too… racy. I want to court you properly."

"Well, okay." I tell him, "Being *properly courted* sounds good to me."

And the best news of all is that I'm writing again. The new play's bumbling along. Not my best work, but I'm back in the flow. Maybe I'll have something to show my agent soon. I swear Charlie's my muse. He always asks me how it's going and I love reporting that it's going well. I tell him all about what I'm working on. In fact, the only thing getting me down is the thing that's always getting me down: Mattie.

"Right before Christmas," I explain to Charlie, "Matt was discharged from this psychiatric hospital out in Connecticut."

"Where's Connecticut?"

I love that he doesn't know where Connecticut is. "Close to New York. And now he's doing outpatient care there and that's good because… he was using meth…"

"Go on."

"Well, I just… I worry about him all the time. Even though we have long stretches with no news about him, it's like a part of me is always on edge. Like I'm living my life, going to work, writing, doing my things, but in the back of my head I'm waiting for the next disaster."

"That's a very accurate description of what it's like to live with an addict."

"You mean a drug addict?"

"Well, yes. In this case, I mean exactly that. But all addicts are the same."

"I'm not sure he's an addict. He uses the meth to self-medicate his mood swings."

"Oh darling girl, you're so naïve."

"Excuse me?"

He pauses. "I'm sorry. I shouldn't have called you that. I actually find your innocence endearing. But I feel I must tell you—that it would be remiss of me *not* to tell you—that you've described an addict perfectly. They're highly unpredictable and chaotic. They suck up all the family's energy and resources."

He totally gets it. Well, most of it. I clarify, "I'm not sure he does drugs because he's an addict so much as he does drugs because he's bipolar."

"Is it only you and Matt?"

"Yeah."

"Kat and Matt?"

I smile. "We get that a lot."

"What does Matt do?"

"He wants to be a gardener, but right now he's just trying to get his shit together."

"Shit is very good for the garden."

I love talking to Charlie.

———

He recites poetry. From Keats to Rumi. He says he's got them memorized.

"No way. You're reading from a book!"

"I swear my father had me learn them."

"Baloney."

"Baloney? Isn't that a strange American meat?" I can hear him smiling.

———

I can't remember what he looks like anymore, and I start to doubt our decision not to video call. "What do you look like again?"

"The most handsome man you ever saw."

"Ha! Do you remember what I look like?"

"Absolutely. Dark skin… blue eyes."

"Uhhhh, no."

"No?"

"I have green eyes."

"Really?"

"Yup."

"Huh."

———

One day Charlie says, "Did you know it rains more days in

London than in New York, but there's more annual rainfall in New York than London?"

———

"What if I fly over for Valentine's Day?"

"What?"

"I'd only be able to come for a few days. But I was looking at flights today."

"You were?" I pop up from my cozy place on the couch, start pacing.

"Yeah," he replies casually. "The prices aren't too bad."

I want to be cool, but I feel like he's being presumptuous so I say, "Listen, it'd be great to see you but, the thing is, you can't stay with me."

He laughs. "All right, Kitty-Kat. Whatever you say."

"Well, let me know what you decide."

I immediately text Lena what's happened then tell her:

> *he can NOT stay with me!*
>
> I still think a one-night stand would be good for you
>
> *Far too soon for us to start having sex*
>
> Because he's THE ONE?!?!?!?

I know she's teasing me, but I don't think it's funny so I don't respond.

———

On Valentine's Day, I'm terrified he'll show up. I text Lena again:

> *what did this Charlie guy look like again?*
>
> No clue. I can barely remember my own name.
> JM has big photoshoot in Cannes so I'm on
> my own with the two kiddos for three nights!!!

So tired—understand why sleep deprivation
is form of torture

Yeah but good he has work, right?

Jean-Marc is a photographer who mainly shoots objects. He used to do Cartier, Chanel, a lot of big names, and then his luck changed. He takes what he can get now.

It's great. V jealous! Wish I was away working,
not cleaning up poop and begging Leo to eat
his food before I go insane

*I'm sure you'll be fine. Listen, what if he shows up
and I don't know if it's him?*

If stranger arrives and wants to make
sweet love, just say yes

That night, Charlie calls and I hold my breath as I pick up. "Hi."
"Hi."
"Where are you?"
"London."
"Cool."
"You sound happy about that."
"Well… yeah."
He exhales a "Hmph."
"Not that I don't want to see you because I do. But if you flew over the Atlantic to see me for Valentine's Day, that's just loaded…" He's silent. "I think you'd be assuming…" He doesn't help me out at all. "I mean…" I feel like a prude, but I'm trying to be sane. "I mean, you couldn't have stayed with me. You would have had to stay in a hotel or something."

All I can hear is his breathing. He makes me wait a long time. Finally, he says, "You're right. It wouldn't have been right for me to stay with you. I certainly would have wanted to and that wouldn't have been sober of me."

"Sober? You mean you'd drink?"

"No, I don't mean "sober" in terms of drinking. I'm saying it in terms of my behavior."

"Oh." Though I've never heard 'sober' used in this way before, I know what he's saying. "So basically I was right and it's too soon for both of us?"

He chuckles. "Sadly, yes."

"I love being right."

"Kitty Kat?"

"Charlie?"

"I really like you."

"I really like you too."

"What are we going to do about it?"

I sit bolt upright, my spidey senses tingling. "I am not having phone sex."

He laughs. "That's not what I'm saying!" Another pause, then, "But what if it was?"

"Sorry, not my thing."

"We should have a date."

"You're asking me on a date?"

"Yes. Here or there?"

"A trip to London? Definitely there."

2

I'm a touch late to meet Mattie at the Taqueria on the corner of 108th and Broadway. In the short walk from the subway, I have to keep my parka zipped all the way up over my chin, and my hands tucked deep into my pockets even though I'm wearing gloves. But I don't care about the cold. My heart's so light I feel like I'm flying. The instant I push inside the restaurant, heat blasts me. My skin feels so good as it defrosts. I wonder if London gets this cold.

Mattie's at a corner table in the back. I immediately clock his weight gain. It's only been two months since Christmas, but his face looks as puffy as the Pillsbury Doughboy's. He's wearing that same crazy yellow flannel shirt he had on at opening night when he collapsed, but with a dark blazer over it. To look respectable? To cover his paunch? He concentrates on getting every last morsel of Mexican goodness into his mouth then says simply, "Hey."

"Aren't we supposed to be there now?"

"Real estate guy's running late." Mattie leans forward in his chair and rubs his face with his hands.

"You okay?" No response. I wait. I hate it when Mattie talks non-stop, but equally can't stand it when he swings into a low mood. "You still doing the out-patient?"

He nods his head affirmatively. Mattie lies a lot about his self-care, but I suspect he's telling the truth now. So if he's sticking with his aftercare, maybe he's not depressed. Maybe this Quiet Matt is Normal Matt.

He looks up at me. "You look different."

"Do I?" A smile creeps over my face, and I have no ability to stop it even though I hate the Grinning Idiot thing people do when they're in love. Because that's the thing: I think I'm in love. I've been grinning a lot lately.

"You're like… glowing." Mattie sounds suspicious. "You and Jonathan back together?"

"God no!"

"So who is it then?"

I explain, "So when I was in London, I met this guy—"

"Wait. London?"

I start with how Charlie dropped us at our hotel even though it wasn't in his direction, and end with how I'm about to buy a plane ticket to have an official date with him. I omit that I think I'm in love with him.

Matt signals the waitress for the check. He says, "Let's go see this place."

He pays in silence, then I follow him out. He says absolutely nothing about what I've just told him, no questions or comments. I drop it as well. I ask, "What are we looking at today?"

"Studio. Brownstone."

Mattie's still living with Mom, but they are, as per usual, at each other's throats. Dad asked me a while ago if I thought Matt should live elsewhere. I suggested again that Mattie move in with him, but Dad said simply, "No." I was forced to agree that if Mattie couldn't live with Mom or Dad, then he needed a place of his own. Then my father called last night and asked me to go look at this place with Mattie today.

Outside I say, even though I've said this before, "I still think you should be back in your old room at Dad's."

Mattie says, "Yeah well, you always think you have the solution but you don't."

"Why don't you insist? It's the room you grew up in."

"Well, finished growing up in. But now Red's all over that place. And besides, Kat, if *you* can't get Dad to let me live there, *I* have no hope."

"What's that supposed to mean?"

"Daddy's little princess?"

I don't know what to say. Mattie's never called me that before. I don't like it, but I don't have a response, so I drop it. Mattie can figure out his own life.

We arrive at 108th and Riverside. The real estate broker walks us up a flight of steps into a gorgeous 450 square foot studio. Parquet floors, spacious loft bed, and small yet sweet bathroom complete with cast iron claw-foot tub. The kitchen is nothing more than a half fridge and a couple of burners. But who the hell needs a kitchen when the Taqueria's on the corner? The building's windows are huge and curved. Curved glass. Outstanding. I can't believe Dad's offering to buy this for him.

Mattie doesn't say much. Just thanks the broker, then we all walk out.

"What do you think?" he asks as we walk back to the subway.

"What do you mean, what do I think? I think you're spoiled rotten."

Mattie sighs. "Kat, I'm really fucked up right now. Just tell me if it's good or not."

"It's good."

"What's your fucking problem, Kat?"

"Nothing."

"Can you stop judging me for like, one second? I mean, what the fuck? You wouldn't have your apartment if it weren't for Dad!"

"All he did was cosign a rental agreement for a place on 170th street!"

"Yeah, and then Jonathan moved in so he could pick up the tab instead of Dad."

"I paid my share! I work!"

"So you live here and I'll live up there! Save Dad some money."

"I can't afford this place."

"That's not the point. The point is that I don't fucking care where I live, Kat, so long as it's not with Mom! So don't you dare judge me when you're just as fucked up as I am."

I give him a look. "You can be so ridiculous sometimes."

"You really think this thing with the London dude sounds like a good idea? You make it sound so impressive and romantic, but who in their right mind starts something up with a guy who lives an ocean away? That trip'll be nothing more than a glorified fuck."

"That's not what it's like."

"Then you're even more screwed up than me because you can't see it." We arrive at the subway, but Matt hails a taxi.

"It must be nice having Dad foot your bill."

"Jesus, Kat, this is the way it is right now. *I'm* supposed to be the one everyone worries about. Not you." He goes. I fucking hate him sometimes.

3

That night, I go online to search for plane tickets, but Mattie's tainted it. Will this transatlantic date truly be nothing more than a glorified one-night-stand? When Charlie calls, I'm ready to ask him just that, but he kicks off the conversation saying, "Go to the airport now."

I smile. "I can get a reasonable weekend fare mid-March."

"I need you to know two things. First of all, if for some crazy reason it works out between us, I'd be able to support you and your writing, financially I mean. Plus I'd introduce you to anyone I could to help out. Though it's not my industry, I'd do everything in my power to help you get set up over here."

What a gentleman! Thank God he can't see me swooning. I keep my voice steady. "Thank you."

"Secondly," a deep breath, "and I mean this seriously," another deep breath, "I don't think this is going to work if we're seeing other people."

"Are you seeing other people?"

"No. And I won't. And I'd like you not to either. It will drive me crazy if you are. We only have a small chance of success here. What we have is incredibly delicate. If our energies are dispersed, there's no way it will work."

I'm shocked. I mean, I'm not interested in anyone else so this is a non-issue. But I'm still shocked. No one's ever proposed exclusivity to me before we've even had a first date. I usually have the "exclusive" conversation with a guy after we've spent a lot of time together, usually after we've slept together multiple times.

"What do you think?" he persists.

"I think..." I remember that the lighting guy from *Annabel* wanted to set me up with a friend of his. But nothing's been arranged and there's no way that could be better than this. No one could be better than Charlie. So I say, "I think that sounds good."

"What's wrong?"

"Nothing!"

"I can hear something in your voice."

"How is that possible?"

"I've been listening to your voice for two months now. I know it very well. So what's wrong?"

I decide to put it out there. "Is what we're doing… real?"

"Actually, Kat, I've been meaning to tell you, I'm just a voice living inside your phone. Very high-tech, but not real at all."

I laugh, then get off the phone and book my flight.

4

I can't sleep. I'm five days away from seeing him. Maybe kissing him. I'm lying in bed thinking about kissing Charlie… when my phone rings. It's 6:45 a.m. on Sunday morning, so 11:45 a.m. in London. I smile and say, "You're calling early."

He sighs heavily. "There's something I feel I have to tell you before you come."

I adjust. "This doesn't sound good."

"Well, I mean, I only thought it fair, before you travel all this way…"

I listen, wait. He says nothing. Oh my God. This is it. This is the end. He doesn't seem to want to spit it out, so I ask, "Are you married? Have a child? Children?"

"No!"

"Okay. Then what?"

He's silent.

"What is it?" This is gonna be bad. "Charlie?" He's freaking me out. "Whatever it is, it's all right." As I say this, I start to believe it. It will be all right because I love this guy. Of course I haven't told him that yet. That would be relationship suicide. Besides, I'm hoping that he'll say it first. No one's ever said it to me first. I should at least hold out till we're in the same country. I should at least find out what he thinks is so terrible. I'm scared again. "Are you ending this insane phone relationship?"

"No."

"Canceling our transatlantic date?"

"No."

"Am I anywhere close?"

"No."

"So then just tell me."

"It's difficult, Kat. It's about me."

"But I love hearing about you."

More silence. More waiting.

"Okay," I tell him. "I'm not going to talk. I'm going to sit here and wait until you feel like you can say it."

A lot more silence. I mute the phone so I can pee. Still silence. I wander into my modest kitchen, put water in the kettle to boil, turn on the burner. I'm meeting Anne later for brunch but much later. Before brunch, I'm hoping to work more on my latest idea for a new play. I've still got flow and want to keep it that way. As usual, Charlie's breathing loudly on his end of the line. I said to him the other day, "You're breathing too loud! Move the phone away from your mouth!" He joked, "We're off to a bad start if you don't like the way I breathe." Now his breathing is the only sign he's still out there. I wait. He breathes. I get out my cafetière, scoop coffee into it. He breathes. My kettle whistles. I turn off the burner. I'm irritated. "Come on, what is it?"

Barely audible: "I'm a sex addict."

My immediate reaction is to keep my tone as light as possible as I ask, "Is that it?" He obviously feels like this is an awful thing. Admittedly, I don't know much about it, but I feel like I should downplay what he's just turned into a dramatic confession. "Why didn't you just say?"

"I'm trying to say now," Charlie whispers. He sounds ashamed.

"Okay. So… what? You sleep with hookers?" I say this like I'm totally cool with that idea.

"Kat! No!"

"Well, I don't know! Why the drama around telling me? What do you do?"

"Can we not get into specifics?"

"Sure. But I don't really understand what you're saying to me. I mean, what this *means*. It's a term that's thrown around a lot these days. Are you like Tiger Woods or Harvey Weinstein? Do you sleep with streams of models?"

"No."

"Are you saying that even though you made such a big deal that we not see other people, that you are?"

"No, I'm not seeing anyone. Only talking with you."

"So… you're not actually doing sex addict-y things right now?"

"No, I'm in recovery."

"Like AA but for sex?"

"Exactly. There's SAA, SLAA, SCAA, all sorts of places to get recovery for it."

"And you're going to those places?"

"One of them, yes."

"Regularly?"

"Yes."

I pour the hot water over the coffee. "Then what's the problem?"

5

After frantically googling "sex addiction," I oscillate between relief and paranoia. The term covers so much. What kind of sex addict is Charlie? The sex offender type? A pedophile? Masturbator? He said he wasn't into hookers or models. Some sex addict behaviors make me want to vomit, while others seem, dare I think it, normal. A few hours later, I drag myself away from my research. Needless to say, I did no work after that phone call.

I brave the elements to meet Anne on the Upper West Side for brunch at our favorite Mexican restaurant. Anne's seated when I arrive. She looks like absolute shit. Sure, it's overcast outside, but she wears her sunglasses inside and clutches her mug of coffee as if her life depends on it, both telltale signs of a wicked hangover. She hugs me. "I look disgusting, I know."

"Mmm-hmm."

"Don't do that head-nodding mmm-hmm thing."

"I'm a New Yorker, that's what we do."

"You're a nice girl from Pleasantville. It's not what we do." She summons the waitress. "More coffee for me and one for my friend, please."

"How was the wedding?"

"I think something was off in the food department. I feel sick."

Anne never admits she's hungover, and I usually play along with whatever excuse she's peddling. But now that Lena made a point about Anne's drinking, I ask, "You sure you didn't just drink too much?"

Anne glares at me. "What has Lena said to you?"

"Lena has a newborn. She hardly has any time to even text me anymore."

Anne stares me down.

"Back in London she may have commented that you like to drink more than we do, but she pointed it out like a fact, which it is! She didn't say anything bad about it because there isn't anything bad to say about it. Why? Have you talked to her?"

Anne crosses her legs. "Well, I do like my booze, but I usually don't feel sick like I do this morning. I swear something was off in the raw bar."

"Okay then."

The waitress brings me a cup of coffee and refills Anne's. A tiny bit of coffee—I mean, like a speck—lands on her wrist. "Ow!"

"Sorry, hon," The waitress makes to dab at Anne's wrist, but Anne moves her hand away.

Anne scowls up at the waitress until she goes. Anne adds creamer, then takes a couple of Advil out of her purse and washes them down with the coffee. "Lena called me last week and gave me about two seconds of her time in order to express her concern about my lifestyle."

"Okay."

"Not really, no! More like, totally obnoxious."

"You guys will work it out, you always do. How was it anyway?"

"How was what?"

"The wedding!"

"Bobby's so happy." Anne says this like it's a bad thing. She's constantly comparing herself to him and he sets the bar high. Ten years older than Anne, Bobby sails through life. He's the first of Anne's four older brothers and he now officially has it all. Which is why I tell her, "I hear you." Then I offer, "You know, I hear the divorce rate these days is fifty percent."

Anne chuckles, slurps down more coffee, then says, "I don't actually wish a divorce on them, and even if I did, Bobby'd end up on the successful side of that statistic."

I ask, "You dating anyone?"

"Don't depress me further. How's Prince Charming?"

"Well," I pause. It's not my secret to tell, but this is Anne. I want her breezy assurance.

"What is it, honey?" There's a genuine softness in her voice.

"He told me this morning that he's a sex addict."

"Bullshit," Anne casually responds as the food arrives. "Oh, I ordered you huevos rancheros."

"What do you mean bullshit?"

"Either he can be faithful or he can't. You don't need to label it. Besides, 'sex addiction' is a mythical illness invented to justify sleeping around."

"Well, there's all sorts of stuff online about—"

"Stop. Can he be faithful? Yes or no?" Anne tucks into her eggs.

"I have no idea. We're barely even a couple. We haven't even had our first date yet. We haven't even kissed yet."

"So you'll find out. And if he can, great. And if he can't, you had a long weekend in London. This is no biggie, Kat."

Anne smiles and I want to believe her. I really really really want to believe her. Like the way I used to want my parents to stay together or Santa to bring me a puppy even though my mother claimed she was allergic (I knew she wasn't). I ask Anne, "What about the sex offenders? Some are Peeping Toms?" I pause then voice my greatest fear. "Pedophiles?"

"Well, is he one of those?"

"I have no idea."

"So you'll go on your date and get to know him better and eventually you'll find out what kind of sex addict he is. If he's any of those oddities, you'll probably sense something weird about him anyway, and it'll be over. You may cry, but you'll live and move on. Simple as that."

Anne's right. I know she's right this time. But for some reason, it doesn't feel *simple as that*.

"What's the problem?" Anne presses me.

"He's just so wonderful, everything about him. I hate that now there's this thing…"

"Everyone has baggage, Kat." Anne sighs an almost imperceptible sigh.

I ask her, "You okay out in Cali?"

"Of course!" Anne sounds falsely upbeat. "What's not to like about sunshine and good-looking people?"

"Tell me who you've been dating."

"Kat?"

"Yeah?"

"Are you sure this thing with Charlie isn't just... I don't know, something you're using to get over Jonathan?"

"What do you mean?"

"Well, you didn't really mean to break up with him. He broke up with you because you were so critical of his lifestyle. You probably wouldn't have left him otherwise. And you still love him, right?"

"Jonathan? Yeah, of course, but won't I always? And this is, like you said five seconds ago, this is just a date, Anne."

———

I research more and more on sex addiction. When I'm saturated, I text Lena with the news.

why can't you pick someone normal?

done a LOT of research. It's totally treatable

well, good then! Besides, it actually sounds
like should be a good thing! ;)

ha. Well... not the way he said it

what do sex addicts do to get better?
Do they have some kind of AA for that?

Yes they have a few fellowships

Is he doing that?

Affirmative

so there you go. I suppose there's as much risk
with that as anything

Sounded really bad. He like... confessed to me

He's exposing himself! Scary for anyone, but
particularly scary if you have an addiction like
that to expose! Kudos to him for being honest
before you even see him in the flesh (which
may be even more fun with a sex addict, non?)

a girl can hope!

Give the relationship time to develop

Crap. Look at what Leo drew

A picture comes through. In the foreground, Leo has drawn a very big stick-figure Lena with her cell phone in one hand, a briefcase in the other. In the background, three small stick figures of Leo, baby Coco and Jean-Marc. Every stick figure has a sad face.

Jean-Marc brainwashed Leo into thinking that
mommy working makes everyone sad

they missed you when you were at work.
Just remind him that you're home now

actually… started working one day a week

Aren't you still on maternity leave?!?

I am! Except for one day/wk

How does that work?

I put Coco in sling and work

What about Leo?

In school half the day, then I try to organize
a playdate for him on the day that I'm working
or give him the tablet or something

do you get anything done?

yeah well I have to—don't want them to replace me

You're a nut

6

I'm sitting here at work, my carry-on suitcase beside me, listening to sparrows chirp a happy song, counting down the hours until I can leave. There's fuck-all to do, which means I could be writing and I should be writing, but I can't focus. I've taken tomorrow off from work because tomorrow I'll be in London with Charlie. It all feels unreal, like I'm five and it's the night before Christmas and I'm wondering if Santa will really come. I want magic.

When I'm in the taxi, I call Charlie and tell him, "This is the last time we'll talk on the phone before we're together." I'm still dying to know what kind of a sex addict he is, but that's a face-to-face conversation.

"They think I'm rubbish." He's talking about his job. I'm a little put off that he doesn't seem excited about me coming to see him, but he's been seriously worried about work recently. He goes on, "I think I'm going to be sacked."

"Sacked?" Another new way of saying things.

"You're laughing? Do you understand I could lose my job?"

The taxi's whizzing out of Manhattan, bringing me closer to Charlie by the second. I tell him, "Charlie, you're amazing and they wouldn't have hired you then *promoted* you if they didn't know that."

"I'm not amazing. You hardly know me."

"I'm a very smart woman. And you are incredibly good at what you do."

"Baloney."

I laugh whenever he says this. And when Charlie chuckles along with me, I feel like I'll implode if the words I'm dying to say aren't allowed out of my mouth. I try to swallow them down for the hundredth time, but they're coming out too forcefully, and part of me cringes yet part of me thrills as I say, "I love you."

Dead silence.

Quietly I say, "Maybe I shouldn't have said that, maybe it's too soon. I know we haven't even had our official date yet, but I feel it and I don't see the point in you not knowing how I feel."

More dead silence. Crap.

He finally says, "I feel it too, Kat. But I'm worried it will all go pear-shaped."

"Pear-shaped? Like a dumpy middle-aged woman?"

"I'm being serious but yes, precisely like a dumpy middle-aged woman."

"If this doesn't go anywhere, Charlie, you can always know that today, March 16th, at 5:21 p.m. Eastern Standard Time, I, Katherine Maureen Callahan, love you."

"That feels very nice, babe. Very nice."

7

Seven hours is a long time to dwell on the fact that he didn't just come right out and say, "I love you too." By the time my plane lands early, all my excitement has been replaced with trepidation. I pray he won't be here yet. I follow the crowd through Immigration, Baggage Claim, Customs, then down a final passageway leading to a set of swinging double doors beyond a final duty-free shop. Before passing through the swinging double doors, I stop. When the doors swing open, I see a wall of faces. Alongside bored taxi drivers holding signs, there's a congregation of husbands, wives, kids, all straining to spot their loved ones. I want to go home. Why am I here? I can't remember what he looks like. What if I'm not physically attracted to him? What if Matt's right and this is all one massive mistake? I turn and, like a fish swimming upstream, push my way through all the passengers leaving. I move as far away from those swinging doors as possible. I make it back around a corner where, even if the double doors are open, the sea of expectant faces can't see me. I try to take a few deep breaths but can't seem to get the air past the top of my lungs. I'm trapped. As much as I'd like to, I can't return to the plane. I'm acting wacko and I know it. Come on, I've come this far. There's nothing to do now but go through the scary swinging doors. I turn. I force myself to walk back to the doors. I push the doors open. I scan the sea of faces. I don't have a clue what Charlie looks like anymore, so I look for someone who's looking for me. I scan, scan, scan. No one is looking for me. My plane was very early and he's not here. He's not here. Air drops down into my body and I can finally breathe. Nice deep breaths. I rest my carry-on by a column. Relieved relieved relieved. Then this grinning man approaches, head cocked, blue eyes sparkling, hand extended. "Kat Callahan?"

I try to smile. Fuck. This is him.

"It is you, right?"

I manage to nod.

He can't seem to stop grinning. He takes my hand in an exaggerated fashion, shakes it formally, as if nine hours ago I wasn't confessing *I love you* in his ear. "I've never seen anyone look so terrified in all my life."

"What do you mean?" I attempt to radiate confidence.

"You looked petrified. Still do!"

I'm so busted. I can't help but laugh and he laughs with me and it's kind of like being with him on the phone, only we're not. He's right here. A brilliant sun beaming down on me. I can't help but bask in his gaze, let it warm me. My fear of not being attracted to him vanishes. It's replaced with a fear of him not being attracted to me.

"Well…" He takes my bag and leads me through the airport. He stops just before the doors to the parking lot. "Kat?"

"Yes?"

"Come here." He takes me to the side. "Can we get this bit over with?"

"What bit?"

He pulls me in and kisses me. A slow, simple kiss. A loving kiss. My heart leaves my body and floats into his.

"I thought I'd make things clear," he says.

"That was pretty clear."

8

In his car, I start to sweat, take off my sweater.

"What *are* you doing?"

"I'm sorry! It's just real hot." This is the truth, but I'm also aware that the t-shirt I'm wearing is low cut in a great way.

"Hot? It's only March!"

"Come on! I've been talking to you on the phone forever, I'm nervous. Ok?"

"All right." He smiles a bit. "But to clarify, it's not hot here. It's been pissing down all day."

"Pissing down? I love that."

"Here." He turns on the air and aims a vent at me. I sit back and try to compose myself. "Better?"

"Yes. Very good."

He shakes his head. "It's like a whole new thing getting to know the in-person-you. I may have to put this you in one room and ring you from another so that I can remember the phone you."

I giggle then blurt out, "When was the last time you did something sex addict-y?"

His eyes stay straight on the road, his wide grin disappears. "What do you mean?"

"I don't mean to be nosy, I just figured if we're potentially getting involved…"

"Ah! But you're sleeping in the spare room!"

"Come on," I gently prod, "I know you have seventeen years sober from alcohol. What about from sex?"

"I see. You're asking how long I've been sexually sober? It's not like that."

"What do you mean?"

"Sex isn't like alcohol."

"Duh. Of course it isn't. But you must either have some kind of sobriety in that area or not?"

"Well," he softens, "yes. And you shouldn't worry. I have a year sexually sober. It's just that it's trickier to define what sobriety means in the sexual arena."

"Oh." I want to know why it's "trickier" as I don't really understand what he's saying, but he looks like maybe I upset him a little so I don't press for clarification. Instead, I reach over and take his hand. "Thanks for telling me. I don't know why I asked." He squeezes my hand in his. God, I like this. It feels like he's energizing me, like we're one. So I steel myself because I want to ask him one little thing, want to stop stressing about a small issue. "And you're not a pedophile, are you?"

He pulls away from me. "Christ no! That's a horse of a different color, Kat!"

"Phew!" I try to lighten the mood because now he's starting to definitely look unhappy. "I didn't mean to distress you. It's a subject I know very little about so I thought I'd ask."

"I'm what I guess is called your garden-variety sex addict. Pedophiles are... they really are a different beast altogether, Kat, and I can assure you that I am not that particular beast. I do have morals."

"Thanks for letting me ask." I change the topic. "Now, about this spare room, I assume I can lock the door from the inside?"

9

Charlie lives in a town called Harrow in northwest London. From how he describes it, it sounds like living deep in Brooklyn or Jersey. His house (he has an entire house) is sparsely decorated and impeccably clean. After his quick tour, I observe, "It doesn't look like anyone actually lives here."

"I do spend a lot of time in my car," he admits. "And I'm sometimes too tired to drive home, so I sleep in the office."

"Isn't this… a lot of space for one person who's not here?"

Charlie shrugs. He takes my suitcase. "I'll pop this up here." He runs up the stairs with my suitcase then back down. He stands in front of me with a big grin and says, "I put it in the spare room."

I laugh. Then we stand there looking at each other.

He finally asks, "Did the flight tire you out?"

"I'm okay."

"As it's still raining—"

"Pissing down."

"Shall we have a late lunch and watch a film?"

I follow him into the living room. While I settle on his blue couch, he brings out nibbles. We slowly tuck into buffalo mozzarella, grilled artichokes, and other delicious bites. I try to be casual and at ease, but the air is charged with sexual alertness, our bodies in tune with each other. When he moves, I adjust. A little dance.

"Why don't you move closer to the city?" I ask him.

"Why don't you move closer to me?" He hooks his foot around my leg and tugs.

"Why don't you lay off the cheese?" I slap his foot.

He laughs then reaches out and pulls me in to him. When his lips touch mine, I melt then melt then melt some more. He pushes my hair back. "You taste better than the artichokes."

"Better than the mozzarella?"

"Yes." He kisses my neck.

"Better than the sun-blushed to-*mah*-toes?" I notice the scar near his throat that I saw the night we first met. It was noteworthy then. I touch it now. "Did you cut yourself shaving or something?"

He pulls away. "This is a bit embarrassing."

"What?"

He takes a deep breath in. "I can't believe I'm going to tell you this."

"What is it?"

"I tried to slit my throat."

"What?" I sit up.

"Yeah. I, well, obviously you can see it's only a nick. I really didn't have it in me to get very far."

"Thank God." I stroke his scar. "Why not the wrists?

He gives a small shrug, "Too cliché?"

"When was this?"

"A long time ago now. When I was an unhappy, overly dramatic teenager and drinking very heavily."

"I'm so very sorry you felt that way."

He kisses me. We make our way upstairs.

Outside his bedroom door, the panic from the airport returns. I see myself walking back down the stairs, getting back onto the couch. I think the things I would say to a girlfriend in my position. *Don't sleep with him on the first date. He won't respect you. If you want it to last, wait!* But I can't listen because the kissing feels so absolutely 100% right and good, and is it really the first date? When you don't live in the same country, don't some of those phone calls count as dates?

Charlie tilts my face up to look at him. "You here with me?"

Gazing into his brilliant blue eyes, we somehow enter his room. I want to stare into his eyes forever. Oh my God, I'm thinking such idiotic thoughts. I giggle.

"What's so funny?"

"This! It's just... surreal!"

He has two flecks of black in his right eye. And then, somehow, I'm lying on his bed and his eyes are gone as he sets out to kiss every inch of my body.

I'm in heaven. I've never been touched like this before. *Completely* touched.

My body becomes more than willing to have sex with him, my mind quickly follows, my clothes swiftly disappear, and it's all going great... really great... until I realize I'm not going to orgasm. And he's working away so gallantly! I feel guilty because I know he's not going to bring me to the place he's aiming for. I tell him in a hushed rushed whisper, "Charlie, it's not going to happen for me our first time so don't worry about that, just enjoy yourself."

Charlie stops what he's doing. He takes my head in his hands, makes eye contact again. "Are you all right?"

"Totally, I just know I won't orgasm and so don't want that pressure on us now."

"It's not about orgasming or not, is it, sweetie? It's about being together."

I laugh again.

"What's so funny now?"

"What you just said is so cheesy!"

"It's true though. That's what this has to be about."

I absorb this. "True," I say. "But I want you to understand that I normally don't have a problem in that area, it's because it's our first time. Once we've spent more time together, it'll be fine. And... I don't want to stop your fun, so... " I smile. "Why don't you go ahead?"

"You sure?"

My answer is the slightest nod of my head combined with the most perfect movement of my hips. We don't take our eyes off each other as he "goes ahead." He looks like he's dying for a moment, like his brain cells are popping, like he's entered nirvana.

Fifteen minutes later, and we're at it again and I scream as I come. I'm coming and he's laughing. "It took you a whole half hour to get to know me better," he teases as he wraps me in his arms. And now my tears arrive. I thought maybe they wouldn't. He turns me around. "My God, are you all right?"

"Yes, I just… sometimes I cry after I come."

"Babe."

"But I swear," I force myself to smile and calm down, "I couldn't be better."

10

When we wake up the next day, it's bright and sunny. Charlie says, "It's been miserable all week. You brought the sunshine with you."

I reply, "Cheesy."

We go to a beautifully manicured park. There are daffodils as far as we can see. While we stroll, I sing to him, songs that my grandma used to sing to me. He holds my hand. When I stop, he says, "Sing me another one."

I sing.

We go home.

We have more sex.

Everything is slow. Every moment counts.

Charlie tells me, "Pack your bags. I booked us a room in town."

He takes me to the Ritz London. We check in before dinner. Our room is gloriously luxurious. We put on our matching robes then take them off each other. They offer dinner and dancing downstairs. We get dressed up and go. My sea bass arrives. It's not very good. Dry, flavorless.

"How is it?"

"Horrible. How's your steak?"

"Rubbish." But we don't care.

We can't take our eyes off each other.

We dance.

We can't take our eyes off each other.

We go back upstairs and make love again.

It doesn't bother him when I cry after sex. He looks at me like he understands.

I feel safe.

We can't take our eyes off each other.

I want to drink in every second of him.

I leave too soon.

11

Back home and I miss him in a way I've never missed anyone before. It's a full body ache. When he calls, I tell him, "That was too much fun."

"I know." His voice is quiet. "I miss you, Kat."

"Where are you?"

"Downstairs on the couch."

I can picture the comfy blue couch downstairs in front of the mega flat-screen TV. I can picture his body stretched across the couch, his shoulders snuggled into one side, his feet dangling over the other, the pillow squished under his head. Less than a week ago, my mind held no image of him; now his face, chest and body are etched in there. And should I forget, there're about a hundred photographs of him and us on my phone. "I wish I was on the cozy couch with you."

"Kat?"

"Yeah?"

"If you talk in that low, slow voice, I'm going to get aroused."

"*Aroused?* Stop it! We are not having phone sex!"

He laughs. "All right, if you say so."

12

We have phone sex.

Without video. We still only talk over the phone. This feels old-fashioned. I love it. The phone sex though, even though there's no video, does not feel old-fashioned. It's something I've never done before (there's been no need) and it's not really my thing, but what can I say, I'm horny too. I giggle the entire time, but the end result is surprisingly great, and at least when I cry no one's looking at me.

13

He visits me next.

"You're here at one of my favorite times of year," I tell him as we walk through Central Park. "Manhattan, in the height of spring."

He kisses me.

"Charlie, look around!" He keeps kissing me. "You're supposed to be soaking in Manhattan."

"Let's go back to your flat."

We do.

———

Then I'm back visiting him for Memorial Day weekend so I can use one less vacation day. I don't want my vacation days to disappear too quickly. We're driving to his place, and I'm bone-tired because I didn't sleep at all on the overnight flight and I'm already hating that I have to leave in three days. The thought *this is insane* creeps into my head as we scoot out of the airport onto the highway.

"Kat?"

"Yes?"

"I have something important to tell you."

I open my eyes. "How important?"

"I think… very."

"Don't make me guess."

"I lied to you."

Alert, "About what?"

"When you asked me about my sexual sobriety."

"Have you been seeing someone else?" I feel a combination of panic and relief. At least I'm finding out now.

"No, no," he assures me. "Nothing like that."

"I'm too tired. Just tell me."

"When you asked me how long I'd been sexually sober? The truth is not a year but a few months. I had a relapse in December."

"When?"

"December."

"I heard you. I mean, what date in December?"

"I don't know. Does it matter?"

"I just happened to sleep with my ex-fiancé in December so it would be weird if it was the same day."

"You don't care that I lied to you?"

I think about it, then: "I suppose we barely knew each other and it's your personal life and it was a bit nosy of me to ask in the first place and you're telling me now. So what difference does it make? I mean, it was before we decided to be exclusive, right?" He nods. "So it doesn't really matter, does it? I mean, have you cheated on me?"

"No. But I have only a few months clean."

"But sexual sobriety isn't like sobriety from alcohol, right?" I yawn. "Are we almost there?" I recline the passenger seat. "Who were you even seeing in December?"

He keeps his eyes on the road. "No one."

"Then how did you relapse?"

"Pornography."

"You don't watch underage porn, do you?"

"Christ no!"

I shake my head. "Then is it really so bad? I sometimes think you make all this sex addict stuff into a much bigger deal than it is. Whenever you talk about it, you're so dramatic. But what's so bad about a little porn? I mean, fine, I guess in your case it's not *a little*. But that's because you're a sex addict, right? So you go to your meetings and forgive yourself and try to do better next time."

Charlie glances down at me. "You're extraordinary."

I get a good look into his blue eyes before he pulls his attention back to the road. My Dad has blue eyes too. Charlie and I could have a baby with blue eyes.

14

I spend the entire summer flying back and forth across the Atlantic. To state the obvious, this is exhausting both physically and financially. I do most of the flying... well, I do all of the flying because Charlie's job demands more time and energy than mine. Lena and Anne, who are never in agreement on anything and aren't really speaking to each other, both conclude that I'm putting more effort into the relationship than he is. I tell them both: "This is about practicality. My Human Resources job is about as far from rocket science as you can get, and that's when there's something to do there. There've been almost no HR issues all summer, so all I do when I'm there is try to write. And at night I'm either doing the same or going to a show or something. So my schedule's mellow. Adding jetlag into it isn't such a big deal. Whereas with Charlie's job... yikes. If he's tired for a big meeting, he could mess up a deal. So showing up for work totally jetlagged and dysfunctional is not an option on his end." They both back off.

Besides, I love it over there. The summer days are so long! Energizing! I'm prolific when I'm there. I'm sure success with a new play sits right around the corner! But by the end of July, I've used up all of my vacation days and a fair chunk of my savings. I hit the pause button. I have to. I mean, I saw it coming and here it is. It won't be until January that I get more vacation days.

Charlie says, "Don't worry, babe. I'll fly over to you." He buys a ticket to come out at the very end of August. That'll be a four-week stretch for us, which is the longest we've gone since we started this insanity.

But then work goes crazy on his end and he has to cancel his visit. I'm so depressed. I miss him so much it's killing me. And I'm not alone with that feeling. Charlie misses me too. We spend long hours on the phone, sometimes just sitting there not saying anything. We video chat now so I can see him. But still, the thought *this is insane* returns frequently. Then I get this email:

Babe,

I have bought you a ticket (see attached). I know it's pushing the limits of sanity as you'll fly out Friday after work, arrive Saturday morning, then fly back on Sunday night to get to work for Monday morning. You'll be wrecked, but I am so eager to see you.

If you feel it's too much, and don't want to make such a short trip, I will be disappointed, but understanding.

Love you, darling.
- C x

PS- Ticket was exorbitant so you'd best get your sexy bottom on the plane.

I cannot believe his generosity, but… *this is insane.* I call him, "Charlie!"

"I have to see you, babe. It's been too long. Do you mind?"

"Of course I don't mind. I'm dying to see you too, but this is nutso. The cost of the ticket alone…"

"Once work calms down for me, things will be different."

———

That Friday, while I wait for the flight, I text Lena. She replies:

This kind of long distance relationship can't be good for you honey

What can I do? I love a man who lives in London.

It's not my fault the geography sucks.

*Besides you spend a hell of a lot of time
away from your family and it works fine!*

no it doesn't! that's my point! JM forever angry bc Leo missed
me to the extreme when I was away on business or even just
working late in the office—yet dying to get back to full-time
work—and now I can hear Coco waking up so ttyl

xxx

Later that night, well, the next day really, I'm lying in Charlie's
bed, about to pass out after some you'll-have-to-get-on-top-because-
I'm-too-tired-to-do-much-at-all sex, when I surprise myself by asking, "What are we doing here?"

"Getting to know that when I kiss your neck just here," he gently strokes the most sensitive spot on my neck, "you'll do just about
anything for me."

Jetlag and sex make an exhausting yet exhilarating cocktail. And
I can feel yet another twinkling inside myself, a distant star springing
back into view. But my head's really wondering what's going on, so I
ask again, "Really? How long can we go on like this?"

Charlie doesn't stop the kisses. "Perhaps I should fly out and
meet your parents?"

I pull away. "What? Why? How is that an answer to my question?"

"If I were a parent, I'd want to meet the man my daughter was
head over heels for."

"Head over heels?"

He kisses that same spot on my neck again. I must admit, I think
he's right about it being my gateway spot. He murmurs, "We only
have nineteen more hours together. I have to make the most of it."

"When do I get to sleep?"

"Once I return you to the airport."

15

Two weeks later, Charlie flies out to meet Mom and Dad. When we're on the train up to Pleasantville, the fall foliage peeping out, I ask, "I thought work was very busy?"

"It is. How extraordinary to grow up with these incredible colors. You were made and shaped in this bizarre country with all its flaws and beauty."

"But if it's so busy, then how could you come?"

"Look at that shade of orange! And that yellow! What a strange country this is."

"Do you think you're obsessed with America?"

"I think we all are. We just don't want to admit it."

My knee is involuntarily shaking.

Charlie presses his hand on it. "Are you that nervous?"

"My knee is."

"Don't be. I'm superb on first meets."

Once in Pleasantville, we start the walk to Mom's house. Along the way, we pass a substantial, white colonial. I pause in front of it and tell Charlie, "This is the house I grew up in, where we all lived before my parents got divorced. It's where my family started out. I mean, I remember the day they brought Mattie home from the hospital and… lots of other stuff. And then when I was thirteen and Mattie was nine, my parents moved, which was a big change. And my Mom insisted that my Dad stop drinking. We moved about half a mile down there." I point down to the left towards Dad's house. "See the big grey house?" Charlie nods. "It's not very far away, but it was considered a major upgrade."

"Did he do it?"

"Do what?"

"Quit drinking?"

"Totally. And so they stayed married until I went off to college when Mom suddenly asked for a divorce. I don't know why she waited so long."

"Because of you and Matt?"

"Well, Mattie was still living at home, so we can't be the reason or she would have waited for him to go to college too."

"Sounds like something happened to spark it."

"Well, I know he cheated on her."

"How do you know that?"

"He was always *at work* which I suspected was code for something else. Then, after we moved and he quit drinking, he was really always at work. We never saw him."

"I'm at work a lot and I'm not having an affair."

"And someone saw him with his secretary at the golf club."

"So?"

"Trust me. He cheated. There was more than one argument about receipts for jewelry that my mother never received. He never fessed up but, with a little hindsight, it's obvious."

"Hindsight is clever that way."

"But I don't think that was the catalyst for the divorce. I feel like that was ongoing." We're both looking up at the house. I tell him, "It used to be orange."

"This house?"

"Yeah, when we lived here it was this peachy orange with brown trim. I don't know why my parents never changed the color. But after they sold it the new owners did."

"Mmmm, now that you mention orange, I can see it shining through the white."

Suddenly I'm slammed with emotions and memories: running away from home with Mattie and no one noticed; watching cartoons while Mom slept on the couch; Dad coming home late every night and sitting at the end of my bed.

We walk on. Charlie heads towards Dad's big grey house. I interlock my arm with his and pull him back on course. "This way.

When they finally did get divorced, Mom's the one who moved out and she moved down here." We walk in silence for a bit. It's nice. I'm used to walking these streets with Mattie who's either overly chatty or taciturn. When we get near to Mom's house, I point it out. "The ranch house there. That's hers."

"Huh."

"What?"

"It's modest. She must have really wanted that divorce. It's almost always the mother who gets the big house."

"Well, yeah. She really wanted to get divorced."

We walk up the pathway to the front door. The house feels peaceful to me. I usually love arriving here, but I'm just so nervous. I knock. The door opens and, when my mother's face appears, Charlie says, "I'm so happy to meet the source of all the loveliness that is your daughter."

Mom gives him a warm smile. "It's a pleasure to meet you too."

"You look like sisters." It's like Charlie winks with his words, a respectful flirtation.

"Oh stop it!" Mom says while soaking in the attention.

"I mean it, Mrs. Callahan."

"Mrs. Callahan! Call me Cynthia and come in, come in."

Mom's put on a little weight since Matt moved in. She was a touch underweight so the extra bit sits nicely on her frame. In fact at 57, Mom looks better than ever. As she walks us through her post-divorce house, she smiles widely. I think Charlie has captivated her. She says, "I hope you'll excuse the state of the house. I haven't been able to clean as much as I'd have liked, what with Mattie in and out. Whoops!" She trips over the edge of a rug, but Charlie grabs her arm before she goes down.

He steadies her. "You all right?"

"Oh goodness! Yes, yes." Mom glances back at me. "Sorry, sweetheart. Your ditzy Mom!"

"'With Mattie in and out?'" Dad never bought the apartment for Mattie as Mattie felt depressed and wanted to "have more energy" before moving. So they decided that Mattie would continue living with Mom and once he was better, they'd get him a place. I've been caught up in Charlie and have not wanted a Mattie reality check. My insides clench as I wait to hear what she's talking about.

But Mom ignores my question. "Come this way!" She leads us to the TV room at the back of the house. Her fine bone china teapot with matching cups and saucers is set out on the coffee table with shortbread on the "good plate for company."

"I want you to feel at home," Mom tells Charlie.

Charlie, who couldn't care less about shortbread and actually enjoys very strong coffee, replies, "This is lovely. Thank you."

Mom's hand shakes while she pours the tea.

"Mom," I try to stay calm, "what do you mean 'with Mattie in and out?' Isn't he living here?"

She says, "Well, actually, honey, he didn't come back home last night."

"And I assume you expected him to?"

"We have an agreement that if he's going to be out, well then, I can accept that he's going to be out. He is 28 after all. But I ask him to tell me when he's going to be out late so that I don't worry about him. And, well, I haven't heard from him since he left the house yesterday morning in a huff."

It's now mid-afternoon. That means Mom hasn't known where he is for almost a day and a half. Charlie thumbs through one of Mom's architecture books that's been a fixture on the coffee table as long as I can remember. He remarks casually, "That's what we call a runner."

I ask, "Why did he leave in a huff?"

"We had a fight."

"About what?"

"I said that he was more than welcome to stay here until he got on his feet, but that I did expect him to get on his feet, and he got very angry. He said I was putting undue pressure on him. I tried to explain that I meant it as a goal for the future, but there was no explaining what I meant. He was offended and angry… and walked out."

"Does Dad know you haven't heard from him?"

"I haven't spoken to your father yet. I wanted to get ready for you and I'm sure that Matthew is fine. He does have a tendency to do this every once in awhile. But hey, it ain't over 'til the fat lady sings, and I don't see any fat ladies singing."

This is Mom's annoying catch phrase of positivity. How she can remain optimistic when Mattie's missing is beyond me. Charlie interrupts my thoughts, asking, "Where on earth did you find this book? It's a classic!"

"Are you a fan of architecture?" Mom asks.

"My grandfather was an architect."

They chat about Frank Owen Gehry's last project in London and a tearoom up in Glasgow designed by someone who died in the 1920's. Mom delights in the conversation. When Charlie goes to the bathroom, I ask, "Mom, I'm worried about Matt. I don't like that we haven't heard from him."

"Well, it's me who hasn't heard from him, not you. And while I equally dislike it when he drops off the face of the planet like this, I did manage to have a chat with Johnny about it and I'm okay."

Mom handles professional speakers. Her main gig and bread and butter is a motivational speaker named Johnny Dower. Johnny travels around the world inspiring people to better their lives with his nine-point plan, which he can break down for you into three sections of three, which will slot perfectly into your morning, afternoon and evening. Johnny Dower is dynamic and people love him. The person who loves him most is Mom, and not only because she collects 20% from his speaking engagements, but also because she's a Johnny Dower follower herself. She continues, "He said that every morning, during my Mind Cleanse, I just have to let Mattie go and get on with my day."

"And you can do that?"

She looks at me, stunned. "Honey, I have to."

I don't really believe her, but the toilet flushes so I quickly whisper, "What do you think of Charlie?"

"What's important, honey, is what *you* think of Charlie."

"Oh my God, Mom, this is why you're so annoying! I'm asking your opinion!"

"Oh, honey," she grabs my cheek like I'm three, "he's wonderful!"

Charlie reenters. "Can I get you another cup of tea?" Mom's asking him but already pouring. "Oh! And I know you're going out to dinner and I shouldn't spoil it, but I picked up a cake from Di Silva's, our local bakery, which happens to be one of the best bakeries in all of New York State. Do you like chocolate cake?"

Charlie looks down, sheepish for a moment, then raises his face to reveal a shy smile. "Cynthia, I'm what you'd call a chocoholic." Mom beams as she heads into the kitchen.

When we leave Mom to have dinner with Dad and his girlfriend, I ask, "How am I going to find Matt?"

"Why is that your responsibility?" Charlie asks.

I quicken my pace. "You probably can't see what's going on. My mom may have seemed all right to you, but, trust me, she's not."

Charlie processes this, then says, "You're right, she did seem all right to me. Sure, a touch stressed about your brother, but nothing she's unable to handle."

"Mmm. I don't buy it."

Charlie puts his arm around me. "Mattie is probably fine. If something truly terrible happened to him, the police would get in touch."

I'm horrified. "Charlie! Do. Not. Say. Things. Like. That!"

"Sorry, love, but it's true. But the good news is that the police have *not* been in touch."

We arrive at Dad's and find Mattie sitting in front of the huge television.

"What the fuck?"

"Hey, Louise."

"What are you doing here?"

He shrugs. "This the London dude?"

Charlie extends his hand. "Charlie. You must be Matthew?"

Mattie scoffs then turns his attention back to the television. He's watching an old *Family Feud*.

I ask, "Where's Dad?" Matt shrugs again. "And why haven't you told Mom that you're here?" A third shrug. Then we hear the front door opening. I whack him lightly on the back of his head. "Text Mom and tell her you're okay, or I'll do it on your behalf and tell her you're not okay." I grab Charlie's hand. "Come on."

Just inside the foyer, Dad helps Red out of her coat. She's made it almost a year. When Dad sees me, he comes to greet me. Red turns to us both with a strained smile and says a little too loudly, "Oh, hi!" like she wants to be a part of our reunion. I pointedly ignore her and turn to greet my father.

"Katherine." Dad beams as he kisses me.

I turn around to introduce Charlie and catch a strange look pass over his face. But then he's smiling his normal smile, shaking Dad's hand.

"And this is Red." Dad presents Red to Charlie.

"Red? What a great name!" Charlie kisses her hand.

Red, as to be expected, says nothing about her name but does give Charlie a playful smile. Dad informs us, "Red's going to change then we can go." Red is wearing what looks to me to be a Diane von Furstenberg wrap dress with accompanying purple pumps and handbag. Why she needs to change is a mystery. But Red disappears up the stairs and Dad turns to Charlie. "Well. Would you like a drink?"

"I'm fine, thank you," Charlie replies.

"Oh right! Katherine mentioned this! A non-drinker! I gave up the booze for many years. I know what it's like."

I cringe a little. My Dad didn't really have a problem with alcohol the way Charlie did. Or even Jonathan. Jesus. I used to have Jonathan coming home drunk every night. There was no way he could stop. Whereas when my Mom asked my Dad to stop, it wasn't a big deal. Sure he started up again as soon as they split up, but Jonathan couldn't teetotal for longer than a Monday morning.

"How long did you quit for?" Charlie asks affably.

"An eternity, Charlie," Dad grins. "Far too long!"

Charlie grins. They stand there grinning at each other, almost chuckling under their breath, as if they've bonded in some twisted, weird way. My stomach starts to turn. Maybe I ate too much cake.

Matt shuffles in. Dad asks him, "Did you change your mind and decide to join us for dinner?"

I ask him, "Did you tell Mom you're here?"

Dad snaps his attention over to me. "What's this?"

"Mom didn't know he was here and she's at home freaking out thinking he's disappeared again."

"Matthew!"

Mattie glares at me. "It's actually none of your business, Louise." He turns to Dad. "Dad, could I talk to you about something?" They disappear into the study.

Charlie looks over to me. "Louise?"

"He nicknamed me after Louise Bourgeois. You know who she is?" Charlie shakes his head no. "A French-American artist who's famous for this huge, creepy spider sculpture entitled 'Maman' that we saw together on a trip to Spain. I wasn't getting along with my Mom at the time."

"Ah."

Matt and Dad emerge from the office. Dad presses him, "Mattie, you sure you won't come out for dinner with us?"

Mattie replies, "Fifth wheel's no good for my already fragile self-esteem."

Charlie chimes in, "We're all pretty fragile."

Mattie looks up at Charlie as if remembering he's here too. "Nice accent." Mattie continues towards the front door.

"Excuse me," Dad mumbles and disappears back into his office.

I whisper, "I bet Matt just got money off my Dad."

Charlie whispers back, "I bet you're right."

———

Over dinner, Charlie comes off as intelligent, kind and funny. A total catch. I get the feeling that Red's a little jealous. Afterward, as Charlie helps me into my coat, he says quietly, "Your Dad's brilliant."

"I know. He's a smart, self-made man."

"No, I mean, he's really brilliant... but do you always kiss each other on the lips?"

"What?"

"When he greeted you, he put his arm around you and kissed you on the lips the way I would."

"Charlie, we may have kissed on the lips, but I can assure you, the way I kiss my father is nothing like the way I kiss—"

"It was closed mouth, of course, but there was something about the way he put his arm around your waist, as if you were lovers."

"Ew!"

"Is that how you greet each other?"

"What is your problem?"

"There was something odd about it. My father would never kiss Florence or Adalie like that. But then we British are so repressed. And why does he call you Katherine when everyone else is instructed to call you Kat?"

"I don't know. Does it matter? He just calls me Katherine. Why is that weird?"

"Because no one else does. You were adamant that I didn't."

"Well, maybe I like it when my Dad calls me Katherine, but no one else."

"And that's not odd?"

"What are you getting at, Charlie? Katherine *is* my name. I just prefer to go by Kat."

"Except with your father."

"So what?"

"I don't know. I just think there's something funny going on."

"Honestly you can really over-analyze things. I mean, I know you're an alcoholic and a sex addict and go to all those meetings, so it's just your way of looking at the world, but come on!"

He doesn't respond.

We make our way out to the parking lot in a strained silence. Dad and Red wait for us to catch up. Then Dad comes to my side and Charlie walks ahead with Red. I loop my arm through Dad's then immediately wonder if *that's* normal. Dad says, "Honey, I thought you were making a mistake when you let Jonathan go."

"Dad." I hate it when he talks about how much he liked Jonathan.

"No, I did. He really loved you. But I've gotta hand it to you, Katherine—" He squeezes my arm. "This one really loves you, too."

"Yeah? How can you tell?"

"I'm your father. I know these things."

———

We're spending the night at Dad's, so we're in my childhood bedroom. All is forgiven and Charlie's working his magic on my body when I hear the front door open and close. For as long as I can remember, that door has had a squeak that travels up to my bedroom. It ruins the moment. I know it's Mattie coming home. It's hard enough having sex in my childhood bedroom. I can't have sex while I'm thinking about my little brother. And I can't not think about Mattie because he seems so much more messed up than I was expecting. I gently stop Charlie and say, "I'll be right back."

He moans. "Where are you going?"

I throw on my pjs. "I just want to see Mattie for a minute."

"It's the middle of the night, babe, and we are very much in the middle of something."

"It's not the middle of the night. It isn't even midnight. And you'll be fine until I come back." He groans.

I sneak downstairs. Matt's rummaging through the fridge.

"Hey." He doesn't respond. "Where'd you go?"

He shrugs, takes out all beef franks and a frying pan.

"Really? It's a secret?"

"Movies."

"See anything good?"

"Not really."

I wait for him to expand. He's focused on covering the entire surface of a bun with butter. When he's clearly not going to expand, I say, "I didn't mean to harangue you before, but Mom was in a panic about where you were."

"So you said."

"Why do you do that to her?" He doesn't respond. I soften my tone. "I mean, I wish you wouldn't do that to her if you could possibly avoid it." He slaps a couple hot dogs down into the pan. "And so, are you like, staying here for good now? After saying for months that Dad wouldn't let you stay here?" Still nothing. "Really? You can't talk to me?"

"Why should I? You have your ticket out of here up in your bedroom."

"What the hell's that supposed to mean?"

"When are you moving to London, Kat?"

"I'm not!"

"You and Prince Charles up there are going to fly back and forth forever? I'm not an idiot. You always want me to tell you what's going on with me, but you never tell me what's going on with you."

He's right. I don't. I watch him turn the hot dogs over with a spatula. I decide to try. "The thing is, I don't know what's going on. We just really like each other and we're getting to know each other, but we don't have any plans."

"Sure." His tone, derisive.

"Aw come on! You can't complain that I don't tell you what's going on and then not believe me when I do!"

"Promise me that you won't leave me here with them."

"What do you mean?"

"When you move to London—"

"I'm not moving to London!"

"When you move to London promise me that you'll come back and see me." He sounds confrontational, but his eyes are wet.

"Oh Mattie! I'll always come back and see you."

He turns the hot dogs over again. They're cooking evenly. "No, I mean like, if you go next month or whatever, come back for Christmas."

"I'm not going anywhere, Mattie!"

"Just promise you won't make me do Christmas without you."

"You're still doing your outpatient program. It's a year long, right?"

"Yes, but, Kat, that's irrelevant! Just promise you'll come back for Christmas."

"Matt, I'm most likely going to be in Manhattan. But if I'm not, I'll come back for Christmas."

"And that's a promise?"

"Yes."

He acknowledges my promise with a raise of his chin and a hot dog peace offering. "You want one?"

"Yes."

When I slide back into bed, Charlie's asleep. I curl into him and he automatically puts his arm around me, warming me. I start to cry.

"What's the matter?"

"I'm just so lucky I have you."

"And I'm lucky I have you."

"Mattie doesn't have something like this."

"I didn't have something like this before either." He kisses the back of my neck. "Now I'm going to fall back asleep."

I eventually have to make some space between us because I get too warm. But when I move, Charlie reaches out and lightly holds my hand.

16

The next week, Charlie's gone. Rather than think how much I miss him, I think how much he's going to love reading my latest play. Charlie will read it and have some insights and they will be so smart.

My phone rings with a number I don't recognize. I pick up and hear Jonathan's voice say, "Hi, baby," and it's like a blow to my gut. I sink down next to my desk, where the last of the day's sunlight streams onto the hardwood floor. "Hi." I keep my voice even, try to make the "hi" say, *I am so happy to hear from you, but even happier without you, so why are you calling?*

"I know it's strange for me to call and you probably don't want to be hearing from me."

"I always like to hear from you." This is painfully true.

"Kat, I was thinking… this stuff isn't any good for me anyway… if I give it up… and I mean, give it all up… can we get back together?"

Time stops. This is the moment I've dreamed of, the moment when Jonathan wants me more than he wants to get wasted. Only what can I do? I'm in love with Charlie. Decidedly in love. And what's real about Jonathan saying he wants to give up… what exactly did he just say he'd give up anyway? All of it. He's going to give it all up so we can be together.

So. Very. Tempting.

But all talk until he actually does it. And *can* he do it? And do I want to put my life on hold while we see if he can? Break up with Charlie for a possibility? I don't. I can't. I can't do that to myself, let alone Charlie. We have the real thing. Why would I mess with it?

"Babe? What do you think?"

"God, Jonathan, there's nothing I want more than for you to have a happy life and I don't think you'll ever get there with alcohol and drugs ruling you. But—" Shit. He doesn't even know I'm seeing someone. "I'm seeing someone."

"Who?"

"It's no one you know."

"Who is it?"

"A guy I met in London."

He starts laughing. A harsh snigger. Finally says, "He lives in London. Good luck with that." And that's it. He gets off the phone.

I fucking will have good luck with it. I fucking will will will have good luck with Charlie!

It's the middle of the night in London, but I call anyway. When Charlie answers, he says, "Babe, you okay?"

I say, "Yes, yes, there's no emergency, except that there is. I need to know what we're doing here. I have to know because I mean… I can't do this the way we've been doing it anymore."

"Sorry?"

"Whatever we're doing, I can't do anymore. I'm sorry."

"My apologies, I was in a deep sleep so perhaps I'm not following you. Are you breaking up with me?"

"No! I will never be able to break up with you! That's the issue here. So I need to know what…" I'm shaking. "Sorry. Yeah. I guess I am saying I can't do this anymore. For starters, I can't afford it. I mean, you bought my last ticket and I really appreciate that. But what? Are you just going to keep buying me tickets now? So that I can fly out for a day here or there until I have more money and vacation time? That's crazy. Secondly, I spend the majority of my time missing you and that can't be healthy."

"Thirdly," he joins in, "we're never going to know if what we have is real or not unless we're in the same country."

"So you know what I'm talking about?"

"Sadly, yes. This isn't sustainable."

"So… we've either got to move it along or end it."

"Yes, it's truly as simple as that," he agrees.

I'm stunned. This is it. This crazy thing has come to an end. He's going to dump me. I close my eyes and try to accept the inevitable. He said it and he's right. *This isn't sustainable.*

"That's why you should move here."

"You think?"

"Yeah."

"But… what about money?"

"Can I go back to sleep now?"

"Charlie, what about money?"

"I make enough for the two of us."

"How much do you make?"

"Enough."

"I won't be able to work over there."

"If you don't work, you'll have more time to write."

"Quitting my job is a big deal."

"I don't mean to be rude, but I'd only just fallen asleep."

"What will I do about my apartment?"

"I wake up very early in the morning, you know."

"I'm sorry, hon, but you can't sleep when we're discussing a major life decision. I'm talking about moving away from my family and friends, across an ocean. It's a big deal."

I hear Charlie sit up in his bed. "Kat, this isn't difficult. I'll set up a joint account and put spending money in it for you to use however you see fit. You'll move in with me, so there are no costs there. Let go of your apartment. If it doesn't work and you need to get a new one, I'll help you out. That's all logistics and logistics are simple. The greater issue, the more emotional one, appears complex but is straightforward as well. Because really, Kat, you have no choice in this matter. You must come and live with me. I won't have it any other way."

"I do have a choice," I say, even though I know I don't. This is the way it has to be. I have to be with him.

"No. No choice. I'm through with missing you so much. You must come live here with me."

"And I won't be earning any money and that's okay?"

"Yes, yes. Hang on." I hear him getting out of bed. I think he needs to pee, but then I hear him fumbling with something.

"Listen," he says.

He plays the beginning of a song I recognize but can't quite place. He sings along about not being lonely, about loving the perfect woman. I lie back on the floor. He screams the chorus. He sings every word of every verse then asks, "Okay?"

"I have never loved anyone like I love you."

"Now can I go back to sleep?"

"Yes, night night."

I will have good luck with this. I really will. I mean, I'm moving to London.

III

When I saw you
I fell in love,
And you smiled
Because you knew.
　　　　—Verdi

1

After two hours of interrogation at Heathrow, it galls me to find Charlie peacefully sipping a cappuccino in arrivals. I tell him, "You should've been with me! They marked my passport!"

"Babe, we've had a full year of back and forth with no issues. How could I have foreseen this?"

"I've had a year of back and forth! Me! Not you! And I asked you to come and help me move my things, but you had work, and now I'm on the system, Charlie. This is the last tourist visa they'll give me! And she said if I leave the country, they won't let me come back in on another one!"

"What is this thing?" He motions to the hideous green piece of luggage I bought on sale. I didn't have anything large enough to move to London with.

"You should have come to New York and traveled back here with me."

"Sweetie, I know you're lashing out at me because you're upset, but honestly, how would my being there have helped?"

"You would have been there when they questioned me."

"Kat, I'm a British citizen. I would've been let through!" He laughs.

"What?"

He keeps laughing and pulling the suitcase and laughing and pulling the suitcase.

"What is so funny?"

"You! You're so incensed, it's hilarious."

"No it's—"

"And this is the most ridiculous case I've ever seen. It looks like a big..." He stops in between a couple of cars and regards the monstrous suitcase. "...a big piece of snot. I name it Big Booger."

"You don't seem to get it. I'm stuck in this country now. They will not issue me another tourist visa. They say I'm a 'foreign mistress!'"

"What does that mean?"

"That I'll be living with you and not paying any rent."

"You're a very cute mistress."

I love that he says that but continue my rant. "It means we have exactly six months to figure out what we're doing."

"Ample time."

"And after that, at the end of April, they throw me out."

"I don't think they literally throw you, babe. Besides, I can always tuck you away in my closet with Big Booger and the authorities will never find you."

"Oh fuck." I take out my cell phone.

"What? Who are you ringing?"

"Mattie." He doesn't answer. I text him.

> *Bad news*
> *If I leave the UK, I won't be allowed back in*
> *So that means I'll be here for Christmas*

I can see Matt's reading my messages but not replying.

"He should have taken your flat," Charlie says. I'd offered it to Matt, but he had moved back to Mom's. He'd said he was sick of being with Red at Dad's and wanted to stay with Mom again, which was understandable financially, but maybe not so healthy.

Charlie hefts Big Booger into the trunk. I text again.

> *Unless we break up by then*
> *I'm sure you're fine but could you just let me know that you're not freaking out?*
> *I need to know you're okay*

"Kat?" Charlie's at my side now. "What is it?" He wipes a tear from my cheek. I look back down at my phone. My last text's unread.

"Sweetie." He pulls me into his arms. "Tell me what's going on."

"I promised Matt that if for some crazy reason I was living here at Christmastime, I'd come back to spend it with him. And now I will be living here at Christmastime and won't be able to go back." Embarrassingly, I hiccup.

"Oh darling one, we have almost two months until Christmas. Tomorrow, or next week even, we can find an immigration specialist to speak with. Maybe they'll let you go home for Christmas then come back."

"Charlie, you know that's not gonna work."

"Well, why doesn't he come here for Christmas?"

I jump back on my phone.

> IDEA: you come here for xmas!
> (or anytime you want!)
> what could be better?

"Come on, love, let me get you to our new home." Charlie gently opens the passenger's door and guides me inside.

A text comes in.

Don't stress Louise. I'm as fine as fine can be.

Just can't really chitchat at the moment as I'm on my way out with Steve and some other guys.

But sure, I'll come see you soon. Don't worry.

Thanks for the invite

"Fuck."

Charlie keeps his eyes on the road. "What now?"

"I think he's doing drugs again."

"From one text?"

"Yup."

"You're terribly presumptuous, Kat."

"I'm not."

"How can you know that from one text?"

"He hasn't been talking to me since I told him I was moving over here. Then when I went up to Pleasantville to say goodbye, he blew me off to hang out with this new friend of his, Steve."

"So?"

"So his depression phase is over and I know he's going up again and when he goes up, he starts making new friends and using drugs to stabilize himself, and I have a feeling that's already started."

"Exactly. A feeling." Charlie pulls onto the M4. I close my eyes and try to chill out.

2

My new home, *our* new home, is a furnished rental in central London, compact and clean. Charlie moved because he didn't feel like it would be fair for me to move here from Manhattan and have to take a train to get into London. I pointed out that I lived way uptown and always took the subway everywhere. But still, here we are in the middle of London.

Showing it to me, Charlie seems nervous. He says, "It's a starter flat, until we have time to find something appropriate. I thought it was sweet. Do you like it?"

"I've never seen such a small bathroom. It's a feat of architecture."

I peek into the living room. Charlie told me he put all his furniture into storage, yet here's his blue couch, squeezed into the room next to another couch that obviously came with the place. I laugh. "The couch couldn't be left behind, huh?"

Charlie laughs. "I wanted something of mine to make it feel like home." He pulls me down on it and starts stripping off my clothes. "You are the best thing that's ever happened to me."

"I need a shower. I feel disgusting from the flight."

He keeps removing clothes. "You can't shower in these."

I kiss the top of his head. "I live with you in London now."

He screws me senseless.

3

"Kat... sweetie..."

"It's okay... I'm okay... I'm sure the jetlag's making it worse."

"How is this okay? How is this *jetlag*? You've been here for three weeks now."

"Maybe it's because I'm missing Thanksgiving at home."

"It wasn't Thanksgiving last week or the week before, or any of the other times."

"It's just... sometimes I cry. I thought you understood."

"Always after sex."

"Sure. Yes."

"Babe, tell me what's really going on."

I say nothing.

"The odd cry after a fantastic orgasm I can understand, but your tears are consistent. It doesn't feel normal."

"I don't know... I... I have no creative outlet. I'm not writing. And writing is the thing that makes me feel better, so it's like I'm in a new place but don't have my thing that makes me feel like me. So I'm unbalanced."

"Writer's block causes your post-orgasm weeping?"

"Right now I think so, yeah." He doesn't look like he believes me, but he drops it.

4

Kitty Kat,

*Apologies for the rushed email. You were sleeping so soundly
when I left this morning (and can I interject that you were
looking tremendously beautiful as well?) so I didn't want to disturb you but I've had a wonderful thought and I'm going to go
ahead and act on it. My next email will be to you and a man
named Rupert Black. I've known Rupert a very long time. We
go to our meeting together on Tuesday nights... you know. He's
a composer and I thought he may be able to help you get over
the writer's block.*

Love you babe.
C x

Rupert old man,
*I'm writing to introduce you to this rather strange American
woman I've dragged here from New York City (cc'd above). She
arrived nearly a month ago and is suffering from severe writer's
block (she writes plays). Further, to be blunt, she could use as-
sistance in the social arena as I'm the only person here who she
knows and, as you well know, I'm useless. Perhaps you and Sally
can help me sort out this Yank?*

See you tomorrow.

Best,
C

Dear Kat,
Welcome to the Big Smoke! I'm always game to meet play-
wrights. You're my favourite lot. Let's make a plan for coffee and
we'll destroy your writer's block. Mobile below.

Best,
Rupert

The fact that this composer, Rupert, is from Charlie's sex addict group therapy gives me pause. Charlie's religious about that group. Never misses a Tuesday night session followed by supper with the gang. But Charlie tells me Rupert's "mega-talented" and it's true I don't have any friends here, so what the hell.

—

I settle into my seat in the Soho café while Rupert places our order at the counter. The first thing I noticed about him, and probably everyone would notice, is that he does that dumb thing of trying to cut his grey balding hair so that it doesn't look like he's balding. He's well into his fifties and how he can't see that he's making it worse is beyond me. Another trait is his self-possession, which is knee-bangingly sexy. Maybe his hair goes unchecked because his air of success, which thanks to Google I know is based in reality, makes him super hot. Once settled across from me, he asks, "So. You're a playwright with nothing to write."

"That's right."

"What have you written in the past?"

I tell him about *Annabel.* He looks impressed.

"So, who's your agent?"

I tell him. He looks surprised. I ask, "What?"

"I'm with the same agency. Will they produce *Annabel* in London?"

"God, I hope so."

"Do you have other shows?"

I tell him how when Jonathan and I broke up, the writer's block arrived and I thought it left once Charlie and I got together. "But now I can't seem to finish anything I start."

"So, you wrote your one hit when you were with your ex?"

"Actually," this only strikes me right here, right now, "I wrote it *before* I was with him. I only edited it when I was with him." I tell Rupert, "I don't know why I've been so sure I was prolific when I was with my ex. When actually, I haven't given my agent any new work for years."

"I think what we can conclude," Rupert says, "is that your writer's block has nothing at all to do with the men you're seeing or not."

"So it seems!" I laugh, but really this whole line of questioning's making me feel like an idiot, so I change the subject. "For a long time now, I've been playing around with a vague idea about a vaudeville sister act."

Now Rupert laughs and I ask, "What?"

"My dear, it's not writer's block if you have an idea."

"Well, it's all I've got and I've been kicking it around for a while now."

He drains his espresso. "Then you have a motivation issue. Let's get to work and plough through it." He motions to the barista for another, then starts asking me questions, making suggestions. I tell him everything I know thus far. The conversation builds on itself and by the end of Rupert's fourth espresso and my second cup of tea, he says, "So to recap, it's the 1930s. We have two sisters. The elder is following her dreams but constantly tripped up by the younger one's crazy schemes. They're orphans from a great tragedy."

"Yes and what about this as a title, *The Amazing Kapakowski Sisters: Bloodbath at the Ritz*. Is that too much?"

"No, that's perfect for this." Rupert sits back in his chair. He taps the table with his finger. "I've only one more question."

"Fire away."

"Are you positive it's a play you're writing?"

"What else would it be?"

"A musical."

I pause. "I hadn't thought about that."

"You must, as an artist, decide which medium best serves the material. And don't you think this just begs to be sung?"

"And you'd like to write the music for it?"

"I'd be offended if you spoke with anyone else. Besides, aren't I the obvious choice?" He has such a charismatic grin. We shake on it and make a schedule.

5

Winter is warmer here than in New York, but I'm always cold. Charlie insists this is because I "feel the cold." I tell him it's because the houses are drafty. Anyway, I'm defrosting in a bookshop café where we're meeting for supper before we head to his friend's 7:30 p.m. show. It's another friend from his wonderful Tuesday night group. Charlie's forty-five minutes late and I'm a little hungry. I don't know if forty-five minutes late is a big deal or not. I call but there's no answer so I text:

I'm here. Hope you didn't forget?

Charlie'd planned to skip out of work a little early today so we'd have some time together. For sure, some work thing's run over. Charlie's worked non-stop since I've arrived. The weekends even. But it's been okay because I'm in some kind of new writing flow. I'm determined to complete a strong draft. Rupert's opened my eyes. So I pour more tea, shove Charlie's tardiness aside, and make notes in an effort to strengthen the outline. But then it's 6:30. Charlie's an hour and a half late and I'm very hungry. I order a salad. I call him again, but it goes straight to voicemail and I don't leave a message. I manage to work for a little longer, then it's 6:52. I shouldn't stress about this.

6:53. Maybe something happened because this isn't like him.

6:53 and 22 seconds. What a fucking asshole.

36 seconds later, I call him again. Voicemail. Hang up. Text him:

??????

Return to outline.

6:55. Call again, leave actual message this time as I want him to hear my voice. "What the actual fuck, Charlie? Are you okay? Where the hell are you?" Then I call his office, get the company's answering machine because it's 6:56 p.m. and no one's there anymore. I key in his extension and it rings and rings and rings until his fucking voicemail finally picks up. I don't bother leaving a message. What would be the point? I have to calm down because there must be a reasonable explanation. Something must have happened. An accident. Why else would it be impossible to call your girlfriend and tell her you're running two hours late?

My fucking salad arrives. I demolish what looks like a delicious salad of buffalo mozzarella and fresh tomato, but I don't taste it. My stomach gurgles with acid as soon as the food hits it. I try to think about *The Amazing Kapakowski Sisters*, but it's impossible to think anything except "Where the fuck is he?"

My stomach aches. I pull out the book I'm reading but read the same page twice, three times, give up.

Gee-zus.

The time is going so

so

so

slowly.

I live through another five minutes of this, resist the urge to contact him again, call Lena instead. Lena doesn't answer, but texts:

I got your present. We love it. It's perfect.
Coco looks adorable in it.

I sent a sweet little dress over for Coco's first birthday.

Can you talk?

not really, what's up?

Charlie like 2 hrs late to meet me

why?

no clue. His phone's off

shit

why shit?

Remember when JM was in that car accident?

don't!

Maybe you should start calling hospitals?

I don't even know where the hospitals are in London. I go to my maps app. I'll find the hospital nearest to his office. Then Charlie appears at the entrance. He looks around for me.

He just walked in

Good x

When he spots me, he comes straight over and kisses my cheek. "Sorry I'm late," he says as if he's five minutes late. It's now 7:07. "We should go if we don't want to be late."

"Charlie, I've been waiting for you for almost two hours." I try to say this rationally, as though I'm just pointing out a fact.

"I know, I'm sorry." He kisses my cheek again, takes my hand. I pull it away.

"What the hell happened?"

"Work. A meeting ran over. It was hell. I wanted to get out of it and couldn't."

"Why didn't you let me know?"

"I just said I was in a meeting."

"You could have sent me a text."

"We don't all sit there with our phones out. That's considered unprofessional, Kat."

"Then you could say, 'Excuse me, as this is running over, I need to call my girlfriend and let her know I'm going to be late.' It's not rocket science. Other people have commitments outside the office too."

He brazenly holds his ground. "I was in a meeting with three different CEOs, babe. I really didn't feel it would be proper to excuse myself to ring my girlfriend."

"You didn't— arrr! You'd rather I sit here waiting for you for two hours, worrying about you, thinking maybe you're dead somewhere than let me know you're going to be late?"

"Calm down. You weren't thinking I was dead."

"Are you telling me none of those CEOs have partners they need to tell they're going to be late?"

"I don't—"

"Of course I thought you were dead! What other reasonable explanation is there?"

Silence. We stand there. Charlie doesn't look at me as he quietly repeats, "We should go if we don't want to be late."

"So you care about not being late to see some friend of yours I never met in his boring play—I read the reviews—but not about being two hours late to meet your girlfriend who flew across the Atlantic to be with you?"

"I don't understand why you're so upset."

"You wouldn't treat a stranger like this." I pull on my coat. "Have fun."

I want to dramatically stomp out the door, but Charlie places his hands on my shoulders and says softly, "Kat?"

I shoot him a look that says, *What could you possibly have to say to me that would make this situation all right, asshole?*

"You're right. You're absolutely right. That was completely selfish of me. I don't think of you like other people. I think of you like family. I think of you like me and I don't treat my family and myself with respect. But I should. I'm so sorry. You're absolutely right to be so angry. I haven't been in a relationship in a while. I was completely caught up in work and that's no excuse but that's the reason and I'm so sorry."

I look at him expectantly. I'm not through being angry so he'd better have some more to say.

He does. "I always place work ahead of my own needs, Kat. I haven't even eaten since this morning. I'm so hungry. Not that you should care about that. I'm telling you so you know that it's not only you I neglected today, but myself."

I cross my arms across my chest.

"I have low self-worth. That's not meant to be an excuse, only an explanation."

He tries to take me into his arms, but I don't budge.

"Kat, please. You're right. You're absolutely right. This is a shitty way to treat you. Please forgive me. I hate seeing you upset and I can't bear that it's me who hurt you. Please don't be hurt. What can I do to make you smile?"

I let him lift my chin so I'm looking into his eyes that I find so goddamn intriguing, especially the one with the delicate black flecks. He whispers, "What if I buy you an ice cream at the interval?"

"It's too cold out for ice cream. I'll freeze."

"What if I promise to make the maintenance of your body temperature my obsession for the evening?"

I smile. "You're pretty smooth."

He keeps his word and wraps me by his side all night.

6

While procrastinating, I stumble upon a link to an American talk show. I stare at a man I'd forgotten about. Holy shit.

He liked my writing so much, told me I had real talent, and even though I knew that the totally shallow, semi-supernatural romp Nick Peters wrote was a piece of shit, I still felt special that a published author thought I was a hot young writer. I was 19. I remember that we got drunk, that he came back to my student housing and that I lay there, frozen, with him licking touching squeezing me. I meekly said things like, "I think we should stop," and, "I don't think this is a good idea," and, "This isn't great for me." But I didn't speak with any force and he disregarded everything I said. I was scared that if I succeeded in getting him to stop, he wouldn't like my writing anymore, wouldn't mentor me anymore, that he wouldn't love me anymore (because he said he loved me, that my writing was sensational, that he really loved me so much, but he wouldn't leave his wife), so I just lay there stiff as a board, mumbling my half-baked objections, letting him molest me, thinking it'll be over soon. He pulled out a condom and I felt both relieved that he was almost through and sickened that it was about to happen. "Wouldn't want our fun to turn into anything serious!" he joked. When he tried to put his penis inside me, I pressed my legs together. He said, "I know from your writing you're not a virgin... your writing... mmm... almost as sexy as you," and so I yielded an inch. "There you go, sexy." I thought I should be happy to have sex with him, while at the same time thinking I should get out of bed and walk away from him, just walk out of the room because I really wasn't happy to have sex with him. Yet I couldn't get up, couldn't seem to make it stop. All I could do was convince myself to open my legs another inch, that this was the right thing to do because he wanted it, and he loved me—he said those words, he told me he loved me—so it must be all right. He spit on his hand, used it to wet me, and then pushed inside, thankfully small, small, embarrassingly small. He was quick, made the most disgusting face as he came, and I wanted to vomit then, and thinking about it now, I want to vomit again.

He's on some show talking about his new bestseller. I shut it off.

That night, locked in Charlie's embrace, I tell him. He strokes my hair. "That's very damaging, Kat."

"I mean, I've never thought about it this way before, but I guess this means that I was kind of raped. Maybe it's date rape?"

"If there isn't consent, and from what you told me, there wasn't consent, then it's rape."

I exhale deeply. "I didn't write for two years after that."

"I can understand why. Could this be the reason why you cry all the time after sex?"

"I don't cry all the time."

"Do you think this could be why? He abused your core."

"What's with the psycho-babble?"

Charlie stops stroking my hair. We lie quietly. He presses my nose with his finger. "I love your nose. It's so wonderfully squishy."

7

"Breakthrough moment!" I explain to Anne on a video call. I've pulled on a red dress, and chat with her while I finish my makeup. "He rang! He was going to be late to meet me for dinner so he rang!"

"Am I missing something? Isn't that what most people would do?" Anne razors through my jubilation, which is annoying because she knows all about him being so late the other week.

"Remember, he's not most people. He has really low self-esteem. I think it's because of the whole sex addict thing."

"Oh my God," Anne scoffs. "Are you joking? Are you seriously going to use that as an excuse for him being inconsiderate and rude?"

"I don't think it's an excuse. It's an explanation."

"Look, it's scary to be in a relationship for most people, Kat, but they still do each other the courtesy of calling if they're going to be late."

"He has an illness, Anne, an actual illness."

"I don't know, Kat. I still feel like this whole Charlie thing is somehow you avoiding Jonathan."

I wish I could reach through the phone and slap her. I ask as casually as possible, "What do you mean?"

"I mean I think you still love Jonathan."

"Huh." I throw lip-gloss into my bag. "I hadn't thought about that. But listen, I have to run in a minute and you still haven't said how you are."

"I did. I said I'm fine. Let's talk later."

I'm very happy to get off the phone with her. Jonathan? It's over. Of course it's over with him. I've moved on. I've moved to London for Christ's sake. Why is Anne bringing him up? It's like she'll never let him go. Annoyed, I hop in a taxi and text Lena.

hey

I'm no longer allowed to be on my phone at home

But you're on your phone?

Yes

Does Anne ever annoy you?

constantly. What'd she do now?

so Charlie called to tell me
he was going to be late

that's great!

right? I thought it was progress.
Anne thought it was a sign
I'm not over Jonathan

lol. French have this expression that
roughly translates to "marriage is like
a closed basket"—meaning no one
can see into it

we're not married

still. All I'm saying is Anne doesn't have
a clue. She's been criticizing me too,
says JM right that I work too much.
Which he probably is, but still—
whose fucking side is she on?

don't know what's going on with her

without my work I'm nothing.
I would absolutely die. Throw yourself
into your new project. It's what's saving me

k

also you have to look at the person
giving you advice. Has Anne ever been
in a relationship that's lasted longer than
three months? how could she have a clue
about someone else's relationship when
she can't sustain one of her own?

Harsh but point taken

gotta run. have fun. Xxxxxxx

Charlie will be late for the dinner we're having with Rupert and his girlfriend, Sally. The elflike Sally lives in a bright one-bedroom apartment on the top floor of a crescent-shaped road in Notting Hill, a seemingly modest property that's probably worth a small fortune. Turns out Sally worked as a banker in the City but gave it all up recently to train to be a chef. Like Rupert, Sally is significantly older than I am. She's in great shape, with an asymmetric haircut that showcases her long neck. I'd put her in her late 40s but don't feel comfortable enough to ask. Everything about her clearly does it for Rupert. He touches her a lot—his hand on her elbow, shoulder, thigh.

Sally talks about her cooking course. "The focus now is on poultry and game, as well as fermented foods." She smoothly slides out from under Rupert's possessive arm, chides him, "You must let me serve the meal before it's overcooked." They beam at each other. I feel like an interloper and hope Charlie hurries up.

Sally's food is amazing. Individual guinea fowl pies with sides of caramelized carrots, beets fermented with ginger and orange, and crispy kale. The entire time we talk about the musical. Sally already knows all about it and asks inspiring questions. I start to feel a little jealous that Charlie's stopped asking about my writing. But it doesn't matter. Charlie's been so incredibly busy with work.

After Rupert's last morsel of pie disappears, he says, "I know I have the privilege of your cooking most days, but I'm rather hoping Charlie's work emergency lasts all night so I can tuck into what we set aside for him." The doorbell rings. "Damn his timing."

Charlie presents a bouquet to Sally. "My apologies. Sorry I'm late."

"Oh please, don't worry at all! I've been getting to know Kat and I think I prefer her to you."

"Most people do." Charlie plants a kiss on my lips, whispers in my ear, "You look beautiful in that color."

Later that night, curled up in Charlie's arms, I'm so pleasantly full and happy. As I'm drifting off to sleep, Charlie says, "You're beginning to fit in here, aren't you?"

"Mmmm. Sally's great."
"You're greater."
"Shhh. Sleep."

8

Mattie refused to come for Christmas. I'm relieved. Whenever I ask if he's okay, he replies, "I'm fine, Louise. Totally cool." Mom refuses to talk to me about him and Dad says, "Mattie's fine. Leave him alone." So I figure it's a total mess over there, a mess that I have a legitimate excuse to miss for once.

We head to Charlie's parents' home. They live on the outskirts of a village called Netley, near the water. His oldest sister, Florence, is hosting Christmas at her home in Dublin. She has four children. To me this seems like a lot of kids. We were invited to the Dublin celebration, but of course can't make it due to my "foreign mistress" status and not being able to get back into the country if I leave. Charlie's middle sister, Adalie, is going there with her husband and two children from a previous marriage. His parents are going in order to be with all their grandchildren, so their house will be empty. This is where Charlie takes me to spend our first Christmas together.

As we pull up the very long driveway, Charlie sighs, "Christ." A woman, who can only be his mother, Ariel, practically jumps up and down from the doorway of the house. Charlie slows the car to a crawl. He repeats, "Christ." When I'd asked when I'd meet his parents, Charlie said, "Hopefully, never. They are royal pains in the behinds." Today, Charlie timed our arrival for once his parents had left, but that clearly didn't happen.

Ariel is as striking as the classic country home behind her. She's a French beauty, mid-sixties, but won't tell anyone her exact age. Her dark hair falls in soft waves to her shoulders. She's dressed to kill in a light wool crêpe, rich purple, A-line mini-dress that you'd think a sixty-something-year-old couldn't get away with, but she's got Tina Turner legs and seems to know it. "Allo-allo!" she cries out to us, standing in the doorway, waving a cream silk scarf. Once I'm out of the car, I can see Ariel's face. She's absolutely ravishing, though she's definitely had some work done. The skin around her eyes looks taut and her lips, overly plump. She wears simple diamond earrings, square-cut. In contrast, I'm dressed like a schlump. I jumped into the car in sweatpants, clunky boots and a warm, bulky sweater. An outfit I would never have chosen to meet Charlie's parents in. But Ariel's not interested in me. After a brief, wooden hug, she extends her arms towards Charlie, displaying her perfectly manicured nails and square-cut engagement ring that matches her earrings. She calls out to him, "*Viens, viens, mon prince arrive!*" Her arms remain extended while Charlie very slowly approaches. I've never seen him move so slowly. We all stand there watching him move into her arms for an embrace, as if he's transformed into a kabuki actor. When he finally arrives in her arms, Ariel squeals like a little girl. "*Viens*, come inside! Your father, he is wanting us to leave so early for the airport. Our flight isn't for another three hours!"

"You told me you were leaving this morning."

"Did I? Oh, I must have gotten confused. Let's have a little something to drink before our *voyage*." She pronounces "voyage" very French.

"Whatever you think is best, Maman," Charlie replies.

Of course I knew that Charlie's mother was French, but I didn't know he called her "Maman."

Ariel calls out to Harry, Charlie's dad, "Dah-ling! They would like to have *un petit verre avec nous!*"

"Tell them that we're on a tight schedule!" Harry's voice booms down from above.

"But I told them, dahling! They won't listen to me!"

Harry storms into the kitchen explaining, "But if we don't go now—" He stops when he sees me. He's carrying a suitcase, but immediately drops it and makes a beeline to tower in front of me. He must be over six feet. His eyes are Charlie's blue with a devilish glint behind them. The rest of his looks are typically British in the negative sense—pale skin, jowls, crooked, yellow teeth. Yet the entirety of him works. He's an attractive older man.

"Oh! You're right of course, Ari," he says, taking my hands. "We must have one drink to mark the day we met the infamous Kat!" And with that, he kisses me on both cheeks, surprisingly close to my lips, then embraces me in such a way that I think he's trying to cop a feel of my ass. Behind him, Charlie smiles a weak apology.

Ariel pours champagne for herself, Harry and me, sparkling cider for Charlie. She says giddily, "I want to show you everything I've bought for you." There's a knock at the door. Ariel snaps at Harry, "You tell that taxi he has to wait!" Harry downs his champagne in one fell swoop then goes to do Ariel's bidding. Ariel turns back to Charlie, all sweetness again, "Look, my darling boy." She opens the fairly large refrigerator. It's stuffed with meats, cheeses, spreads. She grins beside it. "I bought you everything and anything you could possibly desire. Turkey, *filet mignon*, little tender chickens. There is everything. Including," she opens the freezer, "the favorite *choc ice de mon prince*." She kisses Charlie on the cheek. Harry walks back through the kitchen with the taxi driver. "What are you doing now?" Ariel scowls.

"Just getting our luggage! You entertain our guests!" Harry and the driver disappear into the house.

"We should be staying here to celebrate with you," Ariel pouts. Thank God they're not. "This is not right that we're separated for Christmas."

"Yes, but Kat can't leave the country," Charlie explains.

Ariel scowls at me then turns back to Charlie. "Ireland's not like leaving the country. We could take the ferry."

"Oh Maman, you're so funny."

"They don't check the passports on the ferry, and it's such fun!"

Charlie laughs and pulls her into an unexpected hug. "Yes, they do check your passports, Maman." Ariel looks like a five-year-old little girl soaking up her Daddy's love.

Then Harry walks back through with the taxi driver, both men laden with bags, and Ariel pulls away from Charlie to point at the bags, "I'm such an overpacker. But two of those bags are filled with presents!" She claps her hands together. "Oh! Presents! Should we exchange now?"

Faaaaaaaaaaaaaaaaaaaaaak. I asked Charlie what we should get his parents and he said, "Nothing." I asked what kind of wine they liked, if we could bring flowers, cheese, cake. He said, "They're leaving before we get there, and I don't like to buy them alcohol." I asked him to tell me anything we could get them or do for them. And he said, "Honestly, Kat, give it a rest. Nothing. We should get them nothing. They won't care." And now here we are with nothing and I'm going to shit a brick.

Charlie says, "Maman, this year we wanted to *do* something with you. I never see enough of you. So Kat and I would like to take you and Dad to see a show in the West End."

"Oh! That is *fantastique!*" and she hugs him again. It looks like any excuse to embrace him she'll find and use. "And your gifts are under the tree. *Peut-être* is better for you to wait until Christmas day to open them. That way you will think of me though we're apart. *Oui?*"

"Come on, Ariel." Harry reappears. "We must leave now." He holds out her coat, waits to help her into it.

"Oh! Can't we visit with them a tiny bit longer?" She pouts again.

"No, it's time to go. If Charlie had wanted to visit with us, he would have come earlier."

Charlie shrugs. "Didn't know I was invited."

"Don't be absurd!" Ariel's anger seethes expertly, as she lets Harry slip on her coat. "You don't need to be invited to come and stay with your parents!"

The room feels tense, then Charlie smiles conspiratorially to his father and tells Ariel, "Ah, Maman, you'd have to check that with the boss."

His father winks at Charlie. "That's right."

"Boss? You think *he's* the boss?" And Ariel's laughing and all is well and it's clear this is just a weird game they're playing.

When Ariel kisses me goodbye, she whispers in all seriousness, "You take good care of my boy, or I will take care of you. You understand me?" Then she kisses me a second time, puts a big smile on, and sweeps out to the taxi.

They drive off. I wave like nothing's the matter, but Charlie sees my face and asks, "Was it that scary?"

"I think *Maman* just threatened me."

He laughs. "That wouldn't surprise me." He takes my hand. "Come on, I'm starved."

I stand there. "I'm kind of shocked. I really think she threatened me."

"She's mean to you because she knows I'm smitten. She's a jealous child. Don't give her another thought. Let's cook up a feast and watch a film."

I look at him. "Smitten?"

He pulls me inside. "Utterly smitten."

"Good."

9

To attend my first ever midnight mass, I pair a red Santa hat with my new Audrey Hepburn little black dress. This was Charlie's amazing Christmas gift to me, along with a card that quoted Audrey Hepburn, "Nothing is impossible. The word itself says, 'I'm possible.'" My excitement wanes when it turns out I'm the only person in the entire church with a Santa hat. No one is dressed in red. No reindeer sweaters, no tacky ornament earrings that light up, no "Ho! Ho! Ho!" anywhere. I lean into Charlie and whisper, "Why did you let me wear this hat when the dress code here is obviously drab and boring?"

His eyes smile as he whispers back, "Because you look gorgeous." I'm touched but remove the hat. I then suffer through the dullest Christmas Mass imaginable. The unrecognizable songs are more like dirges than carols. No *Silent Night, Away in the Manger*. Not even a *Joy to the World!* I'm grateful when it's time to leave.

Walking out with the solemn crowd (no one humming Jingle Bells), Charlie bumps into an older couple with their three teenage children. "Charlie!" The man engulfs Charlie in a giant hug. The woman looks on, smiling, then moves on to speak to some other churchgoers.

"Duncan, this is Kat."

"Hello," I say, shaking Duncan's hand. He's a very tall, lanky man. Charlie beams up at him.

"It's my pleasure, I'm sure." Duncan's gaze lingers on me for a moment, then he quietly asks Charlie, "You doing all right?"

Duncan's tone strikes me. Underneath his seemingly everyday question sits a deeper query that highlights the possibility that Charlie may *not* be "doing all right." The implication being that not "doing all right" would be very bad.

Is Charlie doing all right? I thought he was. I thought these have been the best days of our relationship. Maybe I'm wrong. I turn my attention to Charlie. He's smiling as he throws an arm over Duncan's shoulders. "Yes," Charlie says. "I'm doing very well." He smiles at me. He's doing very well. Of course he is. I know this.

———

In the car, Charlie explains to me, "Yes, well, he was asking after my sexual sobriety."

"I *hate* that phrase."

"*Asking after?*"

"You know what I mean. I feel like you're saying *vagina* or something."

"What's wrong with vagina?"

"Ew, don't. Just keep explaining."

"Duncan's been a big help to me with my *sexual sobriety!*" he yells. I smirk. "He used to come to the group."

"Ah. The group."

"What?"

"Nothing." But it's not nothing. Charlie's group therapy is presented to me as if it's an exclusive club, as if being a sex addict is cool. And he's religious about it, leaves work early every Tuesday for it, but has yet to leave work early to meet me. I mean, he tried and failed miserably. But every week he manages to leave work early for this group therapy. There never seems to be a work crisis on a Tuesday and that seems weird. Maybe I'm being petty. Charlie works his ass off. So I continue the conversation like an adult, and ask, "Why doesn't Duncan go to the group anymore?"

"Thinks he got better." Charlie zips along the narrow road. Whenever a car comes from the opposite direction, one of them has to pull over in a special lay-by the roads have dotted sporadically along the sides. This often involves reversing which Charlie does at top speed.

"You say that like he hasn't. Why does everyone drive so fast here? It feels like we're always just avoiding an accident on these twisty country roads."

"He's a very good man. And he helped me a lot, but I don't think he's gotten better, no. That said, what do I know?"

We whiz around another corner in silence.

I ask, "Does anyone ever leave the group because they actually get better?"

"Yes. There was a woman named Jane who left for that reason."

"Okay. And what about Rupert? He seems fine. Why hasn't he left?"

"He is fine because he goes to his meetings regularly and comes to group."

"What's the difference?"

"What do you mean?"

"Between meetings and group?"

"They're completely different. Meetings are recovery and the group is group therapy. Kat, you should know this."

I don't want to admit this, but I always thought that recovery was the same as group therapy. Aren't they all just sitting around talking? I ask, "Do you go to your meetings regularly?" Sometimes Charlie also attends a Saturday morning sex addict meeting, but not every Saturday.

"Honestly, no, I don't." Before I can say anything, he continues, "But I go often enough."

"And that does the trick?"

"It does. And besides, I like to sometimes spend my Saturday mornings in bed with you." He wiggles his eyebrows.

"Don't make light of it! This is serious stuff!"

"Jesus, Kat," his voice goes humorless, "I know that better than anyone."

"Of course you do! Listen, from my perspective you're doing really well."

"Don't patronize me, Kat."

"I didn't mean to."

"Sorry, I'm a touch defensive." He nips his gaze from the road to me then back again. "You should know that my exes have consistently described me as a car crash."

"Ha!" I laugh, but then I see he's being perfectly serious. "Oh, cut the crap. It's Christmas! Gimme a smile!" I tickle him under his arm until he laughs.

10

We're out for a drive the very next day, zooming once more along the winding roads. Charlie laughs a self-deprecating laugh. "My last girlfriend said that being in a relationship with me was like being in a slow motion car crash."

"You already told me that."

"Did I?"

"Last night. You really want to be the worst, don't you?"

"What do you mean?"

"You're *The-Most-Difficult-to-have-a-Relationship-With* and *The-Most-Fucked-Up*. Like you want an award for being screwy."

Charlie parks. "Maybe." He sits back and sighs. "I'm sure it has to do with my ego, as everything does. But also, I'm letting you know because I don't want you to get hurt."

"Charlie, I'm an adult. You've been upfront with me about your sexual addiction and you're doing things to keep yourself sober in that area. I'm allowed to choose this relationship if I want it. And I do. I choose it." Charlie looks over at me. I continue, "I'm not a little girl."

He leans in and kisses me. "Definitely not."

"Besides, I'm having the best Christmas of my life. So don't rain on my parade."

11

Charlie's friends with a novelist, Claire Goodkind. Claire lives in L.A. though she's originally from Montana. She's starting off the New Year with a book tour and her first stop is London, so she's spending a couple of nights with us. She must be pretty darn cool as Charlie's home from work early to help prepare for her arrival. We're getting dinner ready for her. I say "we" but it's really me doing all the work. I'm setting our small round table for three for the first time. Charlie's lighting candles around the room and jibber-jabbering. "Have you ever been to Montana, Kat?"

"Nope."

"Have you ever seen a film called *A River Runs Through It*?"

"Yeah."

"It has the best opening line ever." I have nothing to say to this. Charlie continues, "Don't you think?"

"I really don't remember it."

"'I am haunted by waters.'"

"Do we really need so many candles?"

"Isn't that the most fantastic line ever?"

"We don't want to set the place on fire, Charlie."

"It's so deep, on so many levels. Give me your favorite movie quote."

I glare at him. "Who's haunted by waters? That's idiotic." Then I hastily retreat to the kitchen.

But our apartment is the definition of the word small. I can't hide in the kitchen, or anywhere for that matter. Charlie only has to take a couple steps, which he does, and he's jammed up behind me. I'm trying to prep the goddamn salad and he snakes his arms around my waist, kisses my neck and asks, "Why are you in such a bad mood?"

"You can't make it home before midnight when it's just me, but for your writer friend from Montana, you're here at half past six lighting fucking candles."

"Kat, my job's on the line." He releases me.

I'm pretty sure he exaggerates whenever there's a work problem. "Then why aren't you at work?"

"Are you saying I'm not working hard enough?"

"No, not at all."

"I'm killing myself with this job and you're completely ungrateful."

"That's not what I'm saying at all!" I glance at the clock. Great. The Almighty Claire will be here in five minutes. I chop cucumbers. "We don't have time for a fight."

"Then don't tell me I'm not working hard enough when I'm essentially killing myself!"

"I'm just wondering why you can take a night off for this complete stranger, but not me!"

Charlie returns to lighting candles. "Don't be ridiculous. I see you all the time and I never get to see Claire. You'll love her. She's a real writer."

I stop chopping. "What the hell's that supposed to mean?"

"Oh Kat, don't be ridiculous! She's a published author!"

"I'm a produced playwright!"

"It's a little different, don't you think?"

"No, that doesn't make any sense! You're saying she's real and I'm not?"

"Can you give me a break and let me enjoy meeting my dear friend? She's flown a very long way so stop acting insane! I love you!"

I've made lemon chicken with rice pilaf and roasted squash. I make a damn good lemon chicken, if I do say so myself, but how I got roped into catering for a woman Charlie obviously adores is beyond me. "Why don't you just let me know exactly how successful I need to be for you to pay attention to me."

Charlie laughs. "You're hilarious when you're insecure." Then he disappears into the bedroom, probably deliberating over what to wear for the precious Claire, just as the door buzzes. Fuming, I buzz Claire in.

When I open the door and look down the hall to see her step off the elevator, my anger dissolves. Claire Goodkind is enchanting. She has very full, close to black, curly hair. She's voluptuous, Rubenesque, with an open, friendly smile. "Hey, you must be Kat! Charlie said you like dark chocolate." Claire hands me a beautifully wrapped box of chocolates. "Belgian, via L.A."

"That's so nice of you. Thank you!" I'm a sucker for chocolates but was already won over by her amazing hair.

Charlie bursts out of the bedroom. "Claire! The Claire bear!" Charlie gives her a happy smile. He did indeed change his shirt, and I can smell cologne.

Claire cringes. "It's been a while since I heard that."

"When was the last time you were in London?"

"Last book tour. Four years ago."

"You need to write faster. Come in, come in."

———

The next evening, Charlie's home early from work again and we wait for Claire's arrival like she's royalty. Last night, Claire and I talked writing. Charlie knew Rupert and I were working on something, but he didn't know what. He said, "You're writing a musical?" I smiled at him before turning my attention back to Claire. Claire even helped me clarify some of the storyline. As a result of that one conversation about my work, I woke up feeling energized, and Charlie must have done the same because he woke up wanting sex, which isn't usual for us on work days so a very nice treat. After he trotted off with a smile on his face, I got down to work and had a productive day. Now, as we wait for Claire to arrive, I tell him, "I'm happy." It's true. I am happier than I've ever been in my life.

He kisses me. "I'm glad."

When Claire arrives, Charlie asks her, "How were the publishers?"

"They seem to really like the new manuscript. I'm so relieved."

"That was to be expected!" he proclaims. I feel a twinge that he's not as proud of my writing as Claire's. In fact, he stopped reading anything of mine, and we stopped talking about my work, ages ago. But who cares. He supports me, loves me, introduced me to Rupert after all.

"You hungry?" Charlie asks Claire.

"No, no, the publishers took us out for lunch then my agent took me out for dinner. I feel like a stuffed turkey." She collapses on the couch. "You know, I remember this blue couch from your old place. Let me just lie here for five minutes talking to you guys and then let's go out. Even if we just walk around Soho or something, I just want to *be* in London, you know?"

Charlie nods, a big grin on his face. And it occurs to me that these two have known each other forever. I should really let the two friends have some gossip time. I would hate it if Lena were over and Charlie hung around us like a third wheel. But I hesitate. It's not that I don't trust Charlie, but should I really leave him alone with such an attractive woman? I kind of have a girl-crush on Claire. She's not only sexy curvy, but comfortable with her sexy curviness in a way that makes her curves even sexier. Plus, what if Charlie has some sort of thing for American writer-types? But if that were the case, then why hadn't he and Claire ever dated?

Charlie tells me, "Did you know, if it weren't for Claire, I may still be a waiter?"

"And he was the worst waiter."

"Unless I was serving myself." They laugh as though he's said this before, and they think it's just as funny now as they did whenever he said it before. The history of good friends.

I tell them, "I'm going to stay in tonight, guys. You should have some time to catch up." They try to change my mind, but I'm pretty sure they're being polite. I don't want to be the clingy type, and I fall asleep knowing that I most certainly am not.

Later that night, Charlie comes to bed and pulls me into an embrace, whispers, "I love you."

When I roll out of bed in the morning, Charlie, as per usual, has gone to work. Claire's already left too.

12

Charlie puts a super king-size mattress in the middle of our new massive bedroom. He lies on it. He looks like he might pass out. I cuddle up next to him. "Are you going to fall asleep?"

"Mmm-hmmmm."

"I can't believe this is our new home."

"You like it?"

"Like it? It's amazing! It's three times the size of our last place!"

"It's still only a flat. Don't get overexcited."

"Oh hon, Happy Valentine's Day." I kiss him, but he's so tired he lies still, his eyes closed.

We live in Hampstead now. The day after Claire left, Charlie suddenly said, "I can't live in this little space anymore, let's move." So we saw a few properties, and here we are.

"I don't know if I'll be able to deal with the sound of traffic." Even Charlie's voice sounds exhausted.

"I think it sounds like the sea." But he's drifted off.

I listen to the distant traffic. It reminds me of falling asleep to the sound of the ocean at my family's summer rentals in the Hamptons. As Charlie sleeps, the nick on his chin moves up and down with each breath. Thank God he didn't succeed. Thank God I came to see Lena when she was working here and met him. Mattie pops into my head, followed by a deep twinge of guilt that I'm here and he's living at home, doing God knows what. But I shove the guilt away. I live in a two-bedroom Hampstead flat. A flat, not an apartment! The days have been moving from grey and miserable to grey and miserable, but, as if to match my current joy, the sun suddenly streams through our bedroom window. The rays warm my skin. Charlie wakes up enough to pull me into an embrace. "Happy Valentine's Day, sweetie." I'm so lucky.

13

The musical's humming along. Rupert splits his time between London and L.A. His schedule dictates when we meet up. Rupert's great. But spending so much time with him means witnessing how sweetly he treats Sally. Which is also great. I mean, really great. For her. I'm jealous. I mean, the man's a prince. He arranges tickets, buys gifts, and just generally makes time for her. Plus he acts like he can't wait to see her. I guess recovering sex addicts are not created equally. I shouldn't be so ungrateful. Charlie pays for our beautiful Hampstead home. He works hard. It's incredible to have so much time to write or go to a yoga class or explore London. And when Charlie does have time, we have so much fun together it's insane. Smart conversation, mind-blowing sex. Besides, I *like* Sally. And I need friends here.

It's early spring, a sunny afternoon, which I relish so much more now that I've realized London's sky is usually clouded over. We're in Rupert's Soho flat. He's at the piano, tinkling away, and I lean back on his leather couch and let myself pretend just for a millisecond that he's mine. I'm his girlfriend. And he plays for me. And he comes over and kisses me.

I sneak a peek at him. His eyes are closed as he stumbles on a phrase, goes over it and over it and over it until it becomes precisely what he wants it to be. He'd be awesome in bed.

He glances over, excited. "That's it. You hear it?"

Rupert's not thinking about being my boyfriend. He's thinking about the work. What's wrong with me? "Yes," I tell him. "I hear it. That's it." I make a strong cup of coffee.

14

I have one more month on my visa. That's all.

This is, of course, when there's a last minute trip from Matt. My mother told me, "I'm sure your father will call you soon. I have to go on Johnny's annual seminar in Baja this year. I asked Mattie to come. What could be better for him than Johnny Dower and sunshine? But he said not in a million years, and your father has some trip planned with his girlfriend."

"Why can't Mattie just stay there?"

"He can't be on his own."

"Then he should be in a center or something."

Mom paused then said, "I agree with you. How about *you* try telling that to your father?"

When I finally did speak with Dad, he declared, "Won't it be great, Katherine? A visit from your little brother? Let me know if you guys want to go out to dinner, a show, away for a weekend. Whatever you want, it's on me."

I said, "Thanks, Dad. I'll let you know."

And now I'm panicking. Charlie's late at work, as usual. When he finally gets home, I'm folding. There's a great folding technique I found on YouTube. It's keeping me calm. He walks in on me with a YouTube video up and a pile of shirts out. I'm dying to talk to him about what we're going to do about our relationship. But when he asks if I'm all right, I only report the Mattie situation. He sits down on our bed and asks, "You didn't tell them that sending an unstable person on a transatlantic holiday isn't the greatest idea?"

I continue folding. "When my Dad gets an idea in his head, it's impossible to remove it. Besides, he already bought Mattie's ticket."

"Well, don't worry about it then. It'll be fine."

I keep folding.

"Is something else going on here, or are you just having a tidy?"
I keep my mouth shut. If I open it, the word "visa" will fly out.
"Kat? Is something else the matter?"
"No, just Mattie. And like you said, that'll be fine."

———

Sweetly, Charlie decides to go in late to work in order to greet
Matt with me. I'm overjoyed to have the morning with him. We sleep
in, have sex, then fall back to sleep. I wake up to him handing me a
mug of coffee. The sun brightens our bedroom. I'm warm and safe
and loved. Heaven. So I take a deep breath and ask, "You know I have
exactly one month left on my visa right?"

"What are you saying?" He's walking away from the bed so I can't
see his face, but this is not the response I was hoping for.

I downplay, "I'm not saying anything at all. Just that it expires at
the very end of April."

"Yes, Kat. I'm well aware." He returns to bed with his laptop,
sending the unmistakable message that he has work to do.

We sit in silence, sipping our coffees. Charlie starts tapping away.
I don't know what to make of whatever just happened, so I get out
of bed to get dressed. After about twenty minutes, Mattie's arrival
breaks our silence.

Decked out in an oversized, pimpish, fur coat and sunglasses,
super long hair and a goatee, Matt dwarfs what I considered a
spacious living room, a sort of Alice in Wonderland effect. I want to
cry at the sight of him, but hold it in as I receive his bear hug and
counter it with a squeeze that's meant to say, "Be happy! Get your shit
together and be happy now!"

"Louise!!" He lifts me off the ground and spins me. His up-and-
down weight is decidedly down. "You're a London babe now!"

I grin. "Yeah, I guess I am."

"Prince Charles." Matt extends his hand to Charlie. "A pleasure.
Thanks for letting me come hang out for a while."

"The pleasure's all mine. Please make yourself at home. I suspect you'll want to sleep after the red eye."

"God, no! I'm super caffeinated! Ready to roll!"

Charlie says stiffly, "Then I guess it's up to you to show him the town, Kat. I'm off."

I kiss Charlie goodbye then turn back to Matt. "Okay, well…"

"Yeah, well! What are we going to do today? I made a list. Here." Mattie gets out his phone, but as soon as the front door shuts, his eyes bug out of his face as he asks, "What the fuck is up his butt?"

I laugh. "God, I missed you! What do you want to do?"

"The wax museum! And you can answer me about Charlie later if you want, but he was all *the pleasure's all mine I'm off!* What the fuck? Okay, okay, none of my business. Let's go get some pastries for breakfast."

I feel like I should chastise him for drinking gallons of coffee when he's already on the up side of his illness. But instead, I take him to our local café and order a double latte and chocolate croissant right alongside him. My brain needs a serious dose of caffeine to keep pace with his mouth. I chug my latte.

***

Late that night, when Charlie returns home from work, I'm quietly sobbing in bed with all the lights out. "What's happened?"

"Shhhhh!" I snap.

"What?" he whispers.

Mattie is still up watching television. "I told him I was going to bed."

"What's happened, babe?"

"Nothing," I say, eyes streaming.

"Is this about us? I shouldn't have behaved so weirdly this morning, Kat. I—"

"No!" I cry. "What the hell? I can't deal with the visa stuff now. I'm upset about Mattie! Not us!"

"Oh."

"He's just so fucked," I whisper.

"Oh Kat." He gets into bed next to me. "Listen, I was fucked too. Really fucked. I worried my parents no end. And now I've got a great job. I've got a strange, American woman I love living with me. I'm okay."

"I appreciate that you had problems, Charlie, but this is different. Mattie's not an alcoholic. He doesn't even drink."

"He does drugs."

"Yeah but… I'm crying about his mania. He just talks all the time. Non-stop. We went to Madame Tussauds and he talked to the other tourists and the staff. He had a monologue to the wax Madonna. Then we walked through the London Zoo and when we saw the giraffes he questioned the zookeeper about their standard of living. Like, are they getting enough variety in their diet, enough space to roam in, blah blah blah, as if he even knows anything at all about giraffes."

"I hate to point this out, but you knew he wasn't in a good state before he arrived and yet, you allowed it."

"Well, what the hell was I supposed to do? Say no? Reject my brother?"

"As I said before, put up some boundaries. There's still time. You could ask him to see a therapist while he's here. Every day for the remainder of his trip."

"Who?"

"I can ask around and find someone."

"Won't that be expensive?"

"Your father said he'd pay for whatever you want."

"How would you even find someone?"

"I have a lot of connections in this area. You want me to try?"

And the next morning, Charlie finds a therapist, a highly sought-after trauma and addiction therapist. I arrange for Mattie to see her. I tell him, "It's short notice, I know. And I'm not saying that you're manic. Just that you seem like you could be one day soon and I want us to have an amazing ten days."

"Nine days now."

"Well, an amazing nine days then. And she can see you midday today and then every morning at 9 a.m."

"Okay. Sure."

This seems too easy. "Really?"

"Yeah sure, Louise, I love talking about me." He smiles his joking smile. "Besides, I want you to be happy. If you think this is going to make you happy, then I'll go for it."

———

The therapist, a woman named Maria Mancini, works out of her home on Adam and Eve Mews just off Kensington High Street. Adam and Eve Mews is one of those special places that I would never have seen had it not been my destination. Today is beautifully blue-skied. Mattie keeps up his non-stop monologue about weather, minor celebrities, London fashion and his supposed need for more caffeine. "I know that you think I shouldn't drink caffeine, but really that's not the case. Caffeine is what makes me even. At home I add coconut oil to my coffees to counteract the negative side effects. I have ADD, Louise, that's what this therapist is going to tell me. I was incorrectly diagnosed with bipolar."

Maria opens the door and gives us both a broad smile. "Come here!" she says in a thick Italian accent. She pulls me into her incredibly large bosom, decorated with an intricate, very lengthy, gold chain. She says, "First I hug big sister." Then she pushes me an arm's length away. "You are the one living here in London?"

"Yes."

"There is an excellent café down to the right on the high street. You wait for him there." She turns to Mattie. "And you come with me. Do you want me to call you Matthew or Matt?"

"That's a good question," Mattie says as he steps into Maria's house.

Maria winks at me before closing her door.

With the addition of Maria to our daily routine, Mattie's visit acquires a beautiful flow. After he sees Maria, he's significantly calmer. Still not completely even, but no longer talking to passersby. We do London: the Eye, the British Museum, the Tates, shows, sushi, the Shard, Brick Lane, Borough Market. We do it all, all the touristy things I had yet to do.

For Matt's very last day, he cancels Maria and we head out to Stonehenge for a guided tour. It's like I have my brother back. Together, we wonder at the wonder of Stonehenge. We walk around a pathway that encircles the ancient stones from a distance. It's a pity we can't go right up to them. Matt puts his arm around me and says, "Stonehenge is some weird sort of miracle. Miracles happen." He pulls me into his ridiculous fur coat. "So, you going to be living here full time?"

"I don't know."

"What do you mean you don't know? Isn't he the love of your life? Fire of your loins? Cream of your soup?"

"I guess so."

Mattie stops walking. "Louise. What's the problem here?"

"He works a lot."

"Which is why you don't have to work."

"You know, he has emotional problems."

"Don't we all."

"Sometimes I don't think he respects what I do."

"Business-types don't always get creative-types. Don't worry about it."

The tour guide motions for us to return to the bus.

Matt offers, "For what it's worth, I'd suspect that you're over-complicating it, due to the unbelievably awful upbringing we had."

"Unbelievably awful? So I guess therapy went well?"

"I'm just saying our chances of relational success are slim. We have a father with zero ability to commit and a mother who's constantly on the verge of a nervous breakdown."

"Dad was with Mom for decades."

"Yeah, but he was never faithful to her."

"How do you know that?"

Mattie sighs. "I've just presumed based on little things he's said to me."

"Like what?"

"Like… a man is entitled to a regular sex life."

"Maybe I'm missing something. Isn't everybody?"

"Sure, but he was saying, if the man can't get it at home, then because he's entitled to it, it's okay to go elsewhere."

"Ah. Okay." I'm shocked that Dad's said that to Mattie. I mean, Dad has said things to me, worse things, but I don't want to tell Mattie. It would just upset him. We take our seats just before the bus starts up. I ask, "Anything else that makes you think he was unfaithful?"

"Well, you know Doug from my year?"

"Yeah?"

"He told me once that his father saw our father at Jimmie's with some floozy who was definitely not our mother."

"When did he tell you that?"

"Years ago. When it happened."

"But I mean… was that before or after we moved?"

Matt thinks. "I don't remember. Does it matter?"

"And you're just telling me now?"

"Yeah."

"Jimmie's?"

"Yeah."

"That's a dump."

Matt shrugs. "Did you seriously not know he's a cheater?"

"Ummm," I stall. I'm not sure I should share. "I guess I should tell you that when we were little, Anne's mom told Anne that she saw Dad at the club with his secretary."

Mattie hits my arm. "And you're just telling me now?"

"I didn't want to upset you."

Mattie shakes his head. "He's such a dog."

"At least none of those women meant anything to him."

"Exactly my point! Dog! But no matter how you slice it, returning to our conversation, I'd say that you and Charlie are probably doing fine. He works a hell of a lot but most high earners have to."

"Yeah, but my visa runs out next month and well, I guess that'll be that."

"Does Charlie know your visa is going to run out?"

"Yeah."

"I like Charlie. He may have his head up his ass sometimes, but he's a decent guy. Just talk to him."

15

I resolve to do just that the day Mattie leaves. But Charlie surprises me by coming home early and saying, "Get dressed."

"I am dressed."

"I mean, get properly dressed. I'm taking you out to one of my favorite restaurants."

I dress and we jump into the car.

"What's your favorite restaurant?"

"Chez Bruce."

"Where's that?"

"South of the river."

"Is this going to be a long drive?"

"Ish. Yes."

I can't help but wonder if this is the moment I've been waiting for.

To distract myself, I click on the radio. Ahh. *Desert Island Discs*, a quintessential British radio show where the celebrity guests choose their favorite songs. On this evening, a Baroness whose name I didn't catch but who has been a lifelong supporter of education and whose taste in music is eclectic and fab. When she plays an obscure 20's song, my head whirls with ideas for the musical. I open the glove compartment to find something to take notes on. I pull out a folded glossy piece of paper. It's a property listing for a barn conversion in Trunch, Norfolk, set on four acres, near the sea.

Huh. "What's this?" I hold up the listing for the "Impressive 5 Bed Barn Conversion, situated in a superb setting." Charlie's eyes stay fixed on the road. "This is beautiful, but it's a lot of money. Do you have that kind of money?"

"I really don't like you going through my things, Kat. That makes me feel unsafe."

"I wasn't going through your things! I was looking for a piece of paper!" I shove the property listing back in the glove compartment and try to calm down. A barn conversion? Why is he looking at barn conversions and not telling me? It's probably not a big deal, but when we get to the restaurant, I feel so disturbed that I duck into the ladies' room.

I feel like I'm on the verge. I want to talk to my Mom. Thank God she answers. "Honey! How are you doing over there?"

It all comes out in a gush. "Mom, he's taken me out for a fancy dinner and I think he may propose. But on the way over I found the property details for a vacation house or something in the glove compartment of his car and he's never said anything to me about that and now he's acting weird and I fly home to New York in two and a half weeks and we haven't even spoken about my visa expiring and me leaving and I just… I just don't know what's going on."

"Okay," Mom says. "Well, you can't read his mind, can you? Have you asked him what's going on?"

"Not really. No. But I was determined to bring it up today, so I guess I'll do that."

"At this special meal he's taken you out for?"

"Should I wait? I mean, I've been waiting for so long. You see, he's thinking about buying a second home, but not talking about it with me? Is that bad? It felt like he was hiding it from me or something."

"Honey, men are weird. Lord knows what's going on in his head. Listen where are you now?"

"Ladies' room."

"Is there anything beautiful in there?"

"Yes. A bouquet."

"Lovely. A bouquet of what?"

"Roses. Soft pinks and cream."

"Stunning. Do they have a scent?"

I plant my nose on the soft petals. "Yes. A delicate scent."

"You see how there's beauty even in the ladies' room?" Mom asks.

I laugh.

"Go and enjoy the meal. Whether you stay there, or end up back here, I'll always love you."

———

Back at the table, Charlie's ordered me a glass of champagne. "Kat, about the property…"

I inspect the menu.

He sighs. "I was hoping you wouldn't find out about it. It was meant to be a surprise."

"For us?"

Charlie's taken aback. "Who else would it be for?" He stands up. "Now listen. Hang on."

He drops down on one knee and presents a ring box. He says, "Katherine Maureen Callahan, will you please be my wife?" He's looking at me with sincerity and nerves and… love.

He loves me.

Panic crosses his face. "I can't believe this." He starts to get up.

"What?"

"You're meant to respond."

"Oh my God, Charlie! Yes, yes, yes! I'm sorry, I was just—I mean, yes, yes! Of course! I'm dying to be your wife!"

I throw my arms around his neck. He meets me with a deep kiss. The diners nearby applaud. Charlie takes a small bow. He whispers into my ear, "I thought you were going to say no for a minute." He sits back down. "Were you going to say no?"

"No, I'm just… I guess when you said you wanted to go out somewhere nice, I hoped, but the whole property thing distracted me."

Charlie nods. "Well, about this marriage. Shall we buy a second home?"

I start giggling.

"Norfolk? The Cotswolds?"

I start crying alongside the giggles. "Oh my God, I can't believe where my mind went!"

Charlie laughs along with me. "Then you like the idea of a second home?"

"Oh Charlie! Of course! Whatever you want! I mean, I'd love that for us! I've never even been to those places!"

"Cool. We'll go."

"Big enough for us and our children?"

He laughs. "Of course, big enough for us and our children! But I want you all to myself for a little while." He leans across the table and kisses me again. "Shall we get married in your country?"

"Yes! And I have to go there anyway because of the whole visa thing."

"Wonderful. Now, you plan the wedding. Do whatever you like. I'll just show up on the day."

"Really?"

"Yes. I'm sure you have more of an idea about what you'd like, and that way I don't have to be bothered with that part. But I'll plan our honeymoon. It'll be a surprise." Again, he leans across and kisses me. "Is that fair? You do wedding. I'll do honeymoon."

I'm stunned. I sit there laughing and crying.

Charlie reaches over and caresses my face with his hand. "You're such a wonderful creature."

"Oh Charlie, I love you so much I sometimes feel like I'll break."

"Oh babe, I'm the one who's broken."

IV

Then he kissed her so deeply and so completely that she felt like she was falling, floating, spiraling down, down, down, like Alice in Wonderland.

—Liane Moriarty

1

"All the other invitations went out two weeks ago! What's going on, Charlie? Are you trying to keep this a secret?"

"Of course it's not a secret, I just—"

"Do you not want the wedding? Is that what this is? I sent an invitation to your parents, of course, but what about your friends, your sisters?"

"My sisters already have the details."

"Friends?!"

"Babe, relax."

"Are you ashamed you're getting married?"

"Not at all."

"Then what is it? Because if anyone's going to make it, they'll need time to make travel plans. They only have a month now!"

I'm staying back in my old room at Dad's. But right now I'm at Mom's for breakfast with her and Mattie, who's still in bed at 11a.m. We're in the middle of a very hot day. I've been dripping with sweat since I walked over here a couple hours ago, and I'm not in the mood for resistance. I tell Charlie, "You need to invite people, if you want them to come!"

Mom says, "Don't yell at him, honey."

Charlie says, "Is that Cynthia? Let me speak with her."

I continue, "I have done, everything, *everything*, Charlie!"

"And that's what we agreed, babe."

"And it's going to be a breathtakingly beautiful day."

Charlie scoffs on the other end of the line.

"What? It is! It's going to be beautiful, Charlie!"

Mom says quietly, "Sweetheart, give me your phone."

Exasperated, I hand her my phone.

"Charlie, Cynthia here. Tell me what the problem is."

While Mom listens to him, I rant, "I have worked my butt off the past two months doing nothing but wedding planning. And we're a month away! It's insane that his invitations haven't been sent out. And quite frankly, it's weird!"

Mom's focused on whatever Charlie's saying. She tells him, "That's absolutely fine. A perfect solution!" Mom hands me back my phone.

Charlie gloats, "I won! Hahahaaa! Your mother agrees with me so that's that! Bye-bye!" He hangs up.

"What just happened?" I ask.

"Oh Kat, Johnny's always talking about respecting your partner's journey."

"This is about wedding invitations, Mom, not a journey!"

"Yes, but even in the little things, Johnny says you've got to let people do things their way."

"Mom, I have done the venue, my dress, Charlie's vest! The flowers, music, photographer, cake, sent all the invitations for our side! I've even chosen the gifts for our gift registry! All he has to do is tell me who he's inviting!"

"It may sound silly to you, Kat, but it's something I didn't do with your father. I'm not saying that if I'd respected his journey, then the marriage would have succeeded. No sirree, Bob. I'm just saying that it's something I've learned can help. So I'm going to send Charlie blank invitations and envelopes. I'll do it today. He can invite whomever he wants, whenever he wants. It doesn't matter to us."

Ah shit. She's right. As long as we have a headcount a week before, it doesn't really matter. I don't know why I'm so pissed off.

I shift my focus to the real problem at hand and ask, "Why the hell is Mattie still asleep?"

Mom sighs. "Oh honey, I'm just grateful he came home last night. Whenever I wake up at 2 a.m. and he isn't in his bed, I struggle to get back to sleep. But he came home not long after I woke last night. About 2:30 or 3?"

"Oh for fuck's sake."

"Please, Kat. Language."

"Sorry, Ma. Where was he?"

"I don't know. I didn't speak with him. I was in the middle of Johnny's rescue meditation technique."

I don't pull a face or say anything sarcastic. I tell her, "I'm so glad that stuff works for you." And it's true. I am so glad she has a coping mechanism.

"Well, I also took half a sleeping pill."

2

Two weeks later, and Charlie has indeed sent out his invitations. My relief over this is ephemeral, as concern for Mattie increases. Mom's throwing me a bridal shower and sent Mattie and me to the grocery store with a list. In the fruit section of the grocery store, he picks up a big pineapple and says, "Oh pineapple, my pineapple, why are you such a prick? If you let me suck your juice, I'll let you suck my dick."

"Matthew Garrett!" I can't believe him sometimes. That said, he does make me laugh, even if I'm also checking the area to make sure no one heard him.

"Not the middle name! You are *not* using my middle name."

The theme Mom's chosen for the bridal shower is "high tea." When I'm in the tea section loading up on Earl Grey, English Breakfast, etc., Mattie disappears. I look for him down each aisle. I find him in the frozen section. As I approach, he stretches his arms out in front of him as if he's a zombie. He chants, "Iiiiiice Creeeeammm! Yooooouuuuuuuu sccccreeeeeammmmm! We alllllll screeeeeaaaam for iiiiiiiice creeeeeeeeeeeeam!" He's really funny.

I chuckle again, but there's an edge to his silliness. Like, as if he's in pain inside. "Mattie?"

"Si, Señorita, soon to be Señora?"

"Remember when you were with me seeing Maria?"

"Si."

"You seemed so much more *you* then."

"Si."

"You agree with me?"

"Si."

"Now you stay out late and sleep all morning."

"Si."

"You've lost a ton of weight."

"Siiiii."

"You were all gung-ho that it was going to be summer and you'd fix up Mom's and Dad's gardens, maybe get some work. But instead you're out every night, and no one seems to know what you get up to."

He doesn't say anything.

"I'm worried about you, Mattie."

Mattie twists his mouth to the side. "Yeah. I'm worried about me too."

"You gotta get stable."

"This I know. How? I don't know. But man, do I feel like absolute shit today. I feel like I ate a 12-inch poop sub and then a horse came and shat on my face while my mouth was accidentally hanging open."

"Nice one." There's a slight pause, and I decide to seize the moment. "So you're not taking your bipolar medication, but you are drinking and doing drugs?"

"Whoa there. Can you maybe not share that second part with Mom and Dad? I mean, you did your share of drugs too."

"Matt, I'm not you."

"Yeah, but I'm not like a drug addict or anything and that's what you make me sound like. It's just been a super tough few weeks. Just gimme some time to straighten out on my own before you tell them?"

"Please tell me you're not driving under the influence."

"It's the peak of summer!"

"What on earth does that have to do with anything?"

"Most people are out partying, Kat, not hiding away in their parents' house to plan a wedding. For fuck's sake, get a life!"

"Please tell me you're not driving under the influence!"

"Don't mother me, Kat."

"It's better for people to know you're drinking and drugging if it means you don't get into your car—"

"Stop! I'm not an idiot. Fine. If I ever need a ride, I'll call a taxi."

"Promise?"

"I'll promise, if you promise not to tell Mom and Dad."

"I'll give you a week, but then I have to tell them about the drugs." Doom washes over him. "Oh come on, Mattie. Get real. You can get through this. Remember, it ain't over—"

"Oh, shut up."

"It's a nice turn of phrase."

"*Turn of phrase?* What are you, like, British now?"

"I'm just saying I don't see any fat ladies—"

Matt nudges me hard. Right in front of us, opening up the freezer and carefully rummaging through the ice cream, is, indeed, a rather large woman. Matt mutters, "Let's get out of here before she sings." We back away from the fat lady, then hightail it out of the frozen section.

3

That evening, I'm in Dad's study with the lights out. It is so super hot outside and this is the coolest room in the house. This is where I've come to digest the fact that Mattie's doing drugs again. I'm looking out over the backyard. It's a beautiful night, but my mind reels. What if he hurts himself? What if he shows up high on our wedding day? What if he doesn't even show up to the wedding? I don't mean to be so selfish, but he always seems to overshadow anything I'm doing. Like showing up on opening night and collapsing during intermission. I text Charlie:

> *Hi. Just got confirmation that Mattie's*
> *falling apart again. Wish you were here.*
> *I feel like I'm breaking. Love you x*
Give me two ticks and I'll ring

Dad's perfect lawn seems to glitter in the moonlight. It ought to, given the time he spends making sure it's watered and fertilized. I crack the window and hear the quintessential East Coast summer sound of chirping crickets. The backyard light flicks on. Dad walks out holding, of all things, potted flowers. This is odd. Then a woman, a very young blonde who I've never seen before, catches up to him and murmurs something. Dad dutifully places the flowers where she points. What the fuck happened to Red? I guess she went the way of all Dad's girlfriends.

I'd have to convince Dad that Mattie's doing drugs again. Plus, we never told Mom about it before. It could throw her over the edge. But I have to tell them if Mattie doesn't do so by the end of the week.

The woman puts her arms around Dad and nibbles his neck while grabbing his crotch. I close the window and the curtain. I would build another wall if I could. Thank God my phone rings. It's Charlie.

He says, "Sorry I haven't been available, sweetheart. What's the trouble?"

"Mattie."

"Yes?"

"Didn't you read my text? He's doing drugs again."

There's a pause. "Right. Of course I read your text. Sorry, I'm slightly swamped here. What can I do?"

"Come here."

"Sorry?"

"Come here. Help me. I can't deal with this."

"I'm about to take three weeks off for our wedding and honeymoon. I'm working myself into the ground. I'm shattered. I love you, but how can I leave work an extra week early? You're asking the impossible. Besides, he's doing what drug addicts do: using drugs. How on earth would I be of help? Just tell your parents he's doing drugs and send him to treatment."

"It's not as simple as that, Charlie."

"Yes it is."

"Maybe to you, but you're not here. I can't—seeing Matt trying to joke and be himself while I know that inside he must be in such turmoil—it's awful to watch and it's making me so stressed out. You're my partner. I need you here to help me." Silence. I hear in my head what I just said. My God. I am so selfish and pathetic. I backtrack. "Of course, you can't come. Of course, you have work to do. With Mattie fucked up, I just get so stressed. I've lost my perspective. It'll all be fine, I'm sure, so don't worry about it. You're right. I'm asking the impossible."

Charlie says quietly, "I'll be there in a week anyway."

"I know, I know, what was I thinking? I just wanted you here now. For this... shit."

"I'll come."

"No, no, I'm being needy."

"Yes, I'll come. I'll come tomorrow after work. I'll tell them it's a family crisis, and I'll bring my laptop. I can work from there for a week."

I grin from ear-to-ear.

"But you must tell your parents that he's doing drugs before I arrive."

"I said I'd give him—"

"No, Kat, you can't delay. This isn't about you. It's about him. His parents must know the details of what's going on, so that they can get him the help he needs."

I hang up. Fuck. I resolve to tell them in the morning.

4

But there's no need. The very next morning, after the blonde has gone (I hid in my room until I saw her take the soft top off her Jeep and drive away), I'm making coffee in the kitchen when Mom calls. "Well, so Matt's been out all night…"

"Okay." I wonder where this is going because as far as I know he's been out most nights.

"But he came home today…"

I wait but she doesn't continue. I say, "Okay. That's good that he came home."

"No. No, it's not."

"Is he okay?"

"I don't know. He came when I wasn't here then left. But while he was here, he stole my rings."

"What?"

Mom starts crying. "He took my wedding ring and my engagement ring."

"When?"

"While I was out for a walk—I was gone for exactly an hour and a half—and when I came back, it seemed like someone had been here. But Mattie wasn't here. Then I went up to my bedroom to change and saw my jewelry box was open."

"How do you know he took it?"

"The box was in my closet. When I walked into my bedroom, the closet door and jewelry box were both open."

"But how do you know it was him?"

"Who else would know it was in there without having to look for it apart from you? Someone made a beeline to my most valuable pieces. And who else has keys to my home?" She's starting to shout.

This is a new low. I wonder if Matt took Mom's wedding and

engagement rings cause he figured she didn't really need them anymore. That's a nasty thought. I say, "Well, Ma, you gotta call the police."

"I already did."

"Okay. Well, I'll be right over."

"No. Can you please put your father on?"

"Sure." Whoa. Mom's requesting to speak to Dad? As I go to find him, I tell her, "Maybe breaking the law will make it so bad for him that he turns it around and focuses on getting stable and stopping this insanity."

"Oh Kat, if I get my hands on that boy, he won't have a chance to *turn it around* because I'm going to wring his neck."

Dad's reading in his office. I hand him the phone and go back down to the kitchen. I finish making my coffee, not sure if I should be rushing out the door to Mom's instead. When Dad finally comes down, he says, "Why didn't you hand me the phone as soon as your mother called?"

"What?" He puts on his shoes. "Dad, she *just* called!" He's fuming. "Are you sure Mom wants you in her house?"

"Kat, you really don't understand everything." I have to step aside as Dad barrels out of the house. Even though they've been divorced forever, and even though Dad just snapped at me, some small part of me warms to see him on a gallant mission to help Mom.

I text Charlie what's happened. He replies:

Interesting. I strongly advise you not get involved.
On way to Heathrow

5

Once Charlie is with me, he tells me, "I'm going to suggest to your parents that Mattie be put into a treatment center as soon as he reappears." I'm silent. We're back at Dad's house. I concentrate on cutting vegetables for our dinner. "Treatment was my way into recovery, Kat. I checked with the center I went to, Fountain Hills out in Arizona, and they can handle him. They saved my life and could save his too."

"Why did you come here for it?"

"I'm sorry?"

"Why didn't you go to treatment in the UK?"

"A lot of Brits come here for treatment. This is where treatment started. They could really save Mattie's life."

"Well, if his situation were as dire as yours was. Treatment is for drug addicts."

"He's using drugs."

"Because he's bipolar."

"Kat darling, that he uses drugs to self-medicate is a major problem. He needs to be somewhere where both his mental illness and his drug addiction are addressed. What's your resistance to him getting help?"

I look over at him. "I'm not resistant to him getting help. I'm resistant to him not being able to come to the wedding because I want to get married with my most important people present. So I'm questioning whether such an extreme action is completely necessary two weeks before our wedding."

"No wedding's as important as his life."

"That's true. Of course I agree with that statement, Charlie." I turn my attention to sautéing the vegetables. "You must be exhausted."

"I slept on the plane. Are you trying to change the subject?"

"No, I'm sure you're probably right because you're the expert here. But I guess I was hoping that this would come to a head a little later, so that we could still get married."

"We can still get married."

"I don't want to get married without Mattie there. I really don't. So can we just see what he's like when he turns up? Give him a moment to breathe before we start shipping him off to a treatment center? Sure he may have some addiction issues, but his core problem is that he struggles with a mental illness."

"I think they say that if it quacks like a duck, it's probably a duck."

"Who are *they?*" I'm suddenly irate.

"I don't mean to make you angry. Sorry."

A text comes in. I read it then report to Charlie, "Anne's here."

"Because of Matt?"

"No." I exhale in an effort to calm down. "Anne has come to town because we're getting married. Can you put the pasta in once that's boiled?"

"Oh, you mean that she's here *now?*"

I'm already headed to the front door, so I don't bother answering him. I open the door to Anne. I haven't seen Anne in person since our brunch back when I was first dating Charlie. I have to wonder if she stages the lighting on our phone calls because she looks much older in person, visible crow's feet, dried out hair. And more worrying, she's lost a significant amount of weight, which makes her face angular in not a nice way. Plus it's almost as if she's slumping over or something.

"Jesus, Anne, you've turned into a string bean."

"Nice to see you too."

We hug. It feels like Anne ends it sooner than usual, but maybe I'm making that up. I ask, "You okay? Did you meet your new niece?"

"Spent the morning with her."

"Ohhh! How is she? What'd they name her?" Anne's oldest brother Bobby and his wife had a baby girl.

"Emma. She's ... a baby."

"Ha! Don't sound too thrilled."

"I'm not."

We head towards the kitchen area, where I introduce her to Charlie. They shake hands. Charlie says, "It's a pleasure. I can't believe it's taken us this long to meet. That said, Kat has yet to meet many people in my life as well."

"Well, what better way to get people together than a wedding." Anne's giving Charlie her false smile at full force. I get the distinct impression that she's pre-decided to dislike him.

I fill Anne in on what's happening with Matt. Once she's heard it all, she says, "This is just what you need."

And then, because I know exactly what her reaction will be, I rat out my fiancé. "Charlie thinks he needs treatment."

Anne laughs. "Ha! I'm sure he's just going through stuff."

Charlie replies, "When you're in a bad space, life can be very challenging."

"Life can be challenging for all of us, but not everyone needs treatment."

Charlie smiles warmly, says, "Sure." Then he changes the subject. "Kat tells me you're the youngest with four elder brothers?"

"That's right."

"I have two elder sisters. It certainly had its advantages, but it's a strange place to be in the family pecking order, the youngest, yet the first of your gender."

As they chat, I watch Anne defrost. At some stage, she giggles. She actually *giggles*. I haven't seen that in a while. My Lord, he's good if he can get Anne to giggle. She eventually turns to me and says, "This guy you're marrying is funny, Kat. That's something positive to add to our circle."

She stays for supper. We have this happy, joyful little meal. But as soon as she's gone, Charlie asks, "What's her deal? Why hasn't she ever gotten married?"

"She's never had a relationship that lasted more than a few months."

"Fuck."

"I know."

"And I thought I was a car crash."

I laugh.

"I guess it runs in your circles."

"What?"

"Your brother, your friend, you, me."

"What runs in my circles? What the hell's the matter with me?"

Now Charlie laughs. "I'm not sure yet, but there must be something if you're about to marry me." I wince. "I'm only teasing, Kitty-Kat. You're perfect of course. And you were right before, I am exhausted. As there's nothing to do but wait and see if your brother shows up, is it all right with you if I go have a rest?" I show him to bed and get in with him.

6

Three days before the wedding, Dad bolts over to Mom's because Matt finally showed up over there. According to Mom, "He walked in the door and fell asleep. He looks and smells like he's been living on the street, like he hasn't slept or showered in days."

Five and a half hours later, I get the next call from Mom. She's sobbing. She says, "When he woke up, your father, the police and I were all waiting to speak with him. Would you believe he claimed to know nothing about the robbery? Shameless! Then he dropped that story and claimed he was forced into it, but wouldn't say by whom and wouldn't tell us where the rings went after he took them. Then he actually said we should thank him, as he managed to *save* most of my jewelry by not allowing the other guy into the house. Then he said," Mom pauses and tries to calm herself down, "he said I didn't need those rings anymore as neither of you children would use the tainted jewelry from my failed marriage." He spoke my nasty thought. Mom continues, "Your father hit the roof. One of the policemen had to take him into another room to calm him down."

After we hang up, I tell Charlie everything. Then I add, "I know the focus should be on how unwell Mattie is, but I'm so struck by how Mom and Dad are working as a team."

"Could that be why Mattie acts the way he does? To reunite a fractured family?"

"Oh my God, sometimes your psycho-babble kills me."

"Your family unit fell apart, but that doesn't mean there wasn't love there. Maybe Matthew wants to feel that love. Maybe feeling it could help him heal."

I tell Charlie, "Let's go over there and see him."

"If that's what you want."

———

Charlie talks with Mom and Dad in the kitchen while I go in and see Matt. He sits on the sofa like a punished child, gaze to the floor, mouth set in a pout.

"Hi."

He nods.

"How's it going?"

"How the fuck do you think it's going? I'm fucked. You don't know the half of it, Kat. If you think me stealing a couple of junk rings is the worst I've done, then you don't know the fucking half of it. I'm fucked. And you don't fucking understand, so stop pretending like you do, you fucking privileged bitch."

I look to the kitchen, but the door's closed. No one's rushing to my aid.

"What the fuck am I going to do, Kat?"

He looks desperate. I tell him, "You know what, Mattie? You're going to snap out of this. We have over a hundred guests arriving to celebrate. I want you to grow up and be there for us at the wedding. Let me be clear, I'm getting married and I want you there. You. The you who is so great and cool and not doing drugs and being crazy. So what we're going to do is that I'm going to call Anne. She'll stay with you, be like your main buddy. Then you'll also have all of us, all these people who love you, who are here to help protect you. So if you want to run off and get wasted, you're just not going to. It'll be tough shit for you. You're going to stay with Anne and us." He looks up at me. "You're stopping all this bull shit. That's what you're going to do, okay?"

"Okay."

"Then Monday morning, after we're married and out of here, you're going to get a job gardening. Somewhere. Anywhere. It doesn't matter where. All that matters is that you start doing what you love doing. You're going to turn your life around. You could become one of the world's top garden designers. Okay?"

"Okay."

Charlie and Mom come out of the kitchen. Mom has this perma-shocked expression on her face. She says, "Matthew, I just don't understand how nothing has worked. We've been talking to Charlie, and we want to discuss something with you."

I look past Mom and Charlie to my Dad. He won't look at me. Shit. Charlie's talked them into sending Mattie to treatment. I tell them, "It's fine. He's going to be fine." I make sure my voice is calm as I explain, "Mattie and I have talked and we've come up with a plan and we think it will work."

Mom kneels by Mattie. "Honey, I can't take this anymore."

"I'm sorry, Mom, but don't worry," Mattie says. "Kat and I have a plan to keep me safe and it's really all cool." He says to me, "Let's call Anne. Now."

Later that day, while I put together the seating charts, Charlie says for the umpteenth time, "I'm telling you it won't work. You're trying to make a sort of buddy system for Matt. Buddy systems were created with a recovering alcoholic in mind, someone who needs a bit of support in the event he's feeling uneasy and wants to pick up a drink or use drugs."

Anne's agreed to sleep at Mom's house with Mattie and just generally stick by his side. I tell Charlie, "She's just hanging out with him. She's not an official 'buddy.' I only used that word to help everyone understand what I meant."

"All right, babe, but having a buddy is a very real thing that treatment centers use. Professionals! You're not a professional! What you're doing is dangerous."

"I don't need to be a professional to see that he needs support."

"Also, Kat, the buddy system was not created for someone who's using recreational drugs to temper manic-depressive mood swings."

"But I just used that word! This is not the traditional buddy system! Obviously!"

"Oh well, that's wonderful, Kat."

"Should we seat your mother and father at our table?"

"Babe, I don't mean to go on, but please hear me. This is as if you're preparing for a hurricane by putting up a cloth tent. And add to that, the cloth you've chosen to build the tent with, Anne, was not created to be a tent! You've told me yourself that she's a huge drinker."

"Sure, Anne likes a drink, but it's not like she's gonna get wasted with him, Charlie. Not everyone drinks inappropriately."

"This is not going to end well."

"Can you please tell me if you want your mother and father at our table?"

"You're just going to ignore my point?"

"We're getting married in three days. People have flown here from all over the place. You're the love of my life. I'm going to do my damnedest to make sure it goes off without a hitch."

"Oh my love," Charlie sits back, defeated, "yes, let's seat our parents with us."

7

The next day, Charlie goes sightseeing with his parents, sisters and their families, while I hole up in Dad's study getting last minute details sorted. Everything's cool. We're getting married and all will be well. I'm telling myself this when Anne finds me.

After spending Night #1 as Matt's buddy, she collapses onto the floor by the desk and says, "I'm sorry, Kat. I'm so sorry."

I've only seen Anne cry on incredibly drunk evenings. "What's going on?"

"I couldn't handle him, Kat."

"Where the hell is he, Anne? Where is he?" Panic and rage spring simultaneously.

"He's with Lena. Don't worry, he's fine. He's fine. Lena's with him." I calm down. "Lena got in last night. Mattie's with her and Coco, while Jean-Marc's taken Leo to some park or something. They're fighting."

"Who's fighting?"

"Lena and Jean-Marc. There's no way she'll last too long with Mattie either, but I couldn't do it, Kat. I'm sorry. I've never been around anyone like this. He's just so *on*."

"Oh shit. Don't tell me this."

"I know, I know I'm letting you down and I'm so sorry, but he's too much for me to handle. He had this complete meltdown." Her words stumble over each other, as if she's vomiting them out. "He was hysterical for over an hour. And then I suggested he take a Valium of mine—"

"You gave him drugs?"

"He needed something to calm down! Trust me, you weren't there. It was good he took it. I mean, it was crazy. He passed out, like, instantaneously, as if he hadn't slept in days but desperately needed to. He was on this weird high. I don't think he was on drugs or anything, just the way he was acting was so weird."

"God only knows how much he slept when he was AWOL."

"It was mental, like one minute he was motoring around the room, the next he was passed out cold."

"He's been having a really hard time."

"I know, but I just … I don't know." She cries again, then calms down enough to say, "He was so upset and it was like while I was listening to him, I somehow absorbed all his sadness and now I can't, I can't…"

"Shake it?"

"Yeah. And your Dad," Anne pauses and her tears dry up. "I'm so pissed at him. I just saw him downstairs and he asked me how it was going and I told him what I think—"

"Which is what?"

"I think Mattie needs serious help, Kat. He shouldn't be here. There's too much going on. He needs help, Kat!" Anne sounds desperate.

"Okay. So you expressed that opinion to my father and he…?"

"Got pissed off. Told me that Mattie had to be here for you."

"You really think it's that bad? That he shouldn't be here? What happened to the fact that we all need help?"

Anne hesitates. "I've never been around anyone like this." She starts to cry again.

"Okay, okay, okay."

"I know you want your wedding to be perfect, but, Kat, this is insane."

"It's not that I want it to be fucking perfect. I just want my brother there." I pick up my phone, thinking. I tell Anne, "I'll have him come here."

"And do what?"

"Hang out with me here. He can watch TV or whatever."

"No, he can't."

"What do you mean he can't watch TV?"

"He can't stop for long enough to sit down, Kat." Anne wells up yet again. "He's out of control."

I call Mom. Anne lies on the bed and stares up at the ceiling. When Mom picks up, I relay the information. Mom says, "Sweetheart, you have enough on your plate. I'll take care of Matthew."

"But Mom, I want you to enjoy the wedding. You're the mother of the bride!"

"Then I'll get one of my friends to do it, honey. But the point is, let me take it off your plate."

I agree and hang up. Anne has her eyes closed, doesn't move. "Anne?" She looks decimated. "All taken care of."

Anne says, "Mmm?" but doesn't open her eyes.

"Could this be affecting you so deeply because of something going on with you?"

"Nothing's going on but the same old same old."

"Maybe the same old same old is shit."

"You can say that again." Anne opens her eyes and looks at me. "Don't worry about me, Kat. I started therapy."

"That's good. What's your therapist say?"

Anne starts to laugh. "She says I'm depressed!"

"Well, you gotta get un-depressed." I go to my messages.

Anne says, "At least if I'm not looking after Mattie, I can enjoy the champagne toast."

I nod my head in happy agreement, but my fingers anxiously text Lena.

> *Lena! Glad you all made it. Could you possibly bring Mattie to my Mom's asap?*

Course. You know he's not really himself. Also my husband is being the hugest dick in town

> *I know about both. Sorry*

will head to your mom's now. x

When Charlie gets back from town, he insists on accompanying me to Mom's house to see Matt. I tell him, "It's okay. You stay here and rest. I can go on my own."

"Babe, why don't you want me to come along?"

"You can if you'd like. I just wanted to spare you the family drama."

"Is it because I have a very clear opinion of what he should do and you disagree?"

I pause then say, "No. I respect your opinion. Let's go see how he is. He may not be as bad as Anne says. She's having trouble herself. Maybe he can go to treatment in two days. Let's not get over-dramatic."

But when we get to Mom's house, she steps outside the front door and tells us in a hushed tone, "I want him to go to treatment today. Yesterday! As soon as possible." She looks right at Charlie. "I truly appreciate the talk we had in the kitchen and I am completely on board. So is Danny."

"Dad?!"

"Yes, your father and I both agree that he must go immediately. You haven't been here this afternoon, Kat. Matthew is severely depressed. I want him somewhere safe."

"Anne made it sound like he's more manic than depressed."

"You know full well that he can bounce between the two and right now, honey, he's bouncing all over the place and it's very dangerous. When he spikes low, he could hurt himself."

Before I can respond, Mom continues speaking directly to Charlie. "So after our talk the other day, Danny and I looked at Fountain Hills. We've spoken with them, and they're standing by, ready to receive him."

"Excellent."

I ask Charlie, "That's the place you went?"

"Yeah, but they don't only treat addicts, they also specialize in dual diagnosis, which is what Matthew needs. That's what they call it when you're an addict who's also bipolar, or depressed, or anything else."

I can't absorb all this.

Mom says to Charlie, "The thing is, we can't get him to agree. Can you try talking to him?"

Without further prompting, Charlie steps inside Mom's house.

I sink down onto the stoop. The last of the day's sunlight hits my shoulders, warms my skin. Mom sits down beside me. She says nothing. "I... I don't mean to be selfish. It's just... been a lot to organize and it's only a couple days difference we're talking about."

"It's okay to have your dreams, Kat. And if they don't work out perfectly, that's okay too. Charlie has a different perspective because he's been at a bottom before."

"Is that what this is? Mattie's bottom?"

"Let's hope so. To be honest, I'm amazed he's made it this long without dying. I've accepted for a long time now that that could happen, but I always hope that he'll want to focus on doing something about it before it does." Mom puts her arm around me. She's hugging me. She doesn't often hug me. In fact, I can't remember the last time she did. I start to cry. "It's all right, honey. Remember, it ain't over 'til the fat lady sings, and I don't see any fat ladies singing out here."

I want to laugh and tell her to lay off the platitudes, but I can't. I say, "I know it seems like I want Mattie at the wedding no matter the cost, but that's not true. I really just want him at the wedding well. And even though it seems pretty clear that's an impossibility right now, I still wish it could happen."

"I know, honey. I know. Me too."

Dad peeks his head out. "We're all set. He's agreed to go in the morning and they're all waiting for him there. I'm going to go home and organize his flight."

I ask, "Who will go with him?"

Mom replies, "He'll go on his own, sweetheart."

I look up at Dad. "Really?"

Dad says, "That's what the treatment center told us. They told us to get him on the plane and they'll get him off."

While Mom and Dad start talking logistics, I slip inside the house. Mattie and Charlie are on the couch in the TV room. Matt sobs like a baby, his head in Charlie's lap. They haven't seen me so I retreat to the kitchen just as Mattie says, "I just hurt, man, I hurt. I hurt all over and I need it to stop, I need it to stop so badly. You promise me they'll make it stop, you promise?"

Charlie's calm. "Yeah, yeah, that's what they're there for. To make it stop, so you can live."

A couple hours later, Charlie's managed to get Mattie to sleep. Dad's booked the tickets. Mom whispers to us all, "I'm terrified he won't make it through the night."

Dad says, "I'm gonna sleep down here on the sofa. I'll make sure he gets on the plane."

Only then, once everything and everyone has calmed down, do I quietly ask, "So how do I do this?"

Charlie asks, "Do what?"

"Cancel the wedding."

"Why would you do that?"

"We can't get married without Mattie here."

Charlie chuckles, "You're joking, right?"

"Of course not. Dad?"

Dad says, "I agree. It would be mean to have the wedding without Matthew. He's Kat's only sibling, Charlie, and she's his."

Charlie's face falls. "But, Kat, that would be horrifyingly codependent of you to not get married because of Matt's problems."

Dad scoffs. "Codependent?"

Charlie faces him. "Yes. We must go on with our lives and let Mattie's illness have its consequences."

"That's a bit harsh, son."

I interrupt. "I don't know about codependency. I just know that I've been shaken to my core and I want my brother here when I get married."

Mom softly says, "Honey, you kids should have your wedding."

Dad says, "That's absurd! She can't get married without Matthew there. They can delay it."

And like remembering a popular tune, the tension between my parents reestablishes itself.

My mother says, "People have flown across the Atlantic for this event! It's organized and paid for!"

My father rebuts, "The people who want to come will come again."

"Mattie will feel terribly guilty if she cancels."

"He'll feel terribly guilty if he misses his only sister's wedding!"

Mom turns away from Dad. She tells us, "You two go home and think about it. This is for you to decide. Not us."

Walking back to Dad's, we're quiet until we're about halfway there. Then I say, "I'm sorry, Charlie, but you knew I didn't want to do this without Mattie here. And now... I have to ask you something."

Charlie's quiet but squeezes my hand for me to go on.

I steel myself. "Did you push for him to go to treatment because you don't really want to marry me?"

He stops walking. "What *on earth*?"

"Is that what this has been? A way out for you?"

"Are you *insane*?"

"No. I'm very grateful to you for helping Mattie. No one else could have done that. And I agree. He needs to go now. But I just—I can't help but wonder if Mattie's needs conveniently coincided with you finding a way out."

"I'm beside myself."

"Is this what you wanted? A way out?"

"I just got your brother into treatment and you're having a go at me?"

"I want to know if that's what this is, your way out!"

"Call your gang. Get them to weigh in. I can't have this conversation. I'm planning on marrying you in two days' time. If you don't want that, fine." And he walks off.

I'm furious. I call Lena immediately. No answer.

I try Anne, get her on the line, explain the situation. Anne says, "I don't think calling off the wedding is a bad idea at all. This whole thing has been rushed. And there's just so much going on. Don't you want to get married in an atmosphere of peace?"

"Exactly!" I agree. I'm outside Dad's house now. Charlie's gone inside. I pace. "So how do I do it?"

"Jesus, I don't know. I guess you just start calling everyone and telling them it's off."

"Fuck."

"Yeah. Bummer."

I exhale. "Where're you? Where's Lena?"

"I'm at my house. No clue where Lena is. We're not exactly speaking."

"What now?"

"She seems to think I've been, and I quote, 'critical of her since we were seven.' This was after I said one negative thing about her marriage." I don't know what to say to that. Anne can be pretty critical. She continues, "She's really on her high horse these days. If she's not careful, she'll break her back when she falls off."

"Yeah," I'm non-committal. "I think they're just having a rough ride."

"Rough ride? They only got married because she was knocked up with Leo. She didn't even necessarily want to be a mother! It just happened!"

"I can't get into this right now. I have to start making phone calls and… go tell Charlie what I decided."

I hang up just as Lena texts:

I married the FUCKING devil. Called me a bitch!
Saw you rang but sorry can't speak, Coco screaming,
Leo wants to play and husband is dead space. He says
he's fucking tired. Well aren't we all fucking tired?

> *I'm v tired. Mattie going to treatment tomorrow.*
> *Will cancel wedding. Sound like right idea?*

God yes. Never get married. It's a fucking drag and a half

My cell rings. It's Sally. I pick up and tell her, "I have some news."

"I already know. Charlie told Rupert what's going on."

I start to cry. "Ah. So Charlie wants the wedding off too. I guess that's good."

"No, no! He begged Rupert to have me convince you otherwise." I cry harder. Sally continues, "Is it worth my trying? Or are you determined to cancel?"

"Why has this become such a huge deal? Once Mattie's better, we'll tie the knot! As soon as he's out of treatment!"

"Most treatment programs want their patients to stay for three months."

"Oh come on." I kick Dad's hedge.

"But, whatever the time frame, let's think this through. You'll stay living with your parents while your brother is in treatment. And if he goes from there to residential, you'll just stay on with your parents?"

Fuck. "What's residential?"

"Sometimes people who go to treatment live in a sort of halfway house afterwards."

"Yes, of course."

"As I understand it, you've had some sort of visa issue? So you'll be here in the States while your fiancé is back in London. I presume you'll still stay with your parents. Doing what?"

"Well, I can write and Charlie will visit me, like we were doing before. It's not ideal, I know. That's why I was so hoping the timing would be different, but it is what it is."

"And many addicts in early recovery relapse as soon as they get out the door of their treatment center. So if he doesn't get clean on his first go at residential, will you continue to stay here?"

Fuck again. I say, "I take your point, but it all seems too much right now."

"I know how awful it is to witness someone in the throes of extreme illness, but does your whole life truly go on hold while he tries to get better?"

"I understand what you're saying. Really, I do." I say, "But how can it *not* go on hold? All I can think about is Matt. He's all any of us think about. How can I go ahead and have *a wedding*—a day filled with friends and family and good food and wine and dancing and, above all, love—without my little brother, one of the people I love most in the world, without him here with me!"

"Because you must."

"What do you mean I *must*? That's not true. I don't have to and Charlie *knew* I didn't want to do it without Mattie. I mean, I agree that Mattie needs help now, and I was wrong to think about delaying. I know that, but I just wanted us both to get what we need."

"And you can. He can get help, and you can get married."

"But… that doesn't make sense in my head."

"Kat, you are not your brother. Your life and his life are separate. He can be with you in spirit. And the most important thing to do for an addict is to model recovery. Recovery is life. Your life is with Charlie. Not sitting at your parents' house, waiting for your brother to be worn down enough that he wants to get clean."

"I know what you're saying is rational and makes sense. I do. But Charlie knew that I didn't want to have our wedding without Mattie there, and he pushed his treatment agenda through. I know that it's the right time for Mattie to go to treatment, but I can't help but wonder if the timing didn't suit Charlie and he's counting on me to stay true to my word and cancel." Sally hoots with laughter. "I'm serious!"

"Kat, do you really think he'd have rung Rupert and me, in a state of sheer desperation I might add, if he didn't want to marry you?" I'm silent. "What's the real hesitation here? Do you want to marry him?"

"Desperately."

"Then what's stopping you from agreeing with me and going ahead?"

"Well..." I close my eyes. I feel Sally waiting. I tell her the truth, "My father thinks that I should cancel."

"What does that mean?"

"It means that he'll be very angry with me." Sally's quiet. "Hello?"

"Yes, I'm here."

"I don't just mean angry, I mean *furious*."

I imagine Sally absorbing this, factoring in the repercussions. Finally, she concludes, "I suspect that defying your father's wishes may be difficult for you, Kat, a new behavior even. Do you want to live your life ruled by fears? Yours and everyone else's?" Sally pauses, then drives home her point, "Or do you simply want to live your life?"

8

I slip into ivory satin shoes then carefully, oh so carefully, slide my dress over my head. Mattie's in treatment. The center informed us that he arrived safely and Dad even spoke to him before they took away his cell phone. So I'm getting married and Mattie's getting treatment. There's something strange about that. I look in the mirror. Behind me, Lena and Anne smile at my reflection. They've united to be here for me. Lena says, "You look… wow, Kat. Just wow."

Anne adds, "A super-duper hottie tottie wow."

I meet Dad at the top of the aisle in the Pleasantville Country Club's event room. Overflowing vases of cream and soft pink roses, baby's breath, delphiniums and bluegrass greet us. I carry a simple bouquet to match.

I've avoided being alone with Dad until now. After we knew Mattie had been picked up by the treatment center and had settled in safely, I told my parents we were going to go ahead with the wedding, and I made sure that Charlie was with me when I told my Dad. He responded pretty aggressively that he thought I was making the wrong decision to proceed without Mattie. I hope he's calmed down enough to walk me down the aisle. My stomach clenches as he leans into me. In a low voice, he says, "You're a fabulous woman, Katherine. Charlie's a lucky guy."

"Thanks, Dad."

In front of us, Lena and Anne start walking down the aisle. Mom was meant to walk down with Mattie. In his absence, she's opted to skip the walk, so she's seated at the front of the church.

Dad holds his arm out to me. "We'd better get this over with." I take his arm. We start walking, but I freeze. My body will not move. Dad tugs me, "Katherine?" When I don't respond, he prods, "Is this you coming to your senses? You want to delay this? I can tell the guests right now if you'd like."

I look down the aisle. It's not very long. Charlie's at its end, hands folded in front of him, the picture perfect groom. When he sees me see him, Charlie grins. And then, I can breathe. This stuff with my Dad doesn't matter. I can breathe and walk. I can do anything. I tell Dad, "Just get me down the aisle." Dad looks like he makes some sort of internal decision. He faces forward, pulls my hand through the crook of his arm, and starts walking.

As we make our way down the aisle, my smile's so big it threatens to fly off my face.

And we do it. We recite the vows, say the prayers, kiss. A good kiss. A long kiss. A passionate kiss.

A kiss to begin our life together.

9

Charlie carries me across the threshold into our colossal hotel suite. It has three rooms, two bathrooms and a kitchen. It's decorated with random objets d'art that make us laugh as he lugs me into the bedroom. But as soon as he places me amidst the opulent pillows on the massive bed, I say, "Hold on, I'll be right back."

"No showering!" he yells. "Leave that dress on and come to bed!"

I ignore him and disappear into a massive changing room where Anne was supposed to leave a small bag for me. And she did. I carefully remove my gown. It's suffered tonight: a weakened strap, some of the delicate lace ripped. I lay it carefully across two chairs. Then I slip into a see-through cream silk negligee, bought especially for right here, right now.

Charlie's waiting in his briefs on the bed. He frowns when he sees me. "Where's the dress?"

"In the other room."

"Oh no no no! I was not joking! Go put that dress back on! I am making love to you in that dress."

I laugh. "Come on!"

"You come on! I've been watching you in it all night. You'll not deprive me of *that* dress with *you* in it on *this* bed."

"But it's a delicate dress."

"No excuses."

Something in me pauses. Is this abnormal? Weird? Perverted? Of course it's not. My husband wants to make love to me in my wedding dress. This must happen all the time on wedding nights. Now that I think about it, it seems so normal that I don't know why I didn't expect it. I must look like such a prude having taken it off. I should have said to hell with the lace and let him rip it off me. But going and changing back into my wedding dress, I can't help but feel a little rejected that he doesn't seem to care about what I do have on. I agonized over a negligee for tonight. And this one was bought precisely for this moment and I don't mean to toot my own horn here, but I thought I looked smoking hot in it. And then as I'm walking back into the bedroom… fuck. I feel *obedient*. And not in a hot way.

He's still on the bed when I return. I stand in front of him awkwardly. My hand nervously floats up to my head and starts twisting a lock of hair. I expect him to laugh at the absurdity of my putting back on my wedding dress for a frolic. Instead, he exhales a throaty, "Ahh." Then he pulls me down next to him and starts in. His hands, tongue, body, find all the places he knows are there and look to discover more. I know those hands. That tongue. "You are so sexy," he whispers in my ear.

I feel peculiar. But I try to stay in the moment. I pay attention to my breathing. My body starts to respond to him like it always has. See? My body trusts him. I can trust him. I switch my head off and go with the wedding dress screw.

I love you without knowing how,
or when, or from where.
I love you simply, without problems
Or pride.
I love you in this way because
I do not know any other way
Of loving but this.
In which there is no I or you,
So intimate that your hand upon
My chest is my hand,
So intimate that when I fall asleep
Your eyes close.

      —Pablo Neruda

1

My head's glued to the window of the helicopter flying us to the small coastal town of Hermanus, South Africa. I've been to Mexico and the Caribbean, to the more famous European capitals, but I've never been this far from home. As we descend, shapes take form in the ocean beneath me. I gasp, "Charlie, look!"

"I am looking."

"Not at me! Look, look, look!" He kisses my ear lobe. "Are those whales?"

He kisses my neck. "Hundreds of them. This is where they come to give birth."

"My God." I stare. "It's utterly magical." The symbolism of starting our married life in a hotspot of whale fertility overwhelms me. I turn and kiss Charlie back, teary-eyed.

We check into Birkenhead House, a cliff-top hotel overlooking the whale-filled ocean. Our room is at the top corner of the hotel. When I see the view, I exclaim, "This is fucking incredible!" It turns out we can enjoy the hundreds-of-whales vista from our baroque-like bed. So this is what we do.

On our third day of lazing in bed, I'm stroking Charlie's hair when he says, "Kat?"

"Yes?"

"Can I ask you something?"

"Of course."

"I love making love to you…"

"Ew."

"What?"

"*Making love?* What are you, like, 70?"

"What do you want me to say?"

"It's just… the whole thing. *I love making love to you.* Ew!"

"Okay, but I was going to say something else."

"Go on."

"I thought I should raise that I'm worried about how consistently teary you become after you orgasm."

"It's just a release."

"Is it? Or are you feeling anything I should know about?"

I don't want to answer this. I tell him, "I feel so many things. I wish... I wish I were in the middle of my cycle, so I could get pregnant here."

Charlie clasps my hand to his mouth and kisses it. "Well, we'll have to come back when that's happening."

This perks me up. "Really?"

"Really what?"

"Can we start trying?"

Charlie regards me. I wonder if he thinks there's a right or a wrong response. He finally says, "We can start soon. But I'd like to enjoy it being just the two of us for a little while at least. That all right?"

I lie back down. "Yeah. Of course it is."

"Let's give ourselves a year. Then come back here for our anniversary and get you pregnant."

I smile at him.

At breakfast one morning, a member of the waitstaff convinces Charlie to go on a shark dive. I ask him, "Are you sure you want to be locked in a cage and dropped down deep into shark-infested waters?"

"Come with me."

"How about if you go hang out in the shark cage while I go hang out in the spa?"

He jumps up, excited, then leans across the table to kiss me. "Perfect. That's a perfect plan."

So I spend a full day having a body massage, mud wrap, facial, manicure, pedicure and blow dry. That night at dinner I'm more relaxed than ever, while Charlie's completely charged up from the sharks. "First they lure the sharks towards the cage with fish parts."

"Gross."

"They get incredibly close to you. I was scared out of my wits."

"But you were safe in the cage?"

"I'm here, aren't I?" He grins in that way which disconcertingly reminds me of my father.

"Yeah, you're here and you're all hyper. You need to drop down a level."

"You need to move up a level."

"Let's move up to our room."

"We haven't had pudding."

"Oh Charlie, come on. Didn't you know?"

"Know what?" He's still grinning that Dad grin. I tune it out.

I whisper across to him, "Your dessert's being served upstairs."

"I can't believe you call *me* cheesy," he says, jumping up from the table.

We spend our last night the same way we spent all the other nights.

2

For the second half of our honeymoon, Charlie whisks me away to a luxury safari camp. The moment we arrive, the staff rushes us into a jeep to see lions, fresh from a kill, snacking on an impala.

"Aren't they majestic?" Charlie asks.

"I feel bad for the impala," I reply.

When we're eventually brought to our room, I learn that our safari "tent" is a double suite villa made of local wood, steel and thick glass. We're completely safe, but can hear the wild animals. Charlie says, "I won't be able to sleep with the threat of them coming to get us."

"They're not coming to get us, Charlie. Don't be ridiculous."

"I expose myself to you and you shoot me down."

"Sorry. I need to sleep." We lie awake in bed listening to the animals.

"Do you think they can break through the walls?"

"No, hon." I tell him, "I think we have jetlag from being in the States and it's hitting us now."

We toss and turn and toss. I wake up feeling like I just fell asleep. We make it to the early breakfast, after which the safari jeep takes us out again for the entire day. When we arrive back to our room for Night Two, I tell Charlie, "I am utterly zonked." He doesn't answer me. Fuck. He's in that fucking mood where he's removed, like he's trying to hide how angry he is. I say, "We need to sleep. Once we sleep, we'll feel better. Let's go straight to bed."

He grumbles, "You're so bossy."

But we're in bed by ten with Charlie holding me the way he always does. The way that feels so good. We don't make love and that's fine. But I do *notice* that we don't do it because we did it like crazy in Hermanus.

The next day I pop out of bed, feeling lighter, happier. "How did you sleep?" I ask. Charlie grunts at me.

Over breakfast, I ask him, "Anything I can do to help you shake this?" He hears me, but he doesn't say anything, not a single word. Then a stunning young African waitress, her nipples visible through the thin fabric of her halter dress, serves us coffee. Charlie's delightful with her. After she goes, he comments to me, "It's really amazing here. What a place."

"Yes," I agree. In an effort to get his attention back on me, I laud him. "You chose a truly special place for us, Charlie. You're extraordinary at whatever you set your mind to." He gives me what I can only describe as a suspicious smile. For the rest of the day, conversation is sparse and about animals. That night, we don't have sex again.

At breakfast the following morning, while Charlie graces the nipply waitress with his scintillating conversation, I make the mistake of switching on my phone. An email from Dad.

Katherine,

I thought you should know that the treatment center has something called "Family Week." As I have a work commitment, I am not able to go the week they proposed, but will see Mattie the following week. So, as it turns out, your mother will be the only family member there for Mattie during Family Week.
I hope you're enjoying your Honeymoon.

All love,
Dad

I look up sharply from my phone to Charlie.
"What?" he asks.
I'm furious. Family Week? What. The. Fuck. Is this a normal thing that happens at treatment centers? Or just this treatment center? I mean, would Charlie have known about it? He went to this

treatment center, so he must have. I google "family week treatment center." Family Week happens at every treatment center. Fuck Charlie for not warning me about this. And for not talking to me this morning. Fuck him.

"What?" he asks again.

I say, "Could you please pass the coffee?"

We trudge through the day. When we're out on safari, it's fairly easy to pretend like I'm so entranced by the surroundings that I don't need to speak to him. We're on a boat today. Watching hippos mainly. And crocs. It's intense and wild, but I'm furious inside and I know he knows I'm furious. The only way I can think to get over being so pissed off at him is to have sex. So when we're back in our lodge, I try to give him a kiss.

He recoils. "For Christ's sake, Kat! Why would I want to have sex with someone who's steaming angry with me for no reason? For fuck's sake! Why can't you give it a rest for a few nights?" I'm stunned. "I mean, do you really need it so constantly?"

"What? No, I... I just want to feel connected to you."

"And so we have to have sex??"

"Charlie, what the fuck is going on here? It's like you fell into a black hole of negativity after we'd been having such a great time."

"Why must something be wrong because I don't feel like having sex after we have had it non-stop for almost a week? What's wrong with *you*?"

"I don't feel like this is about sex."

"Is it not? Is it not about you using me to deal with some buried turmoil you're too scared to address?"

From somewhere deep inside me, comes a strange, guttural, moan-like scream.

"What on earth was that?"

"You're driving me crazy, Charlie! What's wrong with me is that it's Family Week at Mattie's treatment center next week and I'm not going to be there."

"Ah yes, of course."

"What do you mean *ah yes, of course*? Ah yes! Of course you knew there'd be a family week, but you didn't bother to tell me!"

"Now, Kat—"

"How could you not tell me about that? How?"

"Because it's not important."

"Of course it's important! We should all be doing everything in our power to help Mattie and I've just skipped away to South Africa with my new husband who won't even speak to me! Forget about the sex! What about the fucking conversation? You're happy to speak to the waitress! Are you through with me and ready for her?"

"Jesus, Kat."

"Is this it? Week two of our marriage and you're finished?"

"No, Kat, no." Charlie turns the bedside light on. All of a sudden he's the patient one, waiting for me to look at him. When I finally do, he explains, "This is my sex addiction."

I scoff. "You have *got* to be kidding me!"

"That's what this is. I'm being serious. We've been incredibly close and now I'm freaking out and, therefore, shutting you out." I try to let this sink in. Charlie puts his hands on my shoulder, pulls me down to lie next to him. "I'm sorry you're not there with Mattie. We're leaving tomorrow and once we're home, I'll be able to get to my meeting and you can call the treatment center and try to sort something out. For now, let's just be kind to each other because I love you, Kitty-Kat. Truly I do."

"You mean it?" I inwardly cringe as my insecurity pops out.

"I mean it." He strokes my hair, and I settle back into feeling safe and secure.

3

By the time we're mid-flight back to London, the silence returns. When we blessedly pull up in front of our Hampstead home, it's still relatively early on Saturday morning. Charlie asks the taxi driver to wait while we bring the bags in. Then he turns to me. "I can just make the meeting, if I go now."

"Go." I try not to sound as relieved as I feel. Honestly? I want him to run to that freaking meeting. And not only because he's being a total dick, but also because ever since we touched ground, I want to talk to Mattie and I'd prefer to do so privately.

I pace the living room as I call Fountain Hills. Then I remember that it's the middle of the night there and I hang up. I unpack then take a nap.

When I wake up, it's early afternoon and I figure the treatment center's up. But I discover that patients aren't accessible by phone. I leave a message for Matt and try Mom, who doesn't answer. I'm dying to know how Mattie's doing, so I take a deep breath and call Dad. He answers, "Hello?"

"Hi, Dad."

"Katherine! Listen your brother is very upset."

"Is he still in there? Is he doing okay?"

"He's doing great. But he was very upset that you didn't go and see him. Can you go now?"

"I tried to call him but—"

"You won't get through. They have to get permission to make phone calls, but I doubt he'd be able to call London anyway." He says *London* like it's a foul-tasting medicine.

Tears start. "Can I just show up there? Do I need to speak to anyone about going?"

"Yeah, you need to speak to Mattie. He needs to say it's okay that you come."

———

When Charlie returns with a stylish bouquet of creamy roses wrapped with a hot pink ribbon, I try to hide my blotchy eyes. "Oh Kat, I'm so sorry. I got locked in my head thinking in circles about... ridiculous things. I made the second half of our honeymoon absolutely miserable. I can't go that long without my support network in some form or another and, oh please forgive me. I just thought it would be different because it was our honeymoon. Ludicrous with hindsight. Plus I think the shark thing got me all adrenalized and..."

I start crying again.

"I've gotten you so upset. I'm so very sorry."

I'm crying too hard to speak.

"Come here." He takes me in his arms, sits me down next to him on the blue couch. "Can you possibly forgive me?" He's so earnest.

I force myself to calm down and tell him, "Oh Charlie, it's not just you. Our honeymoon was half wonderful." Then out tumbles the conversation I had with Dad, my guilt over not being there for Mattie, and, hardest of all, my fear that my brother may not get well. "He really might not and I know I'll just have to deal with that, but I want to do everything in my power to help him get better. I wouldn't want the reason he couldn't get better to have anything to do with me not being there for him." Charlie says nothing. He strokes my head, holds me, kisses my hand. But his actions are rote. I know him well enough to know that something's amiss. I ask, "What is it? What have I said?"

"Hmm?" He comes out of his thoughts, as if I've just appeared in front of him.

"Why have you gone all contemplative?"

He speaks carefully. "I was just thinking how I do all this work on myself, and here you are, going through something so extreme, and you don't do, not that you don't *do*, but you don't *have* any support in place."

"You're saying I don't work on myself the way you do? But Charlie, I'm not an alcoholic or a sex addict or anything."

"I'm not saying you need to do what I do, not at all. I'm simply observing that you don't have anyone to turn to with what are, in my opinion, very serious issues. Your brother has fallen apart, and you've decided to marry a sex addict."

"A sex addict in recovery and a brother who's getting help."

"Yes, Kat, that's true." His caresses on my arm feel mechanical.

"What is it?"

"I don't want to start an argument. It was just an observation. Nothing more to it."

"What was the observation?"

"That in terms of people who understand your situation, you're very alone."

I look to him. "I have you, don't I?"

He takes my face in his hands. "Always, sweetie. Always."

4

Hey! We're back!

Yay! Taking Leo to school. How was it?

As I contemplate how the honeymoon was, Lena sends through a picture of Leo on his way to school.

Cute! Honeymoon was magical

Good! And how's Mattie doing?

dunno. I can't get in touch with him and he doesn't seem to want to be in touch with me as he hasn't called me back

?????

I think he must be pissed at me about something. Anyway, quick question?

Shoot

I'm kind of alone out here. Maybe I should get a job now that I can work legally? Just something to support my writing, like I had in NYC?

Defo. Do it

Even tho he earns loads

totally. Work makes you feel good!
Plus you'll probably write more because
your time will be limited so you'll have to focus

you saying I'm unfocused?

NO!!!!

I was thinking so I could meet more people...

I just think job is good idea!!!

bc you think I'm unfocused?

NOOOOOOOO! Just saying that you'll be
even more focused if you have less time,
so get some crappy job and keep writing

5

"I'd be mortified to have my wife working some lowly job. What will you do? Become a barista?"

"Are you being serious?"

"Kat, you're clever and brilliant. You can do a lot more with your life than working in a bloody Human Resources department."

"I worked in one of the world's largest investment banks. It wasn't a nothing job. Don't be so condescending. But anyway, for now, I *was* thinking of getting a nothing job. Like work in a coffee shop or something."

"Are you having a laugh? Please don't do that. You should take this time to pursue your dream, Kat. Don't go backwards, go forwards! Get that musical produced. Go for it, dude." He says this last bit in an American accent. I detest his American accent. "Dude!" Still in the American accent. "Go for it!"

"Stop that accent."

"If you go for your dreams, I'll stop talking like this."

"I am going for my dreams. We're almost ready to send out the musical."

"Good, because going for your dreams," still with the accent, "is the American way, dude. But, dude! If you get some stupid job, dude, then—"

"Shhh!" I cover his lips with my finger. "I just don't want you to think I'm lazy."

"I know you're not lazy, Kat." He finishes the plate of pasta I made him.

I tell him, "We just need to tweak a few scenes."

"You don't need to give me progress reports."

"It's really okay that I don't bring any money in?"

"More than okay. That's the deal."

6

I love my desk. Charlie bought it for me while I was away planning the wedding. The wood's a beautiful teak, and he set it up in a room overlooking the houses at the back. I love looking into the houses across the way. They all have their curtains open, letting the morning sun stream in. I see a mother playing with her child, an older woman cooking something, and a young man working from home. I turn on my computer and realize it's our one-month anniversary.

As if on cue, the doorbell rings. In the next seven minutes, two sweaty men cram the living room with three large, six medium and two small boxes. The wedding gift service I chose is delivering everything at once. This is everything. I open china, a pair of silver candlestick holders, colorful cloth napkins, silver napkin rings, two crystal vases, and a crystal salad bowl. There are all new fluffy turquoise towels and neutral-toned Egyptian cotton sheets, a brand new Le Creuset deep frying pan, as well as their signature cast iron casserole dish. There's a new kettle, toaster, blender, pressure cooker, juicer, and a super shiny horror-evoking knife block. The living room fills with stuff. I can't wait to use it all.

The day slips by and the sweet potatoes with red onions and rosemary are perfectly roasted, the salmon (after marinating in soy sauce and ginger), comes out beautifully, and not one grain of jasmine rice sticks. I set all the food aside. I'll eat with Charlie on our pretty new plates when he's home for our one-month anniversary.

When he arrives, he says, "Jesus Christ, Kat, what is all this shit?"

"Our presents! Aren't they beautiful?"

He exhales. "I can't believe how superficial you are. It makes me sick." Then he disappears upstairs. I hear the shower start.

Funnily enough, I lose my appetite. I put all the food away and head upstairs to bed.

Charlie's sitting up in bed with the light on, working. Once I'm in bed trying to sleep, his very presence annoys me. Finally, he shuts off his light. Then he rolls over to hold me as if nothing's wrong. I fucking hate him right now. I wriggle out of his arms. He laughs, "Are you angry with me?" I can't believe him. "Come here," he tries to pull me over to him.

"Go away."

"Go away?! Fighting words, young lady! Time for me to use the big guns." He rolls on top of me. "I am going to squish you until you smile."

"Cut it out!" He continues. "Charlie, please stop acting like a child." But he doesn't stop. Instead, he sits on my bum and massages my shoulders. "This isn't fair," I protest. But my body melts into his touch, craves it. "You were a jerk. You told me to organize the wedding and that included the gift registry. It was either that or get a bunch of stuff we didn't want!"

"Or we could have asked for no gifts."

"If you wanted to have input as to how we did things, you could have suggested that." He starts massaging my bum. "Hey!"

"If we're fighting, I need to use all the ammunition I can." He slips his hands around my front, while kissing the back of my neck.

"This isn't fair," I say, but my voice sounds weak. We haven't made love since the honeymoon, a month ago now. I haven't told any of my friends. He's supposed to be addicted to sex. On top of which I don't think it's normal for newly married couples to stop having sex.

He slides my nightgown over my head and moves his kisses over to my front side. As he touches me, it feels like we've never had sex before. I panic that we've forgotten how to get from a to b. And then suddenly Charlie brings me there and b is better than I remember it being. I'm utterly exposed while he watches me climax. He watches my tears come, but for all his previous concern, I don't think he minds them right now. Then he gets on his own orgasm face, a face I'm very happy to see, like a long lost friend. When he collapses, I sob more. He holds me until I stop. Once I'm calm, he says, "We should do that more often." I giggle, eyes still closed. "Did you say there was food downstairs?" I laugh. "Is there?"

"Mmm-hmmm."

"I'll be right back."

He returns moments later with one of our new plates overflowing with food. His mouth is full when he says, "You amazing woman! I don't know what's better, the food, or this nice new plate!"

"Happy one month anniversary," I smile at him.

He kisses me. "We really should do that more often."

7

All week, I stay in bed long after Charlie leaves for work. Granted, it's pitch dark outside when he leaves, but I still feel like a slacker. I'm finally willing myself out of bed, when Anne calls. I answer, "Isn't it like 2 a.m. where you are?"

"I'm on the train from Paris. I'm coming to see you."

"You're coming here?"

"Well, I'm going to Brown's. Come meet me for tea?" Anne laughs.

"Why the surprise?"

"Spur of the moment decision. Just wanted to see my girls. I've arrived in London via Paris."

That afternoon, I find Anne sitting with a mimosa, a china teapot, and a silver tiered tray loaded with treats. I sink into the high-backed chair opposite her. She looks haggard, but giggles like she did over the phone earlier. "Isn't this fab?"

"I've never seen you looking so exhausted."

"Jetlag. Totally sucks."

A waiter appears. "Would you like to see a menu?"

I ask Anne, "What are you having?"

"Lady Grey." She's practically singing she seems so happy.

"That sounds perfect," I tell the waiter. He goes and I ask, "So what the hell's going on here?"

"I needed to make peace with Lena."

"And did you?"

"Yes."

"And why did it need to be done in secret?"

"It didn't."

"Then why didn't you tell me you were coming?"

"There are so few surprises in life. Try this." She offers me a sandwich.

I can't really argue with her logic or the sandwich, so I drop my questioning and enjoy the cucumber and cream cheese. Eventually, I ask, "How are you doing?"

"Meh," she says. "All my problems are so first world. How's married life?"

I pause then answer, "It's okay."

"You paused."

"I didn't."

"What's the matter?"

I take a deep breath and explain, "Well, there's nothing really wrong. But I *feel* like there is. The second half of our honeymoon, he freaked out. And then—" I tell her how we've only had sex once since then, and how I just have this weird feeling all the time, and don't feel like I fit in. I talk for such a long time that Anne finishes her sandwiches and moves onto the scones.

As she picks up a second scone, I'm sure she's going to tell me I made a mistake marrying Charlie. I'm sure she's going to mention Jonathan. She says, "Kat, I think this is all in your head." She offers me the scone.

"What do you mean?"

"I mean, you had a hard time growing up. I think it's hard for you to accept when things are good. So sometimes you make them out to be bad, but they're not. Look at your situation realistically. You've lived here for no time at all. Of course you'll be lonely and feel out of place. It's a foreign country. In the same vein, you've never been married before. You've never not worked before. You've never devoted all your time to writing. It's all new stuff you're experiencing and should feel different. But different isn't bad." She puts the scone on my plate. "You should seriously eat that."

Sometimes I feel like Anne jumps at any opportunity to analyze me in an effort to keep the spotlight off herself. But right now, I'm grateful for that.

"It's really nice to see you." I tell her.

She smiles at me. "I love you. You and Lena. I've always loved that there's three of us."

I load the scone with clotted cream and lemon curd. "Yeah, we're a nice combo."

"If one of us isn't feeling great, the other two are there and always have each other."

"If one of us isn't feeling great, the other two are there and have her back."

"Yup," she nods. "That too!"

I bite into my scone. It's heaven on earth. I leave with a massive box of pastries as there's no way we can eat it all and Anne's flying back first thing in the morning. She walks me out onto the street and wraps her scrawny arms around me to say goodbye. It's so funny being hugged by a thin woman after all of Charlie's embraces. It reminds me of when we were growing up. We were always hugging each other.

"You sure you don't want to spend the night at ours?"

"I love you so much, but I have to get up earrrr-lay for my flight in the morning! And I have work to do before I can sleep! Boring, I know." She looks me in the eyes. "You're doing an excellent job at life, Kat. You're married. You're living here. It's all good. Remember that, okay?"

I nod. She waves to me as she disappears back into Brown's. It's weird having my best friend here, yet not staying with me. But Anne's always been a career girl. Whatever work she has to do, she'll want to do it right. I thank my lucky stars she didn't mention Jonathan.

8

One cold night when Charlie comes to bed after yet another typically long workday, I say, "We've been married for three months now and have only had sex once since our honeymoon."

He keeps his back to me as he explains in a subdued tone, "It's completely me, Kat. I keep panicking over being married. It's so intimate. But don't worry, sweetheart, I'm working on it." He faces me, suddenly animated. "I started seeing a therapist who's helped so many sex addicts that she's world-renowned."

I pause. "That's great. When do you see her?"

"Mondays at 11. She's a true expert in the field."

"She sounds like a rock star. How old is she?"

"What kind of question is that?"

"I'm really happy you're in therapy. It's great."

"But you want to know how old my therapist is?"

"I just wonder what kind of female specializes in sex addiction for men."

"There are female sex addicts too."

"Yeah, but you're not one of them."

"What's going on with you? Why are you getting jealous? What's happening with Matthew?"

"Just because I'm asking about your therapist doesn't mean I'm jealous or that something's the matter with Mattie."

"No, babe, it doesn't, but I bet there is."

He's right. On both counts. I'm jealous of any woman who gets to spend time with Charlie and who he's eager to see. And also Mattie finished treatment this week and there's some drama around it that no one's telling me. My Dad will only say that I left the loop and make me feel guilty. Meanwhile, Mom says that Matthew's decisions are personal. She told me that he opted not to go to a residential program, and so has, once again, moved back in with her. These meager scraps of information about Mattie's well-being rile me. However right now, I'm concerned about my new marriage, and I'm wondering who the hell this sex addict therapist lady is. Is she really going to help? Or is this some scam?

But I don't say any of this. I force myself to smile kindly at Charlie. I tell him, "I assume Mattie's doing really well, but I don't have any news."

9

Rupert's sent me another round of thoughts on the musical. We're nearing a final draft so I haul my ass out of bed to focus on these edits. But when I sit at my desk, all I seem able to do is search the web for china sellers. Our wedding china lacks three teacups and saucers, a creamer, half the chargers, and a set of soup bowls. This really bugs me. It's expensive to buy them all retail, so I scour the web for a deal. There's a warehouse in France selling it for half price. I could take the train over, see Lena while I'm there...

I'm looking at the cost of the Eurostar when my phone rings. My mother's number comes up, but I know it's finally Mattie. "Hello?"

"Louiiiiiise. How's married life?"

"Cool. Good. How's post-treatment?"

"How the fuck do you think it is?"

I'm zoomed right back to Mom's TV room when Mattie yelled at me before I set him up to have Anne as his buddy. "I... I actually have no idea how it is, Mattie. That's why I asked." I continue to quietly move my mouse looking for Eurostar deals.

"Louise, listen, I'm not doing drugs. I'm not manic. I'm not depressed."

"You're just angry?"

"Will you let me fucking finish? The problem now is that I'm broke."

"What do you mean?"

"Cashola. I need some."

"And..." I snap to. "Are you asking me for money?"

"Yup."

"I don't have any money, Mattie." I return to looking for discount china websites.

"What do you mean? You're married to a business tycoon."

"He's a management consultant."

"Kat, I'm not an idiot. I do know how to google."

I say nothing. Why should I downplay Charlie's success?

"Mom and I worked a lot on our relationship and I don't think it's healthy for us to be in the same space for very long. But now that Mom and Dad paid for treatment and your wedding, they're less inclined to buy me a place to live and before you ask, I'm not living with Dad again. Been there, done that, and he absolutely doesn't want me there."

"Don't you think it would be good to stay with Mom until you can support yourself and get a place of your own?"

"I do not. I think I'm more likely to get on my feet if I'm not staying at Mom's. Think of it this way: she was a nightmare to live with when I was on drugs, but now *sober*? I can't fucking take her, man. If she tells me about Johnny Dower or the fucking fat lady again, I'll end up killing myself for real."

There's a slight pause as I digest this. I ask, "Were you going to kill yourself?"

He inhales deeply. "Why the fuck do you think I needed treatment?"

"How much money do you need?"

"I have the first month's rent and most of the last. I just need the rest of that and the security deposit."

"How much is that?" He tells me. "Let me see what I can do." We get off the phone.

It's about the cost of the half-price china plus the Eurostar ticket and a few nights out in Paris. I look in our joint bank account. Charlie's generous. I wasn't able to support Mattie emotionally at family week. This is the least I can do. I send him the money.

10

We planned to spend Christmas at Charlie's parents' house again, only his parents decided to stay home with us. To avoid them, Charlie cancelled going to their house and decided we'd have Christmas in London. But his parents call on Christmas Eve. Charlie puts them on speakerphone, listens to them talk at him, and says nothing until he points out, "Kat's here too."

I can feel Ariel's repulsion through the phone. She asks me, "Has he been working too hard?"

"Oh, you know Charlie."

But then his father says something else to Charlie, and his mother switches her attention back to him, and they jabber on for almost an hour.

Once we're finally off the phone, I say, "You didn't say a word to them."

"Did I not?"

"You did not." He flicks on the TV. "Why not?"

He pulls me onto the couch with him. "My parents are incredibly annoying, so I ignore them."

"Oh. When you're quiet around me, is that because I annoy you too?"

"What?" He looks at me and laughs. "You look so funny when you're being paranoid and insecure."

Christmas Day and his parents call again. I would die if my kid ignored me like Charlie does them, so I plan to intervene. Both Harry and Ariel start firing questions at him. As before, Charlie doesn't respond. I find a gap in the conversation and ask, 'How did you two meet?'

Harry replies, "Did you know we met in America?"

"I didn't. What were you doing there?"

Ariel turns her attention to me as well. Though her topic is still Charlie. "It's a delicate balance, Kat, work and home life. He can't do it on his own, you must help him."

I can only have one conversation at a time, so I repeat my question to Harry. "What were you doing in America?"

Harry answers, "Oh, I was very young and I wanted to see the world. So I went to work in New York for a year. You could do that then. I was fresh out of the Army."

He pauses slightly, as if to let Ariel jut in, but she says nothing. He continues, "I worked with a brokerage firm. It was almost what you'd call an internship today. I was the youngest man there. They called me *Britboy*."

I laugh politely.

"Well, and by then I'd met this breathtaking woman here who wanted to live in London so that, as they say, was that."

We all laugh, except Charlie, who's busy staring into space.

I ask, "Where did you two meet?" hoping that this question will get them to tell the same story.

"Grand Central Station," Harry starts. "She sat holding a cup of tea..."

"I was surrounded by parcels..."

"I asked which train she was waiting for..."

But Ariel doesn't complete Harry's sentence. She interjects, "Oh Charlie! I've been meaning to ask you how it's going with Rebecca at work?"

It's so silent I wonder if the line's gone dead. Charlie doesn't look spaced out anymore.

I ask, "Who's Rebecca?"

"What's this?" Ariel's voice sounds so fake. "Has Charlie not introduced you to Rebecca?"

"Not yet."

"Are you sure? Rebecca? His ex-girlfriend?"

"I've never even heard about an ex-girlfriend named Rebecca." I use great restraint to keep my voice even.

"She's not an important ex," Charlie explains.

"Not important? Then why were you with her for two years?" Ariel probes.

"Maman, don't be provocative."

"She was important enough to help get a job."

I feel sick. Who the fuck is Rebecca and why is she working with Charlie?

Charlie looks at me, sighing. He says to his mother, "You're working Kat into a state. Stop it."

"I'm not in a state, but it would be great to know what you're talking about."

"Kat?" Ariel sounds triumphant. "Do you see how I know more about my son than you?" Then she has a good laugh.

Charlie takes my hand, but before anyone can say anything else, Ariel, without missing a beat, smash cuts the conversation back to the previous story. "I told him, *I'm waiting for the train to Boston.* He looked so handsome. He was wearing a three-piece suit."

And Harry continues with her, "I'd been at work."

"And I was on holiday with my sisters."

When we're finally off the phone, I ask, "So who's Rebecca?"

"Jesus, Kat, I knew you would make a big deal out of this, that's why I wasn't going to tell you."

"Tell me what?"

"An old girlfriend of mine, Rebecca Walker, has applied for a job at JCK."

"When?"

"Just last week."

"To do what?"

"She'd be working on my team, as a creative."

"Who is she?"

"Are you seriously going to cross-examine me?"

"Why didn't you tell me?"

"Firstly, we haven't hired her yet. And secondly, I was not only going to tell you all about it, but was also planning to ask if you'd *mind* that we hire her, what with her being my ex and all."

That slows me down but makes me wonder. "Then why haven't you?"

"To be honest, it hasn't been in the forefront of my mind."

"Your mother seems to think she's already been hired."

"My mother is in touch with Becca's mum."

"*Becca?*"

Charlie looks at my face then starts laughing. "Becca and I are friends now. We dated about five years ago."

"Before me?"

"Kat, I didn't even know you five years ago. Of course it was before you."

"I mean, was she the last woman you dated before me?" I'm trying to trick him. The last person he told me he'd dated was Amelia, a Bikram yoga instructor somewhere in Camden.

He pauses a second. "Well, you know about Amelia."

"Oh yes, that's right."

"Well, Rebecca was before her."

"And according to your *Maman* for a significantly longer period of time. So why haven't I ever heard of her?"

He sits on the edge of the couch. "I suppose I didn't want to tell you about her because I behaved abominably in that relationship." He's not looking at me. "And I feel incredibly ashamed."

"What did you do?"

"Oh, you know, the usual." He exhales, defeated.

"I don't know what the usual is."

"You want me to say it?"

I wait.

"Christ, Kat, I cheated on her." God he looks so guilty. He takes his transgressions hard, when, really, non-sex addicts cheat all the time.

I fight an instinct to take him in my arms because I want to get to the bottom of this. I cross my fidgety arms firmly and ask, "Charlie, have you ever cheated on me?"

He stares at me, as if my question's out of left field. But I think it's a valid one to ask a sex addict, so I wait for his answer.

He shakes his head before saying softly, "No." He puts his hand out to me. "Oh what a thing to ask on Christmas day."

"Well, you've done it to everyone else." I take his hand and let him pull me onto his lap.

"I'm a sex addict."

I ask, "Is that the excuse you'll use when you eventually do cheat on me?"

"Come on. That's not going to happen."

"Charlie, are you sure?"

"Oh sweetie," his voice is pained, "I'm sure. You're special. You're different from all my past girlfriends. You're my wife, Kat." He kisses me lightly on the lips. "Come on, I'm going to have to tickle you, if you get too gloomy."

He squeezes my middle until I squeal. He doesn't stop until I'm begging him, "Please! Please! No!"

He kisses me again. Harder this time. Then holding me in his arms, he asks, "Now since we're on the topic, I'd like to know honestly if it would bother you for me to hire Rebecca?"

"That depends. Is there anything going on between you?"

"God no! When you see her, you'll understand why."

"Charlie, you're so rude!"

"You're a goddess. She's—"

"Oh Charlie, don't be mean."

"I'll hire her in the New Year and introduce you then. You'll see you have nothing to worry about."

"Won't it be weird working with an ex?"

"Trust me, Becca wouldn't touch me with a ten-foot pole. Besides, she's married now with two little girls and to be frank—"

"Why would you want to be Frank?"

"Ha. Ha. But like I said, I'm amazed that she'd work with me after what I did to her. I'm thinking hiring her may act as a sort of amends for my behavior."

"You should hire her because she'd be good at the job, not because you feel guilty. This is work."

"You're right," he says. "I'll think it over. But on principle, what do you think?"

I kiss his cheek. "I'm touched that you're asking for my permission. Of course I don't mind. Thank you for running it by me."

11

In the after Christmas sale, I head to Harrods and I'm in luck. Our china is 35% off. I splurge and buy the three teacups and saucers, creamer, half the chargers, and the set of soup bowls we were missing. Bliss. Satisfaction. Hip, hip, hooray! Then I start looking at accent pieces in our range. The addition of a splash of color to our monochrome set…

There's something wrong with me. Using all my willpower, I drag myself away from the china. I end up in the stationary department where I spot a deep blue leather journal. It would match the fountain pen I gave Charlie for Christmas. I get it.

I'm not far from his office and I have nothing much to do, so I start heading over there. Even though most people don't work during the week between Christmas and New Year's, Charlie does. When I asked him why he couldn't take the week off like he did last year, he reminded me, "Babe, I took practically the entire month of September off!" "But weren't those vacation days?" "Most people don't use all their holiday, darling." As much as I dislike Ariel, maybe she raised a fair point that I need to help Charlie with his work/life balance. So I'll deliver his gift in person and try to convince him to come for a walk or have a coffee with me.

When I ring his building's buzzer, security directs me to JCK reception on the 4th floor. Of course there's no one there. But I remember where his office is and head towards it. I'm excited about surprising him. My blood pumps faster.

Charlie's office is the only one with a light on. I walk down the deserted hallway. I hear him talking on the phone.

No. I hear another voice. Someone talking back to him.

A woman.

I turn into his office and see Charlie at his desk. A blonde sits in the chair opposite him.

Charlie stands. He looks shocked. The blonde immediately turns and regards me with a questioning look.

"Hello," I say. I can hear that my tone is overly bright. "Did I startle you?"

"Oh," the blonde says, "are you—"

"This is Kat." Charlie flies to my side and wraps his arm a little too tightly around my waist. "My wife. Kat, this is Rebecca."

It's like I've been punched. *Becca* hasn't been hired yet, so what on earth is she doing here? "It's so nice to meet you." I shake the woman's hand, adding, "It's Becca, right?" to show that Charlie has talked about Becca, that I know all about her and that this is really no big deal. And it's not a big deal. Charlie will explain why she's here. He could be interviewing her. It's not like I walked in on them fornicating.

"I've heard so many great things about you," Becca gushes.

She's prettier than Charlie made her out to be, but not by much. She's on the full side. Her face is very round and she has a slight double chin. Her glasses are stylish, but don't quite work with her face. Ditto her clothes. She sports a striped sweater that's unquestionably an expensive piece, but the horizontal stripes do her no favors. I'm wearing jeans and a simple cashmere pullover. I know I look great.

"We're just about finished here," Charlie says.

"Great. Perfect timing!" I say. I caught that he meant they need a few more minutes to finish up, but I decide to play dumb unless he directly asks me to leave.

So we all stand around for an unbelievably awkward moment. Charlie finally says, "Becca, why don't you get back to your family. We're in good shape here."

"Yeah, we are," she says. Then she explains to me, "I have two little girls at home." I'm smiling like I care. "I thought I'd go back to work after Lily, but Alice came so soon. Rodney and I were really pleased that I could start here before Christmas. Rodney has this whole time off. So he's looking after the children while Charlie's been taking the time to get me up to speed here." I don't bother looking at Charlie, give Becca my full attention. She yammers on, "Rodney's doing the first round of nanny interviews." She shakes her head to express what a nightmare it all is.

I hate Becca but tell her, "You have no idea what a pleasure it is to meet you."

And then Becca is gone.

I snap, "Why did you tell me you were *thinking* of hiring her when you had already hired her?"

Charlie gestures wildly at the space around me. "Because of this, Kat. Your anger. Don't even start, all right, love? This is not a big deal. She was the best for the job and I hired her."

"*Before* you asked me if it was okay?"

"I don't technically need your permission to hire someone for work."

"No," I say slowly, "you technically don't. But it was a polite and kind gesture to ask me if I minded you working with an ex-girlfriend I hadn't heard a peep about. And yet when you asked me if I minded, you'd already hired her!"

He's not looking at me.

I hate it when he does this. "Charlie, come on! Why did you lie? Why on earth would you *pretend* to be doing the kind thing? What are you hiding?"

"I don't know what you're talking about," he says in a hushed tone.

"And now you're pretending like you don't know there's something unusual about hiring an ex to work for you, hiding it from your wife, then pretending like you weren't hiding it!"

"Shhh," he says. "Don't shout. You're embarrassing me."

I quickly check the hallway. "There's no one here!" I scream.

"Kat, please! CCTV."

Out on the street he says, "Kat, listen. I get uncomfortable when you're angry like this and I knew this would happen if I told you I'd hired her. Things are stressful at work and I wanted to get her on this project ASAP and I didn't feel like making a big drama out of it."

"And yet you have made a big drama out of it, Charlie. I care that you lied about hiring her. I don't care that you hired her. I would never care about that. I'm a trusting person, and I trust you!"

"I guess I don't feel that way."

"What?"

"You heard me."

"You don't feel like I trust you?"

"Kat, the look on your face when you saw her in my office was one of pure fury."

"Because you *lied* to me! First your *mother* told me about Rebecca. Then after the cat was already out of the bag, you *lied* about what was really going on! A lie I then discovered not because you came clean, but because I randomly stopped by!" A bit of my spit flies into his face.

"Please don't yell at me," he responds.

"Please don't lie to me!" I yell.

"But don't you see this is exactly why I didn't tell you? I knew you'd be angry."

"But Charlie—" I clench my fingers. He's driving me insane. I force myself not to yell as I say, "I wouldn't be this angry if you had just told me. I'm furious that you lied to me, not that you're working with your ex-girlfriend."

"You say that now."

"And I mean it. I know myself."

"Do you?"

"Ahh! Why are you turning this around to somehow be about *my* character? You're the one who lied. I'm pissed off because you lied to me!" I'm shouting again.

"But if I'd told you the truth, you would have been just as angry."

"We're going in circles." I yank out the journal I bought him. "Here." I shove it in his hands. "It goes with your fountain pen."

"Oh that's not fair." I walk away. He follows. "You can't be extra thoughtful when I'm being a shit. That's not fair." I keep walking. He keeps following. "Where are you going?" he asks.

"Home."

"Come on, let's get a taxi. You're right. I'm wrong. I'll try to do better."

"God, you really piss me off! I don't understand what's going on with you, Charlie, but do you really think it's that easy? *You're right. I'm wrong. Let's get a taxi?* I don't even know whether or not to believe all your apologies anymore!"

He looks for a taxi. All the fight suddenly drains from his face, accentuating dark circles under his eyes. I don't recall ever seeing them there before.

"I'm trying my best, Kat. I really am."

I believe that much. I believe he's trying his best. "Fine. Fine," I say. "It's fine. I don't actually care if you work with her or not, so really it's fine." We get a taxi.

12

Charlie arrives home as I'm popping the first of the hors d'oeuvres into the oven. When he sees me, he stops short. "What on earth are you wearing?"

I do a turn. "You like?" I have on gold Prada heels that I paired with a red mini-dress that does wonders for my chest.

"You're not seriously planning on wearing that?"

"Why? Do I look bad?"

"We've invited about six sex addicts and they could all bring a friend who's a sex addict. Do you really think that outfit is appropriate?"

"Charlie, it's New Year's Eve!"

"Think about your audience."

"They're not an audience. They're our guests." My voice sounds timid, soft.

"All the more reason to behave respectfully in their presence. You look like an absolute slapper."

My cheeks burn red. My eyes well up.

"I don't mean to be harsh, but you should know the truth. You look like an attractive slapper, but all the same, a slut."

I head upstairs and change into a conservative black cocktail dress and much shorter, but still fashionable, heels. But during the party, after Rupert remarks, "You look lovely, Kat," I find myself up in the bedroom showing him and Sally the shoes I changed out of.

Rupert whistles. Sally says, "Put them on before I do."

I strap them on, then do the same turn I did earlier for Charlie.

"Why aren't you wearing them?" Sally asks.

"I was told by my husband that they may be a touch too... provocative."

"They're definitely sexy. Nothing wrong with that though."

"No, but I mean that they're provocative in a way that's inconsiderate to all the sex addicts attending our party."

Rupert and Sally both laugh. Rupert asks, "Did Charlie tell you that?"

Sally says, "Kat, sex addicts have to deal with sexy people, sexy images, sexy all sorts of things, every day."

"Charlie was pretty convincing in his belief that, as their hostess, it would be insensitive of me to dress in a manner that was so alluring." I omit Charlie's use of the words "slapper" and "slut."

"I'm sure Charlie gave you a good argument as to why you shouldn't wear these, but the real reason is probably that Charlie can't deal with those shoes himself."

She may be right. "I want to wear them."

"A rebel," Rupert comments.

"I can tell him that the other shoes were hurting my feet, so I changed."

Sally pipes up, "I think it's important we don't lie to these guys."

I tuck my conservative black shoes back in the closet. "It's not a lie. These other ones were bothering my feet psychologically."

Sally grins. "I like that."

Charlie doesn't notice the shoe change. Even when it's close to midnight and he comes and stands by me and I'm as tall as he is.

13

"China, Kat? You're obsessed and it's insane!"

"Nothing I do is right, is it, Charlie? I mean, last week it was my New Year's Eve outfit. Before that, you didn't like that I like our wedding gifts!" He's silent. "I mean, stop *picking* on me!" I scream so loudly that I shock myself.

Charlie sinks onto the couch. "Good God, Kat, I really can't take this kind of verbal abuse. Especially while on top of it, you're taking advantage of me financially."

"What?"

"You heard me."

"What are you talking about?" I sit next to him on the couch.

"I think it's pretty obvious that I'm the only one earning here."

"We agreed I would work on establishing myself as a playwright here. I may not have done that yet, but Rupert and I sent out the musical last week." I gently put my hand on his knee. He doesn't move, doesn't cover my hand with his. It's like touching a robot. "I'm confused, Charlie. We talked about this."

"Talked about what?"

"Me getting a job. I told you I thought I should get a job and bring some money in while I'm working on getting the musical produced, and you said no."

"No, I didn't."

I search his face for some sign that he's joking because really he must be. He just closes his eyes.

"Charlie, we had a conversation about this as soon as we got back from our honeymoon."

"A conversation about what?" His voice tightens.

"About me getting a job. You said you didn't want me to get one, that you thought it was a better use of my time to write, and... and pursue getting my musical produced."

"I never said that, Kat." He sounds exasperated, like he's lost patience with me.

"But… you did!"

"Kat, why can't you simply hear how I feel? Why are you making excuses? I work very hard and it just feels like it all goes to this bottomless pit that is *you*. I need something for myself. I can't give everything to you."

"I honestly don't understand what's happening here. How is supporting me financially while I make connections and get into the theatre scene here *giving everything to me*?" Then I make a decision. "I'll get a job if this musical doesn't go anywhere. I'm not opposed to getting a job, Charlie. But the deal that we made was that I was going to focus on my work and try to get up and running here."

"And how long is *that* going to take?"

I cringe. "Charlie, we—we *agreed* that I wouldn't work. We talked about this. But if your feelings have changed, that's fine. I can adjust, Charlie, because I don't mind. But I don't see how this is an emergency."

"You don't *mind*? You don't *mind* pulling your weight?"

I cannot believe him. "Do you think I don't appreciate you supporting us? If it weren't for your job, I couldn't have moved here and we never would have gotten married."

He stands up and moves away from me. "The only reason you wanted to come here was so you could quit that job you hated."

"I came here because I love you!"

"Stop yelling at me and admit it."

"Admit what?"

"That you're using me."

"What the fuck are you talking about? I don't use you! I love you!"

He looks like an angry child, a twisted sulking angry child.

"Did something happen at work? Are you stressed? Talk to me!"

"Why are you always yelling at me? Why can't you just listen? You. Use. Me. For. My. Money. Some sky-high bill at Harrods? What did you need from Prada? And what the hell was that transfer to Matthew?"

I pause. "He needed help getting on his feet after treatment."

"Have you even heard of codependency?"

"I didn't think you'd mind!"

"You take advantage of me day in and day out."

"I don't understand. I thought the joint account was for me to use as I see fit! The Harrods bill was for our china! Prada was an indulgence, yes, but you've kind of been a shit lately and I didn't think you'd mind! And then the Mattie thing, well that was just to help him out!"

"Would you have spent that money when you were earning?"

"I didn't realize there was a budget. There's just so much money in there."

"You never listen to me."

"What? What do you mean? Listen about what? We've never talked about this before!"

He heads down to the front door.

I'm astounded. "You're going? Where are you going?!"

But he just leaves.

I don't know what to do. I call his phone but it goes straight to voicemail. I keep calling and calling. I'm mortified, but have to tell someone or I'll implode. So I text Lena who texts me back:

Kat this is just: blah!! You guys are having
post-wedding blues. Lots of married couples
struggle with the first year of marriage. It'll pass.
This is normal. In the meantime, just keep up
your work and get a job for Christ's sake

*I don't think this is just about me having
a job or not*

I also don't think this is just "blah." But Lena disappears, so I try Anne. I can see that Anne reads my text, but she doesn't reply. This has been her norm of late. I contemplate calling Mom but she'd worry. I try Sally. After I tell Sally what happened, she says, "Oh Kat, that sounds like some kind of insane sex addict mind manipulation. The best thing you can do is keep the focus on yourself. My mother always said that a happy woman owns a great pair of shoes and has something to look forward to in her diary. You already have the shoes!" I can't help but smile at that. She continues, "And someone's sure to snatch up the musical. Let Charlie sort himself out and get back to you. In the meantime, remember all the positive reasons why you married him. Literally make a list of all his assets and focus on that."

We hang up and I do exactly what she said.

Funny
Handsome
Supports me
Introduced me to Rupert & Sally
Practically saved Mattie's life—did save Mattie's life
Is being weird and unreasonable but this is what sex addicts are like
Is trying his hardest even though it's hard to be a sex addict
Is honest with me about his struggles
Makes me laugh
Gets me (when he's not being weird—probably even gets me when he is weird even though I can't tell because sometimes I think he might even get me more than I get myself)

I calm down. By the time Charlie gets home, I'm in bed reading. He comes straight to bed and takes me in his arms, as if nothing's the matter. "I went to a meeting then out with the guys after."

"That's great."

"I love you." He takes my head in his hands. "I'm sorry."

"I love you too. It's okay." I place one hand on his thigh.

He gently moves it away and says, "Let's get to a better space. You're going to get your musical off the ground and I'm going to get my head on straight." He pecks me with closed lips then pulls me into a chaste embrace.

14

I call Charlie with the news that this producer wants to read *The Amazing Kapakowski Sisters: Bloodbath at the Ritz,* and he asks, "What's his name?"

"Breckenhauer. You wouldn't have heard of him, but he does great fringe—"

"I've just googled him and absolutely nothing comes up."

"You're probably spelling it wrong. Put in *A Mix-Up of the Mind.* There's a review of it online somewhere. It wasn't the greatest of shows, but it was all original music and this producer Simon Breckenhauer took a chance on that writer-composer team, and they went on to do very well. They were new, too. He managed—"

"Kat, you and Rupert are established and this guy's a nobody."

"Oh come on, don't say that. He's going to read it! What could be better?"

"Someone with some power, some clout. Why aren't you guys sending it to your agents?"

"We did. We don't think they like it. Fucking hell, you are such a buzzkill! *Nothing* I do is good enough for you, is it? Rupert thought this was great news and he knows more about this business than you do! He said it was cause for celebration! He invited us both over to celebrate, but I suppose you're too busy anyway!" Furious, I hang up before he can respond. I'm sick of his condescending voice. And he's wrong. This is great news. I'm going to *enjoy* this small step forward. It's not easy to get things produced.

I email the requested script over for Simon Breckenhauer to read and then get ready to go meet Rupert and celebrate. On my way out the door, I see a missed call and voicemail from an unknown NY number. I pause in the foyer to listen to the message.

"Hi, Kat. It's Bobby Walsh here, Anne's older brother. Please give me a call when you can."

Something's very wrong. His voice says it all. It's not just his subdued tone. It's that Bobby—who left for college so the basement could be our haven, who we never spent time with but stood in awe of—is calling. The mere action of Bobby calling indicates that something is not simply wrong, but exceptionally wrong. This can only mean that something awful has happened to Anne.

I hear a bus going by in the stream of traffic outside. It's either a very useful or useless bus to get me to Rupert and celebrate our step in the right direction.

I concentrate. I want to call Anne. Not her older brother. My call goes straight to voicemail. I send her a text, but it doesn't go through.

I call Bobby. He tells me, "There's been an accident."

This doesn't surprise me.

"Anne was hit by a truck two nights ago." Bobby takes a breath in. "Her body's being flown back to New York today. The funeral will be on Saturday."

The traffic sounds louder than usual. I ask, "Bobby, how did she—?" But of course Anne wasn't hit accidentally, not Anne. When we were teenagers, Anne prided herself on recklessly, yet expertly, crossing the road in a way that let the cars come so close that one time she clipped her pinky finger on a side view mirror. The cars honked; Anne laughed. It was when we were into punk, and Anne wore a flowing black gauze skirt and pointy black leather knee-high boots that buckled up the side. Her skirt would blow up as the cars whizzed past. Both her spatial awareness and timing were exceptional.

"I mean," I stammer, "I mean… she was just here."

"She had some alcohol in her system, but she wouldn't have been in a blackout."

We're both silent. Then I ask, "Was there a note?"

"No." It takes a moment for him to begin telling me the story he's probably already told more than a few times and will be required to tell many more. "An eyewitness says Anne came out of a… a wine bar somewhere… downtown, I guess. She came out and lit a cigarette.

Then she put her purse down by the door of the bar and walked over to the side of the road."

He pauses. I wait.

"This lady says Anne stood there smoking the cigarette and watching the traffic."

I can picture Anne doing this.

"Then a truck—a large, white, bread truck—she says it—it came down the road and Anne calmly walked in front of it and that was it. That was it."

I clear my throat. I want him to stop. I don't want to know that it was a bread truck, don't want details that'll press into my brain to form a memory as if I were there. And yet I ask, "What was across the street?"

"Nothing, Kat."

"But—"

"I asked, Kat. There was nothing across the street, no buildings, no stores, just an empty lot with nothing and no one in it." Oh Anne. "She wasn't crossing the street, Kat."

Oh Anne. My sweet darling, Anne. You came to say goodbye. My Anne. Oh Anne Anne Annie Anne.

15

I've never seen so many flowers. Friends Anne knew from grade school, high school, college, business school, and Los Angeles. Friends of her parents, friends of her brothers. Hundreds of people send so many flowers that the funeral parlor where they're having Anne's wake is wall-to wall floral. Anne's mom, Janet Walsh, trembles. Her grown brothers are all red-eyed. Her father... God, her father. "I lost my little girl," he chokes to me. Everybody says, "She was a beautiful girl who left us too soon."

I kneel in front of Anne's closed casket with Lena. Solid mahogany, very glossy. No expense spared. A heart-shaped wreath of tea roses with a delicate banner across the middle reads, "Beloved Daughter." Behind the casket stands a tremendous bouquet of pale pink and white roses: "Sister, We Love You."

"Anne hated that there was no snow in LA," Lena whispers. I nod. "She would've loved to be here now." A small snowstorm dropped a foot of snow over Pleasantville last night. "Do you think she was homesick?"

I ponder this. "I don't think she missed Pleasantville."

We stand up and move into the packed room. Some I know, some I don't. But man, it's packed. It gets so hot that jackets come off and windows are cracked even though it's still snowing out. Mom keeps checking in with me. "You okay, honey?" I keep nodding. Anne's suicide has made Mom freakishly attentive.

"She would have loved this snow," Lena remarks to no one in particular, looking out the window.

Dad shows up with Mattie. And it makes a change to see that it's not Dad, but Mattie grasping a young woman's hand. Mom sees them too, but comes over to me instead of greeting them. She's hovering.

Lena whispers, "She called me and I didn't call her back."

"When?"

She rests her head on my shoulder. "A week ago. She seemed so happy when she came to see me in Paris. I figured I'd get back to her when things slowed down."

"Sure."

"But I didn't, Kat. I didn't."

"Shhhh… shhhh…"

Dad and Mattie make their way to the casket, leaving the new girl on her own. She wanders aimlessly around the back of the room while they kneel and pray.

Lena goes on. "I haven't *called* her, literally *called* her, in… a very long time. Probably years."

Of course, I'd learned to text both Lena and Anne, but this isn't unusual. I say, "Most people don't have time to talk these days, and most people don't kill themselves."

"I know, but we're all meant to be best friends, and I didn't see this coming."

When Dad and Mattie finish praying, Matt returns to the mystery girl and Dad heads over to me. His eyes are moist with tears. He says, "I'm heartbroken for your loss, sweetheart." He hugs me. He kind of holds onto me. "You're my sweet baby girl, Katherine. No father wants to experience a loss like this. Anne was a sister to you."

Then Mom comes over and says, "Danny?" She basically pries him off me, and he ends up hugging her. It's totally weird. Then she pulls him off and they're talking, but I can't hear what they're saying.

Mattie appears. He also hugs me. Not with his usual gusto. A subdued hug. He asks, "You okay?"

"Shocked."

"Really?" I look at him. "Something was definitely wrong with her back at your wedding."

"What do you mean?"

"She seemed stressed and depressed. And, I mean, she was always moody but worse than usual."

"Don't you think maybe just maybe that had to do with the fact that she was looking after you and you were completely insane?"

"I'm sure that contributed, but I don't know. I've always been nutty around her and she's usually taken it better."

"I just can't believe I didn't get how bad it was."

"Oh, don't even start that bullshit, Louise. Don't go there. You can't save an addict from depression. Take it from me. If my depression won and I wanted to kill myself, none of you could stop me."

"Don't say that."

"I'm just saying you couldn't have done anything."

"I could have talked to her more."

"You have your own life. You were getting married. You live in London for Christ's sake."

He sounds so clear, yet I wonder if he had to process my absence when he was in treatment. Guilt that I wasn't there for him washes over me. "Living in London is no excuse."

"Kat, trust me. Don't fall into the cliché of thinking you could've helped her. You can't help an addict. We have to help ourselves."

"Wow. You sound pretty sure of yourself." I watch the girl he brought look uncomfortably around the room. "But I just want to clarify, for Anne's sake, she wasn't an addict." He laughs. "Don't get me wrong, it's great that you think of yourself as such. But you can't throw those terms around lightly. Anne wasn't a drug addict."

"Addict, alcoholic, whatever, Kat."

"Don't be ridiculous."

Now we both watch the girl take a seat by herself.

"Who the fuck is that, Mattie?"

"Crazy Daisy. We met in Fountain Hills. I was manic and she was depressed so we figured we were the perfect match."

"And she lives in Pleasantville?"

"She moved straight to Queens after treatment. We've just put a deposit on a bigger place to rent together. She's an artist, so she really needs space."

"So the money I gave you went to her?"

Matt exhales, as if trying to keep himself calm. "No, it went to me. To my life."

"But the stuff about not being able to live with Mom, was that bullshit?"

"Don't start, Kat." He changes tack. "Daisy's amazing. I'm going to go hang with her. Come say hi if you feel like it." He goes. I watch him take Crazy Daisy's hand. The wake blurs by.

16

The next day in church, I happen to look around and spot Jonathan. He and a very pretty woman sit in a pew at the back. We stare at each other. He slowly mouths "Hello."

My God. I don't want to stop staring at him. My heartbeat quickens. This feels wildly inappropriate. I turn back around and whisper to Lena, "What the fuck is Jonathan doing here?"

She shrugs. "He loved Anne too."

He and the woman come to the gravesite. The sun sparkles on yesterday's snow. I wonder what Anne would have said about Jonathan and me now. I wonder what she would have said about the stunner he's rocked up with. Jonathan and I are finally close enough to speak. It feels like a cruel joke when he tells me, "Kat, this is Jules, my fiancée."

Jules. The one he was picking up from the airport the day I took the morning freaking after pill. Fucking *Jules*.

Jules wears a simple black silk dress with a contrasting cream silk panel around the scooped neckline. She looks classy in an obvious way. She has pale smooth skin and un-dynamic features. Her hair's neatly pulled back in a chignon with a black pillbox hat and an understated veil. Though Jonathan has good taste in women and this one's probably perfectly fine, I hate her. She's completely dry-eyed. Even for someone who hadn't known Anne, it should have been tough to get through the ceremony without shedding a tear. Plus, her hat's OTT. Who does she think she is? Jackie O?

Jonathan and I embrace quickly, politely. Then I turn my attention back to the priest without looking at Jules again. But the big diamond on Jules' finger flashes in my peripheral vision. I wonder what he did with my engagement ring. I hope it was at least a little difficult for him to let it go.

———

Mourners gather at Anne's parents' house. Jonathan shows up without Jules. We hug. People hug at funerals. This is normal. He smells the same. He holds me the same. My head rests in the nook of his neck the same way it always did. It's like putting on a beloved old sweater. "I've missed you so much."

"I know, baby, I know. Me too. But you're better off without me, Kat. You really are."

"I don't know…"

"I'm the same, baby. I'm exactly the same now as when you left."

"Stop it, you're not."

"I am. Jules hates the way I drink. She doesn't even know that I still do coke."

"Why's she with you then?"

He gives me his smile. It's not disarmingly charming like Charlie's. It never was. Jonathan's smile has always had a sort of despondent grief in it. Like he's doing the best he can but has never been capable of true happiness and has come to accept this as a fact.

We follow fellow mourners down to the basement, the basement where Anne and I slept oh so many nights. It looks like it's been recently renovated into extra living space for her parents. Now it holds the overflow of their family and friends. We hole up in a corner and talk talk talk. I ask about his family. He says it was a pleasure to see mine. We discuss his job, my musical, his engagement, my marriage, though I don't mention that I haven't had sex for months. And that little fact is making this all the more challenging. I want to jump all over him. We're left on our own in the corner, and it's like we're wearing a "Do Not Disturb" sign. He's such a great guy.

———

As soon as he closes the door to his apartment, we're on each other. I can tell from his kisses that he belongs to another woman. We're not in *our* pattern. It's like I'm receiving the caresses he gives to *Jules*.

We're in the short hallway that opens up into his living room. There's a coat rack behind me with all of *Jules'* coats and hats. Jules has, of all items, the quintessential Burberry trench coat. Below it hangs a retro brown leather Coach satchel, and beside that is a classic black Kate Spade. Jules' taste is highbrow, but pedestrian. On the upper rungs, sit a number of her "fashionable" hats. She looks like she tries very hard.

"Does Jules live here now?"

"Well… yeah." He keeps kissing me.

I pull back a little. "Where is she?"

"Work."

I feel bad. But then, Jonathan was mine first.

Whoa. I've lost it.

I do not own Jonathan. He's definitely not "mine." We said goodbye. Years ago now. He kissed my forehead. He got up. He left. Yeah, we may have slipped up after that, but we've said goodbye and he is not mine and I am not his. I am married and maybe I'm in the middle of making a mistake, but he is not mine.

Jonathan cups my chin in his hand, pulls my face to his. Then he changes his rhythm and irrespective of my thoughts on ownership, he starts to possess me. He takes his time. Slowly, so slowly, trickles kisses down the nape of my neck. His hands caress the length of me. His tongue enters my mouth in precisely the right way. I feel our *us* again. And I melt a thousand times over. An "Oh God" slips out of my mouth. Embarrassingly followed by a nervous giggle.

"We should go somewhere else," he says. "We can't do this here."

"Jonathan, honey, before we go anywhere, I have to tell you something." He looks down at me and, oh his eyes! I've missed looking into them and having them look back at me! I've missed them so much! Deep breath. "Jonathan…"

"My Kat."

"Oh."

"You'll always be mine."

Holy shit, holy shit. I laugh again. So nervous. But determined to spit this out. "Jonathan…" another deep breath. "Are we meant to be together? I mean, maybe I married the wrong man. Maybe I was… wrong to ask you to behave differently. Because it feels like it'll always be like this between us, doesn't it? Should we redirect our lives and be together?"

He takes this in. He's silent. He's thinking. He sinks down to the very polished, very clean, hardwood floor, taking my hands along with him so that I sink down too. He expertly turns me around and places me between his legs. My back leans into his chest. We sit there together. My old lover. I thought he was the one and only love of my life. He takes his time to think over my proposal. I know we could make it work if we wanted to. I know we could. The silence ticks on.

It hits me. The silence is his answer. He didn't ask me over today because he loves me and wants to be with me. He asked me over because he lusts for me. Of course, he could love me as well as lust for me, but today is solely about the lust. He's not leaving the kind-of-dull-but-pretty Jules. Our moment passed, or never was. I should've known when he chose going to the airport over talking to me about maybe getting pregnant. Why have I done this again? Why do I expose my heart? I'm an idiot. And now I've betrayed Charlie. I turn around to face Jonathan.

"Baby," he says, "that's really hard for me to hear and really hard for me to respond to. Anything I say would be like being unfaithful to Jules."

I don't point out that he's been kissing me, that I now know his fiancée has a Coach satchel, a Spade handbag, a Burberry trench, and a fondness for hats. I don't point out that he was more than willing to have sex with me. No. I say nothing. It was a moment of madness and now I want to get out of here. I stand. I kiss him on the forehead. I leave.

17

I head straight to Lena's parents' house. Lena lies in her old double bed with the TV on. When she sees me, she sits up and mutes the television. "Well?"

I lie down next to her. "We just made out and then he rejected me for the millionth time and I came to my senses that I'd better not let it go any further than it already had." I cry. I can't help it. I feel like such an idiot, a pathetic cliché of a woman. I tell her, "Anne used to always say I had unfinished business with him."

"I thought she basically came to London and blessed your marriage?"

"Yeah, but that's not what she really thought and she was wrong."

Lena strokes my back. "Oh Kat," she says and her voice cracks, "that girl was wrong about so many things." I nod my agreement. I can't believe Anne's not on this planet with us. Lena tells me, "Not to change the subject, but I tried to quit my job."

"But you love that job."

"My life's out of control. I want time to get my priorities straightened out."

"Wow."

"Think about it. I live in Paris and you live in London, and I haven't even been to see you yet."

"True, but what about reducing your hours?"

"Well, that's the thing about the office, everyone works manically. When I called, it was way after work hours there, but I knew my boss would still be in the office."

"What'd she say?"

"She offered me a raise and an extra week of vacation."

"And you said yes?"

"I said maybe. I called Jean-Marc. I told him my lifestyle was killing me. I told him about their offer."

"What did he say?"

"Well, with the extra money we could hire full-time help. It's either that or I have to quit."

"Which would you prefer?"

"As you rightly pointed out, I love my job."

"Right."

"Don't get me wrong, I love my kids more than my job, but I also just… I love my job. And Jean-Marc also thought that since my boss came back with an offer on the spot, there must be more room on their end and that I should ask for more money and request Friday afternoons completely off, no questions asked, every single week. And if they give me all that, then we'd have a deal."

"So?"

"So I think I married a smart man. And I'll propose that tomorrow."

"Cool."

We watch the muted television for a while. Then I say, "Lena, you gotta tell me what the fuck my problem is."

"I can barely figure myself out."

"Am I stir crazy from no sex yet sleeping next to the man I want to have sex with every night?"

"No sex?"

"We've only had sex once since the honeymoon."

"That's a little unusual."

I feel myself blushing. "Well… it was good the one time we did do it."

"You've only had sex *once* since your honeymoon?"

"Yeah."

"You're still newlyweds!"

"I know, I know."

"Why isn't he here with you?"

"He had a presentation this morning that he'd been preparing for months. So I told him it was fine for him to stay home. Honestly, there's something weird between us and I didn't feel like bringing the weirdness over for Anne's funeral."

"Fair enough," Lena says. "But, hon, you need to go home and have sex with your husband. That's what all this crap with Jonathan's about."

I nod in weak agreement. "Yeah, that's probably true. It's just that. Fuck. I can't believe I kissed him. Do I have to tell Charlie?"

Lena shrugs. "Like I said, I can barely figure my own life out."

18

Back in Heathrow and the texts from Charlie spill in:

> I'm emailing you a name and number. Call Gail
> and tell her you're my wife. She has a big
> production company that does West End shows

> I can't believe your flight is delayed

> I should be at the airport greeting you. I'm so
> sorry I'm not there my love

I have never felt so guilty in my life. Why is he suddenly being so nice when I've been such a shit?

I go ahead and google Gail Talsworth. Gail runs Innovate, a highly regarded offbeat production company that's won a myriad of awards. Most of her fringe shows move to the West End.

The guilt is pushed aside by a wave of fury. I call Charlie. He answers and I snap, "So Gail's a great connection. Why have you been holding out?"

"Oh Kat, I don't know... because I'm an arse? But that producer you found is utter dung. I want you to send your work to someone exceptional. And Gail is exactly that."

"How do you know her?"

"I worked with her father in Seoul."

I try to stifle my anger. I'm supposed to be remorseful about kissing Jonathan. I ask calmly, "Can you get home early tonight? I'm dying to see you."

"Absolutely, darling one."

On the Heathrow Express, I send Gail an email introducing myself.

I make it home and stay up most of the day, but crash out around suppertime, pulled into a dead-to-the-world sleep. When I wake up in the middle of the night, Charlie's asleep next to me. I wonder if he bothered to make it home early.

———

The next night, I'm excited to see my husband. Truly, wildly excited. The way I felt when we first started out. He's coming home relatively early to see me, so I think he must be excited too. He breezes into our living room, finds me on the couch, and before we even kiss or hug, he says, "You can't send your script to Gail."

My fury's instantaneous. "Why not?"

"I'm sorry. I shouldn't have given you her number. I'm not comfortable with this." He drops into his spot on the blue couch.

"Why? Did you sleep with her?"

"What? Nothing like that, Kat. My God, you have such an untrusting nature. I have a working relationship with her father and if this goes badly, it could impact my relationship with him. I need to keep my boundaries in place."

"Charlie! I'm a good playwright! Even your award-winning pal Rupert thinks this musical is the bomb! Why on earth would meeting Gail go badly?"

"I'm not saying that, Kat. God, you always twist my words."

"Then what are you saying?"

"I shouldn't have mixed work with my personal life."

"I don't understand you! All you did was make an introduction for your *wife*, who's trying to make a life for herself in a foreign country that *you* invited her to! Why are you so opposed to helping me out?!"

He speaks quietly. "Please don't yell, Kat. I feel like you expect me to help you. I worked hard to get where I am. It makes me sick how you feel so entitled to a free ride."

"What? How can you *say* that, let alone *think* it?"

"You're constantly using me."

"I don't understand what's going on here, Charlie!"

He makes to leave not only the room: he heads to the front door.

"Where the hell are you going now?"

"Away from you."

"Where the *hell* are you going?"

"Work."

"You just got home!"

"Someone has to make the money to support you."

He leaves.

I can't believe it.

I can

not

be

lieve

it.

I don't know what to do with myself. I don't want to call him. I steam from room to room, willing myself not to call him. But I keep calling him. Over the next hour or two I call his cell phone over a hundred times. He never picks up. I lie on the couch. I keep calling. I stay on that couch and call and call and call. Finally, I drag myself upstairs for a bath. A bath will calm me down. I feel like I've been drugged or something. A strange exhaustion, heavy. I feel like I should phone a friend but to say what? I'm involved in arguments I don't understand? Can someone please tell me what the fuck is going on? I stay in the bath until the water turns cold. I'm ice cold furious.

I'm in bed when Charlie comes home hours later. He calls out, "Kat?"

"Up here!" I call back, trying not to sound like I'm fuming.

He bangs around in the kitchen. I know he's going to come up here any minute and I don't want to still be raging, but I am. When he comes into the bedroom, I wait until he lies down next to me. Then I ask in as calm a tone as I can muster, "How's therapy going?"

"It's fine." He mumbles this, not looking at me.

"Well," I tell him, "something's seriously wrong here. Are you still going?"

"Yes, of course. I wouldn't lie about that."

His phraseology strikes me. "What would you lie about?"

"Oh Kat, it's a bloody expression."

I try to rein my emotions in. I whisper, "Charlie, we haven't had sex in… a very long time."

"Is that important?"

"If your sexual energy isn't in this marriage with me, then where the fuck is it?"

"My sexual energy is totally screwed up right now."

"What does that even mean?"

He turns onto his back. "I don't know, Kat. I don't know."

"Charlie, I think we should go and talk to someone."

Charlie folds his hands across his belly and stares up at the ceiling. His belly strikes me. When did he get a belly? He's still an eye-catcher, but there's no hiding that he's got an extra fifteen or twenty pounds around his middle. And there're those dark circles under his eyes. They've been there for a while now. Also, glimpsing his old scar, positioned exactly in the crease where his chin meets his throat, his chin is no longer singular. He's still staring up at the ceiling, as he says, "All right. I'll set something up. My therapist has recommended a great couples counselor."

My heart soars. "Fantastic! This is good! We have some problems, but if we start tackling them now, we'll be better off in the end. This is great." I take his hand. "Oh honey, I'm so relieved! This is great news." I move my lips up to meet his—

"No, Kat. Sorry but I feel too screwed up. I'll get back on track, I promise, but… well, let's just sleep."

We do. We sleep.

VI

love is…

…choosing each other again and again and again.

1

A shitty, dark, cold, rainy day. I arrive at a fancy, Notting Hill townhouse. An older woman with short silver hair opens the door and tells me, "Come in! Get inside! It's awful out there!" She has a bright American accent. I wasn't expecting the therapist to be older or American.

"Hi, I'm Kat."

"Yes, we know that, dear. They're expecting you. Now, have a seat and tell me what you'd like to drink. Tea? Coffee? I make a mean latte," she brags, and it's clear she's the admin or something. Two oversized couches face each other with a large, glass coffee table between them. A rich red oriental rug lies over a polished, light oak floor. Because the weather's so overcast, it's dark outside even though it's only mid-morning. But the waiting room's brightly lit. "To drink, dear?" she asks me again. "We have everything." She's smiling at me.

"A peppermint tea?" My tummy's twisted into knots. I sit and try to chill out. She eventually brings over a clear glass teapot. The peppermint tea steeps very prettily. "Thank you," I say.

"Don't mention it." She returns to her desk at the back of the room. It's a serene waiting area. Maybe this place really is helping Charlie heal. I hold my tea. I'm so nervous my hands shake.

A business-like woman, late 40s, emerges from the back. She has thick, shoulder-length, blonde hair, with about an inch of white roots that look intentional and give her an otherworldly quality. "You must be Katherine," she says, perfectly British, extending her hand.

"Kat. Yes." The woman has a firm grip. Her large, blue eyes are the only pleasant feature on her otherwise equine face.

"I'm Margaret Klaus. Charles has told me so much about you. He simply adores and thinks the world of you." Margaret says this as if she's privy to Charlie's thoughts, which I suppose she is, as she's

Charlie's therapist. But I feel like she's also letting me know that she holds all the power. I suppose she does. And really, isn't it nice that Charlie adores and thinks the world of me? If Margaret is truly in the know as to his thoughts then that's a nice insight for her to share.

I'm not sure what to say so mumble, "Thank you."

"Did Charles mention to you that I'll be sitting in on the session with you, Charlie and David?"

"No." The couples counselor we're meeting is called David.

"Ah. Well, the plan is that I'll sit in on your first session with David, so long as that's all right with you, in order to give Charles a little, extra support. What do you think?"

I've never done this before, but that sounds strange. Surely if we made an appointment to see a couples counselor, we're here to see that counselor. But Margaret Klaus, the "world-renowned" therapist for sex addiction, must be given the benefit of the doubt. If Charlie didn't need extra support, she wouldn't be offering it. So I smile and agree, "That's fine."

"Wonderful. Now we'll wait for Charles to arrive and then we'll begin." Margaret turns to leave.

"Charlie," I say under my breath. Margaret stops.

When she turns around, she's smiling. "Yes, I know that you know him as Charlie but he goes by Charles in here. His adult name. I believe yours is Katherine." Then Margaret disappears into a back office, closing her door firmly, yet quietly.

I sit back down. I sip my fancy tea. She wants us to go by our adult names. What a load of bullshit, but... whatever. I'm positive Charlie'll be late for our 11:30 appointment, but he bounds through the door at 11:29. I stand to greet him, but he bypasses me, heads straight to the kettle where the American admin meets him. "I can't believe you're on time!" she jokes. "Miracles do happen!"

"Indeed," he says. As he helps himself to tea, I can see his hands trembling like an alcoholic's. I watch him closely. He's probably nervous like me. I mean, my hands were shaking too. He's never done couples counseling before either.

A door to a backroom opens and a well-presented, tall man comes out. He sports a Tom Selleck moustache. "Hello," he says. "I'm, ahh, David." David shakes Charlie's hand, then mine. Despite the dorky moustache, David looks very kind. I relax a little. He takes us into his office. Before he closes his door, Margaret enters. She and *Charles* greet each other while I figure out where to sit. Four wingback chairs are set almost in a circle, but not quite. Two angle in more towards the other two, clearly marking one side for the therapists and the other for the couple in need of counseling. I choose a chair close to the window. It gives me a full view of the room, including the door, which makes me feel better for some reason. Charlie sits in the chair paired with mine. David sits to my right; Margaret, diagonal to me.

"Here we are," says David, then there's a slight pause and everyone looks around awkwardly. I can't glean anything off the therapists' faces. They've obviously done this before. David continues, "Ahh, I think it's good to begin these sessions with each member introducing themselves and stating their intent. I'll start. I'm David. I've worked as a couples counselor for almost ten years. I specialize in sex and love addicted relationships, but don't treat them exclusively. My job here today is to help you, Katherine, and you, Charles, to, ahh, communicate with each other."

"You all know that I'm Margaret." Margaret smiles a horse-like smile. "Katherine, what you may or may not know is that I've worked with sex addicts for about seventeen years now. I've found it helpful for them to have an advocate when they begin couples with their partners. I'm here to be Charles' advocate. But also if you have any questions, Katherine, I'll gladly answer them."

"Thank you," I say. I wonder what the hell I'll have questions about. Then Charlie and I look at each other. One of us has to speak next. Charlie doesn't look anywhere close to opening his mouth. He leans back in his seat and keeps his eyes on me. So fucking typical. He's the one who's been acting like a shit and yet I'm the one who speaks first. I say, "I'm Katherine." Argh. I can't believe I used my full name! I felt like she'd be mad at me if I didn't. I continue, "I'm here because I want my marriage to be one of communication and joy, and it's not." Thank God that's over.

We all look at Charlie. "The pressure!" he exclaims, grinning.

"No jokes, Charles," Margaret admonishes him.

The therapy has begun.

Charlie wipes the smile off his face. "I'm here because I hope to start having honest communication with Katherine. I'm not sure it's possible, but it's my hope."

"Great," says David. He puts his hands on his knees and sits up straight. "Who'd like to start?"

Again Charlie and I regard each other. Again there's a silence. Again I feel like if I'm not the one to break it, we'll be sitting here forever. So I say, "Well, I don't know what's going on, but we've stopped having sex. And I feel like everything I do is criticized in a way it didn't used to be. So I guess... I'm wondering what's going on."

David turns to Charlie. "Do you have anything to say to that, Charles?"

He shakes his head no.

Margaret comes in. "Are you sure you wouldn't like to address that?"

Charlie looks at Margaret like a little boy being forced by his mother to say sorry. He faces me and says, "I've had a relapse."

Boom. Not what I expected. "Have you slept with someone else?"

"No. Not yet."

"Okay." I can hear my voice trembling. "What happened?" His face is all screwed up and twisted. I've seen this face before but never so set on him like a mask. While my question hangs in the air, I search his transmogrified face for the eyes I know but can't find them. My body starts to shake. "Charlie? What happened?" I repeat.

"Breasts. I'm obsessed with them. I've been looking all over London for the biggest ones I can find." I hear his words, but it takes me a moment to absorb them. Then I burst out laughing. "This isn't funny, Kat."

"It kind of is. I mean, you're telling me that the reason we haven't been having sex is because you've been on a quest for big boobs? That's absurd!"

"It's not to me."

"Right. Sorry. So what do you do?"

"I call up prostitutes and ask them the size of their breasts."

"Then do you go see them?"

"If their breasts are large enough, yes."

"What's large enough?"

"A G cup is a starting point but doesn't really do it for me anymore."

I don't know exactly how big that is, only that it's a heck of a lot bigger than I am. "What happens then?"

"Various things."

"But you haven't slept with anyone?"

"No."

"What do you do?"

"I suck their nipples."

I cringe at the bastardization of something so nice in our bedroom. "Is that all you do?"

"No. Sometimes I jerk off in between their tits." He sounds like he's being crass intentionally.

"Is that all?"

"No. Sometimes they suck me off too."

Anger swells in me. "So when you say you haven't had sex with them, you mean intercourse?"

"Jesus. Yes. *Intercourse.*"

"How long have you been doing this?"

"Since December of last year."

"So a few months."

"No, December of the year before last."

My breath leaves my body. I stare at the pristine oak floor for what feels like an eternity. There are no knots in it. It's classy. When I can speak again, I say slowly, "That's before we got engaged. You were seeing prostitutes before we got engaged?"

"No. I was looking for them."

"But you didn't see any prostitutes until when?"

"I started seeing prostitutes just before New Year."

"This New Year or last New Year?"

"This."

"So no prostitutes were seen until about three months ago?"

"That's right."

"But the relapse started about a year and three months ago?"

"Yes."

"And that's what you've done with the prostitutes? Hand jobs and oral?"

"Not just that."

I wait.

"One whipped me."

I look over at Margaret, half expecting her to say this is all a big joke, but her expression tells me to pay attention, he's not finished. "Why would you do that?"

"I don't know, Kat! What the fuck do you think I'm trying to figure out in therapy?" he retorts.

Margaret interrupts him. "Language, Charles. Calm down. This is about giving your wife the information." Charlie glares at Margaret then turns his glare back to me.

"What else do you want to know?"

"I—I don't know. What else do I need to know? Do you want to have sex with them?"

"Not like you think. I want them to rip me apart. I asked one to strap on a dildo and fuck me up the ass."

"Language!" Margaret snaps, as this new image of Charlie hangs in the air.

"And did she?"

"She strapped it on, but then… I didn't do it."

"Is that all?" I ask quietly.

He exhales angrily, looking at Margaret. "Kat, I had a woman in our house."

My breath leaves again. Again I stare at the floor. Oak floor. No knots. Classy. When I can speak: "Was she in our bed?"

"No, in the living room. When you were home planning the wedding. A woman I used to work with. You don't know her."

"What's her name?"

Margaret comes in again. "We don't give names."

I glare at Margaret, telling her to shut the fuck up with my eyes. Then I turn back to Charlie and demand, "Did you have sex with her?"

"I don't think we should focus on her. My interactions with the prostitutes are much more dangerous."

"Did you or did you not have sex with a woman in our house?"

He gives me his stubborn silence.

"For Christ's sake, Charlie, don't torture me, spit it out."

"You don't get it. You'll never get it. I'm a sex addict."

"Don't give me that bullshit line now. Just tell me what you did. Did you have sex with that woman in our house or not?"

"Yes."

"In our bed?"

"I already told you! In the living room!"

I picture our living room where our full china set is on display. One of our wedding vases stands filled with a mixture of sweet peas and roses. Tears start streaming down my face. I've been trying to make our home so lovely, a place where he'd want to be. I ask, "On your blue couch?"

"Yes."

"More than once?"

"No, no. After she left, I never saw her again."

"So let me get this straight. When you said you hadn't had sex about five minutes ago, you were lying."

"I haven't had sex with anyone but you since we've been married."

"Apart from the tit sex, the oral sex and the attempt at anal."

No one says anything.

"What else?"

"Claire."

"We don't give names, Char—" Margaret starts, but I cut her off.

"Claire the writer?"

"Yes."

"Did you have sex with her?"

"Does it matter?"

"But we invited her to our wedding." My God, I can hear my own naivety. Claire was so cool, so nice. She was even helpful to me, interested in what I was doing. I would never have thought...

"And Gail."

"The producer you've set me up with?"

"Yes, but we didn't have sex."

"What did you do?"

"She only gave me a blow job in the car."

My mouth hangs open like I'm in a cartoon. "So you had sex with these women, or blow jobs, whatever, and then invited one to our wedding and got me involved with the other for work?"

"Yes."

"But you weren't cheating on me when I still lived in New York and when I first moved here?"

"No."

"Exactly how did it all start?"

"On the net." He sounds bored, as if he doesn't have time.

"What do you mean?"

"Looking for people."

"Looking for women with big breasts?"

"Primarily, yes."

Of course Claire has large breasts. "Did you sleep with Claire or just ask her to stick her titties in your face?"

"You need to be respectful, Katherine," Margaret says, speaking to me like I'm a child.

"Why? Because I'm being treated with such respect here? Because I've been treated so respectfully the past 15 months? Actually,

Margaret, I think I'm entitled to a little biting sarcasm." I turn back to Charlie. "So jumping back, did you sleep with Claire?"

"Well…"

"I'll take that as a yes."

"Only the second time."

I inhale. "Let's start with the first time. What happened then?"

"I sucked on her tits and she gave me a hand job."

"When was that?"

"You were asleep."

"In the other room?!"

"To her credit, she felt awful. She left at the crack of dawn and would never come inside the flat again."

"*To her credit?* What the *fuck* are you talking about?"

"She felt bad."

"Did it happen on the couch again?"

"Yes. But it wasn't really again. That was in our little flat before we moved. The other woman from work who I had on the couch, was after we moved to Hampstead." He pauses. "Though technically Claire and I had done it on that couch before, but that was well before I knew you."

"Is that like your sex couch?"

"What? No, it's just a couch."

I remember Charlie looking as though he'd like to eat Claire for dinner as she stretched out on the couch. I was sitting right there. That living space was so small I could've reached out and touched Claire with one hand and Charlie with the other. How did I miss this dynamic? I say, "So let's stick with since you've been with me. How many women have you slept with since we've been together?"

"Why are you getting so worked up about the normal women? My addiction is much worse with the prostitutes. I asked one woman to strap on a dildo and fuck me up the arse!"

"Did she?"

"I already told you I didn't do it!" he screams, as if I'm meant to keep track of this information overload, as if my inability to absorb the details is the issue here. "She put it on but as she came over to me, I felt sick. It was a big, black dildo." He really sounds like he's bragging.

"Are you proud that it was a big, black dildo?"

"You wouldn't strap one on for me, would you?"

"I… I don't know…"

"See?"

"You never asked!"

"Oh please, Kat!"

I try to stay on track. "So you felt sick…"

"Yes. I went into the bathroom and vomited."

"You puked?"

"Yes."

"You requested this prostitute put on a dildo for you. She did. And then you puked?"

Charlie nods his head yes and his face shifts so that I can see the blue eyes I remember. He looks like he's about to start laughing and suddenly he is laughing and I'm laughing along with him and we're us again. For a moment. Then I remember what we're talking about. "When was the second time?"

"Second time what?"

"With Claire."

"I already *told* you."

"Did you? No, you didn't."

Margaret interjects, "You haven't told her this yet."

Charlie and I both look at Margaret. Then back at each other.

Why is it always me to break the silence? "The second time. Was it when I was back home planning the wedding?"

"Yes."

"In our house?"

"No, she wouldn't come over. I told you, she felt bad."

"So where did you go?"

Charlie hesitates. He sort of scowls at Margaret then tells me, "Details aren't important."

Margaret, sternly: "Charles. I think this one is."

NINETY DAYS WITHOUT YOU

I wait.

Charlie says, "I took her to Norfolk…"

I wait again. He says nothing. I ask, "Can you please just spit it out?"

"I bought that converted barn—"

"What?"

"—and I took her there."

"You bought that… that property I found in the glove compartment?"

"Yes."

"In Norfolk?"

"I needed to have something for me."

"So you bought a property that you told me was going to be our second home, hid it from me, and brought women there to fuck?"

"I only brought Claire. I felt awful afterwards. I didn't know what to do with the place. I haven't been back and I never want to go there again. It's just… sitting there."

"Why did you tell me it was going to be our second home?"

"Isn't that what you wanted to hear?"

I look at his face again. It's that weird face. I don't know what to believe now. "Are there more women you've slept with?"

"Kat, I haven't had sex with anyone since we've been married."

"You mean intercourse?"

"Yes."

"So you only had sex with people before we got married, when we were engaged?"

"Yes."

"And then you switched to doing everything except intercourse once we got married?"

"Yes."

"And this matters to me… why?"

"Katherine," Margaret says, "there has to be some distinction in the commitment level from when you went from being single to married."

What a fucking bitch. "Sure, Margaret, marriage was meant to be a deepening of our commitment to each other. But we were meant to be sexually exclusive not only during our engagement and our marriage, but also before we even got engaged."

"There needs to be some distinction," Margaret persists.

I hate her. "In my relationship with Charlie, as in most relationships, we were sexually exclusive. This is not an unusual practice. And it was crystal clear between us that we were monogamous." I turn to Charlie. "Was that in any way unclear to *you*, Charlie?"

"No."

"Can you please tell me how many women you've been with?"

"It's a total of thirty-two."

"Thirty-two?"

"Can you please stop repeating everything I say?"

"Exactly thirty-two?"

"Yes!"

"When? Who?"

"Mostly when you were away, then a few women at work, and then I would go out to bars and pick people up. Since we've been married, I've visited at least one prostitute a week."

"And they're all women with big breasts?"

"Except for the men."

"Men. Are you gay? Bisexual?"

"No, Kat, it's not about that. I'm a *sex addict*." He says this as if I will never understand the words "sex" and "addict" strung together. His twisted face accuses me, as if what he's saying is somehow *my* fault. Fucking hell. What the fuck is going on here? This is not my fault. I don't think it's my fault. I feel like I've been blasted in two by a close range missile, and I didn't even know I was in enemy territory.

Everyone sits, doing and saying nothing. David finally moves to cross his legs the opposite way. Charlie's pushed as far back in his seat as possible, legs crossed, arms crossed, head tilted. Not only is his face twisted, but everything about him is twisted. He stares pointedly at the ceiling. When I glance over at Margaret, we lock eyes and I know she can see that I'm undergoing a level of panic I never knew possible.

I stand up to leave. David starts in his seat. "Katherine, ahh, we ask both partners to stay in the room during disclosure. We find that it helps."

I turn on him. "Is that what this is? *Disclosure?* Is that the technical term?"

"Yes."

"I thought I was coming to a couples counseling session." I'm suddenly furious and it feels good, gives me some energy. I need to get out of this room and speak to someone normal so I ignore David and head to the door.

David stands up. "Please, Katherine. I know this is difficult but—"

"Difficult?" I practically spit at him. "I don't know you, and," I look at Margaret, "I don't know you, and," I look at Charlie, "I sure as hell don't know you. So I am walking out of this room and making a phone call."

Margaret pauses, as if deciding whether to fight me or not, then stands up and leads me next door into her darkened office. "We don't get good reception down here. Use my landline." Margaret closes the door behind her when she leaves.

I call Lena, pray she'll answer, start crying again as soon as she does.

"Calm down, calm down, Kat. What happened?" I can't speak. "Come on, Kat. Calm down and tell me so that I can help you."

I tell her. Silence on the other end of the phone. "Are you there?"

Lena clears her throat. "I'm coming."

I would normally balk at Lena dropping everything to rush to my aid. But now I simply say, "Thank you."

Then Lena asks, "Who was that therapist you sent Mattie to?"

"Maria somebody."

"Call her and see if she can see you then call me back."

I do. Maria Mancini commands in her thick Italian accent, "You come to my house the moment you are finished there. I have clients until this evening, but you will stay at my house until I can speak with you."

When I tell Lena I'm going to see Maria, Lena says, "Great. And Jean-Marc and I agreed that I'll leave for the train station now. I just need to go home and pack a bag. Then I'll stay for at least a couple days. I'm coming now. Okay?"

"Okay." We hang up. I sit there. Crying. Above Margaret's desk hangs a beautiful sketch of a nude woman that I'm not entirely sure is appropriate for the wall of a sex addict therapist's office. Does Charlie stare at this nude every week? Oh God. What the fuck am I supposed to do now? I call Lena again. "What do I do now?"

"Go to Maria's."

"I don't have to go back in?"

"Do you want to go back in? Is there anything else you need to say? Or do you want to go straight to Maria's?"

I force myself to think this through. "I'd like to make sure I've been told everything."

"Would that be helpful to you?"

"Yes. And I suppose we should figure out who's sleeping where."

"All right then, go back in. But you can always just walk out the door and go."

"But, Lena, where *will* I sleep tonight?"

"What do you mean?"

"I don't think I can sleep in the same bed as him."

"Of course you can't. He has to move out."

He has to move out. Of course he does. Of course he has to move out. Of course I can't sleep in the same bed or even under the same roof as him.

I hang up and drift back into the room next door, foggy-headed, very aware that I haven't stopped crying. It's not like I'm heaving. The tears flow unaided. I make it to my wingback chair. No one's saying anything, so I quietly propose, "Shall we figure out who sleeps where?"

Charlie volunteers, "I'll move out."

That was quick. Too quick. I say, "Okay." Then I face him again. "Thirty-two men and women?"

"Only three were men. I prefer women. But as I want to be hit and hurt, men are better for that. They tend to be stronger." I absorb. He continues, "To be honest, Kat," the irony of him using this expression, "I've started looking lately at trans women. I think they would do the job better for me." He says this with a sort of casual spite, as if he's in the market for a new toothbrush, a new toothbrush that I have somehow kept from him by the sad-but-true fact that I no longer "do the job" for him.

Who is this man? He's nodding his head at me with that twisted face. I realize I'm holding my breath and force myself to take in air. Everyone's looking at me. "Is there something else I need to know?" No one responds. "Am I asking the right things? I mean, I think I've got it. There were three men and twenty-nine women that he had sex with on some level. One in our new house on the blue couch. In our old flat, there was Claire on the couch while I slept right next door. Then you bought a secret second home where you could have sex with her while I planned our wedding and pined for you. I probably know a couple of the people you've had sex with from work, but you're not going to tell me who they were, except for Gail." I pause. "Is one of them Becca?" Charlie nods his head yes. "Right. So you've also cheated on me with a married woman who has two young kids."

"I don't need you to shame me, Kat."

"And I won't know the rest because they're strangers and/or prostitutes? Unless… you haven't fooled around with Rupert. Have you?"

"God no!"

"Just checking. Anything's possible, right? What about his girlfriend Sally?"

"I do have morals, Kat!"

His hypocrisy staggers me. "You're obsessed with large breasts, have been looking for the biggest pair, and you like people to hurt you. Is there anything else?"

"Who are you to judge me after what you've done?"

"What the hell did I do?"

"Something."

"What are you talking about?"

"Something at Anne's funeral."

"Why do you think that?"

"I can tell when someone cheats."

"I didn't really cheat, but I saw my ex."

"You fucked him?"

"Ha! Hardly!"

"You didn't?"

"I can't believe you thought that," I say, even though I'd set out to do exactly that.

"What happened?"

"I don't know."

"Did you give him a blow job?"

"Jesus no! I kissed him and that was that! I thought I still loved him, but then I realized I didn't."

"I bet you don't love me anymore either." Charlie throws me a twisted look, like he hates me.

"Katherine," Margaret says. "I think you should know that he's still in it."

I turn to her. "What does that mean?" When she doesn't answer me right away, I say, "For fuck's sake, lady, speak so that I can understand you. This is hard enough."

"He's still in the throes of his addiction."

Charlie's still glaring at me with that distorted face, his body pushed back into his chair, as if he's restraining himself from leaping across the room and throttling my throat. Yes. I can see what Margaret means by "in it." It clicks. I know this distorted rage-filled face all too well. I've seen so much of it. If it's the mask he wears when he's in his sex addiction... well then. "Thank you," I tell Margaret, as this clarification is indeed the most useful fact she's provided. "I'm going to go now."

"Would you like to, ahh, schedule another appointment?" David asks.

"Are you joking?"

"Katherine, at least take my details, you may need to, ahh, talk to someone." His look acknowledges my pain, but he doesn't do anything but hand me his stupid card. I take it, then grab the box of tissues as well.

Walking through reception, I don't acknowledge the quirky American lady. I just go. Or at least attempt to "just go," but can't move too quickly because my body feels like lead underwater. A drowning Kat. I push open the door and the fresh air blasts me with a welcome, wet force. It's pouring down with cold rain and though it's pounding my face and neck, I don't care. I suppose I should button up, put the tissues in my bag, but these practical thoughts are muffled by a kind, thick fog that envelops me. The rain sounds louder than normal hitting the box of tissues.

I step out into the street. A driver leans on his horn. I guess I didn't bother looking for cars. As he whizzes past me, his side view mirror hits my hand. I jump back. I'm standing in the road now. A second car comes to a stop rather than hit me. It stays stopped, waits for me to move. But I can't move. I look at the car. Oddly, it's a Mini like Rupert's. It's even black like his. I look to see if Rupert's driving. Of course he's not. London's full of black Minis. The driver, a young blonde woman, stares at me impatiently. I stand there looking at her, tears streaming down my face. Wouldn't it be weird if Charlie had fucked her too? She aggressively gestures for me to cross the road. I think this is a good idea. So I do. But then the Mini doesn't pull away, and I look back to see if Charlie's jumping into her car. But she drives away. On some level, I know I'm thinking crazy. I really don't want to be here when Charlie comes out. So I head towards the Underground. My hand's bleeding where it hit the side view mirror. I take out a thick clump of wet tissues from the box that's now soaked through. I press the tissues onto the cut. Funny, I'm watching my hand bleed, but it doesn't hurt at all. Maybe it didn't hurt Anne when she went. Maybe being hit by a truck is the way to go. The box of tissues is so wet it's beginning to disintegrate. I arrive at the Underground and chuck it in a trashcan. There's a little shop right next to the station. I go in and buy a pack of cigarettes. I haven't smoked a cigarette in years. When I was younger and we all went out, we all smoked. I never liked it but would have one because everyone else did. Now, I want something bad for me. I forget that I don't have matches and have to go back into the shop. After I get the matches and get back outside again, I stand under the awning and light one. It's vile. I smoke it down. I can see how people start smoking. Fuck him. I chuck the rest of the pack in the trashcan and, even though I'm right next to the Underground, hail a taxi.

VII

THIS IS JUST TO SAY

I have eaten
the plums
that were in
the icebox

and which
you were probably
saving
for breakfast

Forgive me
they were delicious
so sweet
and so cold.

—William Carlos Williams

1

Maria opens the door and pulls me into a hug. The warmth of her strong arms penetrates my wet clothes. I'm aware that my limbs are not only wet but also shaking. "Come, come." Maria helps me up the stairs like I'm an exhausted child. As we pass by her living room, I glimpse the feet of someone on her couch. Probably a client. Maria brings me into a bedroom. She says, "Take off those wet clothes," then disappears. I do as I'm told. I stand in the middle of the room, now naked, still crying and shaking. Maria returns with a fluffy towel. "Dry off." I do. Maria pulls clothes from drawers. She hands me a pair of big panties, sweatpants, a t-shirt, and a pair of warm socks. "Put these on." I do. The socks have strawberries on them. "Get into bed." I do. Maria pulls the covers around me, tucks me in tightly. I turn into the fetal position. She rubs her hand over my back. My entire body begins to shudder violently. "There, there. You have taken a blow, a big wallop." I weep and quake as Maria keeps rubbing my back and limbs, up and down. Slowly, the cold starts to leave my back. The shaking subsides but my eyes still stream. "Wait here. I'll be right back." Maria leaves. I stay there weeping. When Maria returns, she carries a tray. "Sit up," she instructs. I sit up. "I need you to eat this soup. It's broth, homemade, easy on your tummy. You eat it all, and you drink this tea. After you eat and drink, you lie there and try to rest. I am downstairs if you need me, and I will be back." She goes. I remain sitting up. I'm not hungry. I take a spoonful of soup. It's so strange how my eyes keep crying. The soup travels down my mouth, all the way down my insides to my belly. I'm a little surprised that I have an inside. It feels like it was blown away. I lie back down.

I wake up and don't know where I am. Then it floods back. I'm at Maria's house because… because…

Even in my own head I can't put words to what happened. What the fuck just happened? My marriage transformed into a bombsite. I cry again for what feels like an endless amount of time or no time at all. I can't tell. But at some point, Maria returns. She starts the rubbing again, my arms, legs and back. I'm vaguely aware that this is not the usual therapist/client behavior. But then, there's nothing *normal* about what happened today.

"There, there. It's going to be all right, my darling. You are in shock right now, but you are safe here. I am trying to warm you up. You are in shock so your body temperature dropped. It's not good that you were so cold and wet. We must warm you up. You are in shock." Maria keeps saying, "You are in shock," then leaving me for a long stretch to see a client, then returning and doing the same thing. At some point, she reheats the soup I haven't eaten and hands me a fresh tea in a bright red mug. She tells me, "I want you to eat." There's a forceful note in her tone, but I can't sit up anymore. I don't even want to try. Maria sits on the edge of the bed. "No?" She leans forward and strokes my cheek. "All right, you can eat a little later. You will see. Appetite won't return for some time, but you eat anyway. You are in shock, my darling. You are in shock. But you are safe here, in this bed."

I am in shock. This is true. *I am in shock, but I am safe here. I'm safe in this bed. I am safe.* I sleep again.

The next time I wake up, it's dark outside. This doesn't mean much though. The rain clouds made it pretty dark all day. Plus, it's only February. The sun still sets pretty early. I can't believe I've slept through the night. I mean, there's no way I've been here that long. But could this still really be the same, miserable day? I don't dare look at my phone, but I have to pee. I pull myself out of bed to use the bathroom. Every muscle aches. The bathroom's littered with what must be Maria's toiletries. It dawns on me that she put me in her own bed, not a guest bed. I feel cold again, so slip back under the covers. The tea and soup sit on the bedside table, untouched. Written on the red mug of tea in bold, yellow cursive is *Love You!* I curl into a ball and cry again.

Maria returns. I'm still shaking. Maria does the same rubbing, consoling routine. "You are in shock, my darling. You have had a big blow. You are in shock."

This time I tell her, "This has happened to me before."

"Ah," Maria says, still holding me, still rubbing. "Good. That's good. We will talk about that. We will make sure that it never happens to you again. I promise you that. We will make sure that this will be the end." I cry harder. She keeps rubbing. "I have one more client then we will talk. All right?" I nod. "You keep resting. And remember I am down the stairs if you need me." Maria notices the full soup bowl. "Tsk, tsk. I am going to heat this soup up one final time. I want you to make an effort to eat it. A good, strong effort this time."

When she returns with the warmed soup and fresh tea in the same *Love You!* mug, I look at her, but I don't sit up. She says, "Kat, I met you only the one time, but I know your younger brother so I know more than a little about your family." Sternness features in her voice now. "If you want, I am well-positioned to help you heal from this blow from the sex addiction. Right now, you are in trauma. You have to work to get yourself better. I can guide you, but it is you who must do the work. Like this soup. I can make this soup. I can suggest you eat it. But you must be the one to pick up the spoon and swallow it down. I promise you, we can work together to ensure that this never happens again. But you are in charge of your healing. I can also assure you that putting something warm inside your belly will help the trauma. So if you want me to help you then you must start helping yourself. You must now sit up and do as I say. Eat this delicious soup."

Still crying, I sit up. Maria places a pillow behind my back as though I'm frail. I hear myself keen.

"Yes, yes, let it out. This is fine. This is good." Maria pulls me to her, rocks me back and forth. "There, there, my darling. You have had a big blow. A big wallop."

My voice stops moaning, though the tears still come.

Maria wipes my hair back from my face. She picks up the spoon and hands it to me. She says sternly, "You will eat now, please," then gets up and leaves again.

Every mouthful's an effort, but I do it. I eat all the soup. I stop crying. I drink down the *Love You!* tea.

The next time Maria returns, she says, "Kat, I want you to get up now. We're going to the living room to have a talk." She drapes a cashmere shawl over my shoulders, then leads the way out of her bedroom down to her front room. I'm struck that Mattie sat in this same room. It was only a year ago but feels like so much longer. Yet Charlie was cheating on me from even before then. Now, dressed in a hodgepodge of Maria's clothes, I shiver as I settle onto the couch where Mattie could've sat. Instead of sitting opposite me, Maria sits down next to me. She takes my hand in hers and notices the cut. It's clotted. The skin's turning black and blue around it. I tell her about walking into the street and almost being hit by the car.

Maria spits out, "Shame on Margaret. She should be ashamed. Letting you leave her office in shock like that. You are in no state to be on your own after such a battering! You could have been killed by that car." Maria's on fire. "Very irresponsible. She should know better. Wait here. I get some arnica cream." She goes.

Her anger surprises me. What she's saying is true. The car could have killed me. I was lucky. It would have been so ironic for me to go that way, following Anne's lead. Did I walk into the street to die? Maybe I wanted a quick out from this torture. Maybe I wanted Charlie to care.

Maria returns with arnica cream. She starts rubbing it onto my hand, and says, "Tell me."

I tell her the story of Charlie and me. How perfect he was, despite his flaws. How when I moved over here, I always knew we would get married, irrespective of his doubts. I tell her how I pushed Charlie for clarity on why we weren't having sex, then the session and the thirty-two people—

"Thirty-two is not so many," Maria interrupts.

"It's so many to me!"

"No, darling, I often hear about hundreds of sexual partners. Hundreds. Men often have a separate phone."

"He had a separate house!"

"Tsk, tsk. Very common with sex addicts."

"He was with some men too."

Maria shrugs. "This is also common."

"To be honest, the men don't bother me. I feel like they should, but it's the women—and I mean the women who aren't prostitutes—they're the ones who disturb me."

Maria nods, encouraging me to continue. So I tell her about the nameless woman in our house, about Claire in the next room of our tiny flat who he then took to the Norfolk house (the house he lied to me about so he could have "something for himself"), about Gail who he introduced me to, and about Becca, the ex he's now working with.

"I don't know when he and Becca fooled around. Or what they did."

"It doesn't matter," Maria tells me.

"It does to me!"

"Maybe now it does but probably not later."

I tell her about his breast obsession, the big black dildo, the desire for trans women.

Images feel etched in my head, as if I can see him with all these people. I tell her, "I feel like I'm dying."

"No, my darling, you are not dying. You have had a big blow and you are in shock." She's said this a hundred times now. "You will not die. On the contrary, if you get through this, you will finally be able to live. Now tell me, you said this happened before?"

"Yeah. I dated a lot of guys before I was with Jonathan. And apart from Jonathan, they all either cheated on me or said that they didn't want an exclusive relationship." Maria listens. "And the thing about Jonathan is that even though he never cheated on me, it always felt like he did."

"Who was Jonathan?"

"The man I was going to marry before I married Charlie."

"Why didn't you marry him?"

"He drank way too much and… used drugs."

"Well then, they were his mistresses." I look at her blankly. "The bottle and the drugs."

I let that sink in. It feels true. I was lonely when I was with Jonathan because he was very busy with his mistresses. I finally say, "But this confession from Charlie… I've never been so deeply betrayed."

"Probably you have not been."

"But, I know this will sound weird, but this is what I felt like when I was little."

"How little?" I sit there. "Kat, how old do you feel right now?"

"I feel like I'm ten or thirteen. Fifteen at a push."

"Who betrayed you?"

"Well… no one. I mean, my father didn't cheat on me. But it always *felt* this way, like he was cheating on me. I mean, I know he cheated on my Mom, and I know that's not me, but I've been feeling this way my entire life." Maria nods her head. "Maybe I'm on the wrong track. Maybe this has nothing to do with my father." Before Maria can tell me that of course it does, I tell her, "Another thing happened to me. In college, I… I think I was raped." I tell her about the teacher in college.

She says, "Dear child, that is most definitely a rape."

I don't cry about this. I tell her, "Right now, it just feels like a fact. I don't feel sad or disturbed."

Maria nods. "Yes, well, right now, your marriage offers enough to be disturbed about. Don't worry. There is a lot of healing we need to do, but healing is possible."

"Do I need to get a divorce?" I sound like a child asking if I have to go to school.

"Eh." Maria gives another shrug. "We talk about that later. Right now, we only need to make a plan for you to get through the rest of this day."

I suddenly remember that Lena's coming over. I tell Maria.

Maria says, "Have her come here. I will tell her how to care for you. She will spend the night with you, then bring you to see me tomorrow."

I call Lena. She's already arrived in London. That was quick, though a clock on Maria's bookshelves tells me it's now after 8 p.m. The "disclosure" was nine or so hours ago. When Lena says she'll get a taxi and be here as soon as she can, I cry because she and Maria are being so nice. Maria doesn't stop my crying.

I hiccup out, "Charlie was in recovery. He went to group therapy, and a meeting every week, and he started therapy with that woman."

"Recovery for sex addiction is very difficult. One meeting a week and a little therapy? Not enough. Even sex addicts who go to many meetings may not get recovery. And you say he is an alcoholic as well? Was he going to his AA meetings?"

"Not that I ever heard of."

"Hmmph. So on top of being an active sex addict, he is a dry drunk."

My mind returns to the nameless woman in our house. Who the fuck was it? I ask, "What if he's slept with lots of people I know? Women who are acquaintances? And they all know how unfaithful he is?"

Maria looks me in the eyes. "It is very possible, my dear, very possible. He is a sex addict, you see." She's studying me. I say nothing. She says, "What do you know about sex addiction? Sex and love addiction? Alcoholism?"

"I didn't have first-hand experience with this stuff, so I googled it."

"You never went to a meeting? You married a sex addict, but you never went to a meeting or met people in recovery or learned about it firsthand? And yet, you married him?"

"I mean, I asked him about it." I hear what an idiot I sound like. In an effort to move the conversation on, I ask, "So what do I do now?"

"Well, my child, you do not end up married to a sex addict who is in this deep a relapse for no good reason," Maria says strictly. "You must look at yourself. We can do nothing about him, but we can heal you."

I don't understand.

"Do you understand?"

"Yes," I claim.

"Don't worry. You will eventually understand." Maria inspects me. "Come here." Once more, I find myself in her arms. She holds me while I cry.

Her doorbell rings. It's Lena. She and Maria speak in hushed tones by the door. Then they come into the living room. Lena hugs me. Maria says, "She has told me about your friend Anne. May she rest in peace. I am so sorry for your loss." I cry anew. "It seems you are surrounded by mental illness and addiction."

I look to Lena. "Not Lena."

Lena says, "I think it's fair to say I have an issue around work."

Maria nods then turns back to me. "Water seeks its own level."

"What does that mean?"

"It means we gravitate towards those to whom we are similar."

I sit back down. Maria talks to Lena about making sure I eat and keep warm.

I'm still dressed in Maria's clothes. As we prepare to leave, she hands me a bag with my clothes in it. When I put on my shoes, I think how much I like Maria's warm, strawberry socks. Then Lena helps me into my coat and we go.

2

Back home. Our home. I'm here with Lena instead of Charlie. The blouse I didn't wear to couples this morning is strewn across the bed; the makeup I put on but didn't put away, splayed over the bathroom counter. I brush my teeth. The taste of that one cigarette lingered and it feels human to finally clean it out. My hand's sore.

Lena brings in water for both of us. As she sets a glass on Charlie's bedside table, it strikes me it may never be "his" side again. "It bothers me," I tell her, "that he hasn't even called me."

"You can call him." I get out my phone. "Do you want me to leave the room?" Lena asks.

I shake my head no. His phone's already ringing. He answers, "Oh Kat, Kat, I'm so sorry."

I sob. We stay on the phone saying nothing. I hear his breathing and remember our beginning. While I cry, Lena sits quietly on the other side of the bed. Finally, I ask him, "Where are you?"

"Josh's flat. In Camden." Josh is his actor friend.

"Did Josh know?"

"No," he answers quietly.

"Did anyone know?"

"Yes."

"Who?" For sure he'll name Rupert, and I'll have more embarrassment with which to contend.

"I confessed to a priest before we got married."

"Why didn't you tell me?"

"Because, Kat... you wouldn't have married me and I wanted more than anything to marry you. I love you."

This is a seriously fucked way of thinking. But he loves me. He wanted to be with me. "Do you still love me?" I ask.

"More than anything," he proclaims.

"I'm going now." I hang up. I lie back in bed next to Lena. Everything's muted and slow. I stare up at the ceiling. I realize Lena's said something, so ask, "What was that?"

Lena repeats, "All this time, I half wondered if sex addiction was bullshit." I nod my head. Lena continues, "I mean, I know Anne was in denial about a lot of things. But we talked about his being a sex addict way back when you first told us, and she said she thought he could either be faithful or he couldn't. Didn't matter what you called it." I nod again. "I guess I can see how it sounds like some lame excuse to get laid without restraint, and right now I hate him for doing this to you, but pornography is rampant in our society. That alone must be a pretty serious addiction."

"Anne would say that he's a shit and tell me to leave."

"I'm sure as hell not going to tell you to stay, Kat. You have my permission to end this one."

"But... but I know he's not just a shit, and... he loves me."

"I'm not going to get into a philosophical discussion about what love is or isn't, Kat. But I will point out that, whether he in fact does love you or not, you can still leave."

I know I'm nowhere near ready to leave him. Even though I've been blasted into pieces, even though part of me hates him, even though I can't believe I'm in this surreal place, the truth is I don't want to leave him. Finally, I tell her, "First and foremost, above all else, I want to figure out how I got myself into this mess because I never want to do it again."

Lena says sweetly, "You could do that, Kat, while you're getting a divorce."

"I'm just not there yet, Lena. I mean, maybe this is the *for worse* part."

Lena looks like I've shocked her. She says, "Okay. Maybe starting divorce proceedings today isn't the right answer. But I don't want you staying in a relationship where you get hurt like this."

"But it's an illness that has a treatment. Maybe he can get better."

"Sure, hon. Maybe." Lena strokes my hair.

———

I cry and sleep, sleep and cry. Lena takes me to Maria, cooks, tells me I have to eat. And I do. I eat and drink because Lena took time out from her family and came all this way. I can't let her down.

The grief comes in waves. I can feel it about to hit me. Then I'm immersed in it, sobbing. I crouch on my knees and howl. Lena watches. She listens to me recount ad nauseam the story of our courtship, marriage and "day of disclosure." I repeat the details of our entire history, what I thought was happening, what was really happening. I repeat it because I *cannot* believe it, cannot believe my judgment was so off. I'm just as shocked by Charlie's sexual exploits, as I am by my inability to spot that something was so terribly wrong. The pain is also physical. I tell Lena, "I feel like I've been stabbed in the solar plexus and then cut open down the full length of my body."

Lena utters platitudes. "Life doesn't have to be this agonizing," and "I know in my heart that you'll get through this and be stronger for it," and "Remember no one's died," and "Time heals all wounds." Normally, trite sayings irritate me, but she's so heartfelt I can't help but feel touched.

She helps word a pointed note for the return of Claire the real writer's wedding gift.

Dear Claire,

In my opinion, the violation of a committed relationship is a serious offense. I have donated the Le Creuset deep frying pan you bought us to a women's charity.

Sincerely,
Kat

Lena holds my hand when I call up Margaret the sex addiction therapist. I tell Margaret, "It was unprofessional of you to drop this bomb on me and then let me walk out of your office. I was in such an extreme state of shock that I walked into the middle of the road and was almost killed."

Lena gets someone to remove the blue couch that I can now only think of as "Charlie's sex couch."

In the midst of all this, I get two emails. One from Simon Breckenhauer, the producer who wanted to read the musical. He's going to pass but kindly explains why with constructive criticism. I forward the email to Rupert with a note saying, "Let's talk about this later. I'm in the middle of some crap." The second email says:

Hi Kat,

How lovely to hear from you. Thank you so much for getting in touch. My apologies for taking such a long time to get back. Your musical sounds fab. I'm always happy to help a friend of Charlie's but especially his wife. I'd love to meet you. But first, why don't you send the script over and I'll take a look at it.

I've just sent a warm hello to your dashing husband, thanking him for sending you my way.

Warm regards,
Gail

I explain the situation to Lena (that Gail gave Charlie a blow job in the back of his car), concluding, "The least that woman can do is help get the show produced, but Charlie asked me not to be in touch with her."

Lena urges, "As this involves your career, why don't you wait until you process your anger, and then see how you feel?" Lena's very smart.

Another smart move of Lena's: she brings me to test for STDs. The results come back clean, and I'm in the clear since we haven't had sex in so long. In fact, Lena never leaves my side. I'm pretty sure this is what Maria told her to do and I'm grateful she's there. I'm aware I'm unstable. This means Lena's there when I answer a phone call from Matt.

Matt tells me, "There's gonna be another wedding, Louise."

"What?"

"Daisy's fucking amazing."

"But you should be focusing on getting better, Mattie."

"I am better!"

My heart starts pounding so hard I can feel it. "But, Mattie...."

"Why can't you just be happy for me?"

"Because, Mattie... I mean, what are you doing for work?"

He laughs. "Jesus Christ, Kat, what do you do for work? For fuck's sake, I'll do whatever! What does it matter? We'll figure it out! Daisy's headed for fame. She just got a huge commission."

"What's she do?"

"Mosaic furniture."

"Okay." I try to sound calm and cool. "I just think that you should figure out what *you* want to do before you change your life for her. I mean, what about garden design?"

"I'm hanging up now. Call me back when you aren't such a miserable whiny old hag."

I turn to Lena, already crying. "My God, Mattie's going to marry this girl he doesn't even know!"

Lena nods her head. "Do you think you should fill him in on what's happening with you?"

"God no!"

"But doesn't this stuff run in families?"

"This stuff?"

"The sex stuff. I mean, your Dad was a philanderer. Now, your husband. It wouldn't be weird if Mattie had a touch of whatever this is."

I chew on this. "Mattie and I have always been very similar. We have the same tendencies, the same instincts. I mean, don't you think?"

"You're a little more tempered, but only a little." I start to hit Matt's number. "Wait." Lena seems to consider her words. "Maybe you should take the time to figure out what's really going on for you first."

I put my phone down. "You're right. I have no idea what's going on."

"And that's okay. No one would expect you to right now."

"I'm going to go through his things."

"I'm going to go through his things." I get up.

"Whoa. I don't think that's a good idea. You could end up getting more upset."

"Yes, but I have a right to know."

"Do what you have to do, but I don't want to participate in that. That makes me feel… yuck." Lena disappears into the kitchen while I make a beeline for his computer.

It's not password protected which makes me think I won't find anything good here, but I still search his files, his histories, everything I can. It's absolutely squeaky clean. I go through his file cabinet, but there are no seedy credit card statements, no secret love letters. Just legitimate business-related papers.

And the deed for the Norfolk house. And a set of keys.

3

After five nights with me, Lena's due to depart on the Eurostar before sunrise. I could not be more grateful to her for taking care of me. But her departure works for me too. Lena's got her bag packed, ready to go. She turns to me and asks, "Are you sure you're okay for me to go?"

I try to act cool. I don't want her to see how eager I am to be without a babysitter. "Of course! I'm fine. I mean, I'm not fine, but I'm as fine as I can be, you know?" Lena doesn't look convinced. "Besides, Jean-Marc must be at his limit."

"I just don't feel like you're right yet."

"I don't think I'm going to be right for a long time."

We hug. She goes. She'll walk down our street then turn the corner to get onto the high street where she'll take the Underground to St Pancras for the Eurostar. I force myself to wait a full ten minutes in case Lena pauses for a coffee or the trains are slow, then I head to the tube as well.

I take the Underground to Euston. Once there, I pay the peak fare to get on the first train of the day. Then I hit the fuck it button and pay for a First Class ticket. I have to find some way of sticking it to Charlie. I find a seat. I only have my phone with me, but I can't read or listen to a podcast or anything. I just want to get there. I stare out at the dreary, never-ending-grey-February countryside. The train can't go fast enough. On the horizon, the sky's pink as day breaks. I will the train to go the same speed as my racing mind. It doesn't. I stare out the window.

At midday, with nothing in my belly but bad coffee and a stale croissant, a taxi drops me off in front of the barn conversion in Trunch, Norfolk.

The idyllic house instantly boils my blood. Though I'm married to

Charlie and therefore part owner of what looks to be a rural paradise, I feel like I'm trespassing as soon as I set foot on the grounds. And this place does have "grounds." I push aside my feelings and unlock the front door. When I step inside, I'm awestruck by a home worthy of *Country Life* magazine. A living area with open plan kitchen occupies about five times the space of our Hampstead flat. It's all done in a mélange of natural woods and neutral fibers. And even though the sun's covered with thick white clouds, a number of oversized skylights brighten the room. From where I stand inside the front door, I can see all the way through to the back of the house where there's a view of green fields that look like they roll straight to the sea. It's exquisitely quiet. And it has that really fresh, brand new smell.

By rote, as if I regularly explore my husband's secret love nests, I step from the foyer into the open-plan kitchen and start looking through the stylish cabinets. There's nothing of interest. In the steel refrigerator, one bottle of Pellegrino sits on an otherwise empty shelf. I cross through the living room and my footsteps echo off the hardwood floor. I walk upstairs and my feet sink into luxurious carpeting. I walk in and out of three smaller bedrooms before finding the main one. It looks like a hotel room, devoid of any personal items. Only the super king size bed looks like Charlie chose it. I stare at it. It's the same rich cherry finish that we have at home. I actually think it's our exact same bed. For fuck's sake. This was the setting for "Sex with Claire the Real Writer, Round II."

I look in the wastebasket. Empty. I open the closets, the bureau drawers. Empty. I go through the tastefully done en suite bathroom cabinets. Apart from towels, empty. I go back down the hall and do the same in the other bedrooms. Apart from bed linens, empty. I return to the kitchen and go through every drawer and cupboard again. Kitchen stuff, all new but nothing interesting. There's no television or laptop for porn. No dildos lying around or even tucked away safely for later. There's no basement. There's another bathroom and room on the main floor, but they don't even have linens or furniture. I go back upstairs to look in the attic, but there's no attic. I wander back downstairs and look around me. It's a beautifully designed house, filled with light and space. I don't understand how he can have this house, this beautiful house, and not just hide it from me, but take Claire—Claire the real fucking writer—take her here and fuck her! How could he do this to me? How? I hear myself screaming. I scream and scream and scream and scream. When I finally stop, I find that I've ended up on my knees on the beautiful hardwood floor. I call another taxi.

4

It takes six hours and four train changes to travel from Norfolk to Netley. I find yet another taxi to complete my journey to Charlie's parents' house and ring their doorbell just after 6 p.m. Ariel opens the door. She wears a navy, soft wool dress, complete with hose and pumps. No lazing around the house in sweatpants for this woman. "Ah!" Ariel exclaims. "*Quelle surprise.*" But she doesn't sound surprised at all. On the contrary, she sounds like she's not only been expecting me but also that the inevitability of my visit is irritating to the nth degree. Ariel leaves the front door open and walks back into the house. I follow her into the kitchen where she puts on the kettle and takes out a teapot. She starts moving about the kitchen. I watch as she tastefully sets the table with folded cloth napkins, a pitcher of fresh mint water, a bouquet of white tulips.

"I think it is a bit early, but still it is fine," Ariel states. Early for what? To leave Charlie? "I hope a basic tea is enough? I dine simply when Harry is away. *Salade?*"

Ah. Too early for supper. "Yes, of course." I sit at the table. "Do you know why I'm here?"

"What does it matter what I know? I'm sure you're going to tell me, so off you go."

I watch Ariel generously squeeze lemon over the salad, add salt, and then she oh so carefully adds three, austere drops of olive oil. When she finally brings the salad to the table and sits opposite me, I tell her, "Charlie cheated on me." Ariel laughs. She actually *laughs.* "He cheated on me and I want to find out what made him this way." She laughs harder. "I thought you would want to help me fix it? Why on earth is this funny?"

"You are such a child! He cheated on you? He is a grown man!

He does what he wants!"

"He's my husband. We're married."

"You think marriage means a man won't want to explore? Sow his seeds? It is the most natural thing, and young stupid women are always complaining about it, so anti-nature." Ariel tosses the salad. "My father, they called him *Le Boeuf*. You know what that means? The Ox! Creature of fertility. Always making *bébés*. Women always coming to the house with their *bébés* saying they were his, and were they lying? *Non!* That was his way. It's only *naturel* for a real man."

I don't have a clue how to respond so go with, "I see."

"And my husband is the same as my father. Well, Harry is not The Ox!" She laughs again as she serves me an anorexic portion of salad. She continues, "I was upset at times, *mais oui, bien sur*, but I would just tell Harry, *Je ne veux pas voire!* Not where I can see! There were never knocks at my door after that. Though he did give me some nasty illness. I had it when I was pregnant with Charlie."

"What was it?"

Ariel wracks her brain. "The clap."

"You had gonorrhea when you were pregnant with Charlie?"

"Yes! Can you believe what that man put me through?"

"But, but… why did you stand for it, Ariel?"

"If I complain because Harry is not faithful, where will I be? I like my life. Harry is an excellent provider. He may want to dibble dabble here and there, but otherwise we are happy. I have happy children and a lovely house."

"But… Charlie's not happy."

"Perhaps not. Perhaps he is. Perhaps it is his wife who is unhappy. Perhaps it is his wife who needs to grow up." Ariel nips a carefully balanced piece of lettuce into her mouth. "*Mange! Mange!* Or perhaps you need some bread and butter?"

I shake my head. I wish I could come up with a verbal deflection to her twisted food jab, but my mind's blank. Besides, an abstemious meal suits me just fine. My appetite has yet to return. It's almost a relief not to be around someone telling me to eat soup or bread or whatever. And even though a very large part of me wants to reach across the table and smash Ariel's face in, I concentrate on balancing lettuce leaves on the tines of my fork, which, despite my American upbringing, I've gotten pretty good at.

5

On the train back to London I'm thinking about one time, and this is years ago now, when I asked Mattie what it felt like to be manic. He explained, "It's like being in a nightmare where I want to stop doing the nutty things I'm doing, but I can't." Maybe I'm manic right now because I know I should go straight home. I've been all around the country. It's hard to believe it's the same day I said goodbye to Lena, but it is. I didn't sleep much last night to begin with, have barely eaten, and yet still, I find myself calling Charlie and telling him, "I think we should talk." Charlie's quiet, then says, "I'm not sure that's a good idea without a therapist." I use my rational, I-am-calm-and-smart voice and explain, "This is urgent. I have to talk to you. Let's see how we do." He relents and we agree to meet at his friend Josh's flat in Camden.

It's almost midnight when Charlie buzzes me up. He opens the door, then quickly turns and walks into the flat, like I'm expected to just follow, mirroring his mother's action hours before. I see he's wearing a new shirt and designer jeans. How could he have gone out shopping? Isn't he as heartbroken as I am? Then I see Josh's incredibly messy living room, serving as Charlie's current bedroom, and Charlie turns to face me. My God. He does not look good. He looks vulnerable, defeated. The black circles appear embedded under his eyes, which look... dull. He's in pain without me. I relax. The poor man. I feel for him, I really do.

We sit on the couch that doubles as his bed and Charlie immediately puts his head in my lap. He sobs. I've never seen him like this. I stroke his head. His sobs subside, but we don't move. When I think he's calm, I tell him, "Charlie, I don't think it's your fault that you're like this."

"What do you mean?"

"I had a long chat with your mother today—"

"You did *what*?" He sits up.

"Well. I didn't mean to go see her. First, I went to the house."

"What house?"

"The one you bought in Norfolk."

"How did you get there?"

"I took the train."

"How did you know where it was? Get in?"

"There were keys and the deed in your file cabinet."

"You went through my things?" He looks like I've committed a grave offense.

I can't help but smile a little, as I say, "Oh Charlie, did you honestly think I wouldn't go through your things?"

"Kat, that's such a violation!"

"Watch what you're saying, Charlie. 'Violation' is not a word you seem to understand the meaning of."

"But this is the point! I don't have anything for *me*!"

"Yeah," I pause, "see when you say that and you have a house that's bigger than anything I've ever dreamed of, and I know the main reason you bought it was to go and have sex with someone else, all I hear is that you don't want to be faithful. You want sex with others and a million-pound house to do it in."

Charlie takes a deep breath in. And then out. And then in. And then out. "Kat. Part of my problem is that there never feels like there's room to be *me* in our relationship, in any relationship for that matter. I always feel like I'm suffocating."

"Your mother told me all about your father and your grandfather. Do you think that's how they felt too?"

Charlie's looking at me strangely. "I don't feel safe around you right now, Kat."

"Oh don't start that! I'm here to help you! I love you! I want to figure this out with you! Let me help."

He sighs. "Well, it's true that this stuff runs in families, very true. Have you ever thought about why you chose to be with me?"

"Because you're wonderful."

"I'm a raging sex addict, Kat."

"Ah yeah, I get that, Charlie!" We stare at each other for a second and I feel all the compassion I'd had drain out of me.

In a childlike voice he says, "I still haven't had sex with anyone but you since we've been married." He says this like it's a gift.

I'm cold now. "Christ, Charlie, oral sex and hand jobs are sex. They're sex!"

"You don't understand. There are lines." Now he's speaking like *I'm* a child.

"Maybe I don't understand you, Charlie! Maybe that really is the problem here, that I don't understand you!" I'm furious. "Or maybe, just *maybe*, the problem is that *you* don't understand you! I mean, for starters, do you realize that you come from a long line of sex addicts and that your mother actually thinks that fucking around is 'normal behavior for real men?'"

"Well, it's normal behavior for me."

"Then I can't be with you!"

"Kat, I told you I was a sex addict!"

"You also told me that you were in recovery and that you were sexually sober!"

"I'm doing better! That's what I'm trying to explain! When I say I haven't had sex with anyone since we've been married, what you don't understand is that that's a big deal!"

"You sound like a fucking idiot. If I said to you, 'I'm an alcoholic. I haven't drunk whiskey in five years, only beer—'"

"It's not the same thing!"

"But would you call that sobriety? No. Because it's not."

He stands up. "You'll never understand."

"You'll never get sober!"

"I'm very sober in some areas. I haven't picked up a drink."

"Ha!"

"What?" Charlie towers over me. "Would you have preferred it if I drank?"

"It would have been a hell of a lot less painful for me."

"So basically you're saying that you'd like me to be dead?"

"Jesus Christ, Charlie! Do you not realize the impact your sexual addiction has had on me?"

"Let's just stay with the point for a moment that you would have preferred that I drank. Is that true?"

"Yes."

"Do you realize that if I drink, I will die? That I am also an alcoholic?"

"You're missing the point."

"No, you're missing the point. You are saying that you would prefer me dead."

"Charlie, you have ripped my heart out!" I stand and face him. "There is a big difference between you having a drink and you fucking a prostitute!"

"I didn't have sex with any of the prostitutes."

"Before we were married you did and you did everything else anyway so what does it matter? These distinctions that you make are just plain—"

"Kat—" Charlie attempts to interrupt.

"Bullshit! You're either sober or you're not and of course I would have preferred your relapse to be around alcohol due to the fact—"

"Kat!"

"That I am your wife!"

"Kat, there are lines!"

"No, Charlie! These *lines* you make up are fucking stupid! There is only one line! You either cheat or you're faithful and you, Charlie, cheat!"

"This isn't about you, Kat. You're just collateral damage." He's looking at me with that twisted face.

"Excuse me?"

"This is about *me*, not you. You're just collateral damage."

I can't believe he had the gall to say it twice. I stare at that twisted face.

I stare at that twisted face and then with all my strength I wind up my arm and smash the heel of my palm across his jaw with every pound of body weight I have because I fucking hate him hate that face want him to die! He doesn't see it coming, reels back, falls onto the couch. His hands move to his jaw. Did I dislocate it? I pause for a moment to have a look, but then the fury overtakes me and I don't give a shit about his jaw.

"You see?" Charlie holds his jaw. "You're insane! I can't believe you've hit me!"

"Don't you dare call me insane when you're the one going to prostitutes!"

"It takes two to tango, Kat."

I see a butcher block of shiny knives on the kitchen counter. "Get away from me," I say in a voice I don't recognize. "Get away from me *now*." My tone ends the conversation. For a heartbeat, we're both right here in the room. I'm thinking about the knives. Charlie looks at me, scrutinizes my face. I hate his very blue eyes, especially the one with the flecks of black. Charlie suddenly grabs his keys and goes. I hear the door slam shut. I'm left alone in his friend's flat.

6

I sit on Maria's couch, still stunned. "I would have stabbed him if he hadn't left." Maria says nothing. "I just saw the knives and saw myself getting one and jabbing him with it, and I mean, I hit him. I've never hit anyone. It came out of nowhere. I mean, I took a self-defense class once, and I somehow managed to remember some move they'd taught us, and I just smashed his face."

"This is rage."

"Yes." I nod in strong agreement. "This is definitely rage and... I had no control over it."

"Because you are out of control."

"But this is very fucked up."

"Yes."

"That said, he did say that I was collateral damage."

"If he had cancer, would you hit him?"

"Of course not. But it's not exactly like cancer, Maria, is it?"

"It is different from cancer, but it is still a legitimate illness that will worsen without treatment."

"I went to see his mother." I recount what happened with Ariel.

Maria explains, "Addiction is often, but not always, handed down from generation to generation. It is the same as substance abuse in that the powerful chemicals released during sexual activity and the activities that precede it, particularly the adrenaline, control him. Adrenaline addiction is very serious and difficult to kick. He has an illness that will become progressively worse and could, without a doubt, kill him." She sits up taller and leans forward. "You cannot let your rage take hold of you like it did. That sort of rage is only for protecting yourself or your children. It's not for domestic arguments and certainly no way to speak to a man who is ill."

"Maria, he has cheated on me and lied to me a thousand different ways!"

"Justification of violence will not be tolerated, Kat," she says firmly. "When we separate your real parents from your childhood parents, you can direct the rage where it needs to go: your childhood parents. With your husband, you can rage at his illness but never him. No. This is not allowed."

"Rage at his illness?"

"Yes, we have no time for addiction. It is addiction that steals our lives. You can rage at his addiction all you like. But not the person underneath."

"Okay. I understand that."

"But we are not here to talk about Charlie's addiction. What about yours?"

"Well, I've been traumatized."

"Yes, of course you are traumatized. But we don't get ourselves into situations like you have, with our eyes wide open marrying a sex addict, participating in a non-intimate relationship, unless there is something ill in us. This is what I am here to help you look at."

I want this session to be over. She has a clock on the table behind her and spots me glancing at it. "Yes, lucky for you we are out of time for today. But I am going to ask you to do something which will be difficult for you." I wait. "I am going to ask you to spend ninety days without speaking to or seeing Charlie. I want us to focus on you."

"But surely I can focus on me and have conversations with him."

Maria adamantly shakes her head. "This is terribly important, Kat. You must give yourself time to heal. And the way to do that is by removing yourself from the main trigger of your hurt who at this moment is Charlie. Otherwise you will be retriggering your rage and I will spend all our time, week after week, asking you to please contain the rage but never getting to its true source. It is not meant to punish him or you. It is a separation to try to save, first and foremost, you, my child, and then, perhaps we will see if the marriage can start to work."

"Okay. Should I call him tonight?"

"No, no contact."

"But surely I should inform him that there's not going to be any contact?"

"You can email him your decision."

"I'm not sure this is my decision."

7

I call Matt. He answers on the first ring. "Mom's worried about you."

"What? Why?"

"They haven't heard from you in weeks. I said you were fine. Are you?"

"Charlie and I... we're having a hard time."

"Isn't it a little soon for the *for worse* part?"

Huh. I reply, "I don't know."

"What's going on?"

If I tell Matt that Charlie cheated even a little, let alone the sordid truth, he'll tell Mom and Dad and they'll hate Charlie. That wouldn't be fair. Charlie's *sick*. I don't want to turn everyone against him, so I tell Mattie, "I don't really want to get into it."

"Ooooooo-kay."

"Mattie, do you think our family's really fucked up?"

"Not any more than any other family."

"So that's a no then?"

"I think it's tough for us, but we get by."

"So that's a yes then?"

"Listen, Louise, can I tell Mom you're okay?"

"Yeah, sure."

"And I mean, yeah, I think our family's really fucked up. A lot of families are messed and it's not like there was any overt physical abuse or anything in ours, which would make how it's fucked up easier to understand. But from my perspective, something fucked up was going on between our parents. And while that was going on, Dad was always working or off doing something or, more accurately, someone, and Mom was pretty depressed and unable to cope with daily things. And now, they're both a little hard to relate to. But I don't know, maybe I'm making excuses, but I think their hearts are in the right places. That said, they're not being cool about Daisy."

"So that's a definitive yes then."

"Yeah, it's a yes. But remember, Louise, it ain't over 'til the fat lady sings."

"Yeah. Thanks."

"No really. It's not. And I don't see any fat ladies singing where I am. You?"

"What are they saying about Daisy?"

"That I've jumped into it too quickly. That I should be taking time for myself. I tell them to look at you and Prince Charles. That moved fast and you're happy."

"No, I'm not."

"What?"

"I'm not happy."

"Oh fuck you! Did they call you and tell you to discourage me from marrying her?"

"You know I haven't been in touch with them."

"I know you haven't been in touch with Mom. Have you been talking to Dad about me again? Oh fuck you all! There I was thinking we were having a heart-to-heart and you've really just called to get on my fucking case." He hangs up.

8

Dear Charlie,

I'm so sorry about yesterday.

It has been suggested to me that I take some time fully out of contact from you. Ninety days to be precise.

This separation is not meant as a punishment and has been framed to me as the best way to save our marriage, which is my intention.

I'm finding this incredibly painful, but still think there could be a way through it. I just want to say again, I'm so sorry for yesterday, especially the physical violence. I feel very ashamed about that.

Yours,
Kat

Dear Katherine,

90 days, eh? Are you aware that that's recovery jargon? I shall save you a seat in the rooms of recovery.

Don't worry about the punch in the face, darling. I'm sure I deserved it.

I have decided to return to my old treatment center for ninety days as well. I will get in touch with you upon my return.

Yours,
Charles

CHARLIE

Just before this whole ninety day thing kicks off, can I ask, why are you calling me Katherine instead of Kat?

can you please lay off the recovery push and respect that I am on my own journey?

what made you decide to go back to treatment?
do you have any hope for us as a husband and wife?

Charlie writes:

Ah Kat, you do make me laugh. See my responses below in bold. Kat Callahan wrote:

CHARLIE

Just before this whole ninety day thing kicks off, can I ask, why are you calling me Katherine instead of Kat? **I'm trying to awaken and live in my authentic, outer adult and to meet yours. This is just a way of reminding myself that I'm doing that.**

can you please lay off the recovery push and respect that I am on my own journey? **Yes. Apologies for that. Was trying to lighten the mood.**

what made you decide to go back to treatment? **Probably the punch in the face! (Joking again, sweetie!) Ahhhh Kat, I don't think I can stay sober here for any significant length of time without intervention and support. And I can't live like this. It's horrendous.**

Do you have any hope for us as a husband and wife? **I married you because I love you. I have no doubt about that. Maybe I don't really know what love is, as I don't really know how to be truly honest and I'm so sorry for that, but if there is** *any way to make this marriage work, the first step on my end will be me having a strong recovery. I wish you all the best over the next few months and will look forward to seeing you upon my return.*

I'm going to sign my name as "Charles" now, so don't freak out.

Yours,
Charles

VIII

Oh oh can't you see
Love is the drug for me
—Bryan Ferry

DAY 1

How dare that fucker say that saving a seat for me in the fucking rooms was "an attempt to lighten the mood?" That's a lie! He was serious! Not everyone goes that way, *Charles*. You fucking dickhead fucking ass dick. I don't call him. I compose a witty response to his last email. I don't send it. I think about calling him. I don't. I think about calling him again. I don't. I think about calling him again. I don't. I write emails to him in my head. I catch myself talking to him while I'm doing the dishes. I mean, out loud. Like a crazy person. I think that we could start the counting from tomorrow, and I could just get this off my chest. How dare he say he'll save a seat for me? Not everyone needs recovery support groups like he does. And how dare he just leave?

I call Maria and book in to see her first thing in the morning. Then I decide I should get some exercise and go for a run. I catch myself talking to him while I'm running. I get home. I still want to call him. I catch myself talking to him while I'm in the shower. I call Lena. She's not home. I call Sally. She's not home. I go to the movies. I can't watch the film because I'm thinking about him. I go to bed early so that I don't contact him.

DAY 2

"Well, yes, he is saying that he's saving a seat for you because you are an addict as well." Maria put me in her own bed when I felt like I was collapsing. She made me eat the soup. She has been nothing but kind and informative, but right now I hate her. "You are like an alcoholic, but you are addicted to love instead of alcohol." I want her to shut the fuck up. "You change any or all aspects of your life at a moment's notice for *love*. You end up empty, shriveled, shivering, cold, in an eccentric therapist's bed, with a husband only on paper."

"That's a little harsh."

"Only because it is true. Yes?"

"It sounds pretty farfetched to me."

"Addiction to love is easy to dismiss as not a real disorder, as is sex addiction, but these sorts of behaviors can very quickly, or painfully slowly, destroy people."

"I married a man who cheated on me."

"You married a sex addict. This is different."

"I'm not saying he's not a sex addict."

"Good."

"I just don't think that because he's an addict, I'm an addict."

"From what you've told me, you suffer from anxiety, low self-esteem and perfectionism."

I squirm, but, "Yes."

"And did you think Charlie would fix you?"

"No! Well, what do you mean? The relationship made me feel whole, but I wouldn't say it fixed me."

"Can't you be whole without a relationship?"

"Of course I can! It's not like I have this antiquated view that a woman's nothing without a man."

"You can have a modern view of the world but still feel like you are not enough."

"The relationship worked."

Maria stares at me.

I say nothing.

She says nothing.

I refuse to let her win so I keep saying nothing.

"Do you really think his sleeping with all those different people was the relationship working?"

Now I just don't know what to say.

"You should know that studies show that the brain chemical dopamine is as high in people in love as it is in cocaine users. Love is one of the hardest addictions to kick."

"Okay," I say, "whether I'm an addict or not, the relationship *felt* like it worked."

"And...?" She wants me to say it clearly didn't work and I don't want to give her that. "Kat, do you want to get better?"

"I'm not sick!"

"Do you want to be in a relationship with a man who is faithful to you?"

"Of course."

"Can you at least admit that being in a relationship with someone who is sleeping around in an addictive manner is not a healthy relationship?"

"Of course! I'm not an idiot."

"Good. Then you understand. It did not work."

"Fine. It didn't work!"

"Finally. Well done. Now, when you were *not* in the relationship with him, did you feel whole?"

"No. I felt whole *in* the relationship. That's why I thought it worked!"

"I am taking a guess here that he does not feel whole outside the relationship either. And I can tell you that no relationship will work when it is built by two people who do not feel whole."

"Okay," I say, "okay, I take your point." We sit there. She has won this one. She is fucking right. "So the relationship didn't work. I have some damage. What do I do?"

"As with all addictions, you must find your own way."

"I didn't say I had an addiction."

"There is a lot of support out there. It's easy to find."

"Wait. Aren't you going to help me?"

"Of course I help you." Maria smiles. "But there is a lot of support out there for the addictive process that you have found yourself in." I groan. She speaks over me. "And I am going to urge you to go and find that support. I am a trauma specialist. There is a distinction between recovery from an addiction and healing of trauma. You don't treat your addiction in here. You find a way to do that out there. In here, we work on uncovering your core trauma, the one that got you into this mess. Now go home and eat a warm meal, and rest, and sleep."

"I can't."

"No appetite?"

"No."

"What is the problem?"

"I'm worried I'll call him. I want to call him. I want him to be in my life. I want to be in touch with him. I want to stay connected to him." Maria nods. I ask, "You know what I mean?"

"Yes, yes, you are love addict, you see. And right now, he is your object."

I fucking hate her.

DAY 3

Fuck me, this is not easy. My whole body wants him, yearns for him. I breathe better when I'm in touch with him. I need him in order to exist. But I have not called him. There's no point in calling him anyway. He's in a treatment center. Surely they've taken away his phone and he has no access to email. But I could call the center and leave a message for him to call me back. I think about it. I want to do it. I soooooo want to do it. I just want to hear his voice. Even though he's betrayed me in a way I never knew possible. This makes no sense, I know, but I want him. I feel cut off. Like a part of me is dying without him. Maybe that part of me needs to die. I start binge-watching a British reality show about blind dates. It's not really that good, but I watch it until I'm exhausted. I get through another day without contacting him.

DAY 6

Maria explains to me, "There are two things happening now. Firstly, you put down your drug of choice so you are in withdrawal."

"Or one could say that I just miss my husband."

"A little odd to miss someone who has treated you so badly, no?"

"He's sick."

Maria seems to take a deep breath and recenter herself. Then she says, "The second thing that is happening now is that you are still in shock. Learning the full extent of Charlie's indiscretions traumatized you. But in fact, it was such a powerful shock, that it served to uncover past traumas from childhood."

"The trauma caused by Charlie's sexual misconduct uncovered *past* traumas from childhood?" I feel like I'm taking a course in hocus-pocus. "How on earth do you know that?"

"From what you have told me."

"About what?"

"That you have felt this way before. From when you were a child."

Why the fuck did I say that? Shit.

"So, the present trauma dug up the old traumas. This is a good thing. Past traumas can be buried so deeply within us that they can only be released by a present-day wallop, and you were lucky enough to get one."

"A wallop?"

"A shock that is bigger than all the past ones. So big that it breaks us open, revealing the old trauma so we can get underneath it, pull it up, examine it, and let it go. One day you'll thank him for his behavior. It has blasted you open so we can see what is hidden inside. Without this blast, you would have continued your life, not knowing what was wrong, thus unable to stop destructive patterns, and never being able to participate in a truly intimate relationship."

I grasp what she's saying, but I don't want to be in Therapy School.

She says, "So tell me how you felt when you were little."

And there it is. She wants me to talk about my feelings *and* my childhood.

"Can you tell me?"

"I don't want to do this."

"Do you want to get better?"

"Of course."

"Then tell me how you felt then."

It comes right out. "Betrayed, broken, abandoned."

Maria nods. "You may not have married the right man to have as a husband. But you married the right man to heal your old family wounds. And the good news—"

I chuckle. "There's good news?"

"The *good* news," Maria stresses, "is that trauma recovery has a beginning, a middle and an end. You are at the beginning. But someday, you will be at the end. When that day comes, you will no longer need to see me."

"Hallelujah."

"Now. Have you been in touch with him?"

"No! Of course not!" I say this as if I haven't obsessed about speaking with him every day since that stupid email he sent me.

"You need help with your addiction. For that, have you heard of sex and love addicts anonymous?"

"That's not everyone's path, you know."

"Of course not. But have you been to one of their meetings yet?"

"No. But I haven't been in touch with him, so I don't think I need that."

"From what you have told me about wanting to call him and having to restrain yourself, it sounds like you are in withdrawal."

"That's offensive. I'm not a drug addict."

She shrugs. "Let me be perfectly clear. In here, we work on your trauma. Out there, you work on your addiction. You do that by going to meetings or you don't come back here." She stands up, meaning our session is over. I get my things. I can't believe she just said that, but what can I say. She walks me to the door. "I hope I see you in a few days."

DAY 7

Maybe there will be no more therapy. I want to call Charlie. I shouldn't need to call him this badly. He's only been gone for a week. That's it. We've had much longer stretches apart. I sit at my desk. My brain's sluggish. It doesn't feel like my brain. But I still manage to review the critical points Simon Breckenhauer made when he passed on producing our musical. I'm pissed off that he passed, but I can see that his reasons were legitimate. I email Rupert. I haven't been in touch with him this whole time. I keep the email about work and write, "Going to redraft, restructure and come up with some new material."

My phone rings. Rupert. He says, "That's a lot of work."

"It needs it."

"Are you okay?"

Argh. He's really saying *are-you-okay-because-I've-heard -you're-a-cuckolded-woman.* I reply, "I assume you've heard?"

"Yeah. Charlie talked about it in group before he went off to treatment." Even though Rupert's no stranger to sex addiction, I feel my cheeks turn red. "How are you holding up?"

"I'm okay at the moment. It's been hard though. Can I ask you something?"

"Of course."

"Did you know before?"

"Before what?"

"We got married?"

"Oh no. I did see him at group, but he neglected to mention he was in relapse." I don't say anything. "Listen, Kat, I take my work very seriously and you're my work partner. Had I known and you not known, I wouldn't have been able to participate in that sort of a triangulation."

"You'd have terminated our working relationship?"

"I'd have requested Charlie inform you of the situation before I did."

I can't help smiling, not only for his kindness, but for the trite reason that he's on my side, not Charlie's. I tell him, "Thank you. That's nice to hear."

"Do you want me to have Sally ring you? See if she can talk?"

He does not offer to discuss my situation himself. No, no, he offers the ear of his girlfriend. Wow. This man is so upright. Would Charlie ever be able to have a relationship with a female that was so above board? Obviously not. He has sex with everyone in his path: old friends, strangers, men, women, married, single. Everyone except me, of course.

I want to get off the phone. "That's very kind, Rupert, thanks. I'll let you know. Right now I just want to get on with the rewrite."

"Are you positive you wouldn't like to speak to Sally?"

"I'm not positive about anything at the moment."

———

Two hours later and I can't even say I've been trying to write. All I've been doing is trying not to call someone who doesn't even have access to a fucking phone. The seconds feel like days. My phone rings. Fucking Sally. Nice Sally. Here to help the crazy person. I don't want to pick up the phone, but that would be so rude.

She asks, "How are you holding up?" I burst into tears. "What are you doing tonight?" I keep crying. "Okay. I'll drop by around six and take you to a meeting."

My brain objects, but all I can say is, "Okay. See you later." She hangs up. What have I done? What have I done?

At least I spend the afternoon worrying about going to the meeting instead of wanting to call Charlie. Promptly at six, Sally arrives looking cool and peaceful. Once I'm in her car, she tells me, "We don't usually end up with raging sex addicts for no reason."

"That's what Maria said."

"Maria?"

"My therapist. Well, she was my therapist, but she says that unless I go to a meeting, I can't continue with her! Isn't that crazy? I'm not the sex addict here!"

"No, but if you don't get treatment for your love addiction, how can she help you?"

"Arrrrgh! That's what she said! On the one hand, I really just want to talk to Charlie. Just like, touch base. I don't think that's so bad. I've been thinking about calling him, or texting. But then I think I'm insane. First of all, he's locked up in a treatment center. Second of all, why can't I go a week without contacting him? What's so essential about having access to him? We even agreed we weren't speaking for ninety days, so why can't my mind drop the idea? It's not like we haven't had times when we didn't speak."

"Yes, but you haven't had no contact. You've always known he was there to ring if you needed."

"But we've gone longer than a week without speaking to each other. We went months not seeing each other when we lived in different countries!" She just drives. "Why aren't you saying anything?"

"Well, I think it's better if you figure these things out for yourself."

"Figure what things out?"

"Let's get to the meeting. You can have a little listen and see if there's anything you can relate to."

We get to the meeting with ten minutes so spare. There's a big sign that says, "SLAA." It doesn't take a rocket scientist to figure out that it's a sex and love addicts anonymous group. If they really want it to be anonymous they should consider different signage. I really don't want to be here. I really don't want to be here! I dash off to the ladies' room in an effort to avoid making chitchat with people. When I get back, I realize I've made a big mistake. Sally saved me a seat in the front. The front row.

The meeting starts. I'm not really listening. I try to see behind me and count how many people are here. I think there are about seventeen. Mostly men. They're probably all pervs like Charlie. Ugh. Not that he's a perv. I mean, sick like him. They're of varying ages. Most of them look normal. One of them reads out: "We become immobilized or seriously distracted by romantic or sexual obsessions or fantasies." I look up to see if the person reading is looking at me. Because that is me. I am seriously distracted. The next statement is one about attaching ourselves to unavailable people. Bingo again. Could anyone be more unavailable than Charlie? I glance at Sally. Did she tell them to read these things for me?

Then a woman speaks for a longer time. It's riveting. She gets to the part about when she finally took a break from her "qualifier" and went into withdrawal. She describes it as a state of "desperate longing" for her qualifier. She talks about wanting to make contact with him, even though she made a conscious choice to "detox" him in an effort to gain much needed sanity and reassess where she was. And here I am wanting to make contact with *my* qualifier even though he just bombed me. She says she was in desperate longing. Desperate longing. How true.

DAY 10

Maria seems happy when I show up for our session, but she doesn't want me to tell her about the meeting I went to. She says, "Your commitment is to go to them and take the suggestions suggested to you. We have other work to do."

We spend the session talking about how I felt when I was a child, what my father did for work, when my parents divorced. Mattie and me in the family are peas in a pod, yet completely separate. The session flies. I talk and talk and talk. I can't believe how much I talk. Maria jumps in, "That is our time for today." I'm surprised.

DAY 11

I told Maria I would go to the meetings, but even though the first one was interesting and I felt a little reprieve from my "desperate longing," I don't want to go. That said, Sally's picking me up. It's nice getting to know her at least. She's been through more than I would have thought with Rupert. Maybe it'll work for Charlie and me. I wonder if he misses me. I wonder if he still wears his wedding ring. I wonder a lot of things. Then Sally picks me up.

We sit in the fucking front row again. And I listen. I don't say anything. Even though Sally has mentioned a few times that speaking would be good, I don't. They all say their names and that they're sex and love addicts, or love addicts or whatever. I'd have to say my name like they do before I speak, and I can't say that I'm a love addict, so I can't speak. Besides, what would I talk about? I'm not like them. I keep listening. Sally drives me home. Before I get out of the car, she gives me a hug. That night, I sleep soundly.

DAY 12

I still miss Charlie. I go see Maria and talk about my childhood.

DAY 13

I really miss Charlie. I go see two movies and then another meeting with Sally.

DAY 14

I write him a letter telling him how much I miss him, how I feel like a part of me is missing, like my best friend is gone. Without him, I understand what depression is. I feel desperate, like having his love is essential and without it I can't breathe, can't survive.

I go see Maria and bring the letter because I don't want to talk about my childhood. I want her to understand that I am in pain about Charlie, my husband. I read the letter to her. She says, "A very clear expression of your feelings." For once, I'm the one nodding my head. She continues, "If you were to keep everything about the letter exactly as it is, but change to whom it is addressed from Charlie to your father, how would that make you feel?"

I feel nauseous.

DAY 15

I wander around an art gallery. Then I go to another fucking meeting with Sally.

DAY 16

I go see Maria and talk about my fucking childhood.

DAY 17

I miss Charlie, but now it makes me feel sick how much I miss him. The meetings give my head a reprieve, but I hate them.

I go to lunch with a woman from the meetings and then go to another fucking meeting with her. She hates going to meetings too. Sally's at the meeting. We tell her how much we hate going to meetings. Sally smiles and nods and says, "Yeah, I hate going to meetings sometimes too." After the meeting, my head is clear. I go home and sleep.

DAYS 18-32

Therapy. Write. Want to talk to Charlie. Feel sick from how much I want to talk to Charlie. Meeting. Write. Therapy. Meeting. A movie, an entire series, social media, anything to distract, anything to distract. Food, videos of other people's lives. Want to talk to Charlie. Want to talk to Charlie. Want to talk to Charlie. Want to talk to Charlie. Want to talk to Charlie. Want to talk to Charlie. Binge snacks and more shows. Try to write. Can't write, thinking about Charlie. Meeting. Sleep. Write. Therapy. Distract distract distract. Try to write. Can't write. Thinking about Charlie. Eat a tub of ice cream. Thinking about Charlie. Want Charlie. I really want Charlie. I miss Charlie. I feel so sick. Don't know if it was the ice cream or missing Charlie.

DAY 34

Therapy. I tell Maria, "I can't go on like this."

"You're right," she agrees, "you cannot."

"What do I do?"

"Today," she stands up, "you will separate the father of now, the one you know and love, from the father of your childhood."

"Okaaaaaay."

"You must understand that people grow and change. Right now, for our purposes, it is imperative that you are speaking directly to the man who you remember as your father when you were young."

As per usual, I'm sitting on Maria's embroidered couch, the same place I've been for weeks. She places a big, old telephone book next to me. I say, "I didn't know they made these things anymore."

"I collect them."

Maria paces behind the couch, like she's revving up. "As you consider how you got to be who you are today and the role your parents played in shaping you, you must remember that your parents were once children too. Though the false definitions of love that got you in this mess are your own, your parents are the ones who taught you how to define love. They taught you that love was betrayal and absence, which are not real love. But they also had parents who gave them false definitions of love. And your grandparents had parents who also had parents, and so it goes back and back and back. What we are trying to do, here and now, is stop the cycle."

"Okay," I say, "that's good. I want to stop the cycle."

Maria moves her usual chair aside, clearing the space. "So I invite your childhood father to join us." She places a plain wooden chair in front of me. "We invite the spirit of your childhood father into this room. We ask him to sit in this chair."

I want to pull a face, raise my eyes to the heavens. I want to leave.

What insanity have I walked into here? But I don't leave. For whatever reason I have ended up here. And I want to move away from the shit I'm in. I don't want to be in the cyclical state of *desperate longing* to *reprieve from desperate longing* back to *desperate longing* anymore. So I close my eyes and try to picture a young Dad with brown hair. He walks in and sits in the wooden chair.

"Now, Kat," Maria's standing behind me, "you are going to tear the pages of that telephone book apart while you yell at your father. There is no room for sympathy now. This is the time to let him have it. This is the man who set you up for this disastrous marriage, and you are going to tell him how angry you are at being set up, while you rip those pages to shreds."

I pick up the phone book. It's heavier than I thought it would be. I take a deep breath in. I feel like a bonehead and cannot believe that my life has come to ripping up old phone books in a strange lady's house. But I have nothing to lose so I shout, "Fuck you, Dad!" as I rip some pages.

"Louder!" Maria yells over my shoulder. "You say, 'Fuck you! You asshole! When I was little you betrayed me!'" While Maria screams, she demonstrates how to really go for the ripping.

I mimic her, shouting, "Fuck you! You asshole! You were always at work! Never around! You fucking taught me that was *normal*!" It actually takes more strength than I thought it would to rip the pages with any kind of momentum. "I fucking *married* someone who was *never around* because *you* taught me that was how men were supposed to be!" I pause. I want to keep going for it, but I feel embarrassed. I mean, I'm shouting at an empty chair.

"Come on, Kat," Maria coaches. "This is it." I look at her. She's like a football coach in the sidelines: knees bent, arms gesticulating. She leans towards me and says, "Kat! Come on! This is your opportunity to heal! Give it to him! Rage! This is the man who modeled to you what to look for in a husband! And now you have a marriage only in legal terms! All you have is a piece of paper! No marriage of the heart, of the spirit! Just legal! See him there in that chair!"

Once again, I let my young father sit in the chair.

"And let him have it!"

"Fuck you, Dad!" I shout and rip. "My marriage has fallen apart and you taught me what family was! And what you taught me fucking sucks! You were never there! I sat around waiting for you to come home from work and you were always late! I felt abandoned and like being left alone meant being loved! I was starved for your attention and would have done anything for it. And do you know why I felt abandoned by you?" I stop to breathe.

Maria says, "Keep going!"

"I felt abandoned because I *was* abandoned. It's a fucking fact that you, Dad, were never around! You left me with a severely depressed mother who didn't get out of bed and a little brother who was starved for attention, Dad! Where were you?" Paper's getting all over me and the floor. "Why weren't you there to protect me? Were you really cheating on Mom instead of being there for us?"

"Was he?" Maria shouts.

"I fucking know you were! Everyone in Pleasantville knew!" Half of the phone book remains. "How could you do that to Mom? She needed you! Me and Mattie needed you! What the fuck, Dad? And guess what? You taught me that was how it is if you're loved. And now my *husband* cheats on me just like *you* cheated on me!" Maria watches, nodding. "He was cheating and I was yearning for him to come home just like I wanted you! And why did you ever think that you could drink? How dare you come home drunk and come into my room and sit at the end of the bed? Didn't you ever think that was weird?" I stop.

"Keep going, Kat. You're safe here. Let him have it."

"You were scary, Dad! I was terrified you were going to do something to me! Why did you talk to me about Mom? Why do I know how much you did or didn't have sex with her? Why do I know that you didn't *like* having sex with her? That you thought she was frigid? Why do I fucking know that, Dad? I'm your daughter you shouldn't have told me." I inhale. Then with less energy: "I felt like I had to listen…"

"Stay focused, Kat! What he did! Focus!"

"You said your fucking wife didn't understand you, but I did! That I was the only one! Well, I didn't have a fucking clue, Dad! But I would pretend to be whoever you needed me to be because I so desperately needed the love you withheld! I was like a stray cat, eating scraps!"

"You were a child!" Maria corrects. "He was adult! Focus on him!"

"You made me feel vile! Gross! Disgusting!" The pages have all been torn once. I go for the torn pages, rip them into even smaller pieces. "Why were you jealous when I had a crush on a boy? Why did you try to take me to East Hampton alone? Why did Mom have to force herself and Mattie to come with us? Why did you take me out to the bar, and why did we laugh at Mom?" Tears well in my eyes.

"Don't you start crying," Maria yells. "He violated you! You let him have it!"

"I was your prisoner! Why did you tell me *in detail* about your sex life? Why did you tell Mattie that a man is entitled to a regular sex life and why, oh why, did you say it was okay to pay for sex? Why did you go on and on to me about how Mom was frigid? Why did you tell me that you loved me more than the women you had affairs with? Why would you compare me to anyone you were involved with? How could you think these things, let alone say them to me? I was 11! 12! 13! Why have you always called me *Katherine*? Why did you tell me I was so special then dump your shit all over me? What kind of sick, twisted man are you! What kind of pathetic loser!"

"Say how he set you up!"

"You set me up, Dad, because I fucking thought I was your wife!" I'm tearing the pages into even smaller bits now. Some of them swirl around me. "And when you cheated on *Mom* it felt like you were cheating on *me!* When you stopped drinking and stopped spending time with me, I thought something was wrong with me! You fucked me over, Dad! You set me up then fucked me over, and it's no wonder on earth why I married a raging sex addict! It's all I know! It's all you taught me, you fucking, fucking, shithead loser!" I pause.

"Are you through?"

"No." I continue, "I wanted a Dad, you fucking loser. Why couldn't you have just been a Dad? Is that too much to ask? Stop calling me Katherine. Yes, I'm a woman, but I'm also meant to be your child. Treat me like your grown up child."

"Good," Maria says. I look up at her. "That's very good. You did very well."

"I was my father's wife."

Maria nods her head. "Yes, yes you were."

It's not like I didn't know this. I did. I just never said it out loud, never even thought it out loud in my head. I place what's left of the telephone book down next to me. I tell Maria, "My father never touched me. He just always looked at me sexually and he used to give me gifts of sexy lingerie and expensive jewelry. The same things he gave my mother. Only I lapped it up while she kept telling him she wanted different gifts, gifts of his time. And I think if my mother hadn't come to East Hampton that time... I don't know, I feel... I mean, I can't imagine that he would have touched me, but I feel like that was a trip planned for lovers, and she butted in and I was so furious."

"Smart of your mother."

"And my Dad... he got so drunk every night. I mean, I didn't know it at the time. But with hindsight, it's clear he drank a lot. At home, this is before we moved, when we lived in the orange house, he would come into my bedroom and lie at the foot of my bed and talk and... I don't know... maybe cuddle me? Stroke my hair? And I really understood how he was feeling and, I mean, I don't know, he said I understood him better than anyone in the world. But at the same time, I was always scared of him. And then he rented a house for a week in East Hampton and Mom got wind of it and was furious. But it was, like, no one could say why the trip was weird. I wanted to go because I loved being my Dad's special girl."

"Of course."

"But instead we all went. And Mom kept asking me to look after

Mattie. And then when we got back home, we were suddenly moving, and Mom made Dad stop drinking. And that was it. He never came to my room anymore. He had said that I was the only person who understood him, so I thought that something was wrong with me when he didn't talk to me or cuddle me anymore. I was mad at Mom. She didn't understand him like I did, and yet she somehow seemed to have taken him from me, even though I *knew* he didn't want to be around her. And so because he couldn't have me and didn't want her, he was just never home anymore. I don't think he was faithful before then, but I think this was when his affairs cranked up a few notches. We never saw him anymore. I was bereft."

"And betrayed?"

"God yes, betrayed. I really believed I was special, that I was loved like no one else." I'm not raging anymore. I feel calm. I feel empty, in a peaceful way. I ask, "But how on earth could he mistake me for his wife?"

Maria gives me one of her shrugs. "Probably happened to him. Abuse is cyclical. But now you will stop it. So when you have a little girl, she will not be abused." The thought that I could somehow have a healthy little girl one day fills me with hope.

DAY 35

I sleep for 15 hours. When I wake up, I'm still exhausted. Of course I go to a meeting. I tell Sally and the new women I'm friends with how tired I am. I don't talk about therapy yesterday, even though I think that's why I'm so tired. I feel deeply ashamed.

DAY 37

In therapy, we're both quiet. I've been crying a lot and I'm sure Maria can see that. She makes tea. I sit on the embroidered couch. Finally, I ask, "Do you think my mother knew?"

"What do you think?"

"Oh come on, I hate it when you do that."

"But you know better than I do. You were there with your mother, so think about it. Do you think she knew?"

I think. "On some level, maybe? I don't know. She made us move. She made him stop drinking. She forced herself on our private vacation."

"Probably she saw your father making you the wife but didn't have the words for it. So even though she knew on some level it was not right, it was too awful for her to be truly conscious of."

"That sounds about right."

"But that doesn't mean she's not to blame. She failed to protect you." Maria pulls out another phone book, stands behind me. I sigh. "It is time to give mother your anger."

"I'm so tired, Maria. I don't think I can."

She looks me in the eyes and tells me, "You have strength in you that you don't know exists."

We do the whole thing again. When my anger towards Mom peaks, I scream, "You knew it was happening and you didn't stop it! You should have made him stop drinking sooner! You should have been the wife! You fucking bitch! I was your daughter and you fed me to him! Abandoned me to him in favor of your depression! Your attempt at protection was half-assed and too late! You let him damage me!"

DAY 42

At one of these meetings, they ask me to read the preamble. I say, "My name's Kat and I'm a love addict," and then I read the preamble. I still don't share during the meeting. But I've been coming enough that I know everyone's drama. It's like a really good soap opera.

Afterwards, Sally tickles me in the ribs. "So you're a love addict, eh?"

"They tricked me into saying that."

DAY 47

I tell Rupert, "I can see now why our agents didn't like it."

"Yes." Rupert eats chocolate cake and starts in on his third espresso. We're in a Soho coffee shop with warm wooden tables and a thousand types of organic beans. We're discussing the new draft of *The Amazing Kapakowski Sisters.*

I go on, "But it's so much better now. I think it's ready to go back to them."

"And this time, they'll like it."

"Yeah," I agree, "I think they will. One question. Do you think it would be weird to send it to that producer, Gail?"

"Why would that be weird? Charlie recommended her and she said she'd be happy to have a look."

"Well, if we're going to send it to her, you should be aware of the dynamic." I take a deep breath. "The reason it may be weird is that Charlie cheated on me with her. He also backtracked and tried to get me not to send it to her after I'd already made contact."

"Ah." Rupert taps his fingers on the table as if it's a piano, something he does when he's thinking. "Kat, if you didn't work with theatre people based on who they did or didn't sleep with in this little town, you'd severely limit yourself."

I laugh then admit, "Well, I may have an ulterior motive."

Rupert raises his eyebrows. "How exciting. A cat fight."

"I'm just curious."

"Call it what you want, if you ever meet her, I want to be there."

I send the new draft of *The Amazing Kapakowski Sisters* over to Gail.

DAY 57

Maria and I have moved on from what happened in my childhood, to what happened with the list of men since then (it turns out Lena was right and I did want to marry every single one of them, even the ones I only dated for a week), to what happened with the college professor and then finally, to what happened with Charlie. We've reviewed my inappropriate behavior, my lack of boundaries, my acceptance of crumbs. We talked about the crying after having an orgasm. Charlie once said it was unresolved trauma surfacing, and Maria agreed. She said, "And we are working now to resolve that trauma." We've discussed Anne's suicide and how now, with hindsight, she was clearly depressed and alcoholic. We talked about Lena's relationship with work. In short, it's become abundantly clear that I surround myself with people who have no time for me because they're caught up in their addictions. And that's not the shocking part. The shocking part is how fine this has all been for me, how normal it feels. I tell Maria, "If I surround myself with people who are busy, it means I don't ever have to be close to anyone."

She replies, "It means you never have to be *intimate* with anyone."

"Yuck."

"What?"

"I hate that word."

"Intimacy? In-To-Me-See."

"Oh yuck."

"Next week we return to the source."

That's what she calls my Dad. I'm happy the time's up. I'm not eager to return to the source.

DAYS 58-63

Rupert and I sent the new draft of the musical to our agents, as well as to Gail. Now, we have nothing to do but wait. I decide to start writing something new. I have an idea about a young boy. At the beginning of the week the idea is vague, but by the end of the week, I have an outline. And then it's time to go back to therapy.

DAY 64

Maria tells me, "It's called incest."

I cringe. I tell her, "It's not like he had sex with me."

"It was physical incest in the way your father looked at you and inappropriately stroked you. Then it was emotional incest for a very long time, technically called *covert incest*, which means he psychically treated you like his wife instead of his daughter." I look at the bright yellow daffodils on Maria's coffee table today. She continues, "It was a violation to treat you like his wife."

"And it makes sense that I would be scared of intimacy, if my experience of it…"

"Your experience robbed you of your childhood, of your core. When a parent abuses a child's core, it sets the child up to choose a life like you have chosen."

"Right. Because I accept what he has given me as the way that people love."

"Exactly."

One of her daffodils is drooping, almost done. I ask, "Will I ever be able to talk to my parents again? Will I ever be able to look at my father again?"

"I don't see why not. It will take time, but yes, you can heal. You can transform relationships if you work at them."

"I have another problem."

"Yes?"

"I want to tell Charlie all about this. I don't want to call him the way I did before. But I mean, he'd get it all. He'd completely understand how impossible it would have been for me to have a healthy relationship without first understanding my past and seeing how it informed my choices." Maria keeps listening. "What I'm saying is that I want to talk to him about this stuff. He always wanted to talk about this stuff with me, and I'd call him cheesy or just change the subject. But now I get it. I get what he was getting at, and I want to talk about it with him." She's still just listening. "And apart from wanting to have this conversation with him that would be on this other level, if I'm honest, I also miss being in bed with him at night. And I don't even mean the sex. I mean, just *being* with him, lying there with him, holding his hand, cuddling, having him as my special person and being his. I even miss his bad jokes."

Maria sometimes speaks to me like I'm a child. This is what she sounds like when she says, "Of course you miss him."

"But he's been an absolute dickhead! There's no way I should miss him! And besides, if I'm attracted to unhealthy relationships due to… all this crap I've found out about myself, doesn't that mean it's not really love?"

"Because you are a love addict does not mean that you cannot also love a person. Truly love them."

"So I don't necessarily have to get a divorce, right? I mean, I'm helping myself and if treatment helps him…"

"The trick, my dear, is to love yourself more than him."

"Yuck, Maria."

Maria leans in, "You learn to say to him, 'I love you, but I love myself more.'"

"That sounds so lame."

"Off you go then."

"What?"

"You practice with me."

I sigh, but I've not only gotten used to doing all these stupid things, but also knowing that I feel better for doing them. So I say, "I love you, but I love myself more."

"Excellent! Well done! You keep telling yourself exactly that."

DAY 76

I get an email from Charlie.

Dear Katherine,

I'm sorry to send an email. I'll start by saying there is no need to respond and I am fine. Doing well, even. Who'd have thought it?

But I'm sorry to be in touch, as I know you specifically asked for ninety days without me and my emailing you does break that. I think, however, that so long as you don't respond, your ninety days still stand, and this email is purely informative.

I'm writing to let you know that I'll be staying on in treatment for an extra month. The work I'm doing here is much needed. I felt that, as my wife, you had a right to know where I was, that I was safe, as well as what I was doing financially.

I hope you're keeping well. I will still be in touch upon my return.

Yours,
Charles

I don't hit reply. A part of me wants to. A part of me wants to scream and yell, "What the fuck, man! I've been *waiting*! How dare you make me wait longer?" But another part of me knows that's not true. I know that actually, at some point during these ninety days, I've stopped waiting.

DAY 90

I wake up alone in my bed. The new norm. There was no need to set an alarm. I have some meetings this afternoon because when Rupert and I sent our agents the musical, I told my agent that I now live and can work in London. He asked why I didn't tell him before. I don't mention that I was too obsessed with my relationship to think clearly about work. I joke that I didn't tell him because I knew he'd want to get *Annabel* produced here, and I am so sick of that play. Turns out he does want to get *Annabel* produced here, and I'm thrilled. This is why I have the meetings this afternoon. We're waiting to hear what he and Rupert's agent both think of the musical. We're also waiting to hear back from Gail. So it's great that on Day Ninety of not speaking to Charlie, I have some work. Sally always says, "Keep the focus on yourself." I'm proud that I made it to ninety days without contacting him. And if someone gave me a truth serum, I wouldn't even say that I want to call him now. If someone gave me a truth serum, I would say that I'm calm, that I found strength in myself that I didn't know was there, that I have regained parts of myself that I didn't even know were missing. I roll out of bed and head to the shower.

IX

Love is the way messengers
from the mystery tell us
things
> —Rumi

1

Somewhere around Day 120, Charlie calls and tells me, "I've rented a place in Chelsea."

Part of me wants to shout, "A rental?! Why the hell aren't you coming home?" But it's a small part. The bigger part of me says, "That sounds like a good idea."

Then he asks, "Would you be able to meet me for a date?" His tone's measured. It's a little off-putting. But then, I'm speaking to him with an equally healthy, boundaried tone. Of course I agree to go on a date with him.

2

I hear from him next on the day of the date. He texts to confirm I can still make it. I reply that I can. Very simple. No flirting. Almost clinical. I look myself over in the mirror. I'm wearing a high cut sundress that doesn't show any cleavage but remains formfitting. I want to be attractive, but not overly so. I want to appear elegant and self-possessed. I don't want him to remember that the last time we saw each other I socked him in the face.

Once I'm in a taxi, I text Lena:

> *Maybe we really are through the for worse part?*

Maybe. Listen, I know he's just a flawed person, but Anne would've said he's been a total fucking dickhead and doesn't deserve a "date" with you. She'd have said that if you want her to put on her whoop-ass boots and come whoop his ass, she'd be there in a heartbeat. Let me know if I need to go buy a pair of whoop-ass boots in her stead

3

Charlie sits in a classic, wingback, velvet chair in a corner of the Lanesborough Hotel's library bar. He doesn't notice me standing in the doorway. Cell phones aren't allowed in the library bar, and I'm a little surprised he isn't surreptitiously checking his under the table. But he's not. He looks like he's writing. He is. He's writing with the fountain pen I gave him for Christmas, in the journal I gave him the day I found Becca in his office. This throws me a little. And he looks healthy under the subdued lighting, like he's been in the sun, shed the weight and found his old confidence. He looks like the man I thought I'd married. A pang of distress fills me. Why couldn't I be the one to help him get to this place where he looks so great? I force myself to breathe, stay present, and approach his table. He looks up, sees me, and breaks into a smile, that wide-Charlie, honestly happy smile. He stands and says, "Hello, stranger." I don't know how to greet him. I don't know how to greet my husband. I don't know what to do with my arms. I don't even know if he still is my husband. I want to look down and see if he's still wearing his wedding band, but don't dare. Then he says, "Come here," and pulls me into his arms. Ah. I know this hug. His cheek presses against mine. He places his hands on my shoulders and takes a step back. He says, "You look more beautiful than I thought possible."

I'm a sucker, immediately feel weepy. "Thank you."

"And you smell," he inhales deeply, "divine. Let's sit." We do. He hands me a menu. As I take it from him, I see his wedding band. Oh thank God.

We order nibbles. Charlie describes the flat he's renting (small), how it is for him to be back at work (stressful but exciting because he thinks he can deal with the stress now). I report in on the musical (exciting), but don't mention sending it off to Gail (we won't go there yet). We nibble on the nibbles. He tells me with pride, "I have almost four months clean now."

"Good job."

He answers a little defensively, "Well, it isn't easy."

"I know it isn't." I want to tell him that I know it isn't easy because of all the work I've done on myself that's been so goddamn hard. I want to tell him that I'm an addict too, but I'm a little embarrassed to say that. Also, I think it's too soon to jump into everything I've been learning from Maria. So I say, "I really get how hard it is, Charlie."

He seems to resolve something internally, then says, "So I've decided what I'd like to do."

This gets my attention. "You mean… about us?"

"Yes."

I wonder if he wants what I want. He must. He must want a real relationship. True intimacy. I ask, "Yes?"

"I want to draw a line." I don't know what the fuck that means, so I give him a look and wait for him to explain. "I want to draw a line under our relationship. I want the past to be the past. Over. And then I want to see if we can build something new from this moment forward."

I need to really understand what he's saying here. So I repeat back slowly, "You want to *draw a line* under our relationship thus far?"

"Yes."

It's still not sinking in, so I tell him, "I don't know what that means."

"Well," he says, then stands up. With his foot, he draws an imaginary line on the ground. "We draw a line!" We both giggle. It's the same old Charlie. "Seriously," he continues, "what I mean is I want a fresh start."

"But we can't just forget what's happened."

"I'm not asking you to. But I don't see any way to move forward without a completely fresh start."

"Okay, and I'm not trying to be argumentative, but what does that mean? What does a fresh start look like?"

"Like this. I take you out to nice places and we chat about our lives and try to get to know each other again."

"I like this."

"Then you like my plan?"

"I guess I do."

"If we decide to be committed to each other, I think we should start up couples counseling again."

"Do you want to be committed to me? Or do you want to be seeing other people?"

He smiles. "You are the only person I want to date. I definitely want in theory to be committed to you. But let's keep it simple and start with regular old dating." Then a cloud comes across his face. He continues in a hushed tone, "It's a screwed up situation. There's no textbook for this. No guidance. We have to find our own way."

I nod. "All right. We can draw a line."

4

"I want to tell him everything I've been learning."

"No. Time with Charlie must be just that: time with Charlie," Maria instructs. "You must not divulge the insights you've had regarding your childhood because you must protect yourself emotionally from him until you know him better *as you would any other man.*"

"Right. Because usually I just spill my guts." This is true. I usually tell anyone anything they want to know about me and a whole lot more.

"Yes," Maria says. "You use false intimacy to build intensity. This is all part of the addictive process. And this time, my child, you will try it differently."

So I try. Charlie and I date. For the next few months, we see each other twice a week. We go to dinner, the movies, coffee, an art gallery. Under strict orders from Maria, I show up looking and smelling good, make no move on him, have a good time, ask a lot of questions and listen to his answers, try to learn things about him I didn't know before. Apparently we love addicts are a manipulative bunch and, according to Sally and some people at the meetings I've been going to, I need to be listening to see what's truly happening and help myself stay in reality.

As the dates progress, I complain to Maria, "He hasn't even tried to kiss me once."

"Child!" Maria exclaims. "No sex! Remember that above all else you are trying to decide if you can be with him, if he's well enough, if you're well enough, if he's trustworthy, if you can trust him. Sex, especially God forbid if it is good sex, will glue you to him instantly. You will lose your distance, lose your rationality. No sex for at least the first few months."

"It doesn't matter what *I* do. The no-kissing's coming from him!"

"That's fine. Good, even. Is better this way."

I keep seeing Charlie and it remains friendly. Absolutely no kissing. And it turns out that Maria's right. I get a clear view of Charlie on these dates. He's a great guy. Insightful, caring, funny. The whole package. And he's clean. He's going to tons of meetings, doing his recovery. I tell Maria, "I feel like I want to be with him. Like, I want to choose him."

"Good, good, my child!" Maria gets all excited. "Because love is meant to be a choice! Not something you fall into that takes you over! That is hormones, adrenaline and addiction! But actually loving someone, making the decision to love him, that's a choice that you must make in your sane brain!"

"I've never done that."

"No, you have not."

"Even with Jonathan I felt like I really loved him, but I think I was possessed."

"Indeed."

"I mean, I never would have broken up with him. He had to break up with me. And later, I was trying to start something up with him again, even though I was married and he was engaged. I was thinking I would leave Charlie and be with him again."

"Swapping one drug that wasn't working so well for another."

I think about this. "So I was just using Jonathan."

"And Charlie. If you push what he did wrong aside, I think you will see that you were using him as well."

"The scary thing is that I can still feel the, like... love addict in me that wants to jump back into the relationship with him. She hasn't gone away. What I mean is, if Charlie said, 'Kat, I want to move back in this afternoon,' I worry that I'd say, 'Cool, great.'"

Maria shrugs. "You have come this far without acting out. You're simply talking about your addiction. Freedom from it is one day at a time. Just pray that you don't do that today. Keep dating him."

5

One night he takes my hand and says, "Kat, let's change things up. Shall we have dinner next week at our house? I could have *Antonio's* deliver and come home straight after work, around 7. We could watch a movie?" Home. He's talking about our marital home! "What do you think? Is that too much?"

My insides go all jello-like. "No, no. That would be wonderful." We haven't completed the three months of dating time that Maria suggested we take but well… almost.

"And I'll bring you the best chocolate cake you've ever tasted."

I don't push at all. Just say, "Yum."

And then he hugs me, and I feel for the first time in all this time that he wants to kiss me. Our first sexual spark. Amazing. I lean back to look into his eyes. And then, he *does* kiss me. It's a soft kiss, tentative. His lips are lightly parted, and I let mine open the slightest bit to mirror his. He presses his lips so gently against mine, lets them linger long enough to not be misconstrued as the kiss of a friend. Then he pulls away to put a couple feet of air between our mouths. He looks shocked. I squeeze his hand. He relaxes and smiles. Normally, I would be exploding inside, but I feel cool. We say goodnight and I decide to walk a while before jumping on the bus home.

6

"He may slip up, Kat. He'll always be a sex addict and it's a terribly difficult illness from which to recover." Sally and I have come out for Middle Eastern food after a meeting.

"But I think he's improved. He seems so much more committed to being sober."

"I should hope that, with all the time he's taken to work on himself, he is. Remember, he'll have been digging around in his childhood just as you have. I'm only pointing out that there's a huge possibility he could relapse. You need to be practical and prepare for that possibility."

"Okay."

"Don't be naive."

"Okay, okay! The thing is, I hear you saying all that, but I know that Charlie can be faithful so long as he's in recovery."

"How do you know?"

"Because that's how recovery works."

"Kat, people relapse all the time."

"If recovery doesn't work, why are you so invested in it?"

"Recovery works for me but not for everyone. It's dependent on the person's level of honesty mixed with some strange, divine outside help that you will have heard referred to as a higher power."

It's true I've heard talk of a higher power in meetings. It really rubs some people the wrong way. I haven't thought too much about it, but in theory, if my being in charge got me to that disclosure, I'm very happy to let go of the reins.

Sally continues, "I believe that if an addict can get that mix of rigorous self-inspection and their own personal, external source of strength, then recovery from any addiction is, indeed, possible." Sally squeezes lemon over a plate of halloumi cheese. "More importantly, it sounds as though over the past weeks you've been able to build something with Charlie and that's wonderful."

"So… can we have sex?"

"You're asking me if you can have sex?" She laughs. "Oh Kat, I can't answer that! All I can tell you is—did you ever listen to that meditation technique I sent you?"

"*Present moment, only moment* and *be where my feet are.* Yes."

"Well, you may want to pick a different body part to focus on, but I can tell you that *present moment, only moment* will blow your mind in bed."

7

On the morning of our stay-at-home date, Charlie calls first thing. When he says, "I'm looking forward to seeing you tonight," I hear sex in his voice. And not a bad kind of sex. Very exciting and also truthful. Oddly pure. "I'll be there right after work," he tells me.

"I'll be waiting," I flirt.

———

I bathe then slip into the sexiest lingerie I own with a pair of casual jeans and a fluffy sweater over it. The Italian food arrives on time, but Charlie's a little late. I'm grateful for the time. I pop the food into the oven to keep warm, then do another quick tidy. I had set the table with everyday dishes, but I swap them out for our wedding china. Then I light candles. Now he's very late. I check my phone, but there's no message. On all our dates the past couple months, he was never once late. The alarm bells sound in my head. Normally I would start calling him now, but I don't feel the need to do that. I blow out the candles and turn on the TV. A rerun of *Friends*.

Halfway through a fourth episode, the doorbell rings. I answer it. It's Charlie. Now over two hours late. He comes upstairs but lingers in the hallway rather than enter our living and dining area. He sees the table I laid with such care.

I don't feel like crying. I can see that his face is all twisted and I know exactly what that face means. He acted out. We're silent. He doesn't move to leave the hallway so I sit on the stairs. Of course, I don't know if he's been with a prostitute, a friend or just on the net. But the details are irrelevant. The end result is that he can't show up for me when he acts out. I wrap my arms around myself. I feel that ancient rage rise up inside me. I feel it start to burn my belly, feel it want to shriek out of me. I feel it in there, feel it but contain it. Not an ounce of it slips out. I take a good look at Charlie. He looks like absolute shit. He can't meet my gaze. The poor guy doesn't need me to shame him. I say, "It's late. I'm very tired. Let's get a coffee in a couple of days." He agrees and leaves.

I turn the TV back on. I think about eating some of the pasta but instead decide to head upstairs and run another bath. I hear a text come in downstairs. It must be Charlie. Inside, a habitual part of me wants to run down and check what he has to say, but that's only a small part of me. Most of me doesn't care what he has to say. It doesn't matter. Right now my entire being shakes from the old hurts his betrayals trigger. I slip into the tub as it continues to fill. I hold myself tightly as I sob.

Much later, I check my phone. The text was from Lena.

Sorry I didn't get a chance to speak with you before your hot date tonight. I didn't want to call and disturb you, but I did want to say that whatever's happening right now I hope that you're okay, and I hope that you know that you can live with this man or without him. No matter the man, I'll always be here ☺

I crawl into bed and write all my anger out into a journal.

I call Sally. She reminds me that Charlie's an addict after all. She says, "This is what addicts do. And you have to watch it because you're an addict too and his chaos and unavailability are your drug."

"What do I do?"

"Know that you're certainly powerless over his addiction to sex, but more importantly, and this is the whole point, you're powerless over your addiction to him. So pray like hell that you keep your sanity and serenity." We hang up. I do what she suggested and pray like hell.

When I next see Maria, I tell her, "I didn't flip out on him, or wail to him about how much it hurt me, or offer him a room for the night, or worse, my bed."

Maria applauds. She says, "Now that is the behavior of a woman."

"Maria, I think I need to go home."

For a moment, Maria looks confused, as if I want to terminate the session, then what I'm saying clicks. "Ah. Ah yes. I think that is a very wise idea."

8

I don't ask anyone to pick me up from JFK. I mean, no one picks anyone up from JFK anyway, but I want to make the journey on my own. I want to feel like a New Yorker again.

Mom knows I'm coming. So when I arrive at her house late morning and she's still in bed, I'm surprised. "Ma?" I'm zoomed back to childhood when she seemed to be "asleep" all the time. "Can I come in?"

"Please, honey, please come in." When she sits up, it's obvious she's been crying. Her eyes are blotchy and red.

"What's wrong?" I ask. I sit on the edge of her bed. She puts her arms around me, holds me.

"I'm just having a morning," Mom says.

No one in my family knows what's going on between Charlie and me. I want so badly to tell her, but instead I ask, "You okay, Mom?"

"Ever since family week at Fountain Hills... well, I know I went there for Mattie, but I opted to get some one-to-one support for myself when I was there too. I should have done this work long ago. It's bringing a lot to the forefront for me. And I know you don't care for Johnny, but I had a long session with him this morning—"

"Mom, Johnny's fine. I talk to a therapist. You talk to Johnny."

She smiles wanly. "And well, the session just floored me." She composes herself for a moment. "So I let myself crawl back into bed." She hugs me tight. "Oh honey, why are you here?"

I blurt out, "I'm having some trouble in my marriage."

Mom nods her head. "I see. I'm so sorry. At least he doesn't drink!" I try to smile but end up crying. Mom says, "Oh Kat, I was so young when I got married. I didn't have a clue."

"I don't think I have a clue either."

"Do you want to tell me what's going on with you guys?"

"Yeah, I do."

Mom moves over and makes a place for me in bed. "Come here."

I climb in and tell her everything. Well, I leave out the big dildo. But I do say, "It all reminded me of Dad."

"Ah," she says, "yes, I can see that."

"Mom, did you think my relationship with Dad was inappropriate?"

She looks shocked. "No! Why? Oh my God, Kat, oh my God, did he…?"

I know she's worried about incest. I can't mention "covert incest." I don't feel like she can take it. I reassure her, "No, no, Mom. Nothing physical, no."

"I knew he was closer to you than to me, and that wasn't right." I nod. "Is your therapy helping?" I nod again. "I'm so glad." She pulls me in close then asks, "What do you want to do now?"

"I guess it sounds cliché but be happy?"

"Is there anything I can do to help?" Mom strokes my hair like I'm a little girl.

"Mom?"

"Yup?"

"There's something else that happened." I tell her about the teacher who raped me in college.

She cradles me and rocks me lightly back and forth. "I'm so sorry, my darling girl. I'm so very sorry I couldn't protect you more." In my mother's arms, I get the comfort I've yearned for but never would have been able to articulate as missing. And then the tears come again: for my challenges, my mistakes, for Anne, for the young me, for the adult me who chose a sex and love addicted marriage. I cry for the sadness I sometimes feel but can't name. Mom cries too. My neck becomes wet with a mixture of our tears. Eventually, Mom says, "This one about your professor we can do something about. Do you want me to help you get in touch with the school?"

"I hadn't gotten that far in my thinking yet. But yes. Yes, that's a good idea."

———

After a good stay at Mom's, I head over to Dad's. I knock. He doesn't actually know I'm in town. I feel anxious. But what can I do? Never see my Dad again? When he opens the door my body starts to shrink back in fear. This is usually where we kiss hello. But then something clicks in me. He's no longer the brown-haired young man from Maria's living room. He's old. Old. He even looks a little frail, with rounded shoulders. He's certainly not going to hurt me. He can't. He's no longer the man from my memories, just as I'm no longer a child. "Hey kiddo! What're you doing home?" he asks. My body agrees to a spontaneous embrace. And there's nothing inappropriate about it. No kiss on the lips. It's just a hug. I'm stiff at first, but then Dad pats my back and it feels like... it feels like my Dad is greeting me. He says, "What a nice surprise! Come on in."

I step inside and see that Dad's not alone. A nice-looking woman stands at the entrance to the foyer. She says quietly, "Hello."

"Oh," Dad seems to remember her, "Debbie, this is my daughter Kat. Kat, Debbie. A friend of mine from the club." He called me Kat. Plus, Debbie from the club looks to be age appropriate. I'm glad he's back on that track. Two small miracles. He turns to me. "Debbie's just made lunch." He looks back at Debbie.

She says, "Oh, there's more than enough food. Please join us."

And so, without even a trace of jealousy or anger, I join them for lunch. I tell them about the musical. I mention that things are rough with Charlie but don't go into it. For the first time, I laugh with one of Dad's girlfriends. I have a good time with her. I feel like a daughter who's having lunch with her father and his girlfriend. Which is exactly what this is. It strikes me that Dad has his own story, and I know next to nothing about it.

Dad sees me to the door. He leans in close to my ear. "Listen, Katherine," he says. The hairs on the back of my neck rise to attention. "Debbie doesn't like to hear about problems, especially not with my children. She says I talk about Mattie too much. She's probably a little shallow."

My senses become hyperaware, and the conversation seems to move into slow motion, as I nod, "Uh-huh."

"But I wasn't born yesterday and I'm pretty sure there's a chance that you may be back here. If that's the case, I want to make a proposal. I want to get you and Matthew a two-bedroom in the city. He's shacked up with some chick in an unheated loft in Queens. I don't know what the hell he's trying to prove. But I'd love to get you kids a place. You won't have to worry about your mortgage. I'll take care of that. You just have to be there to keep an eye on your brother."

"As of right now, I still live in London."

"Right," Dad gives me a wink-wink smile. "Sure *as of right now,* I have a girlfriend."

I'm appalled. "Dad, Debbie just made us a fantastic lunch."

"You're getting off track, honey. Let's be clear. You move back home and I'll look after you."

I'm being challenged. My old response would have been to accept his generosity, masking it as my Dad helping me out, and I, in turn, helping Mattie out. But the price tag's too high. Agreeing to such an arrangement is no longer an option for me. "Thanks for the offer, Dad. If I do move back, I'll want to rent my own place."

"But your brother—"

"Dad, I love you and that's my decision. We don't have to talk about this again." I don't kiss him on the cheek, am careful to maintain actual physical distance from him. When I'm safely down the front path, I call back, "See you later, Dad! Thank Debbie again for lunch!"

———

The next morning, I'm making coffee when an unknown UK number pops up on my phone. I get a queasy feeling but pick up anyway.

"Kat!" A female British voice oozes confidence down the line. "This is Kat, is it not?"

"Yes. Who's calling?"

"It's Gail. Gail Talsworth. Sorry to be so familiar, darling. I'm afraid I've heard so much about you from Charlie that I feel like I know you." Ouch. "Perhaps you'd prefer I call you Katherine?"

"Kat's fine."

"Firstly, my apologies for the time it's taken me to read *The Amazing Kap*. To be honest, when we're sent material from the spouses or children of friends, we always have very low expectations, but, darling, I adore this piece. Absolutely love it. Who else is reading it and when can you come in?"

"Well, I'm in New York at the moment, but no one else is reading it."

"Wonderful. That's precisely what I wanted to hear. Let's do a conference call with Rupert and agree terms."

The conference call happens. Afterwards, Rupert and I chat again about how Gail came to be in our lives. He makes the point again about boundaries, and not basing work decisions on people's sex lives. I tell Rupert, "It's strange. I feel so far away from the betrayal and anger I felt when I first found out." Gail is a powerful producer. We decide to go for it. So, Gail sends contracts to our agents, we sign them, and suddenly I'm needed back in London. I have a reason to be there that's not about Charlie. Amazing.

But before I return, I want to see Mattie. I pick up my Mom's landline and call him. He answers, "Ma, would you stop buggin' me! I'm fine!"

"It's not Mom. It's me."

"Louise! What're you doing at Mom's house? Did it get that bad over there?" I sidestep his question and arrange to meet him on the Upper West Side the next day.

He shows up with Daisy. In fact, they appear to be glued together. Matt looks pretty good. The only problem could be his exuberance. He tells me, "I know you met Daisy at the wake, but since you didn't have a real chance to hang out there, I brought her along. I'd be so happy if you two got to know each other."

This kind of makes me want to puke, but I ask politely, "So you guys met at Fountain Hills?"

Daisy giggles, "I was depressed and he was manic."

They both say, "The perfect match."

Mattie extols, "Daisy's ability at mosaics is extreme."

"Mosaics?" And with no further prompt, Daisy pulls out a tablet. Mattie narrates photo after photo of mosaic tabletops. I remark, "Wow."

As the photos shift from tabletops to mosaic armchairs and couches, Daisy excuses herself for the ladies' room. Still gripping the tablet, Mattie demands, "She's great, right? What do you think?"

I think I'm looking at my younger self, showing Charlie off, wanting everyone to like him so that I can like him. I feel ancient. I can't think of a way to kindly point out to Mattie his need for approval and how it's a slippery slope, so I say, "I've never met a mosaic expert. It's super-duper cool."

"And you like her, right?"

"From what I can see, yeah." Ah, poor Mattie! He's fucked! He's me!

He shows me another photo. "Look at this one." A mosaic lounge chair in sea green that looks pretty darn uncomfortable.

I say again, "Wow." I wonder if he's relying on Dad to make ends meet. This would obviously be unhealthy but is probably what's happening. I don't ask. I certainly don't mention his former gardening aspirations.

He says, "Pretty awesome, yeah?"

Daisy's making her way back to our table. Before she reaches us, I grab Mattie's hand. I lean in and whisper, "You are awesome. You. And I love you."

He flicks to the next photograph, unsettled. "Geez, Louise, lay off the cheese."

9

I'm back in London again. It's been several weeks since Charlie didn't make it to our house for dinner. We've agreed to meet up in his office. I'm running early so rent an outdoor lounge chair in Green Park, along with loads of other Londoners soaking in the last of the summer's rays. Just when I'm tricked into thinking summer could last forever, a biting breeze makes me pull my thin jacket in close. A sweaty woman takes the chaise next to me, carrying a baby boy in a sling. The woman has long, unkempt blonde hair and dark circles under her eyes. She still looks like she could be pregnant with her large belly beneath a flowing blue top. She struggles to take off her backpack. "Here." I help her with her bag.

"Thanks. Thanks so much." As soon as the mother lowers her big body into the seat beside me, her son starts to fuss. The mother kisses the baby's head, murmurs something, expertly removes a bottle from somewhere while simultaneously adjusting the baby so he can have his milk. While the little one guzzles, the mother softly begins a lullaby. The baby's pudgy hand, so small but perfectly formed, presses into his mother's face. His eyelids start to droop.

The fat lady sings. I wish Mattie were here to see this.

I lean back, let the mother's voice wash over me the way it does her baby boy. As the baby slips into slumber, I rise from my seat and start the walk to Charlie's office. The mother's voice accompanies me as long as it can. When I can't hear her anymore, I play her song in my head. I hear her voice singing the lullaby over and over again until I'm standing in front of Charlie in his office.

Seated with authority behind his desk, Charlie once again looks like his handsome, rested self.

I sit opposite him. We smile at each other. I tell him, "You look well."

He scoffs. "Yeah, well, I'm sorry about the other night... being late and all."

I look at him. It's so strange how he can change before my very eyes. As he turns to shut something down on his screen, he looks twisted in his face. Gone is the handsome, smiling man of a moment before.

What's odd is that I feel like I have space to see all of this. I'm just noticing his face, noticing that his smile is gone. I also notice that I don't want to ask about the other night. I really don't. I say, "Look, Charlie, I want to apologize for some things."

This gets his attention. He stops what he's doing and looks at me. "Oh come on!"

"What?"

"I'm the one who's been an absolute shit! You can't steal my role and apologize!"

I chuckle. "Well, what can I say? Too bad." I go on, "You know how we got married?"

"Yes. Very aware of that." He taps his wedding ring.

"I feel that on some level I pushed you into it, that I forced you to marry me."

"Don't be absurd, Kat. No one held a gun to my head."

"I know there was no gun."

"You didn't force me. You didn't say a thing!"

"That's just it. We could have talked."

"There was a visa deadline. That said it all."

"Maybe you didn't feel pressured. But for me, with the benefit of hindsight, I feel that by not having a discussion with you, yet your knowing that I wanted to marry you, that I added more pressure to an already pressurized situation. And while my demeanor may have appeared cool, I know on the inside I was anything but."

"All right."

"In fact, I would go so far as to say that I was desperate for you to want to marry me."

"But I did want to marry you."

"Yes but what I'm saying is that… at the end of the day, we're animals and the words are blah blah blah. What we react to is the energy underneath them. And my energy was a blind maniacal panic. I would have done anything for you to marry me. And I feel I did do everything in my power to, sort of, bind you to me emotionally. It was so much easier to discuss Matt, a topic you could fix. I mean, I know he was legitimately in need of help, but I was so terrified of us not working out that I'd always focus on him rather than us. Even by pretending that I thought you didn't want to marry me, I was trying to manipulate you into wanting to marry me even more. I wanted to be your special girl. And I'm so sorry. I'd like you to please forgive me for my desperation," I inhale, "because it had nothing to do with you."

He's looking at me. This is where I could say that it had to do with my childhood and all that. All this time, and I haven't told him any of my discoveries. But even though that makes me sad, we're just not there. I keep it about the two of us. "I was crushed by the fear that you would maybe let me go. I was determined for you to want me enough to marry me. The wedding was like a marker that would say I was okay. Because I have a hole inside me that I wanted filled by you and a marriage to you represented the filling of that hole. When really, I should have wanted to be with you because of you and me and the great couple we made."

"We were a great couple."

"We had something special."

"But Kat, we're all a little fucked up and that's just your way of being fucked up. I've seen where you come from. I know there's stuff going on there. You can't be other than who you are."

"I'm not saying I could have been anyone else or done anything differently. Just that I can now see how my brand of messed up influenced the way I acted in our relationship. And you're right, that would be the case for anyone with a damaged past. But I'm apologizing for the hurt I caused you, even if I had no other way of acting. I should not have accepted everything that was going on in our relationship. It wasn't right that I accepted things as they were."

"What do you mean?"

"Oh Charlie, any undamaged woman would have realized there was something going on a long time ago. My needs colluded with your addiction, and, in the end, hurt you. For that, I'm sorry."

Charlie smiles sadly. "But I hurt you so much more."

"Being with you has been the greatest lesson of my life. And you're amazing. You're sparkly and kind and energetic and creative and you did your best to save Mattie, but… I just can't do it. I don't have the internal make-up to be cheated on, on any level really, and stay centered. Maybe in ten years I will, and I'll look back on this moment and think I made the worst decision of my life. But I'm not ten years older, I'm me now. And for my own reasons, I get triggered when I'm betrayed and—"

"Actually, when I arrived at your house late—"

"Even if it's just a small slip, Charlie, and even though it has nothing to do with me, and even though it's an illness, it hurts. And right now, I don't want to be in a relationship where there's huge potential for that particular kind of hurt."

"But, Kat, I'm trying to change."

"It's not about you changing or not. This is about me. It's about me knowing that I don't want this anymore, Charlie."

He wasn't expecting me to say that.

"I want a divorce." The words slide from my mouth. I have not said "divorce" yet to anyone. "I'm sorry to say it because I know you're trying, but that's what I want."

He's watching me. He absorbs what I'm saying. Then he nods his head. "I understand." He tells me, "I'm sorry, Kat. I am truly very sorry."

I believe him. I stand. He stands. We hug. I remember our first hug, pulsing with energy. This hug has an energy as well.

The energy of two exhausted boxers when the final bell dings.

ACKNOWLEDGEMENTS

anyone lived in a pretty how town is by E.E. Cummings. Kat quotes Blanche Dubois from Tennessee Williams' play *A Streetcar Named Desire*.

Many people offered input and encouragement before this landed in your hands. Thank you to Susie Little, Maya Parker, Lucy Mair, Allison Quinn-O'Keeffe, Donna Sharpe, Janice Day, Olivia Carballo, Lucinda Gordon-Lennox, Jennie Montgomery, Adrianna Irvine, Candace Simmons, Lee Armitage and Chris Huff. Thank you to the anonymous addicts and alcoholics I spoke with directly about recovery and addiction. You know who you are. I couldn't have done this without you. A special thank you to Jill Schary Robinson and the Wimpole Street Writers group where the seed for this book was nurtured.

Some people gave generously of their creative brilliance. Thank you Emily Sweet, Richard Ward, Patricia Ward, Elizabeth Ward, Valerie Cutko, Mark Doman, Cortright McMeel, may you rest in peace, Dylan Kenrick, Patch and ID Audio, Joanna Scanlan and Anjali Singh.

I am grateful for my immediate family: my mother, father, sister and brother. I love you, your partners and children very much. I'm also blessed with a wonderful extended family. I'm lucky to have you all. Finally, thank you to James and Dillon, for supporting me and letting me love you with all my heart.

ABOUT THE AUTHOR

Jennifer Woodward lives in London, south of the river, with her husband and son. She works as an actress and a voice actor. This is her first novel.

Thank you for reading *Ninety Days Without You*. If you enjoyed it, I would be grateful if you could write a review. I'd appreciate your thoughts, and it makes such a difference helping new readers to discover the book and new writers to get some traction.

I found I wanted to start speaking about the topics raised in the book in real, non-fiction terms. With this in mind, the podcast *Without You* began. You can listen to *Without You* wherever you find your podcasts.

If you were affected by any of the issues raised in this book, there is a wide array of support available both online and in local communities. I encourage you to find the help you need. Recovery is possible.

www.jenniferwoodward.co.uk

Printed in Great Britain
by Amazon

21488009R10210